SEX, MONEY, POWER AND STYLE IN THE L.A. FAST LANE — WHERE A WOMAN NEEDS BEAUTY JUST FOR OPENERS . . . "THIS YEAR'S GLITTER NOVEL!"—*Los Angeles Herald Examiner*

Peach, so rich, so gorgeous, and so willing to risk it all to keep her young lover . . . Laura, the perfect wife until she discovered her husband having sex with an exquisite actress . . . Maggie, climbing higher and higher in the world of high-style success, leaving her husband further and further behind . . . Grace, paying for the sins of her scarlet past again and again and again . . .

"Transports you to a fabulous world of limos and love affairs.—*Long Beach Press Telegram*

"Four remarkable women learning to take control of their own lives . . . engrossing . . . an absorbing page-turner . . . Highly recommended!"
　　　　　　　　—Fred Mustard Stewart
　　　　　　　　author of *Century* and *Ellis Island*

"WONDERFUL"—*Dallas Morning News*

Here, from a great new talent . . . a glamorous, deliciously sexy novel of two very desirable women in the glitter-filled world where movie-making and high-finance connect . . .

Golden Triple Time

Zoe Garrison

Brimming with glamour and intrigue, this is the ultimate story of women in business and in love— a high-powered experience that will take you on a breathless spin into a world of dazzle and desire.

An original hardcover novel from NAL
0-453-00478-4—$15.95 U.S./$19.95 Canada

FAME & FORTUNE

A Novel by

Kate Coscarelli

A SIGNET BOOK

NEW AMERICAN LIBRARY

PUBLISHER'S NOTE

This novel is a work of fiction. Names, characters, places, and incidents either are the product of the author's imagination or are used fictitiously, and any resemblance to actual persons, living or dead, events, or locales is entirely coincidental.

NAL BOOKS ARE AVAILABLE AT QUANTITY DISCOUNTS WHEN USED
TO PROMOTE PRODUCTS OR SERVICES. FOR INFORMATION PLEASE
WRITE TO PREMIUM MARKETING DIVISION, NEW AMERICAN LIBRARY,
1633 BROADWAY, NEW YORK, NEW YORK 10019.

This is an authorized reprint of a hardcover edition published by St. Martin's Press.

SIGNET TRADEMARK REG. U.S. PAT. OFF. AND FOREIGN COUNTRIES
REGISTERED TRADEMARK—MARCA REGISTRADA
HECHO EN CHICAGO, U.S.A.

SIGNET, SIGNET CLASSIC, MENTOR, PLUME, MERIDIAN AND
NAL BOOKS are published by New American Library,
1633 Broadway, New York, New York 10019.

First Printing, March, 1985

5   6   7   8   9

PRINTED IN THE UNITED STATES OF AMERICA

To my husband Don,
Who has always believed in me . . .
And to my children, Don and Cyndie,
Who set the pace . . .
With all my love.

A special word of appreciation to Joan Stewart and Toni Lopopolo, who are all that an agent and an editor should be, and who have become my friends.

_1_

The Farewell

PEACH MALONE put her arms around her daughter for one last hug. There were tears in her eyes but she wanted to keep the farewell lighthearted. "It was a wonderful visit, Anne. You've given me the strength I needed. Thank you for everything." Peach then turned and hugged her son-in-law. "Federico, thank you for your patience and kindness in putting up with an old lady for two months."

Federico looked at the tall blond woman who was so exquisitely beautiful that admiring eyes followed wherever she walked and replied, "It was my pleasure, Peach. I look forward to your return."

Anne handed her mother the extravagant raincoat lined with golden sable that Peach had bought while there and her carry-on bag from Gucci. "Here, don't forget your big purchase. It might be chilly in Milan and it'll come in handy. I've arranged for you to be met and escorted to your flight home. Come back soon . . . promise?"

The flight from Florence to Milan was short, and just as Anne had arranged, Peach was met by a Pan Am representative who took her to a private waiting area. She sipped a cup of espresso and tried to concentrate on the *Herald-Tribune*, but her mind kept returning to the disturbing talk she'd had with her attorney, Horace Beller. How was it possible that she could be the widow of Drake Malone, one of the world's wealthiest men, and yet have her banker and her attorney dictate how she spent her money? Had Drake really

9

given them the power to destroy his own son's hopes and dreams?

A young man in a uniform interrupted her reverie. "Signora Malone?" he asked.

"Yes?" Peach responded, thinking the flight must be ready to board.

"There is a telephone call for you. Please . . . this way."

Peach slipped her arms through the coat—it was easier to wear than carry—picked up her purse and bag and followed him out of the room and down the corridor to a telephone mounted on the wall. "Please, signora, your call will be transferred here."

She set her bag down on the floor and picked up the receiver but heard only the dial tone. Perhaps she needed to wait for it to ring. She put the receiver back. Nothing happened. She felt foolish just standing there staring at the telephone, but she was afraid to leave it. Maybe Anne was trying to reach her. She was the only one who knew where she was, and something might have happened. Perhaps Steve had called . . . or Horace. Wouldn't it be wonderful if they'd managed to straighten things out without her?

Suddenly, she felt something hard pressed against her rib cage, and a man's voice hissed into her ear, *"Silenzio!"* She turned and found herself looking into the face of a young man with tightly curled brown hair. His eyes were obscured by narrow, wrap-around sunglasses, and he was dressed in a closely fitted gray gabardine suit. Peach was momentarily confused until she felt her arm on the other side grasped, and she reacted instinctively.

"Let me go!" she demanded and tried to pull away.

"Keep your mouth shut and do as you are told!" another voice commanded, and what she now knew was a gun was shoved harder into her side. Good God, it was happening! She was being kidnapped! The one danger Drake had always feared most and tried to guard against.

The second man picked up her case, and they propelled her forcefully along the corridor, through the rush of people hurrying by. She realized they were taking her out of the terminal, and she knew she had to find some way to stop them. She must not let them get her away from the crowds. Drake had often warned her that it was far better to take risks when there were people around, because once you were alone, you had no option but compliance.

Her mind raced as fast as they walked. How? What could she do? If they were brazen enough to abduct her here, would they also dare to kill her in the presence of dozens of witnesses? If she made a scene, would they run? If she screamed, would anyone come to her aid? Could she scream? Would the fear that stiffened her throat permit her to make a sound loud enough to startle them . . . to direct attention to her . . . and perhaps draw help?

She looked ahead. The doors were less than twenty yards away, and a policeman was standing there in his splendid uniform. It was now or never. In one quick movement, she dropped her large purse, and in the brief second that her captors were diverted, she pulled away and pitched her body forward. The sound of her own scream filled her mouth and her ears . . . loud and clear and compelling. Almost simultaneously, the sharp bark of a shot rang out, and as she crumpled to the ground, she wondered if she was dying.

_2_

Peach

THE WHEELS of the jumbo jet touched down in Los Angeles, bringing her back after eight weeks in Florence and one long terrible night and day in Milan, and Peach thanked God she was alive and home again. The hostess handed her the coat that had saved her life, and she ran her fingers through the holes in the fabric and fur that had been made by the deadly bullet meant for her body. Drake must still be out there somewhere watching over her.

Once more she had followed his advice, and it was right, as it had always been. Although the police tried to convince her that it had not been an ordinary kidnapping, that it appeared to be more of an assassination attempt, she was not convinced. Kidnapping was a common occurrence in Italy, and Drake had always feared that someday someone would make an attempt on his family. Although he never feared for his own safety, he was meticulous in protecting his children. From the day he first learned Peach was pregnant, he took steps to join the ranks of the reclusive rich. Not once had he ever allowed pictures of his children to be published, and he managed to turn his high visibility profile into a very low one.

They had lived a private life. He tailored his investments to direct attention away from himself. He used his attorney and his bank to protect his anonymity, and he enjoyed maneuvering behind the scenes. As the years passed and no attempt was ever made on them, Drake's family felt safe and secure.

12

Now Peach rejected the idea that someone was trying to assassinate her. It was simply outrageous. Who would want to kill her? She didn't have an enemy in the world, and in spite of her wealth, she had no power or control over it. Drake had apparently left that in the hands of men whose judgment he trusted more than hers.

As soon as the police permitted it, she had telephoned Anne to warn her. Her abductors had escaped and she was afraid that her daughter might be their next target. She begged Anne to return home with her, but in her usual stubborn, truculent way, she refused. Italy was her home now, and the only concession she would grant her mother was that she would hire a driver until things settled down.

Bigger children, bigger problems, some sage had once observed. How true. First Steve and his problems at the winery . . . now Anne. Without Drake, could she protect either of them?

Miles was, of course, waiting for her at the gate. He was always the perfect servant, proper and punctual. She restrained the urge to throw her arms around his tall, skinny frame and instead warmed her greeting with a smile.

"I'm sorry you had to wait so long, Miles. Those idiots in customs treated me like some kind of dope smuggler."

"Welcome home, ma'am. Are you all right? You look a bit pale."

"They wanted proof that I wasn't trying to smuggle in my engagement ring. As if I haven't had enough problems on this damn trip."

"Is something wrong, ma'am? You look a trifle upset."

"A couple of hoodlums tried to kidnap me in the Milan airport. It's their favorite sport over there, I guess. Luckily, I got away, but they ruined my new coat." She held it up so that the light could shine through the holes.

"My God, ma'am . . . they almost killed you!" Miles exclaimed, his normal composure shattered. "Perhaps we should call Mr. Dooley and put him back on the payroll."

"I'm not sure it's really necessary, but I'll think about it. I feel so much safer now that I'm home. I do wish that Anne and Federico would come back here to live. Have you moved into the penthouse yet?''

"No, ma'am. Tomorrow is the day we'd planned on, although Mrs. Hammond has it all ready for you. Of course, under the circumstances, you'll not want to stay there alone tonight. I'll wake Sarah, and we'll bring our things over right away.''

"Miles, you will do no such thing. I don't intend to let this incident get blown out of all proportion. We're in the United States, not Italy, and I'll be fine. After all, I chose that particular building because of its exceptional security. Now, don't worry. Just drop me off and go on back to Sarah. I'll see you both first thing in the morning. How's Winnie?''

"She's waiting in the car, ma'am. She's been one lonely little dog, and the general upheaval in the house has been difficult for her. She's getting up in years.''

Half an hour later, Miles turned the Rolls-Royce into the driveway of the high-rise on Wilshire Boulevard. The doorman helped Peach out of the car and, carrying her tiny dog, Winnie the Poodle, she hurried into the high-ceilinged and spacious lobby. The coldness of the white marble floors and walls and the heavy crystals on the chandeliers chilled her. Had she committed herself to living in the Dorothy Chandler Pavilion, for God's sake?

Her private elevator slid upward silently, carrying her to the twentieth floor, which was all hers. Willis, the doorman, slipped a key into the elevator's control panel, which permitted the doors to open. Quickly, he gave her a briefing on the various security systems, but there were so many buttons and combinations that she was confused.

"Good grief, I can't absorb all this right now. Can't I just lock myself in for the night and get briefed on all this tomorrow when I'm not so tired?''

"Sure, Mrs. Malone. There are three of us downstairs on duty all of the time. There's a red panic button in every room. Just press one of them if you need us. Goodnight, and welcome home.''

Willis left, and Peach pressed the master switch and flooded the rooms with light. Dear God, this is it, she thought, the results of her first major decision as a widow. She'd spent a fortune on this place. Please let it be all right. She'd been so sure it was the thing to do when she'd asked Horace to buy the penthouse so hurriedly, but as the weeks passed in Italy, she began to have doubts. Now she was about to take her first look at the only home she herself had bought. She was forty-five, and although she had lived in many houses, tonight she would sleep in the first home that had ever belonged exclusively to her. And she was completely alone. No husband, no children, no servants. Just Peach. All by herself. "Except you, Winnie. Come on, let's see what it looks like." She put the little dog down and surveyed the splendor before her. She was desperately hoping to be overwhelmed with joy, and she was. The entry flooring was pale polished wood, inlaid with darker woods forming a stylized but readily identifiable peach. She knelt down to admire the workmanship, to stroke the wood, to absorb its beauty through her fingertips as well as through her eyes.

She looked around at the warm beige walls, admiring the color and the simple, heavy glass sconces. There were no chairs or benches. The foyer was empty except for a life-sized ballerina by Monya, which stood composed with eyes downcast, her feet in perfect fifth position. The body of the sculpture was of highly polished brass, only her hair was finished in a rough, anodized texture. Three small spotlights from above lighted her, and the effect was dramatic. Peach moved to the sculpture that Drake had bought for her and put her arms around the cold metal and rested her cheek on the dancer's head. The memory of Drake Malone, her husband of twenty-six years who had died just ten weeks before at the age of seventy-one, filled the room. In their years together, he had been her lover, her protector, her constant companion, the father of her children, and to the end, the center of her life. Could she live without him? The muscles in her throat began to constrict painfully, but she didn't want to cry. "No tears . . . no tears tonight in my new house . . . in my new life," she whispered.

She lifted her head, patted the dancer lightly, and began the tour of her new home. She walked slowly, her eyes taking in every rich detail. God bless Maggie Hammond! Each room was more beautiful than the last. Maggie had decorated the place in the owner's favorite colors—peach-toned beige and cocoa brown. The effect was smooth and uncluttered. Maggie had wisely decided not to put paper on the walls to avoid conflict with the priceless art collection that Peach and Drake had accumulated over the years for joy and not for investment.

In her grief after Drake's funeral, Peach had decided to leave the big house in Bel Air as quickly as possible. The last five years there, after the stroke that confined Drake to a wheelchair, had not been very happy ones.

Throughout his illness, she had watched over him lovingly, trying to give him back some of the strength with which he had surrounded and protected her for all the years of their marriage. When she realized that he was willing himself to die, she knew she could never again live in their home without him. It was his house, his alone, and if she was ever to become a complete person without him beside her, she would have to begin in a place not touched by his dominating personality.

Now she had her new home, and she loved it. Maggie Hammond was a genius, and she was proud that she had been the one to discover her. Maggie was not an interior decorator, she was a witch. She had done a super job, and in so doing had reinforced her employer's belief in her own ability to make decisions. Peach wanted to call her right then, but it was much too late.

She took off her coat and went into the bedroom, where she pulled off the handmade Tanino Cresci boots she'd bought in Florence. With a sly sense of satisfaction, she realized she had forgotten to declare them while going through customs. It served them right for making such a fuss over her diamond ring. She had worn the ten-carat, emerald-cut stone on her finger for so long it had never occurred to her that anyone would think she'd bought it recently. She was still smarting from the nastiness of the customs officer who'd treated her like a common criminal and charged her a bloody fortune in duty on the coat.

She stripped off her clothes and walked through the apartment feeling hedonistic and free. Looking out the large windows at the City of Angels sprawled below, she realized how good it was to be home again. She could not understand why anyone would want to live anywhere else. Smog, traffic, the unreality of never-never-land were all minor in comparison to the blessings of the weather and the sunshine. Why had her children abandoned this city so easily?

On the bar rested a silver wine cooler filled with ice and a bottle of Chardonnay from Steve's winery. A small white card was propped underneath, and the words "Welcome Home" were printed neatly on it. How nice. Miles must have put it there for her. Maybe she'd have a glass. She was still nervous and edgy, not quite recovered from the nightmare in Milan. Too bad the police had let those outlaws escape. She shivered. She'd better hurry and get into the tub before she caught cold.

Carrying the wine, a corkscrew, and a large Baccarat wineglass, she returned to the bathroom and turned on the water in the huge apricot onyx tub. While she waited for it to fill, she opened the wine, poured a little into the glass, and set it on the side of the tub. She put some aromatic bath oil in the water and then stepped in. The whirlpool jets were on full force, and just as she was about to sit down, her feet slipped, and she grabbed for the side. She landed hard on her bottom, unhurt, but she managed to knock the bottle and glass to the floor, where they both shattered, sending fragments of glass and golden liquid everywhere.

"Damn! How clumsy can you get?" she scolded herself.

She tried to ignore the mess and relax, but Winnie ventured in to see what all the commotion was about.

"Oh, God! No! Out, Winnie! Stay away. You'll cut your feet!"

Groaning at her own ineptitude, Peach pulled herself out of the water, gingerly stepped around the mess, and scooped up the little dog, who was eagerly sampling the tasty vintage running all over the floor.

Grumbling and annoyed, she went into her bedroom and slammed the door on the mess. She couldn't deal with one more thing tonight. Miles could clean it up in the morning.

She dried herself off and curled up in bed under the electric blanket. Winnie jumped up and tucked herself close to her owner's back, and they were both comforted. Peach was exhausted and depressed. Steve had troubles . . . she was worried about Anne in Italy . . . and she felt alone and filled with self-pity.

Anne's harsh words returned to haunt her. Had she really sacrificed too much of herself worshipping her husband? "He was just a man, Mom . . . he wasn't the god you made him out to be, and his words weren't the gospel. Isn't it about time you started thinking for yourself?"

Easy to say. Could she do it? Had her will and her spirit atrophied through all the years of disuse?

"Kitty O'Hara, come out, come out, wherever you are," she pleaded.

—3—

The Money and the Power

KITTY O'HARA sat in the office of the director of personnel and waited nervously as he read her application for employment. Although she didn't have much hope, she had, at least this time, made it past the receptionist.

"Miss O'Hara, why are you applying for this job?" he asked wearily.

"Because I need the money, Mr. Powell. My father died recently and I have to find work soon."

"But a factory job? Really, look at your hands. Do you know what one day of handling shoe leather will do to them?"

Kitty looked down at the whiteness of her long thin fingers, and she wished her parents had not been quite so protective. "I know, sir, but I'm really desperate. I've tried, I really have, but I haven't got any business training. I was supposed to enter Washington University this fall . . . I had a full scholarship . . . but I can't now. I really need this job."

The slight tremble in her voice and the brightness of her eyes as the tears surfaced convinced him that she would not be suitable for factory work, and ten minutes later she was back on the street. She walked to the bus stop feeling useless and miserable. She didn't know where to go next. She couldn't stand the thought of returning to their flat where her mother would be slaving away in the midst of a clutter of fabrics and pins. Maybe she would go see Anna Barry. Although it had been four years since she had attended dancing classes, Anna might give her some advice.

Her teacher had not changed. She was nearing seventy, but her tiny figure was still lithe and shapely in its black leotard and pink tights, and her horn-rimmed glasses still perched precariously at the end of her nose like a huge butterfly ready to swoop away at the slightest disturbance. Her dark eyes skewered Peach as she greeted her. "Where have you been, girl? You're probably all out of shape."

"I just graduated from high school in June, Anna, and you're right, I am out of shape," Kitty replied, not intimidated by the abruptness of her welcome.

"How's your mother? Is she still sewing? We miss her needle here at recital time."

"She's all right, I guess. My dad died suddenly this summer." Kitty's eyes filled, and Anna's composure melted. "Oh, my dear, I am so sorry." She put her muscular arm about Kitty's waist and led her into the office and closed the door. Kitty gave her the sorrowful details in words that tumbled out awkwardly and hurriedly, and when she was finished she was embarrassed. "I'm so sorry, Anna. I didn't mean to take up so much of your time with my troubles."

"Kitty, my child, I am never too busy for my friends. Now, the past is history, we must go on from here. You need a job, and you can't find one because you haven't been looking in the right places. You do have training, you know, the best . . . from me."

"I'm not a ballerina, Anna. I was never very good, you know that," Kitty protested.

"Neither am I, my dear, but I have taught many youngsters who went on to do what I could not."

"I don't know if I could . . ."

"Well, you can try. I must warn you that the hours are long, from one to nine every day and all day on Saturday. Six days a week. If you want to have a go at it, I'll start you at fifty dollars a week."

Kitty accepted the offer eagerly and hurried home to tell her mother the news.

*   *   *

Kitty and her mother managed to exist on their combined earnings until Hazel's eyes began to give her trouble, and she was told that new glasses would not help much, that she had cataracts and would eventually need surgery or lose her vision altogether. Hazel was in despair, but Kitty was young and was not afraid of carrying the burden alone. She decided to look for a second job. She had until one o'clock in the afternoon each day; surely she could find some way to earn some money in the mornings.

With a little work experience behind her, Kitty managed to get a job as a maid at the Park Plaza Hotel on the morning shift. The hourly pay was not much, but she was assured that there would be significantly more in tips, and her uniforms were supplied. Kitty's ordeal began. She awakened at five, packed a lunch, took a bus and then a streetcar to the hotel. There she scrubbed and cleaned the rooms and the baths of the early risers until noon, when she boarded another bus and ate her lunch while riding. At twelve forty-five, she arrived at the dance studio in time to change and get ready for her first class at one. Saturday she taught all day, and on Sunday she worked a full day at the hotel.

Hazel protested, but it was futile. Kitty was both tired and exhilarated at the same time. She had a problem, but she was solving it, and hard work was not a great price to pay for that. She began to save for her mother's surgery.

She even found the work at the hotel less unpleasant than she had thought it would be. The rooms were lavishly furnished, and she took pride in cleaning and straightening them. She was strong, and she worked fast. She loved to look at the beautiful furs and clothes hung in the closets, although she was amazed at how untidy wealthy people were. Glasses were frequently set on the tables, where they left rings on the rich wood. Cigarettes were ground into the thick wool rugs, and shoes were polished with the white terry-cloth towels. Toilets were frequently clogged with sanitary napkins and condoms.

To Kitty's disappointment, tips were not as generous as promised. Some guests would leave a dollar or two on the dresser, but most did not. Kitty envied the bellhops who were rarely denied their gratuities because they could look people straight in the eye. Maids were, for the most part, invisible and usually forgotten.

One cold winter morning, she arrived at the hotel and was told by the housekeeper that she would have to clean the penthouse suite immediately. A very important guest would be arriving early, and everything had to be in perfect order. Kitty dragged her cart to the elevator and pushed the button for the top floor. She wished she felt better. Everyone wanted the penthouse detail because the tips there were usually excellent, but she felt wretched. Her period had started in the middle of the night, and she'd had to get up and change her pajamas. Her cramps had been worse than usual too, and she hadn't slept well. Most of all, however, she was simply exhausted from the grind of never having a day off.

She inserted the key into one of the huge wooden doors and pushed her cart of fresh towels and cleaning supplies into the hotel's most expensive suite. The richness and beauty of the furnishings enthralled her, and the spaciousness of the rooms was awe-inspiring to a young girl who had known nothing but a cramped, cold-water flat.

She was tempted to spend a few minutes browsing through the rooms, but she knew she had to rush. She hurried into the largest bathroom to begin. As she bent to scrub the huge tub, she could not help fantasizing. She imagined herself soaking in it, luxuriating in a thick white bubble bath. Her hair would be piled on top of her head in big curls just like in the movies, and her fingernails would be long and red. Of course, there would be a white telephone nearby so that she could talk to her rich suitors.

She imagined herself stepping out of the bath and seeing her reflection in the large gilt-framed mirrors. She stood up and posed and saw a tall, gaunt figure. Her uniform hung on her like a rag. The months of working two jobs had taken their toll of her flesh. She stepped on the chrome bathroom scale. She had lost ten pounds! She was surprised that Anna

hadn't mentioned it, but then, Anna believed that a dancer could never be too thin.

When she finished cleaning the rooms, she pushed her cart into the hallway and returned for one last look around to be sure she had left nothing undone. In the main bedroom, she looked out the huge windows overlooking Forest Park, which stretched out for acres below. Her father used to take her to the zoo there when she was little. He'd hold her hand and tell her stories about the animals and buy her pink cotton candy.

A wave of acute depression swept over her usually optimistic persona. She began to cry tears of grief and fatigue and hopelessness. She sat down on the deep, down-filled cushions of the chaise longue and gave in to all the fears and anxieties that she had managed to suppress. She buried her face in the softness of the cushions until she exhausted her tears and her body, and she fell asleep.

Two hours later, Drake Malone stepped into the private elevator with the hotel manager and a bellman who was carrying his bags. The manager tried to make conversation with this notoriously rich and successful man, but Drake Malone was tired, and he just wanted to be left alone. He had flown all night through bad weather to get there for a meeting with some jackasses who had botched up a land acquisition, and he had no time for obsequious hotel employees.

The elevator doors opened at the top floor, and there stood Kitty's cleaning cart piled high with towels and used dust cloths. The manager was humiliated. "I'm so sorry, sir. I can't imagine how this happened. . . ."

"Just get it out of the way," Malone snapped, "and set my bags inside. My own staff will be arriving this afternoon. See that I'm not disturbed until then. No telephone calls either." He walked into the suite, waited until the bags were set down and slammed the door on the retreating men.

He strode to the bar and poured himself a tall glass of tomato juice and sat down at the desk. After calling several key people in his organization, he ordered breakfast sent up. Damn, he missed Fawcett. He was not accustomed to taking care of himself. His valet-manservant-butler Fawcett usually

did everything for him, but he had been struck down by a heart attack and could no longer function for his long-time employer.

Drake needed food and rest. He wanted to be alert for the afternoon briefing. Helen, his secretary, would not arrive until late in the evening. She had taken on most of Fawcett's duties temporarily and she was also running the Los Angeles office.

He took off his coat and tie and unbuttoned his shirt as he drank his juice. He was of medium height, powerfully built, and at forty-four years of age, remarkably fit. His hair was still thick and almost all white. His skin was tan from the California sun, and his heavy eyebrows were black. His appearance and sense of his own power intimidated men and fascinated women.

Drake Malone was a man of enormous wealth. Although he was accustomed to having minions surround him ready to carry out his commands, he was singularly alone. He had built an empire of investments that included real estate, oil, and communications. He had backed plays on Broadway and owned a major league baseball team, but although the latter had been only vanities, these, like all of his other ventures, turned out to be profitable. The tabloids had labeled him Midas Malone.

When he was forty years old, his wife died of cancer. Throughout their twenty years together, she had not been able to give him a child, and her death left him alone. For more than a year he mourned her and was filled with anger at being able to buy anything he wanted except the health of the woman he loved. Bitterly he realized that he had suddenly become the world's most eligible and desirable bachelor.

There were women—beautiful, young, bright, and well educated—available to him at all times. As secure and attractive as he was, he was also realistic enough to know that his fortune was the greatest lure, and although marriage was always on the minds of the women he met, it was never on his.

He enjoyed their flattery and attention and convinced him-

self that by having only casual or strictly physical relations, he was remaining true to the woman he had loved and lost. Even though his body was not faithful to her memory, certainly his soul was.

Now here he was in St. Louis, all alone for the first time in years, and he felt frustrated and annoyed. Why the hell did Fawcett have to go and get sick? He contemplated his suitcases. He should take out his clothes and hang them up. To hell with it.

He picked up the telephone and placed a call to Los Angeles. After a few rings, a sleepy voice answered.

"Horace? What's wrong?" he demanded. "You sound like you just woke up."

"It's six in the morning, Drake. Are you in St. Louis?" Horace answered with only a shade of rancor in his voice.

"Sorry, I forgot. Anyway, open your eyes and make a note to call Tim at Merrill, Lynch and tell him I want as much of that new issue as he can get . . . you know, the Bailey thing we talked about."

"There's a big demand for that one, Drake. He's already promised me as much as he can. I just don't think I can lean on him any harder."

"Yes, you can. Tell him if I don't get ten thousand shares, I'll get another broker."

"Okay, okay, but he's a nice guy. I'd hate to see him get fired over this," Horace answered, trying to be more conciliatory.

"I didn't say to change brokers . . . just threaten him a little. Horace, you've got to learn more about manipulating people. Didn't they teach you that in law school?"

"Sure, boss. Any other orders for the day?"

"I'm going to sleep for a couple of hours. Be sure Helen has all those contracts before you put her on the plane."

"I delivered them to her at three this morning. We worked half the night."

"Thanks. What would I do without you? Now, take a couple of days off. But don't get too far from a telephone. I might need to talk to you when the negotiations get heavy, okay?''

"Okay, boss. Anything else?''

"Go back to sleep.''

There was a knock, and Drake opened the door to admit the waiter, who pushed in a cart set with crystal, silver, and fresh flowers. There were hot croissants, toast, grapefruit, eggs, and coffee, just as he had ordered. He declined the waiter's offer to serve and waved him out, then proceeded to the bathroom to wash up. As he entered the bedroom, he saw Kitty curled up on the chaise. She was still sound asleep.

"What the devil?'' he exclaimed as he strode toward her, suddenly understanding why the maid's cart had been parked outside his door. He hated slovenly employees, and he was determined to hang this lazy little bitch out to dry. He intended to shake her awake, but as he approached her, his annoyance turned to curiosity. She looked like a baby with her arms cuddled up close to her body. Her long blond hair had fallen out of the knot she wore when she worked, and there were still tears puddled in the hollow between her eyes and the bridge of her nose.

When he realized that she had been crying, he was touched. He reached down and pulled the silky strands of hair off her face. She was sleeping soundly. He ran his thumb across the curve of her cheek and felt the warm soft texture of her skin. Her innocence and vulnerability moved him, and he wished the moment could freeze in time. He felt like the prince who has just come upon Sleeping Beauty.

Kitty felt his eyes upon her, and she awakened to a kindly face smiling down on her. It took her a few moments to realize where she was, and she struggled to orient herself. When she did, she put her hands over her face. "Oh, my God, what have I done?'' she gasped.

"You just fell asleep, that's all.''

"I'm so sorry, sir. I'll get right out.'' She sat up and tried to stand, but Drake put his hands on her shoulders and stopped her. He was not about to let this treasure escape.

"Stay there. I want to talk to you. You do owe me an explanation, you know."

"But I've got to get back to work! They'll fire me for this. What time is it?"

"It's nearly ten."

"Oh, no! I have a whole floor to do, and I've got to be at class at eleven."

"Class?" His heart sank. Was she a mere schoolgirl? "Do you go to school?" he asked.

"No, I teach ballet at Anna Barry's."

"Two jobs? No wonder you fell asleep," he responded, relieved. How old could she be?

"I really have to go," she protested.

"Please, no. Don't worry about your jobs. I'll see that everything is taken care of. I'm Drake Malone."

His name brought no sign of recognition, no flicker of avarice into her eyes. She had no idea who he was, and it was quite obvious that she needed money very badly. "Young lady, I don't know who you are or what your name is, but I expect an explanation before you leave here. Come into the sitting room. We'll have breakfast and discuss it."

The unquestioned authority in his voice warned her to comply. She followed him meekly into the sitting room where they sat down together, ate, and talked. Drake asked her probing questions and learned the history of her short life. Kitty told him everything, even about her mother's failing eyesight and the grief she still felt for the loss of her father. She found him to be an attentive listener who seemed terribly interested in all of her problems. She was comfortable in his presence, and as they talked, her burdens seemed to be transferred from her weakness to his strength.

At last, with great reluctance, she rose to go. She hated to leave him and the beautiful suite. What a lovely visit they'd had. "Now that I've lost one job, I had better go and make sure I keep the other one. Thank you so much for being nice to me. I'm sorry I fell asleep on your couch."

Drake could not stand the thought of her disappearing from his life. "Have dinner with me tonight," he urged.

"I don't finish teaching until nine."

"Then we'll have a very fashionable late supper. Where shall I pick you up?"

"Anna Barry's Dance Studio on Olive. Everyone knows where it is." She was now standing in the doorway and was about to disappear. Drake put his hand to her face and caressed her cheek. "Peach down," he murmured.

"What . . . do you mean?"

"Your cheeks. They're soft and downy like peaches. That's what you remind me of . . . a peach."

"But peaches have hearts of stone," she protested, smiling.

"I certainly hope not." He paused thoughtfully. "You know, I think I shall call you Peach. Sweet and delicious Peach."

Kitty smiled uncertainly and left the suite. She could think of nothing to reply, but she was pleased and flattered and happy.

Drake watched the door close and felt both a loss as well as a sense of great excitement. He was a man of many hungers, and he wanted her more than anything he had ever desired. He wanted her for her sweetness and softness and for her innocence. But, above all, he wanted her for her need. He knew how much his love could change her life, and he was grateful that he had the money and the power to perform miracles for her.

The streetcar ride to Anna's went rapidly. Kitty was in a rapturous trance. Never in her life had she met a man so dynamic as Drake Malone. He was the handsomest person she had ever seen in real life, and he was obviously very rich. He was also powerful, yet tender and kind, and most of all, she sensed that he liked her more than anybody had ever liked her before, except her parents, of course.

Later in the day during a break between classes, Kitty asked Anna for a favor. "Anna, I have a dinner date right after work tonight. Would it be okay if I asked Marina to take the last half-hour of my eight o'clock class?"

"Marina's not coming in tonight. It's her mother's birthday. What time is your boyfriend arriving?"

Kitty could not bring herself to think of Drake Malone as a boyfriend. It was almost sacrilegious to put a juvenile label like that on him. "Anna, he's not my boyfriend. He's a nice man I met at the hotel this morning."

Anna bristled. This young lady was going to get herself in trouble picking up strange men at that hotel. She had no business working there anyway. "And who is this stranger, may I ask? And how old is he?"

"His name is Drake Malone, and he's very nice. I don't know how old he is, forty maybe."

"Drake Malone? *The* Drake Malone? You must be mistaken. How exactly did you meet him?"

Kitty told her the whole story, and Anna listened to every detail with a growing sense of horror. When she finished, Anna's guns were aimed and ready to fire. "My dear child, do you have any idea who Drake Malone is?"

"I know he's a very handsome and very sweet—"

Anna cut her off. "He's one of the world's wealthiest men, that's who he is. He is at least forty-five years old, and he has a taste for beautiful young women. Do you understand me?" Anna's voice was full of indignation.

"I think so but . . ."

"No buts about it. You must not go out with him. Your reputation will be ruined . . . to say the very least."

"Just for a quiet dinner?" Kitty was incredulous.

"Especially for a quiet dinner. Drake Malone isn't interested in just eating with you. He has other plans. And if you appear in public with him, you'll probably have your picture taken by the newspapers. Word is probably around that he is in town, and the press is surely watching for him."

At first Kitty was swayed by the information about Drake and the fervor of Anna's warning, but the thought of denying herself an evening with a person who made her feel so good was intolerable. "Anna, I know you mean well, but you've never met him, and I have. He's nothing like you say he is."

Anna knew when to retreat. She shrugged her shoulders and

turned away. "Have it your way, my sweet little booby. But believe half of what you see and nothing that you hear."

"What about my eight o'clock class?"

"I'll take it for you."

Kitty watched the stern little figure march indignantly away, and she smiled at the sight. How she loved Anna, and although her words had been harsh, Kitty knew they were spoken out of love and ignorance. No matter what anyone said, she knew that Drake was a fine, caring person. Anna would realize that when she met him.

The day passed quickly for Kitty but slowly for Drake. To the surprise of his staff and his business adversaries, he was tolerant, amenable, and uncritical. He was generous and agreeable to compromise. There were men who met him that day for the first time who would henceforth spread the word that his hardheaded, toughminded reputation was a lie, and they would be forever considered gullible and foolhardy by those who had been bruised in previous encounters with him.

By seven that night, Drake had dismissed them all. He was eager for the evening to begin. Standing nude and scrutinizing himself in the same mirror that had reflected Kitty's figure just hours before, he held his hand up to shield his face, and he was satisfied that the body before him was as hard and lean as that of a twenty-five-year-old. His skin was a bit leathery on the face and arms from too many years of golf and tennis. And although his hair was white, he still had it all, maybe too much actually, for like his old friend and distant cousin Jack Kennedy, he had trouble controlling it and found it necessary to have weekly trims. He had heavy black eyebrows and the piercing blue eyes of the Irish. His teeth were large and white and all his, and his smile lighted his face. His frown, however, was menacing and barely concealed the threat of violence that always lurked just below the surface of his personality.

He thought about Mary, and for the first time in four years the pain was bearable. Was time beginning to heal that terrible, bleeding wound her death had inflicted? Was it possible that the young girl he had just encountered could stanch the flow? A wave of guilt spread through him. "Mary, my love, if I could bring you back, you know that I would. I would give all that I own to have you at my side again," he whispered, and the longing, the loneliness, the need for someone to love pierced him.

Drake arrived at Anna's studio early. Anna's sharp eyes spotted him through the glass partition, and she left her class to confront him. "Are you looking for someone?" She did not feel friendly toward this lecherous tycoon, and her manner was frosty.

"Yes, I'm looking for Miss O'Hara, but she doesn't seem to be around."

"She's in the shower room. I suppose you're Drake Malone?"

"Yes, I'm a bit early. I had hoped to watch her teach . . ."

"Mr. Malone, what do you want with her? She's just a child."

Drake was startled by the directness of her approach and her bright, dark eyes that stared intently into his. "Well, Mrs. Barry, I intend to take her out to dinner, and what's more, I believe she is not a child but a lovely young woman. And I intend to treat her with a great deal of respect."

Anna was not mollified. "Mr. Malone, she is a good girl, and she is quite innocent. Please leave her as you found her. God will punish you if you don't . . . and so will I!" Having warned him, Anna left abruptly and resumed teaching her class. Drake was not offended. After all, it was only natural that she would regard him as a rich old lecher, but he knew he was not . . . was he? Exactly what were his intentions toward this exquisite young woman?

Kitty emerged from the shower room scrubbed and clean. She had on no makeup other than a touch of coral lipstick. Her hair was damp, and ringlets of curls edged her face.

"Hello, you're here early," she greeted him.

"I thought you'd still be teaching, and I wanted to see you dance."

"Anna insisted on taking the whole class for me so that I'd have plenty of time to shower and dress."

"She must be nice to work for."

Kitty laughed. "She's a tyrant, but I love her. Everyone does, even when she's yelling at us all for being lazy."

"Are you hungry?" he asked.

"Starved."

"Good, then let's be on our way. The chef at the hotel is preparing something special for us."

"The hotel? Oh, please no. I'd feel funny going there and having people I know wait on us."

"Nonsense. Maurice will be disappointed if we don't show up. And besides, you're not going to work there anymore, remember?"

Kitty felt a pang of depression. She would have to start looking for another job. Drake noticed her change of mood. "Forget it, my little Peach. You were not meant to clean up other people's messes. Let's go." He took her arm and started down the stairs, then he turned back to wave at Anna, who was watching them leave. Two memorable women in one day, he reflected, not bad.

Downstairs the driver hurried to open the door of a long, black Cadillac limousine. Kitty held back. "My goodness, is this your car?" she asked.

"Not at all. It's just rented . . . and so is he," Drake answered.

Smiling nervously at the driver, Kitty stepped into the luxury of the car, and as she allowed herself to sink into its plush upholstery, she awakened to a style of life she thought existed only in the movies.

They arrived at the hotel and were escorted to a table close to the dance floor. There was a string quartet playing dinner music. Fresh roses filled a silver vase in the center of the table. The room was beautiful, and Kitty felt like Cinderella who had gone to the ball without the help of her fairy godmother and with no glass slippers. Drake sensed her discomfiture as they were seated. "What's wrong? Don't you like this table? I can change it."

"No, the table's fine . . . it's me. I'm not dressed right for a place like this. Look at the beautiful gowns the other women are wearing.''

Drake studied her brown pleated skirt and plain pink cotton shirt and wondered at the brilliance of her. "You're the loveliest woman in the room," he assured her. "No one is looking at your clothes. Would you like a drink before dinner?''

That afternoon Kitty had asked Mrs. Ulrich the pianist what she should order in a fancy restaurant and had been told that smart and fashionable people always had a martini before dinner. "Why, yes," she replied, "I'll have a martini, please.''

Drake was amused at her attempt at sophistication. "Fine, and I'll have a Haig & Haig Pinch with soda," he told the waiter standing by.

The drinks arrived, and Drake watched Kitty closely. He was pretty sure she had never tasted a martini before. "To new friends," he toasted. She took a sip, and the raw taste of gin filled her mouth. She had to force herself to swallow it. Hazel's cod liver oil had never tasted that bad.

"A martini is always pleasant before dinner, isn't it?'' he asked slyly.

"Yes, it is," she replied without conviction. She looked at the full glass and was dismayed that she would have to drink it all, or at least more of it. How could sophisticated people drink something so vile before dinner?

Drake watched her looking at the drink with revulsion, and he took pity. "I'm not thinking straight. Our first evening together rates something special.'' He called the waiter and ordered a bottle of Dom Perignon. The silver ice bucket was set beside their table, and the sommelier popped the cork. Two crystal glasses appeared as if by magic, and the sparkling wine was poured. Drake signaled the waiter to remove the martini, and he raised his glass in another toast. "To you, my dear," he said softly as they clinked glasses. "Thank you," Kitty responded and sipped gingerly at the bright and effervescent liquid. The taste was dry and tingly and yeasty, but it was wonderful.

"This is so good. What is it?'' she asked.

"Why, it's champagne, of course.''

Kitty was embarrassed. How dumb he'd think she was.

Time moved swiftly. Kitty talked more than she intended, but Drake encouraged her with his interest and attention. He in turn told her all about Mary, whom he had never discussed with any other woman. With Kitty it seemed natural and not at all disloyal. Kitty's interest in him seemed to be honest and without guile, and he was certain there was not a trace of avarice anywhere in her. Her youth and her innocence charmed him utterly, and he felt an enormous sense of freedom to be himself with her.

When the evening ended and they arrived at her flat, Kitty invited him to come inside and meet Hazel. It never occurred to her to be ashamed of her meager life-style or the clutter of her mother's sewing. Hazel was, as usual, still working, huddled under the glare of two floor lamps, struggling to see the tiny stitches. At first she was not aware that her daughter had brought a guest.

"Mother, it's too late for you to be still working," Kitty scolded as she entered.

Without looking up, Hazel answered, "I promised Mrs. Ford I'd have her suit ready for a luncheon tomorrow. How was your date? Was he a nice boy?"

"Mother, I want you to meet my friend Drake Malone."

Suddenly aware of another presence in the room, Hazel looked up and tried to focus on the figure across the room. She stood up and moved closer. "I'm sorry . . . my goodness, honey, you shouldn't bring anyone into this messy house. How do you do, Mr. Malone?" As she neared him, she saw that this was not a boy but a man nearer her own age.

Drake took her hand and pressed it tenderly. The courage and grace of these two lonely women touched him. "Mrs. O'Hara, I'm so happy to meet you. You have a lovely daughter, and now that I've met her mother, I can understand why she is so beautiful." He spoke so earnestly that Hazel found herself beguiled. Surely this was a very important man. They chatted only briefly, but Drake managed to convince Hazel over her strong protests that she must join them for dinner the next evening.

Kitty followed him to the door as he left. "Thank you for the best night of my whole life," she said shyly.

Drake looked into her dark eyes that at times seemed more purple than brown, and then he lifted a strand of her long blond hair and touched it to his lips. "My darling Peach, I cannot stay in St. Louis very long. Would it frighten you if I told you that I do not intend to leave alone?"

Before she could respond, he was gone, the black car disappearing into the night. Kitty stood at the door for a long time watching and feeling a deep sense of loneliness. Was Drake Malone real or was he a phantom prince who had appeared for a shining moment and had now vanished forever? When she went back into the house, Hazel said, "Honey, you better get to bed. You're not getting enough sleep, and you're going out again tomorrow night."

"I can sleep in tomorrow, Mother. I lost my job at the hotel." Hazel put down her work to listen, and as Kitty's story unfolded, her mother felt the stirring of a faint, almost forgotten hope that someday her daughter would marry a man who would cherish her and provide her with security. Although her faith told her that a life of hard work was a life spent as the Lord intended, she secretly prayed that her child would be spared some of the hardships she had endured. Her Kitty was special, and she deserved better.

Drake's days in St. Louis were crowded with business meetings and his evenings spent with Kitty and her mother. He refused to allow Hazel to stay at home alone, partly because he enjoyed treating her to expensive food in elegant restaurants but mostly because he wanted no cloud of suspicion over his intentions toward her daughter. Even Anna's disapproval wavered when she learned that he was including Hazel in their outings.

On the evening before he was scheduled to leave, Hazel was adamant in her refusal to accompany them, and Drake did not protest. She wanted them to have some time alone together so that their relationship could progress beyond its present status. Nothing in her simple background could have prepared her for the wily campaign Drake had already devised to acquire Kitty for himself.

Seated side by side on a banquette in a little French restaurant, Kitty sipped at a glass of Dom Perignon, the drink that Drake had encouraged her to enjoy. She felt it was wicked to spend so much money for the pale, fizzy liquid, but it was delicious and just one glass made her feel carefree, although it wasn't working that night.

In all their previous meetings they'd had so much to talk about, but now Kitty was quiet. Drake would leave the next day, and she would go back to her drab life. It was as though she had lived in darkness until Drake had brought the light, and now she was to be plunged back into all the dim yesterdays.

A violinist came to the table and played "Tenderly" for them. Drake took Kitty's hand and held her fingertips to his lips as the music played. After the musician had moved on, Drake said, "That's how I shall always love you my sweet Peach . . . tenderly."

"But you'll be gone tomorrow," she said morosely.

"Why don't you come with me?" he asked.

"To California? Are you proposing?"

"No, my darling. I would marry you tomorrow, but you are too young. You need time. I don't want to sweep you off your feet with my money and my life-style. So, I propose that you come live in California. I'll arrange a separate place for you and your mother. If, after a while, you feel that you could love me, then we'll be married. If not, I'll provide for you both, either here or wherever you choose to live."

Kitty was stunned. She drew her hand away from his. This wasn't happy ever after! She was young, in love, and romantic. "No, I won't come to California with you like that. If I said yes to such a proposal it would break my mother's heart. She would never agree to such a cold-blooded arrangement as that. If you want me . . . really want me . . . you'll have to ask me to marry you . . . now."

Drake smiled. Everything was going according to plan. He would never have to feel guilty about cradle-robbing. After all, wasn't this sweet young thing setting the terms herself?

"So be it," he said, and took from his pocket a small purple velvet box, which had been delivered that afternoon by messenger from Cartier in New York. Kitty watched in fascination as he opened it and set it on the table in front of her. Nesting in the richness of the velvet was a ring so brilliant and large it took her breath away. She reached out her long slim fingers to touch the square-cut stone, to feel the icy coldness, and to assure herself that it was really there. "Is . . . is that for me?" she asked.

"No other," he replied softly.

"Is it a . . . diamond?"

"Of course it is."

"I didn't know they came that big."

Drake laughed delightedly as he took it from the box and slipped it on her finger. God, he was going to enjoy spending his money on her. "My love, I'll buy you bigger ones later. I just felt that a ring larger than ten carats would be a trifle gaudy on such a fragile young thing as you." He pulled her close to him and held her, looking deeply into eyes that were filled with trust and adoration. "Peach, my love, I shall cherish you for as many years as God will give me. You will never have to be afraid of anything or anyone again."

Kitty experienced a sense of comfort and longing as she pressed herself deeper into his arms. He was the most wonderful man who had ever lived, and she could not believe that he had chosen her. She felt as if she were in a dream.

"Do you love me, Peach?"

How could she find words rich enough to tell him? "More than my life, Drake," she murmured.

He kissed her tenderly, restraining the passion he felt. There would be plenty of time for that later. He did not want to frighten her, for he remembered too well the emotional trauma Mary had suffered on their wedding night. He was no longer a frustrated, fumbling youth, and he intended to see that Kitty learned to desire and enjoy sex as much as he did. She would have to, for his drive was demanding, and she would have to satisfy him. He was determined to be as faithful in this marriage as he had been in the last.

Three weeks later in St. Louis Cathedral, in the presence of tycoons, princes, politicians, the world press, Grace Gable, Hazel, Anna, Helen, and all the little ballet students, Kitty O'Hara became Peach Malone.

_4_

Maggie

MAGGIE turned over in bed and faced the warmth that was Kirk still sleeping. With her eyes closed she slid her hand over to his back and wished that this was all there was to life, just warmth and comfort and touching. Sharing a bed was the nicest part of marriage, she mused, as she allowed herself to drift into the half-sleep where conscious and subconscious are one. Just two months more and they would have been married twenty years. Twenty years . . . twenty times three hundred and sixty-five . . . that's seventy-three hundred nights, she sleepily calculated. Incredible. Hmm, that was almost sixty thousand hours that she had lain beside this man . . . slept with him, made love to him, comforted him, and was comforted. How many of those hours had been angry ones? Not many, for on the nights that either one had gone to a bitter sleep, the mornings had usually been congenial. Both of them were able to work out their antagonisms during slumber. But this night was different.

She turned over and pressed her back up against his, and Kirk moved slightly. Why did she always feel so much closer to him when they were in bed together? The grandfather clock in the hall tolled. Only six. Why had she awakened so early today of all days? Usually Kirk was awake long before she was, and he was frequently irritated at her ability to sleep late.

Today, however, was different, for dawn had arrived to find sleep long gone while she lay worrying. If I could only switch off my mind as easily as I can turn off the damn TV, she grumped to herself.

She buried her face in the pillow. God, why was she so afraid to tell him? After twenty years of sharing everything, why had this one piece of wonderful news presented such a dilemma for her? Because she knew it would upset him, and she was afraid that he would take the matter out of her hands.

She turned over again and put her arm around his waist and snuggled close. We've been touching intimately for twenty years, she mused, and yet, I'll never forget the feeling of the first time. She had grown up unaccustomed to physical contact. Her father was cold and unapproachable. He had rarely hugged or kissed her even when she was a child. Her mother, Angela, although warm and loving, was always in the midst of food preparations or housework, and she never initiated contact. Perhaps her enormous size made her keep her hands to herself for fear that her obese body would be as repulsive to others as it was apparently to her husband and to herself. Even as a teacher, Maggie had learned not to touch her students. A teacher was to communicate with words and keep her hands off.

Kirk had helped her to discover the wonders of touching, and she had loved it. It had been such joy to hold and cuddle her daughter when she was a baby. She administered to her hurts with hugs and kisses as well as Band-Aids.

Yes, Kirk had uncovered a new Maggie, but she was no longer content with herself. She wanted to find out if there was more to her.

Kirk raised his head and looked at the clock-radio on the bedside table. "It's only a little after six. How come you're awake?"

"I shouldn't have had coffee last night, I guess," she lied.

He began to stroke her gently, lifting her nightgown. His fingers moved lightly up and down, then farther and farther down until they were touching the warmth between her thighs. He lifted her hair and kissed the back of her neck, then her shoulders, until she turned on her back. Slowly he moved to her eyes, her lips, and her breasts with his mouth while his hands explored the body that was so familiar to him.

He moved over and into her, and their bodies moved and responded to each other. As the minutes passed, and he realized that this was one of those times when she would receive and enjoy his body but would go nowhere herself, he ascended to his climax then lay down with his arms around her.

"Hmm, you're nice. I wish you would be this awake every morning."

"I'm a night person, remember, and I don't fall asleep in front of the TV like you do," she protested, sensitive from years of needling.

"What's on your schedule today?" he asked.

"A lot of thinking. I have a big decision to make."

"Really, what about?" She could tell he was only half listening, but she decided to forge ahead and tell him. It was time he faced the fact that she had something of her own that was important.

"Drake Malone's widow has asked me to decorate her new penthouse for her." She knew she had his full attention now.

"Are you kidding me? Or is someone kidding you?"

"No, it's quite true. She called me yesterday."

"Where did you meet her? Not at the supermarket, I presume."

"Not likely." Maggie felt a thrill at her husband's awed response to her announcement. It had been a long time since she'd had such respectful attention from him. She stretched the moment, for she had to choose her words carefully. This would be frightfully difficult if he chose to oppose her, and the job itself was terrifying enough. "Laura recommended me to her. Jim was Drake Malone's doctor when he died."

"That was just last week. She's sure not wasting any time spending his money."

"It's not like that at all," she protested, realizing he had already managed to put her on the defensive. "She's leaving for Italy soon to spend a couple of months with her daughter who lives there. She bought a large place on top of one of those expensive new high-rises on Wilshire, and she wants it completely decorated in two months.''

"Does she know you have no formal training? That you've never been paid a cent for all the help you've given your so-called friends with their houses?"

"You know I wouldn't lie. She liked Laura's house and asked her who did it. Laura told her it was just a hobby with me . . . I didn't need the money . . ."

"That's an understatement. I don't want you making any money. I'm having trouble enough sheltering the money I've made this year."

"But if I take the job, I will be making money, Kirk . . . significant money."

"Forget it. Besides, you can't get tied down to anything now. If the Japanese thing works out, I have to be prepared to leave on short notice, and I want you to go with me."

"How is that deal coming along? That's the first time you've mentioned it in a long time."

"Fine, nothing new."

"That whole deal has been on and off for ages now. What makes you think it will happen in the next two months?"

Kirk was annoyed. He knew she was right, but he did not intend to concede anything. "Forget it, honey. You've got a job here in this house. I don't want you working for some rich bitch who'll think she owns you."

Maggie resisted the urge to snap back that he didn't own her either, but she tried to be persuasive. "Kirk, Peach Malone may be rich, but she's not a bitch. I had a long talk with her on the telephone, and she's very sweet. This is a golden opportunity for me. Do you have any idea how thrilling it is to have someone actually offer to pay me to do something I enjoy doing?"

"I don't get it. That woman had enough money to buy any decorator in the world. Why would she want you?"

"Thanks, dear, for that vote of confidence. I know it's hard to believe, but she told me she didn't want the place to look like anyone else's . . . and she didn't want someone who was involved with any of her friends. She wants me precisely because I haven't got a lot of nosy clients. She's a very private person, and she doesn't want anybody to know what she's doing."

Kirk realized he might lose the battle, so he began to retreat as gracefully as possible. "Okay, okay, as long as you don't get in over your head." He got up and headed toward the bathroom.

Now was the time to accept his grudging permission and end the discussion, but Maggie wanted also to extract from him an understanding that he could not expect things to go on as usual. She heard his razor snap on, and she knew it was too late. He'd hate it if she brought it up again at breakfast. Relaxing with his coffee and the *Times* was the best part of his day, he often declared, and she knew better than to interrupt that. "The devil with it. I'll call her today and take the job and fight it out later," she hissed as she threw back the blanket and swung her feet to the floor.

_5_

Amazing Grace

"GRACE, there's a call for you on line one . . . a Mrs. Malone. I told her you were busy, but she insisted."

"Gary, you should know by now that I take her calls regardless of how busy I am." The very thin, fashionably dressed and coiffed woman waved her employee out of her office and picked up the telephone. "Welcome home, stranger. How was Italy?"

"Fine, I suppose," Peach responded. "Could you do me a really big favor, Grace?"

"If I can."

"I desperately need my hair done today. I know it's awfully short notice, but it's really important. I've got a dinner meeting tonight with the trustees of Drake's estate, and I'll need all the self-confidence I can get," Peach said.

Grace hesitated only briefly. "Any particular time?"

"About three. I'll shampoo it myself. I'm at my new penthouse . . . do you know where it is?"

"Yes, I'll be there."

Grace replaced the receiver. Damn, now she couldn't meet her daughter at the airport, but Casey would surely understand. She knew about the promise she had made to Drake. She then called Eve and asked her to come into the office. Almost immediately an attractive woman wearing tight white pants and a turquoise silk shirt cinched at the waist with a fuchsia cummerbund arrived. "Amazing Grace's," the hair salon of many of Los Angeles' weathiest people, both men and women,

44

had all of its employees dressed at Alan Austin's in Beverly Hills.

"Eve, are you doing anyone special this afternoon?" Grace asked.

"I was supposed to do Ghilly Jordan, but her housekeeper just called to cancel. She's in the sack with somebody great, she says, and doesn't want to quit while she's ahead."

"While she's giving it, you mean. Who's the new stud she's balling lately?"

"She hasn't told me, which is weird. She usually describes every grind, suck, and tickle. Sometimes I think she has an orgasm just telling about her conquests. But she's been awfully subdued the last couple of weeks."

"Eve, would you mind picking up Casey at the airport for me this afternoon? She's arriving on American's three-thirty flight from Chicago."

"How come you're not meeting her yourself? You haven't seen her for months."

"I can't. Peach Malone just called."

"God, how stupid. You know very well that Mrs. Malone would understand. Let me go for you."

"No, I promised Drake . . ."

"He's dead now. I'll go do her hair and explain . . ."

"Nothing, you'll explain nothing. His death doesn't change anything."

"Okay, okay, but Gary will have to get off his butt and help with that group of Japanese tourists."

"He's got dermatitis on his hands from the dye."

"Too bad, let him wear rubber gloves. You baby him too much."

"Eve, who's running this shop . . . you or me?"

"Sorry, I guess I've been here too long."

"Nonsense, I couldn't manage without you."

"Then how about a raise?"

"I gave you one last month."

"I know, but what have you done for me lately?"

Grace smiled and felt a rush of warmth for this intelligent woman she had known so long. Eve had left the shop several times to try to find herself, but nothing ever worked out for her, and she always came back. Hairdressing was the only creative outlet where she could make enough money to support herself. She also loved beautiful clothes and associating with celebrities. Hollywood's rich and famous had a penchant for treating their hairdressers as social equals.

Grace, however, never placed herself on the same level with the people who flocked to her salon. She treated all her customers with consideration and respect, and everyone who worked in what she called "Gable's Stable" cultivated the same courteous attitude, or she fired them.

She summoned Gary into her office and told him that he would have to work that afternoon. She was amused as his anger mounted. He was so incredibly handsome, and the customers adored him. "Grace, you know I can't," he began, but she fixed her eyes on the bulge at his crotch, a technique that always managed to unnerve him, probably because there was not as much there as advertised. A lot of women had tried to find out and failed. Gary was not only gay, he was also discreet.

"This is an emergency, Gary. I'm sorry, but I've got to send Eve to pick up Casey. You can wear rubber gloves. These are Japanese tourists, and I'm sure there'll be no coloring to do."

His manner changed abruptly. "Japanese? Can I charge more? They've got lots to spend, you know."

"Okay, but keep it within reason."

Gary left and Grace leaned back, sinking into the soft leather of the tall turquoise chair which she had imported from Italy. The walls were covered in a pale, blue-green ultrasuede fabric that was almost obscured by the dozens of autographed pictures of famous clients. In the world of the young and the trendy, the ambitious and the gay, the monied and the celebrated, she had triumphed. A chubby, uneducated bumpkin from Illinois had become the doyenne of hair in the capital of glamour. She had worked hard to get this far. She had raised her daughter, who was now a Ph.D. teaching English literature at the University of Illinois, and she owed nothing to anyone except Drake Malone and his widow. It was a debt that would never be repaid as long as she or Peach lived. If she had not met Drake Malone, God knows what would have happened to her and her child.

It was a cold snowy night in Champaign when Jerry Casey offered her a ride in his Pontiac after the coffee shop closed. He had been there all evening with his fraternity brothers, and Grace had been fascinated by his height and ruddy good looks. Jerry Casey was the only person at the University of Illinois who could manage to stay tan all winter long.

Grace worked nights in the shop to help pay her expenses at school. Her father had saved very little for her education. The small grocery store in Mount Vernon, Illinois, made just enough to support his family. Her two older sisters had gone to beauty school and moved to Chicago to work, but Grace was very bright and wanted to be a schoolteacher.

The night Jerry offered her a ride, she hesitated only a moment. He had a reputation for being very fast, but she was not afraid of him. She was full-breasted and had been fighting off urgent young men since puberty. Anyway, Jerry had always been different from the others. He had never grabbed at her or eyed her breasts, at least not obviously. He spoke courteously and never made suggestive or leering comments. And he was so good-looking.

It was snowing heavily, and her dormitory was a long way from the coffee shop. She accepted his offer and went in the back to get her coat. She picked up the old rubber galoshes her mother had given her, but she couldn't bring herself to put them on. She would look tacky. She stuffed them under the cabinet and put on her coat and tied a wool scarf around her head. She would ask him to drop her right in front of the dorm entrance.

Jerry helped her into the car, and after getting in, he turned on the engine, the heater, and the radio. Tony Bennett was singing "Because of You." Grace shivered with the cold and the thrill of being there with him. He reached into the back seat and pulled a lap robe to the front. Carefully, he tucked it around her, his fingers lingering a shade long as they pressed the blanket under her thighs. "There, that should keep you warm," he said.

"I'm fine, really," she replied, "and besides, it's not a long ride to the dorm."

"Are you in a big hurry to get there?" he asked.

"Well, uh, no, I guess not."

"Good, I've been wanting a chance to talk to you."

"You have?"

"I wanted you to know that I don't think it's nice of the guys to make remarks like they do." He eased the car into gear and pulled slowly away from the curb.

"You don't?" she asked, faintly bewildered.

"I think it's shitty the way they're always sniggering about, you know, your bustline."

In spite of the cold, Grace felt her face grow hot as she blushed. She had always been sensitive about the size of her breasts, and she tended to wear clothes that diminished or hid them as much as possible.

"I guess you're used to it, but it makes me mad, and I've told them so. A woman is so much more than just a pair of big tits."

"I'm not used to it at all, Jerry. I hate it, I really do. It's so embarrassing."

The car moved slowly through the white and silent streets while they talked about classes, people, and music. Grace was amazed at how often they agreed on things. She was almost unaware when he stopped the car and turned to face her, giving her all his attention, hanging on every word she said. She found herself confessing private thoughts she had shared with no one before.

His arm slid across her shoulders, and they moved closer together on the seat. It was warmer that way. When at last he began to kiss her, it was sweet and comfortable, and she had no desire to stop him. It was not long before she felt his hand under her skirt, slowly stroking its way up her thighs. Other boys had always touched her breasts first, and she had rejected their advances. In his wisdom, he bypassed her upper torso and went directly to his primary target. Grace was aroused to the point where she welcomed his touch, and when she opened her legs for his hand, he knew he was in control.

Gently stroking and kissing her, he eased her to a prone position on the seat under him. He pulled off her now soggy underpants and unzipped his fly. With a quick stroke, he pressed himself inside so rapidly that the pain of her splitting hymen was smothered in the convulsion of her first orgasm. He was not finished with her, and he pressed into her harder as he continued his thrusts. He brought her to climax once more before he reached his own.

Lying on the seat of his car with her seducer exhausted on top of her, Grace felt his semen and her blood seeping from her. She hoped she had pleased him enough so that he would want to see her again.

Jerry Casey raised a hunger for sex in Grace that his own libido could barely satisfy. Every night he would pick her up in his car, and they would devour each other's bodies for hours in the back seat. Since conquest, not sex, was his real passion, his interest lasted less than a month. He stopped coming to the diner where she worked, and calls to the fraternity house were met with sniggers and offers from the brothers to fill in for him. Being pragmatic, she finally acknowledged that the big romance was over, and she tried to have no rancor for him, until she missed her period and realized she was pregnant.

Suddenly, her confidence was shattered. She had no one to help her. Never, ever, could she tell her parents what she had done. They would consider her a slut and would probably disown her. In the 1950s only women with a death wish would have an abortion, for they were expensive, dangerous, and illegal.

She would have to leave Illinois and go to a place where no one knew her. She would go to California where the sun always shined, but she had to have some money. She would confront Jerry Casey and ask for his help. It would be wonderful if he offered to marry her, but she was not stupid enough to expect that to happen. It took her two weeks just to catch him alone on campus.

"Hi, Jerry, where've you been? I've been trying to reach you."

"Yeah, well, I've been pretty busy."

"Jerry, I'm pregnant."

"I don't like that kind of joke, Grace. I've got to go to class."

"It's no joke. I need your help."

"If you've got some crazy idea that I'm going to marry you, forget it. You enjoyed those rumbles as much as I did."

Grace managed to keep her dismay at his response hidden. She decided to be as callous as he was. "Don't be an ass, Jerry Casey. I wouldn't marry you if you were the last man on earth. I wouldn't want a husband who cheated, and you'll always do that."

"What do you want then?" His face was sullen and suspicious.

"Enough money to get me to California."

"All I've got is fifty bucks in my bank account."

"That's not enough. Call your father."

"I can't. I've already borrowed on next semester's allowance."

"Call him, Jerry, or by God, I will."

"Okay, okay, but he'll never let loose of more than two hundred."

"When can you get it to me?"

"Tomorrow."

"Why, you creep. You've already got that much. You lied."

"A deal's a deal." He smirked snottily.

Grace wanted to slice off his cock and make sure he never screwed anybody else again, but she knew she was beaten. "Tomorrow. I'll meet you here at this time," she declared.

"Yeah, well, before I give you any money, I want a letter saying I'm not the father of your kid. This'll be the last time you get any money out of me. Understand?"

"You bastard!" She turned and hurried away. She did not

want him to see that she was crying. Didn't the son of a bitch care that she was going to be the mother of his child?

The next day they met and exchanged the letter for the money. "So long, honey. Have a good trip. Maybe those big knockers of yours will get you in the movies."

Grace's hostility was monumental. "You're just jealous of my big tits because you've got such a small cock. It's not nearly as big as Duncan's or Harry's, you know."

Jerry's face showed his dismay and shock. "You cunt, you've been screwing my friends too! How do you know it's my baby?"

Grace smirked. "I don't."

She hurried away into the crowd of students before he could get his hands on her. She was enormously pleased with herself. Getting the last word with a jerk as sleazy as Jerry Casey was damn satisfying.

Grace got up from her desk and walked out to the salon to check on things. She did this constantly, for somewhere in the back of her mind there lurked a fear that everything was just an illusion, a dream that would disappear, and she would find herself back in Illinois, alone and pregnant. It seemed ironic that she could have made her fortune catering to women's need to remain young, when she herself looked back on her own youth with abhorrence. She strolled through the salon watching her employees attempt to perform miracles and the coldness of her memories was warmed by the reassurance that this beautiful salon was all hers. No one else owned any part of it, and her debts were paid. All except one.

Grace left school two days after her final confrontation with Jerry. She boarded a Greyhound bus and headed for Chicago, where her older sisters Eldona and Blanche worked as hairdressers. She wasn't sure of the reception she would receive, but she knew it would be better than going home in disgrace. She had always been the darling of her parents, for she was pretty and bright, and she excelled in school. Her father, in the absence of a son, had vested his hopes in her to become a lawyer, or a doctor, or a teacher, or at least to graduate from college. She suspected her sisters resented her.

To her surprise she was welcomed warmly. Perhaps her sisters were relieved that she, after all, had proved to be less than perfect. Although their apartment was small, they let her sleep on the couch, and to help with her keep, they got a job for her as a shampoo girl in the hair salon at Marshall Field's, where they worked. Although she felt guilty about it, she did not reveal to her sisters that she had two hundred dollars. Once her child was born, she intended to leave Chicago and make a new life in California.

Blanche bought her a wedding band at the dime store and insisted that she change her name to avoid embarrassing them. Eldona, who was an avid movie fan, chose the name Gable after her idol Clark. Grace didn't mind. Chicago was just a way station for her.

Working at the shop with her sisters was enjoyable. She loved all the perfumes and the clean smell of the shampoo. She was a hard worker who endeared herself to everyone with her eagerness to be helpful. She was quick to sweep hair from the floor, keep everyone supplied with clean combs and curlers, and serve coffee.

When her pregnancy began to show, the manager provided her with a larger uniform to help conceal it. He was paying her less than she was worth, and he did not want her to leave. Eldona concocted a story about Grace's husband deserting her and joining the Navy, and everyone was sympathetic to her plight. Although the baby was due in September, Grace told everyone that the big event was not till November. She was hoarding every nickel and dime she got in tips and adding them to her savings account, and she wanted to work as long as possible.

Grace returned to the apartment one night to find a letter from her mother. It had been almost two months since she had written them that she had left college to become a hairdresser. She had not mentioned her pregnancy. She dreaded opening it.

Dear Grace,

Your dad and I wish you the best of luck. We are sorry you quit school, but it is your life. We are disappointed, but we love you because you have always been such a good girl. Stay that way.
Your loving mother.

Grace cried all night.

After a labor of over nineteen hours, Grace gave birth to a seven-pound daughter in the charity ward at St. Ann's. She named the child Casey. If her father would not give her his last name, Grace decided she would at least have it as her first name. Since she had registered as Mrs. Gable, that was the surname listed on the birth certificate. The father was listed as Paul Gable, address unknown. No one would ever know that her daughter was illegitimate.

Grace decided to nurse the baby, because it would be a long ride across the country and impossible to provide bottles of formula. She told no one her plans, for she did not want to be persuaded to spend one more miserable winter in Illinois. She was going to find the sun.

Early in November, Grace boarded a bus with three hundred dollars hidden in a homemade belt tied around her waist under her slip. She carried her baby, a small suitcase of clothes, and a box of stiff, paper diapers. She left a note of thanks to her sisters with a promise to keep in touch.

The horror of the long ride and the ensuing weeks of panic were memories Grace seldom resurrected. She found Los Angeles to be a dirty, uncaring city, so huge and spread out that people without cars were prisoners of the neighborhoods where they lived. Grace could find no one she trusted to take care of her child, and she could not take the baby with her to search for a job. She was stranded in a cheap downtown hotel where she was surrounded by whores and winos. She felt that she had been damned and sent to hell.

One morning as she was descending the dark stairs to go to the grocery store, she was stopped by a young woman on her way in. Her makeup was heavy, and her clothes were garish and tight.

"Hi, can I see your baby?" she asked.

Grace hesitated for fear the woman might have a disease, but her smile was kind, and Grace was hungry for a friend. She opened the crib shawl covering Casey's face, and the woman leaned over. She made no attempt to touch the child. "Gee, she's gorgeous. How old is she?"

"A little over two months. How did you know she was a girl?"

"Pink blanket." The two women laughed, and they eased into a conversation. Grace learned that the woman had a three-year-old boy living with a foster family, and that she called herself Lily after the opera star Lily Pons. She invited Grace to have coffee in her room, and with some misgivings, Grace joined her. Over coffee and stale doughnuts, she told Lily her problems.

The next morning Lily awakened Grace early. "Kid, I got an idea for you," she said. Grace invited her in and listened while Casey nursed. "Look, you can't keep the kid here. It's too dirty. I called this woman who's got Bobby, and she said she'd watch Casey for a week so you could look for a job. Then you can pay her. She's a nice lady and could use the money."

"How far away is she?" Grace asked.

"We can take a bus. Let's go. I gotta get back and go to bed. I had a big night."

The neighborhood where Mrs. Goldhammer lived was tidy. Located in the Fairfax area, the houses were small, but the lawns were trimmed, and there were geraniums growing everywhere. The house where Lily stopped had pink stucco walls and a red tile roof. She rang the bell and a heavyset woman answered.

"Hi, Mrs. Goldhammer. Here's my friend Grace Gable, and this is Casey. Isn't she cute?"

The woman smiled and opened her arms for Grace to give her the baby. "How nice. Come in, won't you? Here, let me see the little darling."

Suddenly a whirlwind of chubby arms and legs came flying out the door and slammed into Lily. "Mommy, Mommy, you're back!"

Lily gathered her little boy in her arms and hugged him. Grace was astonished at the onslaught of love and joy that suddenly transformed the streetwise and tough Lily into a vulnerable and loving mother. Mrs. Goldhammer hurried them into the house. "Come, come inside. Hurry. That nosy social worker is all the time snooping around."

They sat down in the living room. The hardwood floors were polished. The furniture was old, the rug was worn, but there were clean and starched hand-crocheted antimacassars and doilies on the couch and the tables.

As they drank Mrs. Goldhammer's strong tea, they talked about Grace's need to find a job. Then Mrs. Goldhammer made her proposal. "I will keep your little girl for one week, and when you get a job, maybe we work out babysitting during the day. I need money too. These social workers don't pay much for foster kids, and what's a poor old widow to do, I ask you?"

Grace liked the woman, but she had learned to distrust her feelings. Although she didn't want to hand over her child to a perfect stranger, she couldn't bear to think of returning to the wretchedness and despair she faced alone at the hotel. "Mrs. Goldhammer, I'm nursing Casey. She's never had a bottle. If I leave her for a week, I'll lose my milk."

"You gotta do it sometime. You can't go to work and nurse a baby too. I'll mix her up a formula with some Carnation milk and Karo syrup. You see, she'll be fine."

Grace was overwhelmed by the authority in the woman's voice and her own inability to think of a better solution. She had to go to work or they would both starve. Reluctantly she agreed to the arrangement. She nursed Casey for one last time before leaving her. She was frightened and heartsick at abandoning her baby, and she sobbed uncontrollably on the bus ride back to the hotel.

Grace tried everywhere to find a job . . . beauty salons, restaurants, department stores. Her breasts became engorged with milk and hard and painful. She tried to express some of the milk to get relief, but the pain was excruciating. She longed for the soft sweet mouth of her baby cuddled to her breast to nurse away the misery. Just thinking of her child caused her nipples to stiffen, and she had to pad her brassiere with toilet paper to keep the milk from leaking all over her clothes.

By the end of the fifth day, she was desperate. Her money was disappearing in bus and streetcar fares, and she was running a fever. She felt ill, and she was worried about Casey. She decided she must see Mrs. Goldhammer and beg her for more time. She was also anxious to see if Casey was all right.

The shortened days of winter brought darkness early. In her feverish and frightened state of mind, Grace became confused. She wished she'd waited for Lily to come home. The houses looked so different at night. She walked up one street and down another, but she could not locate the house where Casey was being kept.

At last she decided she'd better find a telephone book and look up the address. She had been stupid and foolish to think she could find her way back alone. She walked down Pico Boulevard looking for a telephone booth. Cruising cars filled with young men would occasionally slow down and follow her, but she tried to ignore them. Some called to her with obscene proposals and nasty gestures. Some shouted to her in a language she could not understand, but there was no doubt in her mind what they wanted.

She was tired and weak, but she forced herself to walk faster, to put purpose in her step, to look neither to the left nor to the right. She was afraid, and she felt very much alone. She saw an open liquor store and she hurried inside hoping to find refuge there. The brightly lit interior was comforting momentarily. She barely observed her surroundings, so intent was she on making contact with someone, anyone, to escape the overpowering hysteria of isolation. A thin, sharp-faced man, his hair slick with oil, eyed her coldly.

"Please, may I take a look at your telephone book? I left my baby at . . ."

"There's a public phone two blocks down at the gas station."

The man's hostility chilled her, and afraid as she was to return to the street, she was even less inclined to stay in the store with him. She returned to the darkness of the night where the wind had begun to blow. She shivered, although the cold felt good on her face, which was inflamed with fever. She was exhausted, but nonetheless moved with an urgency that compelled her to find her daughter as soon as possible.

Having been born and raised in the security of a small town and always surrounded by people who knew her, she lacked the sense of self-preservation inculcated in city children. She had not been taught to be suspicious of strangers, and she was now experiencing a fear for her own safety that heretofore had been alien to her. Her self-confidence and belief in her own ability to survive was nearly shattered. Her heart beat faster.

At last she reached the station, and with relief she sprinted toward the telephone booth back in the corner away from the boulevard. She enclosed herself in the booth and, with fingers fumbling, lifted the heavy book and began her search for the address of the woman who had her child. The light was dim, and her eyes were swollen and red from the fever and her tears. It was hard to read the small print. "Dear God, please let me find her," she whispered.

Grace was unaware that five young men had driven into the station and were holding the attendant at gunpoint while they emptied the cash drawer. Angry that there was less than they expected, the man holding the gun slammed it into the side of the attendant's head, knocking him unconscious and opening a large wound. The assailants piled into their car and were about to speed away when they passed the telephone booth and saw the lone young woman.

"Hey, lookit that, man . . . we gonna get us some pussy."

"Yeah, let's git 'er."

One of the husky young hoodlums jumped out of the car as it stopped within inches of the telephone booth. He watched Grace for just one moment to make sure she was alone, and then he hurled himself at the door, pushing it open.

Grace screamed as she felt the pain of the folding door slamming into her back, pinning her against the telephone. Quickly, the youth slapped his hand over her mouth and pulled her toward him roughly. She struggled and kicked and tried to fight him off, but he was strong and rough, and her efforts were useless. Within moments, she found herself pressed on the floor of the back seat with six heavy feet and legs on top of her body and her head. She tried to scream, but a heavy shoe slammed into her face, and she heard the click of a switch-blade knife being opened and then thrust at her throat.

"Shut yo' mouth, you lousy bitch, or I cut you good!"

She whimpered slightly, but she made no more effort to scream or to fight. Through her terror, she felt the pain of the men's feet stomping on her sore breasts. She tried to think of some way to save herself, but she knew there was none. She considered screaming and forcing them to kill her instantly so that she would not have to endure the ordeal that lay ahead, but the will to live for her child was strong, and she found the courage to remain silent until the car finally stopped in a dark alley.

"Let's do it here . . . c'mon, I'm in a hurry . . ."

"Shit! We all's in a hurry. Get yo' ass away from her. I seen her first. I git it while it's nice and tight, you heah?"

Grace was dragged from the car, and rough hands tore at her clothes, exposing her soft and sensitive skin to the cold night air. Her legs were pried apart, and she was smothered by the weight of a heavy body on top of her. A large hand covered her mouth so that she could not scream. Suddenly she felt the pain of a large, dry penis forcing itself into her body, thrusting hard and deep. Hands pinched and poked at her sore breasts, and she felt a large mouth covering her nipple, sucking and slobbering and chewing at it.

"This muttha's got milk!" he screamed as he reached his

climax with a last pelvic thrust that almost penetrated her womb. He was pulled off her, and she was quickly mounted again. The pain was less severe now that she was lubricated with semen.

"Hurry up, shithead! Ma prick is gonna 'splode."

"Stick it in her mouth, asshole!"

Suddenly Grace found her head covered by the weight of a heavy torso. "Open yo' mouth, cunt, and suck!"

Almost smothered and barely able to breathe, Grace tried to turn her head, but the cold blade of the knife was thrust into her ear. "Suck, bitch, or I stick it in."

Grace opened her mouth, unsure of what was expected of her since she had never heard of oral sex. She had to force herself not to clamp down with her teeth and bring on her immediate death. The body pressed down over her face, pumping at her, making it impossible for her to get air, and his penis filled her mouth and pressed into her throat causing her to gasp and gag helplessly.

She tried to remove her spirit from her body. She prayed to a God who did not hear. She knew that she was dying at the hands of men who had no regard for her humanity. If they could abuse her so brutally, then her life or death could have no meaning to them. She was nothing. She longed for unconsciousness to escape the thrusting and prodding at her body. At last, she lost track of time as her spirit began to drift away. The rapists used her again and again, until suddenly the headlights of a car flashed over them, and they leaped away from the battered flesh of what had been a vital young woman minutes before. Rushing into their car to escape, they left her barely alive. The lights of the patrol car advanced rapidly toward Grace's body in pursuit, but the driver saw her in time or the wheels of the law would have finished what the criminals had begun. Grace was not aware that she had been rescued. The policemen got out and flashed their lights over her bruised and battered body.

Semen and blood ran from her mouth, her vagina, and her anus. Blood seeped from knife cuts on her face and body.

There were huge welts raised on her face, and her eyes were swollen shut.

"Jesus, what a mess! D'ya think she's alive?"

"I dunno. C'mon, let's put her in the car and get her to emergency, fast."

Quickly the two young officers put Grace into the back seat of the squad car. They did not bother to cover her nakedness. As they drove off with their siren screaming, one of them remarked, "This is one little hooker who won't turn any tricks for a while."

"Yeah, if ever."

Grace the woman survived, but Grace the girl was left dead in the alley. Three days later, she remembered what had happened to her. Four days later, she found the strength to ask a nurse to find Lily at the hotel, but she had to wait more than a week to see her. In addition to her injuries, Grace was also suffering abscesses in both breasts, and the doctors had lanced them to release the infection and pus that was congesting them and keeping her temperature elevated.

When she was strong enough to see her friend, Lily's appearance convinced the hospital staff and the police that Grace was, as had been assumed, a prostitute. Grace was too ill to comprehend their opinion of her, and she was thankful to get the news of her baby's well-being. Lily was wise enough not to question her friend about her nightmare, and she kept the conversation centered on Casey. She told her that Mrs. Goldhammer had gladly agreed to take care of her daughter until Grace was on her feet again. Lily did not tell her that she was giving her money to do it.

Days later, when she was able to walk without help, Grace asked a nurse why the police had never been in to question her. Weren't they trying to find her tormentors? She was bewildered by the nurse's smirk as she replied that they probably felt it was a waste of time.

Grace was released from the hospital three weeks after the attack. She was thin and weak and still unable to sit down comfortably because of the stitches in her vagina and anus. The swelling around her face had diminished, and the bruises were fading from purple to yellow. The young intern who had stitched her eyelid had been nervous, and the scar was beginning to give her left eye a sinister droop. Her breasts grew smaller each day, almost as if her body was trying to recede from its own sexuality.

If her youth was helping her to heal physically, it was failing her mentally. Her days and nights were filled with terror. Asleep or awake, the ghastly experience kept recurring in her imagination. Her days in the hospital were days of uncontrollable weeping, and her nights were filled with fear and dreams. At first the hospital staff was understanding, but as time passed and the horrible screams in the night continued, they lost patience with her.

Grace herself was disgusted with her own inability to put the experience behind her, and when the physician suggested that she might be better off at home, she agreed. But where was home? With Lily, the only friend she had. The rapists had not only stolen her youth and her spirit, they had also taken all of her money.

Lily came to the hospital to pick Grace up in a taxi driven by a customer of hers. As Grace stepped outside, a shiver of fear swept through her. How was she to survive and take care of her child? Defiled as she now was, home and family were even more remote than they had been before.

It was a beautiful day in Los Angeles. It had rained the night before, and a cool breeze had blown away the smog. The sun was bright and clear, and snowcapped mountains were visible in the distance. For the first time, Grace was thankful that she had not died.

The cab pulled up in front of the pink house that had eluded her that dreadful night, and Grace realized she was going to see Casey again. Mrs. Goldhammer appeared on the porch with Casey in her arms, and Grace pulled herself out of the cab and hurried toward her baby. Understanding her eagerness, the older woman relinquished her bundle to Grace, and then she put her own arm around the mother to support her. The emotion of the reunion was so intense that Grace began to cry, and so did Lily and Mrs. Goldhammer.

After their visit, they returned alone to the hotel. Lily helped her up the stairs. "Look, Grace, I hope you don't mind. I can't afford to pay for two rooms, so the guy downstairs moved a rollaway bed in my room for you. Okay?"

"I don't know how I'll ever repay you. I couldn't get a job before, and look at me now." She walked to the dresser in the small room now crowded with two beds and looked at her image in the mirror.

"Give it time . . . a little makeup . . . you'll be fine, believe me," Lily said, trying to reassure her.

Grace did not wait a week before she began to experiment with Lily's makeup to try to hide the damage that had been done to her face. She was in a hurry. She had to get well so that she could escape the terrors of the nights alone in the hotel room. She was unable to sleep, a victim of her fears and her memories. She had come to a painful and frightening decision.

"You what?" Lily screamed when she told her.

"I've . . . decided to do . . . what you do."

"You're nuts! You got an education, you dummy. D'ya think for one minute I'd be hookin' if I could do anything else?"

"That's the point, Lily. I can't do anything else. I can't find a job. I don't even have bus fare to look for one, and I can't keep living off you."

"Lord, Grace, listen to me. Every night I'm out there I'm scared shitless. I worry all the time that what happened to you might happen to me. It don't have to be no gang either, just some nut with a knife . . . or a gun. Kiddo, there's more crazies out there shoppin' for pussy than nice guys. You don't know what it's like. It ain't fun . . . it's lousy."

"Maybe the odds are in my favor now, Lily. It's already happened to me. Maybe I'm safer than you are."

Lily shook her head in disgust. "I don't get it. After what you went through, how can you even think about fuckin' anybody."

"I might as well sell it, Lily . . . I sure as hell could never do it for enjoyment again . . . never."

Grace's decision was not easy to implement. Night after night, she would walk the streets with Lily, but she could not bring herself to follow through. If a john responded to her appeal, she would back away and leave him bewildered. Lily refused to give her any encouragement. If Grace was determined to be a whore, she'd damn well do it by herself. Lily felt that she already had enough sin on her immortal soul without adding that.

As time passed, Grace grew weaker. She did not want to eat Lily's food, and she was afraid to sleep because the demons in her psyche would take control and torture her in her dreams. She longed to hold Casey in her arms. Lily was making less money than usual because she was afraid to leave Grace alone too long, and they were existing on canned spaghetti and coffee. Grace's figure became more wasted, and her drooping eyelid became more prominent in her gaunt face with its haunted eyes. She began to lose all hope.

Salvation sometimes appears in the guise of tragedy, and so it was with Grace. One night she took to the street again, determined this time to conquer her fears and turn her first trick. She had not seen Casey for over a week, and she was desperate for bus fare. She spotted a nice-looking young man standing alone on the corner. She approached him cautiously, trying to remember the patois of the streetwalker. She was nervous as she managed only to rasp a weak, "Hi."

"Hi, yourself," he answered, looking interested. Her mind blotted out all the catchy approaches she had heard the women of the street make, and she stood there gaping at him silently. "Well," he said, "how about it? You interested in making some dough tonight?" Stiffly Grace nodded her head. The stranger moved quickly toward her and lifted his hand to signal a waiting car parked down the street. The headlights flashed on, and the vehicle moved rapidly toward them. "This is your lucky night, little lady. We've got a whole fraternity house full of young studs with bulging pockets and cocks . . ."

Terrified, Grace saw the car draw up beside them. Inside were five or six men. She tried to pull away, but the young man gripped her arm firmly. She had to run . . . to escape! She swung her leg back and kicked him in the shin as hard as she could. He released his hold, and she dashed away as fast as she could go. She darted across the street into the path of a long, black limousine speeding down the boulevard. She did not see it nor did she ever have any memory of the impact when it struck her.

Two weeks later, she awakened in the hospital once more, but this time it was different. She was not in a ward but a private room. A bouquet of red roses sat on the dresser across from her. As she tried to move, she realized that her left arm and leg were immobilized in casts, and a bandage covered her left eye.

When the nurse entered the room, she was startled to find Grace awake. She hurried to the bed and looked at her closely. "Thanks be to God!" she exclaimed as she took Grace's hand and pressed it warmly. "Can ye hear what it is that I'm sayin' to ye?"

Grace smiled and answered softly, her voice sounding strange to her own ears. "Yes, I can. Who are you?"

The older woman crossed herself quickly and lifted her eyes upward in thanksgiving. "Dearie, I'm Katie, your private nurse, and I've been watchin' over ye day and night for Mr. Malone. I must be callin' him right away with the good news."

For the next hour, Grace's room was a flurry of activity. Nurses, aides, and interns stopped in to see for themselves that the mysterious young woman was indeed out of her coma at last. Grace was too bewildered by all the attention to ask questions. It was enough to bask in the glow of their concern.

When she was alone with Katie, she asked the most important question. "How is my baby, Katie? Is she all right?"

"Baby? Ye had no baby, dearie, ye had an accident. Mr. Malone's car hit ye . . . don't ye remember?"

Grace was confused. She had no recollection of the accident or the events leading up to it. As she struggled to assemble her thoughts, a tall, handsome man entered with an entourage of nurses. He stood beside her bed and smiled encouragingly. "Well, well . . . at last. You've had a long sleep, young lady."

"How . . . how long?" Grace asked.

"Two weeks. By the way, I'm Dr. Allison."

"Two weeks! Oh, God, my baby!"

Katie drew the doctor aside and told him what she had heard. As they conferred, Drake Malone strode into the room, and ignoring everyone, headed directly toward Grace. He stared into her face intently to assure himself that she was really conscious and muttered, "Thank God."

"Help me, please," she begged him.

Startled by the fervor of her plea, he leaned toward her. "Anything . . . I'll do anything that is in my power to do for you," he promised.

"Find my baby . . . please find her for me."

"Tell me everything. If your baby is on the face of this earth, I'll find her for you!"

Haltingly, she struggled to find the right words, the names and the places that tried to elude her. Drake Malone listened and then began his quest to put Grace's life back together again. It was not easy. Lily had been arrested and then evicted from the hotel. She had disappeared. Mrs. Goldhammer had turned Casey over to the authorities. Daily, Grace remembered more details, and eventually Drake's people located the foster home where Casey had been placed.

When Grace was released from the hospital, she was taken to Drake Malone's house with Katie, and there she was reunited with her child. Because of the extent of her injuries and her poor physical condition, she needed a long convalescence. Drake saw to it that she had everything necessary to help her recover, and although he was frequently away on business, his staff provided her with all the amenities.

Grace began to heal in body and in spirit. The serious concussion she had sustained helped her to push the memory of the rape into the shadowy recesses of the coma she had lived through. The skilled plastic surgeon who repaired her face also fixed her eyelid, and she began to recover her strength.

She started to worry about her reliance on Drake Malone. Although he was rich and powerful, she knew that he blamed himself for her misfortune and was determined to atone for it. With the return of her health and vigor, however, came also the renewal of her own spirit of independence.

One night after dinner on one of his rare evenings at home, Drake invited her to go for a drive in his new sports car. Casey was in the tender care of Katie, who had become like a mother to Grace and her child. Heretofore, in spite of the fact that she lived in the same house and occasionally dined with him, their relationship had been quite formal. She agreed to go, for she wished to tell him that she did not want to keep on being a burden.

As they drove with the air blowing her rich brown hair, Drake began the conversation that was to change the course of her life. "Grace, I can't tell you how sorry I am about everything."

"Mr. Malone, it was an accident. It wasn't your fault. You weren't even driving the car. And besides, I ran right in front of you. I'm very grateful for all you've done, but I don't in any way hold you responsible."

"Maybe not, but I know better. I was in a hurry, and I was annoyed at the prospect of missing the opening curtain at the theater. I told the driver to forget the speed limit . . . that I'd pay the fine if he got a ticket. It was thoughtless and selfish . . . and it would never have happened if my wife had been alive and in the car with me. She was the one who was always caring and considerate of others. I can only thank God that you're alive."

Grace wondered if she should tell him the truth and free him or if she should be silent and use his guilt to buy security for Casey and herself. She looked at his strong profile and observed a vulnerability in him that only a few people would ever see. "No, Mr. Malone, you were not the one who hurt me. The real truth is you saved my life. Please go on driving as I tell you my story. Don't look at me or I may not be able to go on."

She took a deep breath. She knew that by telling Drake her

story, she would have to relive the agony and misery again, but she had no choice. She had to repay his kindness to her. She told the grim history of her young life and omitted none of the details. After she finished, he drove home. As he helped her out of the car, he took her in his arms, and they stood there for a long time saying not a word. When they finally separated, he broke the silence. "Grace, there is an old saying that if a man saves someone's life, he owns it." He paused and then continued, "Perhaps you're right. Maybe I did save your life, through carelessness or divine intervention, who knows. But now that it's saved, we must salvage it. I want you to put everything that's in the past away. Tomorrow we'll plan your future, and that's the only thought you must take to bed with you tonight. Remember, you're not alone anymore."

He raised her hand to his lips and kissed it. Then he turned swiftly away to return to his room. Although the horror story he'd just heard had moved and distressed him, he was also filled with admiration for Grace's courage. She deserved help.

The next day it was decided that Grace would study cosmetology. Drake's secretary located an apartment near the school for her, and Drake insisted that it be furnished comfortably. He promised that he would have a check deposited to an account for her each month so that she could learn to budget her own money and pay her own bills. He did, however, insist that Katie go along to live with her but remain on his payroll until Grace finished school and had a job. Then, and only then, would he permit any discussion of her independence.

As time passed, Grace was successful beyond her own fantasies. Through Drake's influence, she got work as a hairdresser on many of the big studio movies, and with the contacts she made she ventured into opening her own shop. On several occasions, she borrowed capital from Drake, but she always repaid him with interest. Their friendship was special to them both.

One day shortly after she had assumed responsibility for

her own expenses, Drake called from St. Louis and asked her to fly out to attend his wedding. She helped the young and beautiful bride with her hair and her makeup, and it was then that Drake asked her for the first time for a favor.

"Grace, she's young and beautiful like you. I love her deeply, and I want to be sure she is always surrounded by friends. If ever she needs you, please be there for her. Will you promise me that?" She assured him that she would.

The proprietress of "Amazing Grace's" paused to survey her domain and remind herself that it was all real. Then she went out to her Mercedes and sat down beside her driver, Rudolfo. As the car pulled away, her thoughts turned to Casey, and she wondered why she had decided to come home on such short notice. A small knot of anxiety tightened in her chest. Would she never stop worrying about her daughter?

—6—

Laura

"Jim, please . . . I don't want to go without you," Laura whimpered as she stood in line to board the jumbo jet.

"Nonsense, honey, you'll be fine as soon as the Valium takes effect."

Guiltily, Laura fingered two tablets she had dropped into her jacket pocket. Jim had wanted to give her an injection, but she had refused and insisted on pills instead. She would be traveling alone, and she wanted to be clearheaded. Besides, the terrible fear she had when flying was not helped by medication. Valium only added depression to her problems.

Everyone else was aboard, and the flight attendants at the entrance to the plane were watching her expectantly. Jim kissed her lightly, but she continued to cling to his arm. "Don't do this to me, please. I don't want to go alone," she whispered. Unheeding, he propelled her forward. Nodding to the flight attendant, he declared, "I'll just walk her to the door, and I'll be right back."

As they passed through the narrow corridor, Laura's heart began to pound so hard that the sound of it seemed to fill the air. Her hands and knees trembled, and she leaned heavily on her husband's arm, afraid that her legs would give way and she'd fall, embarrassing him and humiliating herself.

Jim kept up a quiet litany of encouragement as he moved her toward the entrance to the plane. "You'll be fine once the plane is in the air. It's nonstop to Chicago, and I've arranged for a limo to pick you up and drive you to Winnetka. Just because I can't go doesn't mean you should miss the wedding. After all, you did introduce Marge to Hawley, and one of us has to be there." He kissed his wife briskly and turned her over to the stewardess. "Have a good time. I'll call you tonight."

Quickly he left her before she could protest further. He was certain she would not create a scene. She hated scenes. The stewardess guided her to an aisle seat in the first class section and helped her to fasten her seat belt.

Laura looked around her. She was the only woman in the section, and the seat next to her was empty. She was extremely frightened and felt alone and isolated. She was sure she was going to die there, surrounded by total strangers. She looked across the aisle at a man with his briefcase open, reading some papers. She tried to take some comfort from his confidence and lack of concern.

Why was she so afraid? There was a time not long ago when she had not been so fearful. They could seldom afford to travel by plane then, but when they did, it had always been an exciting adventure, and her fear added a small measure of thrill to the flight. She did not experience bone-chilling panic until that flight five years ago when she and the twins, Shannon and Dac, had accompanied Jim to a convention of cardiologists in New York.

Laura shivered, remembering that flight. She touched her forehead and realized that it was wet with cold perspiration. A flight attendant leaned down and asked, "Are you all right, Mrs. Austin? Can I get you something to drink?"

Laura shook her head and declined. "No, thanks. I couldn't swallow anything right now." She heard a sound, and she did not have to turn her head to know that the cabin door had been closed. She was now sealed into her tomb. Although it seemed hardly possible, her heartbeat accelerated. She clutched the armrests and closed her eyes. She would pretend she was somewhere else. She would focus her mind out of the airplane to a place where she was not afraid. The powerful jet engines were started up. She wanted to scream, to rush to the door and demand that they open it and release her before the plane moved, but fear suffocated and paralyzed her, and she remained rigidly in her seat.

Unable to control her thoughts, her mind again returned her to the flight with her children, the flight that had affected her so mortally. They had boarded the plane and let Shan and Dac each have a window seat. The takeoff and flight had been perfect, but when they arrived in New York the landing gear would not lock into place. Laura could never forget the panic of those next minutes. The terrible rush of fear, not only for herself but for her family. They were trapped up in the sky, and the possibility that all of them might be destroyed filled her with a terror she had never known before.

Now, alone on an aircraft for the first time since that ghastly trip, she experienced again the quiet hysteria she felt then, even though the plane had finally landed safely, surrounded by emergency vehicles and flashing lights. She wondered if any of the other passengers on that flight had been scarred with the same haunting and unreasonable fear that plagued her.

Each flight she had endured since then had been with Jim at her side, and they had all been almost unbearable. Now he had forced her to try it alone, and she was certain she would not live through the ordeal. Either the plane would crash, or she would die of fright before they landed in Chicago.

It wasn't death that worried her. She really was not afraid of being dead. Dying was the problem. The terrible moments as the plane plunged toward the earth, the awful realization that a violent death was only seconds away—this was what filled her with cold, numbing horror.

She sat quite still, sure that the slow passage of time was only her panic stretching the minutes into hours. Then she became aware of movement around her and the silence of the engines, which were no longer throbbing. A man's voice was speaking, and as she opened her eyes, she observed that some of the passengers had gotten out of their seats and were standing in the aisle. Confused, she signaled for the attendant. "What's . . . what did the pilot say? I was . . . uh . . . napping."

The steward tried to reassure her. "There's a little problem with the number two engine. Maintenance is checking it out now. Nothing to worry about. It should be all cleared up in a few minutes."

"What about my connecting flight in Chicago?" the man across the aisle demanded.

Laura snapped to a decision. She had been given a reprieve. Fate had stepped in and saved her, and she was not about to ignore it. Unfastening her seat belt, she jumped up and grabbed her purse and carry-on bag. She hurried to the door, which was still closed. "Please open the door for me," she demanded of the attendant close by.

"I'm sorry, but we aren't letting the passengers off. It's only a minor—"

"I said I wanted the door opened. I am not staying on this plane," she declared, and although she tried to keep her voice down, the words came out much louder than she expected. The look on her face and the quaver in her voice warned the young man not to defy her. "One moment please," he said as he rushed to the nearby telephone. After a hurried consultation with the captain, he returned. "Just one minute, please. The ramp must be returned before the door can be opened."

Laura waited stiffly, feeling the eyes of everyone on her. She was acutely embarrassed. She hated drawing attention to herself, but she just had to get off that plane.

At last the door was opened, and she rushed out, avoiding their questions as she raced toward the ladies' room. Bolting through the door, she barely managed to enter a toilet stall before her churning insides made their violent exodus. Leaning over a toilet, she retched and heaved until her nose and throat were raw from stomach bile.

When it finally ended, she picked herself up from the floor, aware of her surroundings. Naturally fastidious, she was shocked to realize that she had been clutching the public toilet seat. She hurried to the sink to wash away the vestiges of vomit and fear. A glance in the mirror was painful. She was pale and pinched, and her fresh hairdo had gone lank. She felt a wave of disgust for herself.

When she was reasonably sure that she looked presentable again, she headed toward the ticket counter to ask for her luggage to be removed, but it was too late. The plane was already on the runway taking off. She went directly to the nearest telephone to call her husband. She would tell him she'd gotten ill and had to leave the plane. It's true, she reasoned . . . she didn't have to lie. She'd never been more ill than she had been just a few minutes before.

"Molly, this is Laura. Is Jim busy?"

"Mrs. Austin? I thought you were going to Chicago this morning?"

Laura didn't feel like explaining. "The flight was delayed. May I speak to Jim, please?"

"He's not coming in today. Dr. White is taking his calls."

"Where can I reach him?"

"I'm sorry, Mrs. Austin, but he hasn't called in yet. I'm sure he will soon. Can I give him a message?"

Laura hung up the phone, perplexed. Jim always kept in touch with his office, even when he took time off.

Since not many people used cabs in Los Angeles because of its huge sprawl, she had no trouble finding one available. She settled down for the ride to Sherman Oaks. As the driver eased the car onto the San Diego Freeway heading north, she wished that he were going in the other direction and taking her back to their old house in Long Beach.

Whenever she thought about the house she had left less than two years before, she experienced a crushing sense of loss. She tried not to think about it anymore. It was foolish to grieve over a house. Jim was happy now with the money and the celebrity of his new practice. As she had so many times in the past months, she promised herself that she would try harder to fit in with his new life and new friends.

It was midday, and traffic moved swiftly through the mountains into the valley. The taxi pulled into the circular driveway in front of a big Cape Cod house on a tree-lined street that wound up the hill. She paid the driver, and in a moment of recklessness, handed him a ten-dollar tip. He thanked her and then hurried away as if afraid she might realize her mistake and want her money back.

Laura looked up at the wonderful familiarity of her home. She was so glad to be back. Fervently she apologized to the house for all the nasty thoughts she had directed toward it. It didn't look so huge anymore. She might even learn to love its location, perched precariously on the side of a hill. It did have a spectacular view, and even during the terrible mudslides of 1980, it had not moved an inch. It was a good house, and she vowed to be happy in it from now on. No more complaining.

Inside it was still and cool just as she had left it that morning. Everything was in perfect order. Her sense of relief and contentment did not last long, for she still must confront Jim. He would be so annoyed . . . no, disgusted with her for being such a coward. But she was not a bit sorry she had escaped. When the plane crashed, she would be vindicated. She caught herself. Oh, dear God, she didn't really want all those people to die just so her husband would not be angry with her.

What a jackass I am, she thought as she hurried upstairs to bathe away all traces of her morning's ordeal. Half an hour later, she felt warm and relaxed from the long, hot shower. Wrapped in the soft pink cashmere robe Jim had given her for Christmas, she sat down at her dressing table to call him once more. It would be better to break the news on the telephone than to see the disgust on his face. She hated it when he was angry with her, as he was so often lately.

Suddenly she was aware of voices downstairs. Who could that be? The twins were away at school. Jim never came home in the daytime. A prowler? She had been careful to lock the door and turn on the security system when she came in. Of course, it was probably that ridiculous oversized television set with the remote control coming on by itself again, triggered by a signal from an airplane. She was certainly having problems with aircraft today.

In her bare feet, she padded noiselessly out of the bedroom and across the carpeted hall to the balcony overlooking the foyer. There inside the front door stood Jim with his arms around a woman. Their bodies were pressed tightly together, and he was kissing her. Transfixed, Laura stared, unable to assimilate what she was seeing. Sensuously, the two began to grind their pelvises against each other. Their desire and passion seemed to fill the air, stealing the oxygen, depriving her of breath. Hypnotized by what must surely be illusion, Laura could not tear her eyes away.

She watched as the woman slid her hand down and insinuated it between their bodies. She unzipped his pants, and his penis sprang out full and rigid. Slowly her body snaked downward against his until her mouth was level with his crotch. Holding him with her hand, she began to slide her tongue over and around him, and then she took him into her mouth. His pelvic thrusts came rapidly, and he wound his fingers in her long blond hair. "God, don't stop!" he begged, and the sound of his voice shocked Laura out of her trance. This was not a nightmare . . . it was real! They must not see her! Striving to make no sound whatsoever, she backed slowly toward her bedroom, her eyes not leaving the spectacle below. She was afraid if she moved too quickly she would attract their attention. She knew from the sounds that her husband was making that his climax was near, and she did not want to witness it. Too late, his spasm came, the woman's mouth still enclosing him. Laura continued to watch as the coupling ended, and Jim lifted the woman's head up close to his so that he could kiss her on the mouth. My God, she swallowed it, Laura's mind screamed. Jim held the woman close to him and stroked her hair. "That was great, Ghilly darling. You're terrific," he murmured.

"Don't think you're finished yet. After we have a drink and your little friend is ready again, it'll be his turn to return the favor," she replied.

"He's ready now."

"Maybe so, but I'm not. I need a drink and something to eat first."

"You've already had something to eat . . ."

"Tell me, and that stuff's fattening, you know." They

both laughed and walked toward the kitchen. Jim did not bother to zip up his pants.

Laura's shock had turned to revulsion and panic. She wanted to shout at them. She wanted to let them know she had watched the whole ugly scene. She wanted to kill them, but more than anything else, she wanted to erase the memory of what she had just witnessed.

Softly she crept into her bedroom and eased herself quietly onto the bed. Her mind and emotions were in a turmoil. The act that had just been performed before her was now etched into her mind with acid, and she knew that it would replay itself again and again in her head like a scratched phonograph record that repeats the same dreary note, over and over. A cacophony of angry questions beat rhythmically on her skull. Had he done it before? No! Yes? Who was she? Did he love her? Does he love me? Would I do what she just did? Could I?

Somewhere in all the brain-breaking clatter, one thought of self-preservation seeped into her consciousness. He must never find out that she had seen them or her marriage would be at an end. No man would want a woman who had so little self-respect that she could continue to want him after seeing that disgusting display.

For the second time that day, she found herself trapped, but this time there was no escape. She could not get out of the house. If she moved around to hide in another room, the floorboards might creak and betray her. If she stayed here, they would surely find her when they decided to use the bed for the second round.

Perhaps if she pretended to sleep . . . but she could never manage that. Her eyelids would twitch and betray her. If she could really fall asleep . . . that would be the answer. She tiptoed into the bathroom and opened the drawer filled with samples of medication that Jim brought home from the office. She could hear them talking and laughing loudly in the kitchen. She had to hurry or the pills would not have time to take effect. She found several packages of Seconal. Silently she turned the faucet handle very slightly so that warm water would trickle into a glass. The sedative would have to work fast. Her hands shook as she broke four capsules and spilled the powder in the water. It was a heavy dose but she knew it would not kill her. Pity.

She drained the glass and swallowed the empty capsules. She started to throw the packages away, then thought better of it. She set the glass and wrappings on her bedside table, took off her robe and slipped into a nightgown. She settled herself under the blanket and shivered. She prayed she would go to sleep quickly.

Ghilly sat at the breakfast bar in Laura's kitchen while Jim rummaged through the refrigerator. "Terrific," he exclaimed, "there's a bottle of champagne here." Ghilly shook her head. "No, thanks. It gives me a headache, and I have to be on the set at five this afternoon. We'll be shooting most of the night. Just a little orange juice and vodka and something to eat," she said.

Jim took the juice and a bowl of chicken salad from the refrigerator. "How's this? My wife fixed a lot of food before she left so I wouldn't have to eat all my meals out."

"Nice lady. Just a little on my plate, and no bread. I've got a nude scene in this one, and every extra pound looks like ten on the screen."

They sat down at the kitchen table to eat Laura's food. "Umm, this is great stuff. You didn't tell me your wife was a good cook."

"Yeah, she's a great cook, all right, but . . ."

"No good in bed, right?"

"No, that's not it. She's fine . . . not very exciting and still a little shy, but she's always willing."

"How come you're screwing around?"

Jim thought before replying, "I don't know."

"Been doing it long?"

"Sure . . . no, not long. Just since last December."

"You're kidding? All those years with only one woman? How boring."

Jim laughed. "Yes . . . all those years. And you want to

hear something even funnier? Until last December, Laura was the only one . . . ever. We lost our virginity together.''

"You mean all through medical school . . . the nurses?" she asked incredulously.

"I was busy. My passion was always medicine."

"You must have been a real grind."

"A real grind," he echoed, laughing, "and speaking of grinding . . ."

"Let's go then, but in a bed this time. I'd like to get a little sleep before I go to work."

They finished their drinks, and Jim put his arms around her and kissed her lightly. "Do you have any idea how many men in the world would like to be me right now holding the beautiful Ghilly Jordan in their arms?"

"How many?"

"Millions." He kissed her tenderly, and arm in arm, they moved toward the stairs. "I should carry you," he said, and reached down to pick her up, but she resisted. "No way. Jack Lemmon tried it once for a scene, and he dropped me. Forget it. I'd rather walk."

Halfway up the stairs, Jim remarked, "I just thought of something. I'm now one of the few men in the world who's had his cock in the world's sexiest mouth."

Ghilly said nothing but smiled a trifle ruefully. There was no point in telling him that he had not joined a very exclusive club.

They reached the door to the master bedroom, and Jim opened it. "Who's that, for Christ's sake?" Ghilly demanded, but she kept her voice to a whisper. Horrified, Jim signaled her to back out of the room, which she quickly did. He inched quietly toward the bed to confirm his fears. It was Laura! But how? Why? He turned and waved frantically to Ghilly to move away from the door, and then he reached under the blanket and checked his wife's breathing and her pulse. She was in a heavy, drugged sleep. He picked up the empty Seconal packages and left the room. Ghilly was waiting in the hallway.

"What the hell is going on?" she hissed. "I thought you put her on a plane to Chicago this morning."

"She must have gotten off after I left her, come home, and taken a bunch of sedatives."

"Oh, my God, do you think she saw us . . . downstairs?"

The thought that she might have been watching made his stomach churn. It was impossible. She couldn't have. "No, I'm almost certain she didn't. She left these empty packages on the bedside table. It's a stiff dose, and she'll probably sleep a long time. She's terrified of flying. Something must have happened. I'll keep an eye on her till she wakes up."

"Well, I'd better be on my way. God, to think that she was up there while I was down . . . poor thing. I hope you're right . . . for her sake. Call me tomorrow when you find out what happened."

"Sorry about this, Ghilly."

"Yeah, so am I."

Jim watched as the voluptuous body of Hollywood's latest sex symbol bounced down the stairs and out of his life. She might never come back because she hated complicated liaisons. All she wanted, she had informed him, was a pleasant, unfettered fuck.

He returned to their bedroom and sat down beside his wife, putting the Seconal wrappings down. He would know the truth when she awakened. In all their life together, she had never lied or deceived him in any way. She was incapable of duplicity. Was their marriage over? Did he really care? Was he supposed to spend the rest of his life repaying her for supporting him through medical school . . . for bearing his sons . . . for shouldering all the burdens of home and family while he devoted himself to medicine? Did he really owe her his life? Somewhere deep inside him a small voice whispered yes, but he could barely hear it.

— 7 —

Pretty Please

PEACH put the telephone down and heard a light knock at her bedroom door. "Is that you, Miles?" she called.

"Yes, ma'am. Sarah and I just arrived. Would you like breakfast?"

"Yes, please. I'll be right out."

She threw back the covers and hurried out of bed. She wanted that mess in the bathroom cleaned up before Winnie got in there again. Wrapping herself in a robe, she went to greet her servants. While she talked to Sarah, Miles went into her bathroom armed with mop and broom to set things right once more.

"Sarah, I just talked to Mr. Beller. If it's not too much of a strain so soon, I've invited him and Mr. Petrone to dinner this evening."

"No problem at all, ma'am. We stocked the pantry and the freezer day before yesterday."

The telephone rang, and it was Maggie calling to see if everything was all right. "Maggie, dear, I love the place. It's absolutely perfect. I wouldn't change a thing. I'm completely satisfied. Did you have any problems?"

Maggie hesitated. She still had difficulty discussing money. "I hate to mention this, but I haven't been paid my retainer for the last four weeks."

Peach was shocked and asked her why. There was a long pause while Maggie groped for words that would not inflame an already heated situation. "Mr. Petrone put a stop on paying the bills. The only way I could get him to release the funds so I could finish the job was to agree not to take any more salary."

"Oh, my God, why would he do that? I am so sorry, Maggie. And after the wonderful job you did for me too. He had no right to do that."

"I didn't know what else to do," Maggie continued. "My husband wanted me to quit, but I just couldn't walk away and leave the job unfinished."

"Maggie, I'll take care of everything tonight. You have my word. Your check will be sent tomorrow without fail. And I want you to know that I appreciate all that you've done more than I can tell you."

"I knew you'd take care of everything, Peach. Thanks for having the confidence in me to let me do it. I enjoyed every minute . . . except when I had to deal with Mr. Petrone."

"Let's have lunch together next week. Have you seen Laura lately?" Peach asked.

"I've been too busy to see anybody."

The conversation ended, and Peach was shaking with anger as she dialed Steve at the winery in the Napa Valley. A woman answered. "Is Steve Malone there?" Peach inquired.

"He's busy right now. Who's calling?"

"His mother."

"Oh, wait a minute, Mrs. Malone. I'll get him right away."

Within seconds, she heard the voice of her son. "Mom?"

"I got on the first plane I could. My God, honey, what's going on up there?"

"Are you all right, Mom? Anne called me and told me what happened at the airport in Milan."

"I'm fine, honey . . . and nothing happened to me, really, although I must say I'm glad to be back in the good old U.S.A. I tried to talk your sister into returning, but you know Anne."

"She's not at all convinced it was an ordinary Italian-type operation, Mom. She said one of the men spoke English. I think you should call Doug back on the job."

"I'll think about it. Now, tell me about your problems."

"Since I talked to you, things have gotten worse. Dom cut off all my operating funds. And it's harvest time, for Christ's sake!"

"Why would he do that?"

"He's pissed off because I bought that new crusher . . . but we needed it."

"What did he say?"

"Same old stuff. The winery was too big a drain on the estate. He said if I didn't get in the black soon, he'd put it up for sale. Can he do it?"

"God, I don't know. He's acting as if he can do damn near anything he wants to. Look, I'm going to talk to him this evening, and I'll straighten everything out. Now stop worrying and go back to work. By the way, who was that who answered the phone?"

"Penny. Jesus Christ, Mom, I'm scared shitless. He must have some reason to think he's in the driver's seat."

"Don't panic. I've known Dom and Horace for years, and your father had complete confidence in them. I'm sure they have only our best interests at heart."

"Mom, don't let them take this place away from me."

"I'll call you tonight."

As Peach put down the telephone, Miles returned to the kitchen. "I'm sorry about that mess, Miles."

"It's all taken care of, ma'am. Should I take Winnie out for her morning walk?"

"Please. She's probably curled up on my pillow still asleep."

Moments later, Miles returned, but the dog was not with him and his face was ashen. "Mrs. Malone . . ." he said.

"What is it?"

"It's Winnie . . . she's gone."

"Gone . . . where would she go . . . oh, no, Miles." Too quickly she understood the terrible meaning of his words, and she rushed into the bedroom. Gathering the tiny still body in her arms, Peach broke into tears of sorrow and hysteria. This was too much. Why did she have to die now?

Sarah came into the room and tried to comfort her mistress.

"Oh, ma'am, she hasn't been herself since you left. I had to coax her to eat every day. Your return must have been too much for her poor little heart. She was almost twelve, you know."

For a long time, Peach held the dog that had brought so much love and joy to her and her family. When she finally exhausted her tears, she surrendered the small cold piece of fur to Miles. "Shall I take her to the pet cemetery, ma'am?"

"I think maybe we ought to have her cremated. Call the vet's office and ask them what to do."

Gloom surrounded them all. Sarah bustled about trying to get Peach to eat some breakfast, and Miles disappeared for an hour. When he returned, he reported that everything had been taken care of, which sent Peach into another paroxysm of weeping. Finally, Sarah took matters into her own hands. "I'm going to call Miss Grace and have her come over this afternoon. Mr. Beller and Mr. Petrone will be here this evening, and you'll feel much better if you have your hair done."

Pulling herself together, Peach said she'd make the call herself. When it was done, she asked Miles to give her a rundown on the situation at the house in Bel Air. Miles told her that the staff had been dismissed by Mr. Beller with good severance pay, and he was pretty sure that there was a serious buyer on the horizon.

At three o'clock, Grace arrived and was escorted to Peach's bedroom. "Grace, it's so good to see you!" Peach exclaimed, and they hugged briefly.

"I've missed you," Grace replied, and Peach told her about the traumas she'd suffered the past two days.

"Jesus . . . it never rains but it pours, right? Have you called Doug yet? I think it would be a good idea," Grace responded.

"Not you too? Is everybody trying to make me paranoid?"

"Well, that's what Drake would do . . . he never took silly chances, you know."

Tears of emotion came into Peach's eyes. "I don't think I'll ever get used to living without him, Grace."

Their eyes met, and their combined memories invoked the spirit of the man who had meant so much to them both, and his essence filled the room.

"Time heals everything, Peach. Believe me, I know."

Peach knew most of the details of Grace's early life. Drake had told her so that she would understand his close relationship with her and his generous support. Because she was always secure in her marriage, she had never been threatened by Drake's concern and parental interest in an attractive woman so close to her own age. Although she loved him, Grace returned his kindness with a friendship that was loving and loyal both to him and to his wife. She had never attempted to lure him into a sexual liaison. Drake loved his wife passionately, and she respected his marriage.

"How was your trip otherwise?" Grace asked, and broke the emotional intensity of the moment.

"Pretty good. I enjoyed my visit with Anne more than I expected to under the circumstances."

"Drake probably made all the arrangements for you from somewhere up there."

"I wouldn't be surprised."

As Grace combed through Peach's damp hair and tried to talk her into letting her color it, Peach asked about Casey.

"She's coming home this afternoon. Eve is picking her up at the airport right now."

"Good grief, why didn't you send someone else to do my hair?" Peach protested.

"You needed me more than she did today."

"You're a good person, Grace. How long has it been since you saw her?"

"Almost six months, and it sure seems strange that she's coming home now . . . at midterm."

"Maybe she's getting tired of the place."

"Don't I wish! Every time I've talked to her, she's been ecstatic, damn it. She's found all the happiness back there I didn't have. You know, my parents died without ever knowing the truth about her."

"Why didn't you ever tell them?" Peach asked, but Grace's penchant for lying was not new to her.

"I was afraid they wouldn't love her."

"Grace, that's so unfair. She was their only grandchild."

"I know, but I made that decision a long time ago, and over the years, I've learned to be comfortable with those lies. I've told Casey so many tales about Paul Gable, I've almost come to believe in him myself."

Peach worried about the inordinate number of lies that surrounded Grace's relationship with her daughter, and although Drake had constantly counseled her to stop giving advice, she couldn't resist. "Casey's a grown woman now . . . intelligent and educated. There's no stigma to being born to a single woman anymore."

"Lay off, Peach. I can't tell my daughter that her entire life has been a lie . . . not just one, but many."

"How can you have so little faith in her?"

Grace bristled defensively. "If Drake were here, he'd tell you to mind your own business. He never once tried to tell me how to run my personal life."

Peach was stung by the harshness of the reprimand. Was her relationship with Grace to change too now that Drake was gone? "I'm sorry. I won't meddle anymore."

Grace's manner softened. "That's okay. You can give me advice. Just don't get mad when I don't take it. Believe me, I've agonized over this plenty. I wanted Casey to have everything, even a father, so I just made one up. Is that so awful? She loved him. She'd pester me all the time for more stories. I'd have to write them down so I wouldn't get mixed up. You know you really have to be careful what you say when you're not telling the truth. God, she'd never forget a thing. Anyway, there's no sense in changing things after all these years."

Peach couldn't resist one last dart. "Well, it was lies that sent her to Illinois, remember? You had to tell her so many fairy tales about your glorious days at good old alma mater that she just had to go back there and experience it for herself."

"Your point. Now drop it, okay?"

Later that evening when Grace had gone and Peach was dressing for dinner, she resolved to keep her mouth shut in the future. She was all alone now, and she could not afford to alienate her friends.

She put on a dress designed by Karl Lagerfeld, of pale blue wool as light and airy as fine silk. From the proliferation of jewels in the wall safe, she chose a multistrand necklace of tiny blue pearls with a large sapphire and diamond drop, and sapphire and diamond earrings. She stepped into a pair of blue calf Andrea Pfister pumps, walked to the tall three-way mirror, and surveyed herself. Her blond hair was a bit faded, she had to admit, but her waistline was still slim, and she was pretty, except for the tiredness in her eyes. She was as ready as she ever would be for the encounter with the men in control of her fortune, and she knew from long experience that men were far more attentive and flexible when dealing with a woman who was beautiful.

Peach entered the living room where her guests were being served cocktails by Miles. They sprang to their feet as she appeared. "Peach, my dear, you look lovelier than ever."

"Why, thank you, Horace." Peach embraced her lawyer and kissed him on the cheek. He was a frail-looking man, pale and almost bald. His face looked like that of a wrinkled cherub, and it did not match the long, thin, almost cadaverous body on which it was perched somewhat tentatively.

"Good to have you back," Dom announced in his gruff way.

Dominic Petrone was the president of one of the state's largest chain of banks. He was tall and solidly built, and his gray hair was carefully combed to cover a slight balding spot. He had been a football star at college, and his manner was still reminiscent of a locker room. He considered himself a man's man. He and Drake had been close friends and golfing buddies for many years, and he had promised his now dead comrade that he would continue to oversee the Malone estate personally.

Miles brought Peach a glass of champagne, and they all sat

down. Peach opened the conversation. "Dom, why did you give Maggie such a hard time? She was working long hours to get this job done."

"The bills had gone out of control. First of all, although I like the penthouse, I still think Horace spent too much for it. Ten million for a damn condominium? And another million to furnish it? Isn't that being a little self-indulgent, Peach?"

Peach was startled. "Ten million, Horace? I thought you told me it cost six?"

"You misunderstood. Six million for the large unit on the floor below, remember?" Horace countered.

Peach shook her head. "No, I don't, but I was distressed and confused. There were too many decisions to make then, and I was so upset." Why did they always make her feel so incompetent?

Dom continued. "And the house in Bel Air still has not had a valid offer. I've been forced to sell some stocks at prices that are not that great to meet the mounting expenses. You're a wealthy woman, Peach, but you can't go overboard."

"Is that why you've cut off Steve's operating funds?"

"Well, not really. The kid just made me mad. I told him to hold the line, and he went right out and ordered some fancy piece of equipment from France. I'd told him to cut out the capital expenditures until the place started making some money. When I got the invoice, I just overreacted, I guess."

"You know, Peach," Horace interjected, "I think we should start looking into getting a buyer for the winery. It will take a lot of capital to make it go."

Peach was horrified. "No! Absolutely not. That winery is his life. I would never permit it."

"Well, I'm sure with the right kind of deal, it could be arranged to keep Steve on to run the place," Dom declared confidently.

"I don't even want to talk about that now. I want you to give Steve whatever he needs, and I don't want him harassed anymore. Any objections you have, I'd like you to discuss with me first."

"Okay. I'll go along with it for another six months. Then

we'll have to sit down and take a hard look at the figures again. We'll work something out," Dom agreed.

"I also want you to pay Maggie Hammond immediately. I want her to receive a bonus of a hundred thousand over her retainer fee. I promised her that much if she finished on time and to my satisfaction," Peach lied.

Dom looked surprised. "You actually promised her that much? Why didn't you let Horace make the financial arrangements with her?"

Were they deliberately trying to make her look like a fool, she wondered, or had she actually made a poor deal?

"Well, perhaps I should have, but time was so short, and I just wanted to get it over and done without any fuss. You will pay her, won't you, Dom?" Her voice was low and contrite and effectively transmitted the image of a woman asking for help.

"Of course he will, Peach," Horace intervened. "Now, I have a stack of things for you to sign. Why don't we get it done before dinner?"

Eventually they moved into the dining room, where Miles served a delicious dinner that included a pink and tender rack of lamb with garlic sauce, topped off by a dessert of fraises des bois with crème fraîche. Both men consumed it with great enthusiasm. Peach was too distracted to notice even the little she did eat. She was having trouble digesting the realization that for the rest of her life she would have men telling her what she could and could not do. Had Drake really intended to continue controlling her from the grave?

In her distress, she completely neglected to tell them about the attack on her in Milan. Was it because she also did not want to reveal that she was thinking of putting Doug Dooley back on the payroll?

After they'd gone, she called Steve and told him the money would be forthcoming, but she did not mention the subject of selling the winery. There was no point in getting him upset right now.

That night she went to bed angry and miserable. She needed Winnie to cuddle with, but she was dead. Drake was gone, but she could not muster any sorrow for him. How could he have been so insensitive?

Suddenly, guilt was layered on her resentment. She should be grateful. She had all the money she needed to go anywhere, do anything, buy whatever she wanted. All she had to do was ask the men in control. Just ask. Pretty please.

—8—

A Terrible Joke

GRACE finished Peach's hair and hurried to her waiting car. "Rudolfo, get me home as fast as you can!"

Within minutes, she was rushing up the walk toward her rustic brick house in Beverly Hills. She did not stop to notice the colorful flowers bordering the sidewalk, for she could think of nothing but Casey, the daughter she loved more than anything in the world. Eve's car was not in the driveway. Her heart skipped a beat. Had the plane landed safely? Was Casey all right?

Her hands shook as she inserted the key in the lock and opened the door. The buzzer on the alarm did not sound. She was certain she had set it that morning. Cautiously, she entered the foyer, looking about. Suddenly two strong arms grabbed her from behind, and she screamed in fright.

"Surprise!" Casey said, and released her. Grace almost collapsed with relief and joy. She gathered her adored child in her arms and hugged her. "Casey, you rotten kid. You scared the hell out of me."

"Sorry, Mom. I couldn't resist. You looked so funny creeping in like that."

"Let me look at you . . . it's been months, you know."

"Mom, you look terrific, as usual. I like your hair that light color. Makes you look younger."

"That's the secret word . . . but actually I've put on a pound or two. You look awfully pale, honey. Are you okay?"

"Now don't mother-hen me. I'm fine. I'm wonderful, as a

matter of fact. I'm pale only because the sun doesn't shine all that much in Illinois.''

"But you're skin and bones."

"Now, no nagging for the first ten minutes."

"Okay, okay. Let's sit down in the living room to talk." When they were settled on the couch together, Grace asked, "Now, why the sudden trip home? Is something wrong?"

"Nope. Everything's wonderful, matter of fact."

"How long can you stay?"

"Depends. At least six months."

"Six months! What about school?" Grace's question did not conceal her delight.

"I've resigned, Mom. I'm not teaching there anymore."

"Why? I thought you loved my old alma mater?"

"I do, but it's a long story. Are you ready for it?"

"I'm not sure." She looked warily at her beautiful child. Casey's blond hair and heavy dark eyebrows were a counterpoint to her olive skin and brown eyes. She was the image of her father, but Grace pushed that to the back of her mind just as she had buried his memory so many years ago. She stood up and walked to the bar, which was hidden behind a pair of mirrored doors. "Let's have a drink. I have a feeling I'm going to need one."

"Nothing for me, but go ahead."

Silently, Grace filled a glass with ice from the small ice machine and then poured a splash of Tanqueray gin over it. With a tiny silver syringe she put two drops of Vermouth in the glass and then sat down. "I haven't had one of these in a long time," she remarked.

"How come?"

"It's just simpler, and less calories, to have a glass of white wine. I assume your news calls for something stronger, right?"

"Maybe. Mom, I'm in love."

Grace's spirits picked up. Casey was almost twenty-eight, and Grace was starting to worry that school and studying were too dominant in her life. "That's good news"—she paused—"isn't it?"

"Sort of . . . he's married."

"Where does that leave you?"

"He's going to ask his wife for a divorce. They haven't slept together for years."

Grace was not happy. "Who is this man?"

"Mom, don't get that tone in your voice."

Grace tried to be more positive, but it wasn't easy. "Go ahead, honey. I'm all ears."

"He's an English professor . . . the head of our department."

"How old is he?"

Casey hesitated before answering. "Mom, he's very young-looking. He runs six miles a day, and he's the most attractive man I've ever met."

"How old is he, sweetie?"

"Forty-eight," Casey answered.

"Forty-eight! My God, he's old enough to be your father! Why, he's even older than I am." Grace was indignant at the idea that some old lecher had violated her beautiful child. She was sure Casey was no virgin—hardly anyone was anymore—but this was disgusting.

Casey had gotten up from her chair and moved over to sit close to her mother on the couch. "Mom, please don't judge him until you've met him."

Grace tried to regain her poise. Her life had been spent manipulating self-centered and difficult personalities. Surely she could handle a daughter who was reasonable and intelligent. She took Casey's hand in hers and looked down at her long tapered fingers. After all the brightly polished acrylic talons she saw every day, Casey's short unpolished nails looked so innocent and refreshing. "Sorry, honey. Go on."

"It all started three months ago," Casey began. "We had been working together on next year's curriculum, and I wanted to develop a study of sexism in American literature. He offered to go over my notes and critique them. He got interested in the project, and it became a joint-effort. From my very first day there, he has always been kind and friendly. Anyway, we worked late one evening, and he invited me to dinner, but all the restaurants were closed by that time. We wound up at my apartment, and well, one thing led to another, and he spent the night.''

Grace tried to put the image of copulation away from her. "I take it he was not the first?"

"Hardly, Mom, but there had actually only been two others. Reggie Marshall in high school . . . he was the first, and it was so, well, dreadful that I decided never to do it again. The second was Bill Watley in college."

"You went with Bill for almost two years, didn't you?"

"What a drag. I only slept with him because it was expected. Everybody was into sex and talking about orgasms . . . but I didn't enjoy it . . . not once."

Grace could not put into words her sympathy and understanding, and so she squeezed her daughter's hand and listened as she continued. "I hated taking birth control pills too. They made my waistline thick and gave me migraine headaches. After graduation, I broke up with Bill and took a vow of celibacy until I got my doctorate."

"Was it very difficult to keep?" Grace asked.

"Not at all. I was busy and always so loaded down with work that I was rarely tempted. Then, I started dating Harry Hartman, and he got all upset when I refused to sleep with him. He had some problems with sex himself and felt utterly rejected so I told him I was a lesbian."

"Casey!" Grace was not too jaded to be shocked occasionally.

"Actually it worked out rather well. We became good buddies. He never had to feel uptight about performing, and neither did I."

Grace handed her daughter her now empty glass. "Here, this is too much for me. Fix me another drink before you tell me anymore. Are you sure you don't want one yourself?"

"I can't have any alcohol."

"Why not?"

"I'm pregnant."

"Jesus!" Grace's heart did a quick slide into her stomach, and her mind raced back through the years to the moment she realized she was going to have a baby. Guilt engulfed her.

Had the sins of the mother tainted the child? She put her arms around her daughter and held her close. "Poor baby," she murmured.

Casey pulled away. "It's okay, Mom. Don't feel sorry for me. I'm thrilled."

"Have you told him yet?"

"Of course, and he's as happy as I am. His wife couldn't have children, and he didn't want to adopt. Now I'm the one who'll have his baby."

"Has he told her about you?"

"No, and he won't unless he has to. He thought it would be better for me to be away while he was going through the divorce thing. She's well liked at the university, and he doesn't want me connected with their separation. He feels it will be easier on me later after we're married."

"But doesn't he want to be with you during your pregnancy?"

"We can't have everything, Mom. If things get settled quickly, he'll come out here during school vacation. He'd like to be here when the baby's born."

Grace was relieved. Because of her own miserable experience, she tended to be cynical about men and sex, but perhaps this man was all right. "Do you love him so much?"

"More than anything in the world. I can't wait for you to meet him. He's tall and handsome and terribly intelligent. He's opened a whole new world for me. I had begun to think I was asexual, but he's proved I'm not."

Grace listened to her daughter's rhapsodizing, and she was caught up in her bliss. "Would you like to be married here at home?"

"Oh, yes, I would . . . as soon as his divorce is final. Then, I guess we'll have to take your grandson back to Illinois."

"Ah, now, how do you know it will be a boy? You might have a daughter like I did."

"It really doesn't matter. It's just that I feel in my bones it's a boy. And I've decided to name him Paul, after my own father."

Him again, Grace thought.

Casey continued. "You know, Mom, I've also decided to keep my maiden name."

"Whatever for?"

"Several reasons. First, because I'm so damn proud of both of my parents, and secondly because I earned my Ph.D. as Casey Gable, and I intend to use that name professionally for the rest of my life."

"I see."

"Besides, if I take Jerry's name it will sound silly. Can you imagine being called Casey Casey?"

An ice-cold serpent of fear coiled around Grace and began to squeeze the breath from her. Had she heard right? "Jerry Casey . . . is that his name?"

"Yes, is that the first time I mentioned it?"

It couldn't be! What kind of God would play such a terrible joke on her? No, it had to be a coincidence of names.

"Mom, are you okay? You look so pale."

Grace's face had been drained of all color, and it was obvious that she was ill. She tried to get to her feet. "Honey, help me to the bedroom. I feel faint. Please . . . hurry." She tried to focus her eyes, but the room had begun to darken until all she could see was a pinpoint of light on Casey's face, and in the distance, she could hear her calling, "Mom, Mom!" Her legs refused to support her, and she realized she was falling, but Casey held her and eased her onto the couch. Although the room continued to spin, there was light again. She had not fainted, thank God. She closed her eyes, and the memory of Jerry Casey leaped across the years to bedevil her again.

"Mom, are you all right?" She saw the anxious face of her daughter hovering over her, holding an ice pack to her forehead.

"I'm fine now. I just got a little faint."

"What's wrong?"

"Nothing. I'm fine. I just shouldn't have had that gin. I'm not used to drinking it."

"Are you sure my news didn't upset you?"

"No . . . no. I'm perfectly fine. Just let me rest for a few minutes, and then we'll go out to dinner."

"Forget it. You're staying home. I'll fix something here."

As Casey started toward the kitchen, Grace called to her, "Casey, do you have a picture of . . . him?"

"Jerry? Yes, but the roll is still in my camera."

"Good. I'm anxious to see what he looks like." Grace relaxed. It was a stupid coincidence of names. She was sure it could not be the same man. It couldn't be. "Honey, there's some homemade bread in the freezer," she called.

_9_

Let It Be a Dream

LAURA turned over to touch Jim as she always did when she awakened at night. And then she remembered. Dear God, let it be a dream! A nightmare.

She started to sit up in bed but then decided against it. The room was dark, and she was weak and ill. She wanted to go back to sleep and shut out reality once more. She pulled the blanket up and buried her face in the pillow, but she could faintly hear the sound of Jim's voice. Dear God, were they still here? She raised her head to listen. She heard the hum of the clock-radio, a car passing on the street, and the vibration of . . . was it the furnace or the pool filter? But no more voices.

She looked at the clock. It was nine-thirty. The empty Seconal packages still lay on the table. Had Jim ever come into their bedroom? Did he think she was in Chicago? She lay down again, and the revolting scene replayed itself again and again. Every detail was as vivid as the moment it had happened. Then she remembered the humiliating display she had made of herself at the airport. She was a ridiculous woman. No wonder he wanted someone else.

The door opened, and a shaft of light crossed the bed. "Laura, are you awake?"

She wanted him to go away, but she could not feign sleep anymore. "I just woke up."

The door opened wide, and her husband entered the room and sat down on the bed. He reached for her hand, but she did not want him to feel her racing pulse. Quickly, she sat up and held out her arms. "Oh, Jim, I'm so sorry."

He put his arms around her and held her close. "About what, Laura?"

"I got sick on the plane and had to get off."

"Sick . . . or scared?" he asked tersely.

"Both. The flight was delayed because of a mechanical problem. The longer I sat there the more nauseous I became. I realized I was going to vomit, so I got off and ran to the ladies' room. By the time I finished heaving out my insides, the plane was gone . . . with my luggage and everything. I've got to call Marge." She moved away from him to get up.

"I just talked to her. She knows how afraid you are of planes. She sent her love and said to tell you she understood."

Laura was overwhelmed with misery. If Marge only knew. Her eyes filled briefly, but she managed to control the tears. Jim was watching her too closely.

"Why did you take the Seconals? That was a stiff dose."

She became wary. She had to convince him he was safe. She was not ready for a showdown now, and perhaps if she could avoid it, things would be normal again. "That was stupid, I know, but I was so jittery . . . and well, to tell the truth, I couldn't bear facing you and having you know what a sniveling coward I was. I know how unhappy you've been with me since we left Long Beach."

"Why do you say that?"

"Because it's true. I just don't fit in with these Hollywood people."

He stiffened and pulled away. She had succeeded in diverting him with the same old nagging complaint.

"You just won't try," he said accusingly.

"I have tried . . . besides it's you I'm worried about anyway. How could you give up important research to be a nursemaid to a bunch of self-centered, vain, egotistical . . ."

"I did it to make money for you and the kids."

"We don't need the damn money! I don't want to talk

about it anymore. I feel awful. Maybe I really do have the flu," she complained.

"Why don't you come downstairs and try to eat a little something?" he asked, and his manner became solicitous.

Laura swung her feet to the floor and stood up to go to the bathroom. "Good idea . . . would you mind putting some water on to boil for tea? I'll be down in a few minutes."

Jim watched as she walked away from him. "Laura, I'm glad you're here and not in Chicago," he said softly.

What a hypocrite, she thought. She wanted to look him in the eyes, but she was afraid he might try to touch her, and her paper-thin façade of normality would crumble. "I am too," she replied as she entered the bathroom and closed the door behind her. She prayed he would not follow her.

She locked it, hoping he would leave so that she would have a few minutes to compose herself. She pressed her ear to the door to listen for his movements, and her throat began to throb with the pain of repressed weeping. She snatched a heavy terry-cloth towel from its rack and covered her face in an attempt to smother the strangling sounds. She wanted to let go, to dissolve her terror and sorrow in an orgy of tears, but she could not. Tears turned her into a red-eyed, runny-nosed mess. Quickly, she turned on the shower and spun the handle to cold. Stepping out of her gown, she plunged her naked body into the icy torrent of water, hoping that the shock would subdue her emotional outburst. Shivering violently, she held her ground under the cold deluge and refused to back away. She found relief from her agony in the punishment of her body, and her helpless weeping stopped. She had regained her composure and would be able to face her husband again.

Fifteen minutes later she joined Jim in front of the fireplace. To her surprise, he had fixed a pot of tea and made sandwiches. Since he had always considered cooking and housekeeping to be solely her responsibility, he rarely prepared food. She sat down on the couch beside him, but not close.

"How nice," she said as she reached out to pour the tea at the same moment he did, and their hands touched. He felt the coldness of her skin, although she recoiled reflexively. He took both of her hands into his and began to rub them briskly. "My God, your hands are like ice."

She wanted to pull away but dared not. She never rebuffed his touch. "I took a cool shower to try to clear my head. Those pills made me groggy, and I hate that feeling."

"How come you took so many? You've always refused sleeping pills before, and that was a heavy dose."

She had to be cautious. The less she said the better were her chances of deceiving him. She took a sandwich as she answered, "I don't really know. I was awfully depressed and experiencing a lot of self-hatred, I suppose. I just wanted to blot out the world, and I hated the thought of facing you." She was pleased with herself. It all sounded true and plausible.

"How did you get home?" he asked.

"I took a cab."

"Why didn't you call me?"

"I did, but Molly said you wouldn't be in today." She did not want to ask, but she had to. "Where were you?"

Jim was prepared. While she slept, he had checked with his office and learned of her call. "I was at the hospital. I stopped there after I left you, and Tom dragged me into a consultation. It was interesting, and I just got involved."

Laura was relieved. Obviously he did not want her to know. She hoped it was because he wanted to preserve their marriage. As she sipped her tea, she looked at him. He was more handsome now than when they married. He was intelligent, brilliant really. And until today, he had been a good husband and a caring father. A sickening thought occurred to her. Had he been cheating on her all along? Was that woman just one in a succession?

Shakily she set her cup on the tray. She had to get up and leave. Her life was cracking into little pieces like a shattered windowpane. Dear God, if she had only stayed on that plane!

Jim noticed her sudden paleness and uncertainty. "Laura, are you all right?"

"I don't know. I must have some kind of bug. Would you help me back up to bed?"

"Here, I'll carry you." He reached down and caught her at her knees, and she suddenly found herself cuddled in his arms. She closed her eyes and pressed her face against his shoulder. "Please God, don't take him away from me," she prayed silently as he carried her up the stairs and laid her on the bed.

"I'm going to the car and get my bag. You don't look at all well. I'll be right back."

He hurried to the garage as his heart pounded and a terrible realization drummed its dreaded message into his head. She had seen them in the hallway!

_10_

Don't Try to Force Me

MAGGIE felt guilty for having neglected Laura for so long. If it had not been for her recommendation, she would never have had the opportunity to work for Peach Malone, and now that the job was over, she decided to call her. The telephone rang ten times before a voice that sounded muffled and faraway answered. "Laura, is that you?" Maggie asked, but there was no reply. "Laura, this is Maggie Hammond. Are you okay?"

"Yes . . . I'm fine."

"Well, you don't sound fine at all. Is something wrong?" There was no answer, and she realized that the line had gone dead. She dialed the number again, but after it rang more than twenty times, she hung up. She was sure she had heard Laura's voice. Something was wrong, and she was a good forty-five-minute drive away. She called Jim's office, but his secretary said he was at the hospital and couldn't be reached.

She dressed quickly, although she continued to dial Laura's number every five minutes or so. When she was ready to leave she called Kirk to tell him where she was going, and he urged her to find out if Laura was okay. "I'll see you tonight, honey. We'll eat out, so you don't have to hurry back," he said, and she replied, "I love you."

"I love you too . . . and I'm glad you're finished with that house and back to being a wife again."

The drive to the valley was long, and traffic moved slowly. It was a typical Los Angeles overcast morning, and the gray skies added to her sense of gloom. She was worried about Laura, but she was also experiencing a severe letdown now that the Malone job was finished.

She hoped that once the word got around and people saw the place she had just done that she would have lots of offers. That was the way it was supposed to happen, but she was pessimistic enough to believe it might not. She felt some ambivalence about the whole career thing anyway. There had been mornings in the last two months when she yearned to stay in her robe and have a second cup of coffee. She loved to read the *Times* at breakfast, but lately she'd only been able to scan the headlines.

Her closets and drawers had become a shambles too, and she was plagued by cleaning women who were indifferent and clumsy. She had lowered her expectations regarding cleanliness and order, but it had not been easy to accept the notion that if she continued her career, controlled chaos would become a permanent condition in her household.

She parked her car on the street in front of the Austin house and briefly paused to admire the grandeur of the place. Laura had been foolish to protest moving here. She had tried to convince her that Jim had made a wise purchase, but Laura could be terribly stubborn when she wanted to be.

She rang the doorbell, but there was no response. After knocking forcefully, she checked the garage to see if Laura's car was there. The gate was locked, but by pulling herself up on it, she could see that her friend's new Seville was in its place, and she was alarmed. She had to get into the house.

The front door was locked. She surveyed the locked side gate and figured that she could have climbed it if she had worn pants instead of a skirt. She looked around and saw that the street was empty, then stepped out of the tight skirt and draped it over the gate and took off her shoes. In pantyhose and sweater, she hoisted herself to the top of the wooden fence, straddled it, then swung the other leg over, and dropped into the side yard. If anyone saw her, they'd call the police for sure, but she was pleased with her own boldness and derring-do. Wait until she told Kirk about this at dinner! He'd love it. Damn! She realized she had left her shoes on the other side. She put her skirt on again and noted the runs in her pantyhose and the splinter in her behind.

Padding gingerly along the flagstone walk toward the back of the house, she tried to convince herself that she was being foolish, but she had a strong feeling that something was wrong. She reached the backyard and was reminded once more of Laura's reason for objecting to the house. The yard was small, and there was a steep drop at the property line in the back. The view was glorious, however, although Laura had often complained that the house would slide down the hill some rainy day. It was not a neurotic fear, for the ground was not stable in the area, and homes were frequently lost in mudslides during torrential rains.

Maggie pounded on the locked back door. When there was no answer, she dragged a lawn chair near the breakfast room window and stood on it to peer inside. Her heart rolled as her fears took form. Laura was seated in a chair, her head resting on her arms atop a glass table. A cup of coffee had been tipped over, and the sleeve of her robe had absorbed the brown liquid. Maggie shouted at her and pounded on the window, but the inert figure of her friend did not move.

Maggie jumped down from the chair, pulled a stone from the border surrounding the flower bed, and strode toward the French doors which she herself had designed. As she expected, they too were locked tight. "Damn!" she muttered as she slammed the rock into the beveled glass panel and shattered it. Carefully, she snaked her arm into the hole and reached the bolt, which slid back easily. She turned the handle, and the door gave way. She stepped quickly over the shards of glass and hurried to her friend.

Tenderly she pulled Laura's head up and felt for the pulse in her neck. It was slow but steady. What had happened to her? A stroke? Maggie picked up the telephone to call the paramedics. She was as frightened as she had ever been. She had to do everything right or she might lose her dearest friend. God, what was the number? As she waited for the operator to answer, there was a terrible thud. She whirled around to see that Laura had slumped to the floor. As Maggie dropped the telephone and rushed to her, Laura's body began to convulse and vomit started to spill from her mouth. In a flash, Maggie remembered that drug victims often strangled on their own regurgitation, and she turned her friend's body on its side and held her face down. For what seemed an eternity, Laura retched and heaved, and when it was ended, she gasped and groaned.

"Laura, are you all right?"

Laura opened her eyes and tried to focus them, but she could not distinguish Maggie's features. "It's me, Maggie! Can you sit up?" Laura managed to lift her head slightly.

Trying to avoid the mess on the floor, Maggie dragged Laura's dead weight across the tile floor onto the carpeting in the adjacent family room. She pulled two pillows off the sofa and propped them under Laura's head. She then raced back into the kitchen and wrapped some ice cubes in a dishtowel and found a bottle of ammonia under the sink. She put the cold pack on Laura's forehead and waved the open bottle of ammonia under her nose. Instinctively, she suspected that Laura had taken some kind of drug.

One whiff of the ammonia and Laura responded. She gasped and coughed and lifted her hand to push the bottle away. "Laura, listen to me. Did you take any drugs?" Laura nodded affirmatively and continued to cough. "How many? Were you trying to kill yourself?" she persisted.

Laura began to cry, shaking her head no. Maggie went to the telephone. She called Jim's office and demanded to speak to him. "I'm sorry," the nurse replied, "he's with a patient, but if you'll leave your number—"

"Put him on! This is an emergency!" she demanded.

"Are you a patient of the doctor's?"

"I said this was an emergency, you fucking nitwit! Put him on! His wife is ill."

The next voice she heard was Jim's. "Dr. Austin, who is this?"

"Jim, thank God! It's Maggie Hammond. Get home as fast

as you can. Laura's taken something, and she needs you. Please hurry.''

''It'll take me at least twenty minutes. Should I call the paramedics? They can be there sooner.''

''No, just hurry.''

Maggie returned to Laura, who had fallen into a stupor again. She pulled her to an upright position and began to rub her arms and legs briskly. Occasionally Laura would come to life and open her eyes, but it would not last long. Maggie began to fear that she had made a wrong decision. Suppose Laura had taken a lethal dose and needed immediate attention? But if she hadn't, the stigma of attempted suicide might also destroy her.

Jim arrived and found his wife barely conscious and Maggie pale and frightened. He felt Laura's pulse and listened to her heart. He took her blood pressure and then gave her an injection. At last, he lifted her in his arms and carried her upstairs to bed, and then he said the words Maggie had prayed for. ''She's okay. Now, tell me what happened?''

His face was a mask as Maggie told her story. ''I know it's none of my business, but what the hell is wrong? Laura doesn't take drugs promiscuously.''

''She hasn't set foot out of this house in over four weeks,'' he replied stoically.

''What?''

Jim shook his head. ''She says she can't. She won't even go to the grocery store or the hairdresser. We get invited out a lot. She accepts, then cancels at the last minute. She complains of a headache or an upset stomach. The last time, she insisted she was having a heart attack. I examined her but couldn't find anything wrong.''

They were standing a few feet from Laura's bed, talking softly, when they heard her move. Her eyes were open. ''Maggie . . . why . . . what are you doing here?''

Maggie sat down on the bed and took her hand. ''I came to see you, but you didn't answer the door, so I broke in and called Jim. What kind of medicine did you take?''

Laura's eyes were riveted on her husband, and he asked, "Did you take Seconal again?"

Laura shook her head. She closed her eyes and answered, "No . . . they were all gone. I took the last ones last night before I went to bed."

"What did you take, then?" Jim's voice had become angry and accusatory.

"I didn't feel well when I got up . . . I took some Valium. I was jittery and nervous about going for my annual checkup this afternoon."

"Valium? Jesus, where did you find them? I thought I threw all that stuff in the drawer away. How many . . . what color were they?"

"Four . . . I think . . . the blue ones."

"Four? Christ, no wonder you passed out. Look, Maggie, stay here for a while, will you? I'm going downstairs to call the office. I'll have Molly call Sid and cancel your appointment."

When he was gone, tears began to stream down Laura's cheeks. Maggie put her arms around her and tried to comfort her. "Can you tell me what's wrong? Maybe I can help."

Laura shook her head. "No . . . Maggie, I need to go to the bathroom."

Maggie managed to get the wobbly woman on the toilet. Jim appeared and was relieved to see his wife up and moving about. "She's up, good. Maggie, could you stay with her for an hour or so? I need to get back to see a patient who is really ill. Then I'll close up the office and come right home. Okay?"

"Sure, Jim. Take your time. Laura and I have lots to talk about."

When Laura was back in bed, Maggie left her briefly to clean up the mess in the kitchen. She brewed a pot of tea and fixed a tray with two cups and crackers for Laura and a cheese sandwich for herself. She rang up the glazier and ordered a new pane of glass for the door, and then she returned to the bedroom.

As they talked, Laura seemed to rally a little, but then

Maggie suggested they call Peach and set a date to meet her for lunch the next week, and Laura retreated again. "No . . . I can't."

"What do you mean, you can't? Of course you can."

"Please, Maggie . . . don't try to force me."

"Nobody's going to force you to do anything, but what's this nonsense about you never leaving the house anymore?"

"Did Jim tell you that?"

"Laura, you can't stay cooped up in the house all the time. You must make yourself go out." But as Maggie tried to reason with her, a veil of intractability closed on Laura's face. "I just need time, Maggie. Really. I haven't been feeling well lately. That's all."

Jim returned two hours later, apologetic for his tardiness. As Maggie was about to leave, she decided on one last parting bit of advice for her friend's husband.

"It's probably none of my business, Jim, but we've been friends for a long time, and I care about you both. Laura told me nothing, but I can tell that there's something very wrong in this house. She's in big trouble, and you had better do something about it."

"Thanks for the help, Maggie. Tell Kirk I said hello."

He said nothing more, and she left the house feeling helpless and frustrated. She retrieved her shoes from the front yard, got into her car, and drove away, glad to be away from the melancholy she had found there. What had happened to them? she wondered.

Maggie recalled the night Jim had announced that he was leaving the Veterans Administration hospital to join Everett Allison in private practice. Until that night, they had been close friends, spending one night a week together playing bridge or seeing a movie. Since then, she had continued to see Laura, primarily to help her furnish the house, and Kirk met Jim for lunch occasionally in Los Angeles, but that had been the extent of their relationship for almost two years.

Maggie remembered how upset Laura had been that night. As Jim regaled them with anecdotes about Allison's celebrity patients, Laura was unusually sarcastic. She considered it unethical to discuss a major star's menstrual problems or a country singer's hemorrhoids, but Jim ignored her, which was not all that unusual.

Allison had offered him an incredible deal financially, which he just couldn't pass up. By aligning himself with him, Jim would immediately get half of everything the practice brought in. He would become the social equal of the glittery aristocracy of the beautiful people. Allison needed Jim because he was dying of cancer of the pancreas, a terminal illness that chemotherapy would not stop and would only make his last weeks of life miserable. He decided to let nature have its way with him.

Everett Allison had lived a rich life. He had married three times and fathered six children, but he had saved nothing and was almost out of time. All he had left was his home and his practice, and if his patients learned of his disease, they would quickly abandon him out of their own insecurities and distaste. His only hope was to entice a doctor to join him to take over the practice and maintain it. He chose the brilliant and charismatic Jim. After his death, it was agreed that one-third of all income from his current patients would be paid into a trust for his children until the youngest reached the age of twenty-one, in five years' time.

Maggie remembered being impressed by the whole arrangement. Neither she nor Kirk had been sympathetic to Laura's objections. Jim had already devoted more years to pure medicine than most physicians, and his desire to reap some material rewards seemed only natural.

At the beginning, Laura accepted her new life-style and enjoyed the luxury of buying anything she wanted for her house. Her relationship with Peach Malone became important and flattering to her. Jim had been on constant call at the Malone house while Drake was dying, and Peach had reached out to Laura in guilt for the time she demanded from Jim. Laura responded with warmth and sympathy and gave Peach a great deal of support in the final days.

Where the hell had it all gone wrong? Maggie wondered.

She arrived home just before six to find her secretary waiting for her. "Dee, how come you're still here?"

"Great news, Mrs. H. I had to wait and tell you myself. It's just too exciting to write on one of those little pink pieces of paper."

"Tell me!"

"Belinda Cornwall called. She wants you to come to her house tomorrow for a consultation."

"Seriously?"

"Seriously. I even called her back. I pretended I was just checking the address, but I really wanted to make sure someone wasn't playing a joke on us."

"Belinda Cornwall! Good grief!" Maggie collapsed on the sofa as her secretary beamed in triumph.

"I could hardly wait to see your face."

"Dee, do you realize that Belinda Cornwall is the absolute doyenne of Los Angeles society?"

"I know. Guess what else?"

"Jane Fonda called."

"Nope, but a check came from Mrs. Malone . . . delivered by special messenger, no less."

Dee had been holding her hands behind her, and she suddenly whipped her right arm forward, and with a flourish worthy of D'Artagnan, she swept the check under Maggie's nose. Maggie gasped in astonishment. On top of her salary, Peach had sent a bonus of one hundred thousand dollars . . . a bloody fortune! She could not believe her eyes. Whoever said the rich were parsimonious had obviously never met Peach Malone. Wait till Kirk got home and saw this!

"Mrs. H., I hope I did right in setting up the appointment with Mrs. Cornwall. She was very insistent."

"Of course. What time is it for?"

"Ten in the morning, tomorrow."

"Terrific. Now call Kirk and find out what time he's coming home. Then call Ambrosia and make a reservation for two an hour after that. Tell them to ice a bottle of French champagne for us. I'm going to treat my husband to a very special dinner tonight."

"Right away."

"And deposit this check . . . no, do it tomorrow. I want to see Kirk's face when he sees it."

Maggie hurried to her bedroom to strip off her clothes and take a shower. As she pulled off her skirt, she noticed bits of Laura's vomit still clinging to the fabric, and her euphoria faded. Laura! God, she'd forgotten the whole miserable day in the excitement of Dee's news.

Fortune had not treated her friend so well it seemed. What did it have in store for her? She stripped every piece of clothing off her body, rolled it all into a ball and stuffed it in the wastebasket. She wanted nothing to remind her of the unhappiness she had witnessed that day.

_11_

That Little Debacle

DEAREST MAGGIE,

How can I thank you for all you did yesterday? Even though I was not quite myself, it was a pleasure to see you again after all these weeks. You look just wonderful. Working must certainly agree with you.

I'm anxious to hear all the details about Peach's new house. I'm sure you have lots of stories to tell. As soon as I'm feeling better, I'll call you, and we'll have lunch together. Providing, of course, that the popular decorator will have time to fit a dull housewife into her schedule.

I can't imagine what you must think of me for being so stupid as to take that much Valium. It was really a terrible mistake. I thought the yellow ones were strongest. It was very silly of me. It's a mistake I won't repeat, you can be sure of that. I rarely take medicine of any kind, you know, and from now on, I intend to be my old Spartan self and just ignore the headaches.

Life has been so busy, you see. I rarely have any time to myself at all. We're always going to dinners and parties, and it's a struggle just keeping my clothes in order, much less taking care of this big house. It's so difficult to find reliable help. The boys are away at school now, and that helps some, although I miss them terribly.

Please give my best to your darling husband. Tell him I miss being his bridge partner. We never have time for cards anymore.

You are a dear friend, Maggie. Please don't be concerned about that little debacle yesterday. Everything is fine. I'll call you soon.

Love,
Laura

_12_

A Fairy-Tale Princess

SHE was so stimulated by her sudden wealth and the impending meeting with Belinda Cornwall that Maggie found it impossible to sleep. Her insomnia had not been helped by the rich food and champagne she and Kirk had consumed late the evening before. She looked at the clock and saw that it was only four in the morning, but she just could not lie there another minute longer. Slowly and as quietly as possible, she eased her feet onto the floor and sat up.

The room was dark, and she was forced to drop to her knees to fumble for her slippers. She could find only one. She dared not go in the bathroom for her robe, or Kirk would certainly hear her. There was a creak in the floorboards that could wake the dead. Shivering slightly, for the house was cold, Maggie inched her way out into the hall. Grasping the rail, she made her way to the stairs and went down. She took Kirk's baggy sweatshirt out of the hall closet and pulled it over her head. It was so old and stretched out of shape that it covered her torso completely. In the laundry room, she found several unmatched socks in the basket and pulled on one black and one brown and then shuffled into the kitchen to fix herself a mug of instant coffee.

She settled on the couch in the study to mull over the day's events and plan what to wear to Mrs. Cornwall's. She was worried about Kirk too. His reaction to her check and her impending meeting did not get the positive response she had hoped for. She looked up and saw him standing in the doorway watching her. "Isn't it a little early in the morning to go trick or treating?" he asked.

She smiled. "Don't you like my outfit?"

He sat down beside her and pulled her close to him. She snuggled into his arms and pressed her face against his neck. She loved to have him hold her close.

"Nervous about your big meeting?" he asked.

"A little."

"Don't be. You don't need her . . . or anybody for that matter."

"I need you."

"No, you don't. Not anymore."

"Darling, how can you say such a thing?"

"You've already made almost as much this year as I have, and it looks like you'll make a lot more."

"So? It's our money, not just mine. For years you've been supporting me. You mustn't be upset now that I'm contributing too."

Kirk said nothing for a while. Then as if the words were exploding from deep inside his soul, he said, "I don't want your money. It's not ours . . . it's yours. I want you to keep it for yourself. Put it into the bank or spend it. Buy yourself a Rolls or a diamond . . . whatever. I don't want any part of it."

Maggie could see that he was really upset. "Kirk, what happened? Last night you were happy when I showed you the check, and now . . ."

"I thought about it all night. I had trouble sleeping too."

Maggie was unprepared for his mood swing. She must retreat quickly before she forced him into taking a stand so rigid she could never budge him from it. She wrapped her arms around his neck and kissed him lightly on the mouth. "Okay, you're the boss. I'll keep it if you insist. We'll discuss it later when we find out if there will ever be anymore. In the meantime, let's forget about the filthy stuff and go back to bed." She flicked her tongue across his mouth lightly and looked directly into his eyes. "You know, we haven't had a good morning orgy for weeks."

He kissed her passionately as his hand lifted her nightgown to expose her lower body. He moved down to kiss her navel, then gradually he moved his lips to the softness of her belly and into the wiriness of her dark pubic hair. They were both aroused, and Maggie's heart began to beat rapidly as she relaxed her legs and opened them to him. As he slipped to his knees in front of her, he lifted his head to meet her eyes. Impishly, he whispered, "How did you know that I get turned on by women wearing men's sweatshirts and socks that don't match?" He buried his face again into the moist, pink recesses of her body.

Somewhere a bell was ringing. Maggie could hear it in the distance, insistently forcing her to rise from a deep sleep. Disoriented, she saw the sun shining through the louvres of the shutters, and she disentangled herself from Kirk's arms to look at the clock. Good God, it was eight-fifteen! The door-bell rang again. Dee was here early, thank Heaven. She leaped from the bed, snatched a robe from her closet to cover her nakedness, and hurried downstairs. Kirk sat up. "Jesus, what's all the commotion?" He looked at the time and bolted out of bed. Maggie opened the front door.

"Good morning, Mrs. H. I thought I'd come early this morning . . . you're not dressed!"

"Don't stand there telling me what I already know. Come in! Thank God you're early. We overslept."

Dee hurried into the house, her arms filled with roses just picked from her yard. "I brought you some—'

"Thanks, put them in a vase and make some coffee. I've got just thirty minutes to get dressed and out of here."

She rushed into the bathroom, but Kirk was already at the sink shaving. "I can't believe we slept so late," he exclaimed.

"I know. Do you mind if I take the first shower?" she asked.

"Sorry, honey, I'm in a big rush. I've got an important appointment in L.A. at nine-thirty," he replied.

"You'll never make it," she answered with a touch of rancor in her voice.

"Yes, I will. Just stay out of my way, and I'll be out of here in ten minutes."

Tempted as she was to declare that she was in a hurry too, to remind him that she had an appointment with one of Los Angeles' wealthiest and most influential women, Maggie restrained herself. This was no time to argue, and she retreated gracefully, but not without a full measure of resentment. Vowing to organize the guest bathroom with her own makeup and toilet articles, Maggie went to the bedroom to lay out her clothes. She checked the time on her Cartier tank watch and wound it. Kirk was still in the shower.

She hurried downstairs and out to the garage. She was fairly sure she knew where Hancock Park was, but she would have no time for wrong turns. She took the map book out of its pocket in her car and checked the street and freeway routes. That done, she ran into the kitchen. The coffee was still dripping into the pot.

She dashed upstairs again. Surely Kirk would be out of the shower by now. She pinned up her hair as she hurried along, whisking past her dripping husband as he dried himself. She jammed the shower cap on her head and stepped into the stall.

"What's the big rush?" he asked.

"I've got an appointment at ten, remember?" She was irritated that he could so easily forget those things that were most important to her.

"Oh, right. I forgot. Sorry I dominated the bathroom. Why didn't you remind me?"

"That's all right. Just stay out of my way, and I'll make it."

Although she took a fast shower, Kirk was already dressed when she emerged. He called to her as he was leaving. "I may be late tonight. I've got a heavy schedule. If I'm not going to be home for dinner, I'll let Dee know. 'Bye." He left without kissing her or wishing her luck. Damn him!

By the time she was ready, it was after nine. She gave Dee hurried instructions and left the house. She had to stop for gas, which annoyed her for she did not want to be even two minutes late and lose the job, whatever it was, by default.

It was ten o'clock exactly when she parked her car in front of the massive white Georgian house with its wide pillared portico that stretched across the façade. The lawn was as lush and clipped as a golf course green, and the walls were bordered by tiny rows of pompoms in bloom.

Trying to quell her nervousness, Maggie strode the distance of the long brick walkway and up three steps to the porch. There seemed to be no doorbell, so she lifted the heavy brass knocker and rapped on the door. Immediately, a butler in morning coat and striped trousers answered. Before Maggie could speak, he said, "Good morning, Mrs. Hammond. Please come in."

The foyer was large and cheerful. The ceiling soared two stories high, and sunlight streamed through a stained-glass skylight sending colored beams of light onto the hardwood floor. An ornately carved wooden table stood against the wall and was flanked by two matching high-backed chairs upholstered in needlepoint. Rising ten feet above the table was a tall, gilt-framed mirror which reflected the grand curving staircase. The polished wood stair treads were carpeted with a deep rose runner held in place at each tread with a shining brass rod. The gleaming brass banister was supported by wooden balusters, also intricately carved. Three enormous crystal chandeliers hung at descending levels along the staircase. The prisms of the crystal drops sent more rainbows of light twinkling around the white walls. Maggie surmised they were from Baccarat. The wall behind the stairs was hung with an old Aubusson tapestry.

Whatever in the world did Belinda need her for? Maggie wondered. If the rest of the house had the perfection of the entry, it would be sacrilege to change a thing.

The servant opened a door and led Maggie into a large library, and as she crossed the threshold a voice rang through the room. "Come in, Mrs. Hammond. Come in and sit down."

As she approached a wing chair placed in front of the tall,

diamond-paned windows, a tiny figure rose from the chair to greet her. Maggie could not believe the vision before her eyes. Was this diminutive woman dressed in what looked very much like a wedding gown the monarch of Los Angeles? Was this the woman to whom the rich and the powerful genuflected? Could those intense blue eyes be the eyes of the socialite who entertained lavishly yet never permitted one word to be printed about her parties? How could this fragile little woman be so influential that she could make staying out of the social columns fashionable?

Maggie approached her, and Belinda Cornwall extended her hand to give her visitor a warm, firm clasp. Her fingers were so tiny they disappeared into Maggie's larger hand.

"How nice of you to come on such short notice. Now have a seat here beside me." She pointed to the other wing chair. "And Mason, please bring us some coffee. Is that all right?"

"Fine," Maggie murmured, trying to settle herself comfortably but feeling anxious and on edge.

"You're probably wondering why I called you here on such short notice," the older woman commented.

"I assumed you had spoken to Mrs. Malone," Maggie replied.

"Actually no, I have not seen our dear friend Peach since Drake's funeral. I was inconsolable at his passing. We had been friends for many years. In fact, at one time we thought we were in love, but we were very young and soon came to our senses. We were far too much alike to be able to live under the same roof." Her eyes drifted away momentarily, and then she continued. "I learned from private sources about your arrangement, and I have kept track of your progress with the penthouse. I hear it is quite lovely and that you finished ahead of schedule."

Maggie was both flattered and disconcerted that someone so prominent had been watching her progress. "Do you know my background in design?"

Belinda chuckled. "Only that you don't have one to speak of."

Maggie's laugh was forced. Her hostess sensed her discomfiture and hastened to add, "I do know, however, that you have taste and sensitivity and a fresh approach, and that you regard beauty and comfort above flash and 'statements,' as they call them. I don't want any decorator making statements in a house of mine!"

Mollified, Maggie was about to reply when Mason arrived wheeling a teacart toward them. The women watched in silence as he poured the coffee and offered a tray of tiny sweet rolls. "Have one of these, my dear," Belinda urged, "they are delicious. My pastry chef is a genius, and you were probably too nervous to have breakfast."

"Not really. I overslept, which is very unusual for me."

Mrs. Cornwall's eyebrows soared in astonishment. "It's not that I wasn't nervous," Maggie admitted. "I just couldn't sleep all night, and then I dozed off at dawn."

"Well, that's better. Goodness, I'd hate to think I hadn't intimidated you at all."

Maggie laughed and helped herself to one of the feathery light pastries.

"You may go, Mason. We can pour for ourselves."

The self-effacing butler seemed to dematerialize, so silently and quickly did he leave the room.

"Tell me, what do you think of my dress?" Belinda asked abruptly.

"Why, it's lovely."

"Don't you think it's a trifle elaborate for the morning?"

"Are you happy wearing it now?"

"Extremely."

"Then you should wear it, by all means."

"Don't you think it would look better with a veil and bouquet?"

Maggie looked directly into the mischievous expression on her hostess's face and realized she was being baited. "If you're asking me if I think it looks like a wedding gown, yes."

"That's what it is. I wear them all the time. I love them."

Maggie's surprise was evident. "Really? I didn't know that."

"Why should you? As you know, my name never appears in any of the social columns, so you would have to know someone who knows me, and that's unlikely. We don't move in the same social circles."

"How do you manage that . . . staying out of the papers?"

A smile lurked in one corner of the older woman's mouth. "I manage." She did not elaborate.

"Why wedding gowns?"

"I like them. Always have. When I was a little girl, I dreamed of being a fairy-tale princess on my wedding day. By the way, isn't it sad what has happened to those two lovely words, fairy and gay? Anyway, I finally realized my dreams. I married Prince Charming, you see. He was marvelous . . . handsome, rich, kind . . . and very loving. My wedding day was glorious. I can remember every little detail. I had everything I ever wanted from that day until the day he died twenty-five years ago."

She paused and turned her head to look out the window. The room was silent. Maggie could hear the faint sounds of life emanating from the garden . . . the whir of a lawnmower, the calls of birds, music from a radio somewhere.

"Sometime after he died," Belinda continued, "I tried on my wedding gown. It still fit perfectly even though I was no longer the beautiful young princess. Standing there looking at myself in the mirror, I relived the happiness of that day. It was then I decided that if wearing a wedding gown could make this old lady happy, why not wear it?" She was smiling, relishing the story.

"Do you have many of them?"

"My dear, I am like the lady who went to a psychiatrist because she liked pancakes. When he assured her there was nothing abnormal about that and that he liked them too, she replied, 'Wonderful! Then come to my house. I have closets full of them.' Yes, I have so many gowns I have to rent a vault to house them safely."

"Fascinating," Maggie commented.

"I am a collector, you see. Many of them are antiques and very valuable. I don't wear those, although I have exact

121

copies made in my size. Right now I am negotiating with several museums. I am prepared to donate sufficient funds to display and maintain them . . . but let us proceed to the reason I have called you here."

Maggie was relieved. The conversation had been interesting, but her curiosity was killing her.

"My son is getting divorced."

"I'm sorry."

"Don't be. Congratulations are more in order. It was not a good marriage at all. It should have happened years ago."

"I see. Does he live nearby?" Maggie could not imagine what her son's divorce could have to do with her.

"He lives in New York City. His wife Bittsey wouldn't live anywhere else. It was my own fault. I sent him east to college, Harvard, of course. That was a bit of snobbishness for which I paid dearly. In my stupidity, I never dreamed he would fall in love with a girl who would refuse to leave New York."

Belinda lifted the silver pot to pour more coffee as she continued her saga. "Bittsey has left Connor. Now that their children are grown and gone . . . they are, by the way, both in California, one at Stanford, the other working in our San Francisco store . . . *she* wanted out." Belinda's voice lifted in indignation. "She said she needed . . . *space!*" The last word she spat out like an obscenity.

"How long were they married?"

"Twenty-three years. He gave up everything for her. He was to become head of my family's retail operation, but because of her, that mantle fell upon my nephew Martin's shoulders."

"And your son?"

"Connor opened a branch of the store on Fifth Avenue and called it Cornwall's. He elevated the quality of service and merchandise so successfully that we started a second chain of higher class stores. He has done very well, but the base of power in our operation is here."

"A lot of marriages are ending in divorce nowadays, Mrs. Cornwall," Maggie said.

The woman shot her a glance of withering coldness. "I know they are, and I think it is a disgrace. A woman's first duty is to her husband and family."

Maggie opted for silence. Belinda was not a person to challenge.

"Tell me, Mrs. Hammond, what does your husband think of your new career?"

This was not the time for truth. "He's quite happy with it. He's proud of what I do, although I have not allowed it to interfere with our life. I love him very much."

She could tell she had responded properly by the warmth of expression that returned to her hostess's face.

"Good. Now I want to enlist you in my cause. I intend to lure my son home, and you shall help me prepare the bait."

"I don't understand," Maggie said, bewildered.

"My nephew Martin is not well. This is very confidential, you understand. The diagnosis is leukemia."

"I'm sorry."

"Yes, we all are. He wants to retire next year and turn the presidency over to his twenty-seven-year-old son. I will not have it! That job was always meant to be Connor's, and now it will be." Her voice lowered. "But first, I must convince him to live here."

"How can I help you?"

"He loves the beach. I have made a very judicious purchase of a home in the Colony at Malibu. Are you familiar with the area?"

"Yes . . . no, not really."

"It needs work . . . in a hurry. Can you do it for me?"

Good grief, Maggie wailed inwardly, is this to be my lot in life, to be an instant decorator? "I don't know. I would have to see it."

"You performed miracles in record time, I've been told."

"That's probably true, but it was very costly for Mrs. Malone to do it so quickly."

"It must be obvious to you that money is no problem for me either, and I want my son back."

"I don't think a house can do that for you."

"Of course a house won't do it, but it cannot hurt. I want the place ready in three months. Connor will be here for the annual meeting of the corporation, and I have asked him to arrive early so we can celebrate his forty-fifth birthday here. I want to give him a beautiful home on the beach. That coupled with the offer to assume the presidency of the corporation should do it."

"I see." Three months would be a breeze. "When would you like my answer?"

"Why, this moment, of course. I have arranged for you to fly to New York tonight on the company jet to meet Connor. You will pose as my new secretary bringing papers for him to sign. You will see his house, get to know him, and have a chance to find out about his likes and dislikes. I have asked him to entertain you tomorrow since the jet will not be returning until the day after."

"He's expecting me?" Maggie was incredulous.

"I hope I've not been too presumptuous."

"But . . . I have to talk to Kirk, first."

"Would you like to use the telephone?"

"Oh, no, I must see him." Maggie resisted her pressure.

"Go then. You have no time to waste. The plane leaves at six, although naturally they will wait for you."

Maggie looked at her watch and saw that it was after eleven. As she stood up to leave, she realized there had been no discussion of money. "Mrs. Cornwall, we have not talked about my fee."

"I shall pay what Peach paid plus ten percent for your newly acquired experience."

"Are you quite sure?"

"What did you receive from her?"

"Six thousand a week and a bonus of one hundred thousand because the job was completed to her satisfaction."

Belinda's face registered her surprise. "Was that what you asked for?"

"No, the bonus was much larger than I expected."

"Hmph, a fool and his money are soon parted."

"Shall we forget about the ten percent?" Maggie offered.

"Do we have a deal?"

"As soon as I clear it with my husband."

Maggie raced through the halls and past the startled butler standing near the door, which he barely managed to open before she scooted through. She had a million things to do if she was going to make the plane at six, not the least of which was to break the news to Kirk. She hoped he could handle it.

_13_

Help Me

Dear Miss Jordan,

You've never met me, but we have a great deal in common . . . my husband. It seems that he's screwing both of us. I hope he hasn't told you that we no longer share the same bed, because we do.

I love him, you see. I've loved him since the first moment he touched me. You've had many men, but I've had only one. Why do you have to have him too when you can have anyone you want?

I feel certain that if you sent him away, he'd come back and love me again. Let him go.

I'm just a housewife. I was pretty when I was young, but I'm almost forty now. My hair is fading to gray, and my eyes look tired all of the time.

I saw you that day in the hallway. I never did anything like that, although I would have if he'd wanted me to. I've done everything he's ever asked of me.

I cannot compete with someone as beautiful as you. I just hope you will find the compassion to send him away. I need him. I would rather be dead than live without him.

Help me,
Mrs James Austin

_14_

A Big Star

PEACH put down the telephone. She couldn't believe it. Maggie was on her way to New York on a job for dear old Belinda, the lady with the "whim" of iron. She hoped she could survive in such tough company.

Peach was also worried about Laura. Maggie had asked her to call the Austin house, but she was vague about the reason. She dialed Laura's number and was about to hang up after seven rings, when the receiver was picked up but no one spoke. "Laura . . . hello, is that you?"

"Peach?" Laura's voice sounded faraway.

"Yes, but I can hardly hear you."

"Is this better?" Her voice was more audible.

"Yes, how are you?"

"Pretty good, and you?" Laura answered.

"Much better than I ever thought I would be. I can't believe how well I'm adjusting to living alone."

"Really? Did you enjoy Italy?"

"I did. Let's have lunch, and I'll tell you all about it. I'm so anxious for you to see the beautiful job Maggie did with the house. After all, you're the one who gets the credit for finding her, and I'm extremely grateful. How about tomorrow? I'll send the car for you."

"No, no, not tomorrow. I'm . . . busy."

"The day after then?"

"No, I can't make it then either."

127

"Well, you tell me what day is good for you. I have lots of free time."

"I'll . . . have to call you."

"Laura, is anything wrong? You don't sound like yourself."

"I haven't been feeling well lately, Peach. I have terrible headaches."

"I'm so sorry. Have you seen a doctor?"

"No, I haven't."

"What does Jim say?"

"I haven't told him."

"Laura, how foolish. Why not?"

"He's busy. He's not home much anymore."

"If you're going to be home, why don't I drop in for tea this afternoon?"

"Thanks, Peach, I appreciate your concern, but I'm sure I'll feel better next week. I'll call you then."

Troubled by the conversation, Peach called Jim's office and made an appointment for a checkup. The other line rang, and she picked it up to hear the voice of her old friend Arlene Silenz, wife of one of Hollywood's most durable producers of screen epics. "Arlene, it's so good to hear from you."

"Darling"—Arlene rushed into the conversation—"we're having a little dinner party here tonight. The first answer print of *Sandman* will be delivered from the lab today, and we're showing it to our best friends. Can you join us? Drake's been gone long enough now for you to come out of mourning."

"Arlene, I haven't been wearing a black veil. Drake made me promise to start life again as soon as possible. I'd love to come."

"Wonderful. Sevenish, darling."

"How are you dressing?"

"Oh, casual black tie, I suppose. Have to rush. 'Bye now."

Peach was pleased with the invitation. It had been a long time since she had dressed up and gone to a dinner party, and this would be an exciting evening. *Sandman* would be the big picture of the year. It was based on an old comic book hero, and it was rumored that it would surpass the *Superman* films

128

in popularity. Like most Los Angeles residents, Peach kept up with the activities of the film industry, and although she had friends in the business, she was still intrigued by the big stars.

She rang for Sarah, who appeared almost instantly. "Sarah, I won't be home for dinner. I'm going to Mrs. Silenz's this evening."

"How nice, ma'am. Are they showing *Sandman?*" Sarah was fascinated by Hollywood also.

"That's what she said."

"How exciting. What will you be wearing?"

"Black tie casual. What in the world is that?"

"Why don't I ring up Bessie over at Mrs. Silenz's and find out what madam's planning to wear?"

"Good idea, and call Grace. If she's busy, ask if Eve can do my hair this afternoon."

Sarah returned a few minutes later with a perturbed expression on her face.

"Can't Grace come, Sarah?"

"She wasn't there. I spoke to Eve, and she said Grace hadn't been in the salon for two days."

"Oh? I forgot, of course, Casey's in town. Will Eve come?"

"She can't get here until four."

"Fine, what did Bessie say?"

"Mrs. Silenz is wearing something new. Giorgio's is delivering it this afternoon."

Promptly at four Eve arrived with her bag of tricks to make Peach look beautiful. Sarah ushered her into the lush bedroom.

"I'll be right out, Eve. I just washed my hair."

Minutes later Sarah arrived with coffee for Eve just as Peach came in wrapped in a taupe velvet robe with a small satin peach appliquéd on the collar.

"Can we hurry? The shop is chaos without Grace," Eve said.

"Let's go, then. How's Grace enjoying her visit with Casey? She hasn't called me."

"Okay, I guess. I haven't talked to her much either. She called me the morning after Casey arrived and told the receptionist to tell me to carry on. She said she needed a vacation."

"That doesn't sound at all like her."

"That's for damn sure. She's always at the salon, hovering over everybody like a hawk."

"Maybe there's a problem with Casey."

"I don't think so. I picked her up at the airport, and she looked terrific and happy."

"Hmm, well, let me tell you something, the things that make daughters deliriously happy, men usually, often make parents miserable. Anne drove us up the wall from the time she was thirteen. Drake swore her mind was being controlled from outer space."

"Yes, but Casey's not exactly a kid anymore."

"True, but I'm sure Grace still wants to make all her decisions for her."

"I still can't get over Grace letting her go to Illinois."

"She didn't have much choice," Peach replied.

At seven that evening, Peach stepped into her Rolls for the ten-minute drive to the Silenz home in Trousdale Estates. She was wearing an ivory silk floor-length Valentino, cinched at the waist with an eighteen-karat tubular gold mesh belt from Ilias LaLaounis. The only other jewelry she wore was a pair of nine-carat radiant-cut canary diamond stud earrings set in yellow gold. Although she had removed her wedding band on the day after Drake's funeral, she continued to wear her ten-carat, emerald-cut diamond engagement ring.

As the car pulled away, she admitted to herself that she was a bit nervous. This would be her first foray into the social life of Los Angeles as a widow. She had heard that women alone were not often welcome because they were considered a threat, which was laughable. She had never really flirted with a man in her life. She had always been so secure in Drake's love, and while she liked men, she did not need them to confirm her beauty or her desirability. Drake had done all that for her.

The car turned into a circular driveway surrounded on both sides by tall cypresses. The door of the huge, one-level house on top of a hill overlooking the massive sprawl of the city was opened by a butler, and Peach entered. She was suddenly seized from behind and caught in a bear hug. "Honey, you look prettier than ever."

She managed to turn her head and see the flushed, smiling face of her tall and portly host, Burt Silenz. "Burt, it's so good to see you. Let me turn around and give you a kiss."

"Fair enough." He released his hold, and she kissed him on the cheek and gave him a hug.

"God, you're still one of the most beautiful women in this town, Peach. It's great to see you again."

"It's good to be here, Burt. I was so pleased when Arlene called today. I didn't think anyone even knew I was back in town."

"Well, you know Arlene, the town crier . . . knows all . . . sees all . . . tells all."

"Come on, Burt. She's not like that."

"She's been my eyes and ears around this town for a long time. I'd have never made it this far without her."

"What awful things are you saying about me now?" a familiar voice demanded. The hostess had suddenly appeared, and she too hugged Peach, but as women do, they kissed the air over each other's shoulder to avoid smearing lipstick. "Peach, you look gorgeous. I'm so glad you could come."

"So am I. You know this is my very first party since Drake . . ."

Arlene squeezed her hand. "I'm honored. Now come in and have a drink. We have to serve at seven-thirty sharp. The film's running time is one hundred and forty-one minutes, and I don't want anyone to fall asleep because of the late hour or too much booze."

"I'll kill anyone who falls asleep!" Burt thundered.

"Burt, you know your pictures are so full of action nobody ever dozes off," Peach assured him.

Burt lowered his voice to a confidential tone. "This is the best goddamn picture I ever made. It's so terrific even I can't believe it. Just wait till you see Jason Darrow. Beautiful, that's all. Not only is he the handsomest hunk since—"

Arlene interrupted him. "Stop trying to prejudice her, Burt. We want her honest opinion."

"The hell we do, I want her to love it," and he winked at Peach conspiratorially.

Arlene gave Peach a little nudge and remarked sotto voce, "Jason is here tonight. He's even more gorgeous in person, if that's possible."

Flanked by her host and hostess, Peach entered the spacious library where thirty or more men and women were standing in little groups talking animatedly and drinking cocktails. She realized at a glance that all the shakers and movers were there to see if Burt had done it again.

Arlene steered Peach from one group to another, introducing her and putting a glass of wine in her hand. She exchanged pleasantries with Lew and Edie Wasserman and Lorraine and Sid Sheinberg of Universal, and Marvin Davis, the owner of Fox. Although she was introduced to almost everyone she did not know, the names were dropped so casually that she had difficulty sorting them out.

Before she had drunk half her wine, Arlene announced that dinner would be served on the terrace immediately, and she found herself on the arm of a tall, extremely handsome young man whose name had eluded her in the confusion.

"I take it you're here alone?" he asked.

"Yes, I'm afraid so," she replied.

"Good. So am I. Shall we sit together?"

"Well, if Arlene hasn't put out place cards . . ."

"She hasn't. I wandered outside during cocktails and checked to see who I'd be sitting with. I'm new to all this, and I don't know any of these people, except what I read in the trades."

"I know some of them, but I've been out of things for so long . . ."

"Have you been away?"

"My husband was ill for a long time before he died two months ago. This is my first party."

"Well, that's great. I mean, I'm sorry about your husband, but I'm glad you're going to parties again."

Peach smiled up into dark eyes that glistened with cheerful amusement. He was quite sensational looking. His hair was thick and sandy-colored and slightly curly. He was very tall, and his evening clothes were perfectly tailored and looked brand new. His ruddy, suntanned, and slightly freckled countenance and broad muscular chest, however, indicated he was more at home in dungarees and sweatshirts.

The guests passed through the French doors on to a broad marble terrace that overlooked the lights of the city. Round tables for eight were set with lilac-colored cloths with centerpieces of purple iris and Waterford crystal hurricane lamps. The entire terrace was enclosed in glass, like a large greenhouse, and there were numerous planters of thick greenery placed about. Everyone moved quickly to the chairs and sat down. Peach and her escort paused at the doorway to admire the beauty of the setting.

"Lovely, isn't it?" Peach murmured.

"Good God, yes. How can everybody take it all so, well, so for granted?" he asked.

"We're used to it, I'm afraid."

"I hope that never happens to me. I want to go through life enjoying the magic of every moment as beautiful as this."

"I'm sure you will," Peach commented, impressed by his sensitivity. She wondered who he was and why he was here alone.

"By the way, my name is Peach Malone," she said as they sat down at the nearest table.

"Peach? What a terrific name. Did your parents like peaches or what?"

"My husband named me that when we first met, and he refused to call me anything else. In fact, he even had it changed legally one year as a birthday gift."

"He gave you a new name for your birthday?" he asked, amused.

"Not for my birthday, for his. He was so proud of naming me that he wanted it as a gift for himself."

"Unusual man."

"Very."

Arlene sat down at the table beside Peach and whispered into her ear, "Well, you haven't lost your touch," then grinned and winked. When all the guests were seated, there remained two empty chairs at their table. White-coated waiters began serving the soup, and conversation settled down to a mellow hum. Arlene leaned toward Peach and spoke softly. "Those chairs are for Jim Austin and Ghilly Jordan, but they'll be late as usual. I think they have trouble getting out of the sack. I just hope they don't arrive in the middle of the film or Burt will be furious."

Peach was disturbed and shocked at Arlene's casual innuendo. "Why is Jim bringing Ghilly? What about Laura?"

Arlene just shrugged her shoulders indicating she didn't know.

"Have the Austins split up?" she persisted, realizing at last the reason for Laura's recent strange behavior.

"I really don't know. Burt went in for an examination last week, and Jim said nothing. Naturally, I asked Ghilly, but she told me to mind my own business."

"But I think he's still living at home," Peach replied, trying to remember exactly what Maggie had told her.

"I don't know, but lately he's been seen everywhere with Hollywood's grand horizontal." Arlene terminated the discussion by turning to Sid Sheinberg, whose studio would be distributing *Sandman*.

Peach was distressed by the information she had just received, and she lost her appetite. She set her spoon down and gazed out over the city. Something had to be done about Laura. Maggie was in New York. It was up to her.

A deep voice whispered in her ear, "The children are starving in Europe."

"What? What did you say?"

"That's what my grandmother always said when I wouldn't eat my dinner," the young man next to her said.

"I'm just not hungry anymore."

"You're upset by those people who aren't sitting there, right?"

Peach hesitated. Laura's life was so private that she couldn't bear to think it was being served up at every cocktail party in town. "Yes, Laura is a dear friend. Her husband is too. He was my husband's doctor during the last months of his illness. They are both kind, wonderful people. Very dear to me." Her eyes brimmed with tears, and she dabbed at them carefully to avoid smearing her mascara.

"Think about it tomorrow, like Scarlet did. There's nothing you can do this evening. Don't let your friends' troubles spoil your first evening out. Tomorrow you can do something."

She smiled up into his face. Goodness, he was surely the most remarkable looking young man. "That sounds like something Drake would have said."

"Your husband?"

"Yes, he was a brilliant, wonderful man."

"I'm flattered. Now eat."

Peach managed to eat some of her dinner all the while being entertained by her companion who was determined to keep her so preoccupied that she would forget the empty chairs. Their conversation ranged across a myriad of topics until it reached the sea, which was his obsession. He told her his dream of someday owning a yacht big enough to take him anywhere, and she confided that she too loved the sea, a fascination that seemed to be shared by many landlocked Midwestern expatriates. Her husband, however, had always been in a hurry and preferred airplanes so there had been little of the maritime in their lives.

Arlene's voice interrupted everyone's conversation as she announced, "When you have all finished your raspberry soufflés, please come into the screening room. We have coffee and liqueurs there, although, as you well know, Burt allows nothing to be served during the film. I don't want to rush you, but we must begin soon. It's a long film, and there'll be a contract out on anyone who leaves before it's over."

The group responded immediately. Film was serious business to all present, and they extended the same courtesy to the Silenzes' multimillion-dollar project that they would expect for their own.

Peach and her dinner partner led the way into the house. He held her arm, and she could tell that he was nervous for his hand was shaking. She saw tiny drops of perspiration on his forehead and upper lip. "Are you feeling all right?" she asked.

"I'll be okay. This is my first private screening."

"Really? Well, you're in for a treat. Burt has the finest screening room in the business."

They walked through the dining room and down a long hallway toward a pair of heavy wooden doors which were standing open. Peach entered first, then turned to see the expression on her escort's face as he followed. His eyes opened wide, and he let out a long, low whistle. "Jesus! This is incredible."

The room was very large and dim. Across the back were three rows of lounge chairs all covered in heavy velour in shades blending from dark brown on the far side to pale beige near the door. The rows were spaced widely and elevated, and between the seats there was a narrow brass table to hold drinks. The walls were covered in a rich brown fabric, and brass sconces provided a soft light. About twenty feet from the first row was a large screen.

In the back row at dead center was a console with controls and telephone. To the left of the screen was a small brass bar with a bartender ready to serve.

"Let's go in," Peach said. "I'm afraid we're blocking the door."

"Sure, would you like something to drink?"

"A splash of cognac to sip, maybe. And you?"

"I better not. I'm a little queasy."

"Oh? Where would you like to sit? I'll stake out two places while you go to the bar."

"How about the back row?"

She said softly, "Better not. Protocol sort of demands that we leave that for the big boys."

"Anywhere then, just as long as it's near the door." He headed toward the crush of people at the bar, and Peach sat down. Moments later, he returned with her cognac and a glass of dark liquid for himself.

He grinned shakily as he sat down beside her. "I got a Coke. My mouth's pretty dry."

Chattering noisily, the guests settled quickly in their seats. Heretofore, the evening had been merely prelude. Everyone was anxious to see the film that had been Hollywood's best-kept secret for the last year. Burt had made everyone in the cast and crew sign pledges of silence, and he had permitted no interviews with anyone connected with the film except himself. When questioned about the covertness of his project, he would only say that he was trying to avoid having his idea usurped in advance by a cheap, quickie movie made for television.

Because of the power of his films at the box office, Burt had even managed to keep the top brass at the studio from seeing it in advance. The control Burt had was the envy of every producer in the business.

The audience quieted as he strode forward and faced them from the center of the screen. "My friends," he said, "here is *Sandman* . . . at last."

He hurried to his seat at the console, pressed a button, and said quietly into the intercom, "Roll it." The lights dimmed until the room was in total darkness. Peach could feel a tremor of excitement in the young man's arm. Suddenly, the screen came alive with a brilliance of flashing light and stirring music as the titles sprang into view.

Peach was instantly caught up in the wonders of the film and the fascination of the story as it unfolded. Then the legendary *Sandman* swirled into view, and she realized that the star of the film was sitting beside her. His eyes were riveted to the screen, and his face was a mask of terror. She reached over and took his hand to comfort him. No wonder the poor boy was frightened. His hand felt cold and moist, and he clutched hers until her ring dug into her finger, but she did not pull away for she was pleased to be helping him weather the crisis.

She turned her attention back to the screen again with renewed interest, and was easily caught up once more in the unfolding panorama. She found herself thrilling to the dynamism and masculinity of the character on the screen, responding to the character of Sandman like a young girl watching an idolized movie star. Her vision was consumed by the beauty of the man's face and his body as the sheer folds of clothing revealed its contours, but above all, she was delighted with the style and wit of his performance.

From time to time, she would remember that the godlike creature on the screen was sitting beside her, clutching her hand like a frightened child, and she was amused that he could so stir her on the screen. She was having a terrific time. She felt young and rapturous. Although she wanted the movie to go on forever, too soon the final credits began rolling, and it was over.

The audience broke into a spontaneous torrent of applause, and the lights came on. A flushed and grinning Burt was out of his seat and running toward the front of the room. As he passed, he grabbed the young star's arm and dragged him out of his seat and whirled him around to face the enthusiastic group. "Here he is! He's gonna be bigger than Gable!" Burt cried.

Peach found herself rising to her feet along with everyone else. Calls of "bravo" and "terrific" . . . "a hit" were heard. There was a surge forward as everyone tried to be the first to shake Burt's hand and congratulate the new star.

Peach stood at the periphery of the group watching her handsome young friend's triumph, and she was happy for him. What an exciting and wonderful time she'd had. She must tell her hostess. She circled around the group and found Arlene by the bar supervising the pouring of champagne into tall crystal glasses. "Arlene, this has been marvelous. I can't tell you how much it meant to me to be here tonight."

"Peach darling, I loved having you. Here, take a glass. We must all drink a toast to success."

Rapidly Arlene and the bartender served champagne to everyone, and as the glasses were raised, a voice called from the group, "Here's to Burt . . . the fat, balding George Lucas!" Everyone laughed at the insiders' joke, but Burt was pleased. Money was what the movie business was all about, and it was a compliment to be compared to the biggest winner of all time.

Everyone drank the special Taittinger Comtes de Champagne, and as the group became more subdued, Peach managed to say a few quiet words of thanks to her host and hostess. She wanted to say goodnight to Jason, but he was surrounded, and it was time to leave. She asked the attendant at the door to call her car for her, and in just a few moments the Rolls appeared. She was about to get in when she suddenly found herself gripped around the waist by two powerful hands that pulled her back. "Hey, where are you going in such a hurry?"

Peach turned around to see a glowing and triumphant Jason behind her, grinning. "Why, Jason! Congratulations on an absolutely brilliant performance. I wanted to tell you but you were so—"

"Did you like it? Really?" he interrupted her eagerly.

"Like it? I loved it. You were sensational. I can't remember when I've enjoyed watching anyone on the screen as much as I enjoyed watching you as Sandman."

His eyes sparkled as he hung onto every word she said. He looked so boyish and happy . . . he was irresistible. There was a moment of silence, which Peach finally interrupted. "Well, I must be going. Again, congratulations and best wishes. And thank you for making my first evening out such a memorable one."

She extended her hand, and he took it in both of his own and held it. "Send your car home," he urged her. "Stay with me awhile. We can go for a drive in my car. I'm so excited I could burst. I don't want this night to end so quickly . . . please?"

Peach was tempted, but she asked, "Surely you have someone to share it with . . . a friend . . . a girl?"

"I have no one . . . really . . . and I need someone to talk to who has seen the movie and can share it with me. Please don't make me go back to my apartment . . . or to a bar alone."

The urge to refuse politely, to go home dutifully was strong, but she questioned her inclinations. Why not go with him? She had no one in the world to answer to . . . no one. She was free to do as she pleased, and she wanted to be with him. She turned to Miles, who was standing at the car door. "Miles, go on home. I'll be in later. Don't wait up . . . and leave the security system off."

"Goodnight, ma'am." Although Miles displayed the decorum of a proper British butler, still he could not completely mask his disapproval of Peach's sudden friendship with such an eager and boisterous young stranger. Peach saw the look and was annoyed. "Miles, I may be quite late, so don't worry about me."

The Rolls drove off, and immediately an attendant pulled up in a bright red Porsche that was obviously brand new. Jason held the door for her as Peach lowered herself with minimal difficulty into the passenger seat. She was grateful for the two months she'd spent in Italy tucking herself into her son-in-law's Maserati. Jason got into the driver's seat, reached across and fastened her seat belt, and they were off.

"New car?" she asked.

"How'd you guess? Burt gave it to me last week. He said it was bad for my romantic image to drive around in a Datsun pickup."

"That was generous of him."

"Maybe, but I think he finally realized he'd gotten a bargain. I didn't have an agent when I signed to do the picture, and I outsmarted myself. What did I know about deals and percentages?"

"Too bad. You've got one now though?"

"None of them, the big ones in particular, would even talk to me before, now who needs them?"

"You do. Drake always told me that there was no place in

business for grudges or hurt feelings, and agents are a way of life in this business.''

"You seem to know a lot about it. Was your husband involved?''

"He was involved in everything, Jason. He put up the money for Burt to make his first film.''

"That must have been a good investment.''

"On the contrary, it was a very bad one. The picture never did recoup its negative costs, but it was a marvelous film. The critics loved it, and on the basis of that, Paramount financed Burt's biggest hit ever, *Crisis*, and as you know, that made jillions.''

"So your husband gave Burt his start?''

"Yes, but everyone forgot about that except Burt and Arlene. That's why I was in that crowd of heavyweights tonight.''

"I'm glad you were there.''

"So am I.''

They drove in easy silence for a while, then Peach asked where they were going. Jason just shrugged his shoulders. ''I don't know. Got any ideas?''

It was after midnight. There would be few places open at this hour on a weekday. Los Angeles was an early-to-bed town, not like New York. "Would you like to go to my place? Sarah has wonderful goodies to eat, and I'll make a pot of tea. Does that sound terribly old and stodgy? Would you rather go to a bar? Perhaps Harry's in Century City is open.''

"I hate bars. I'd much rather have tea . . . and goodies. We might even catch the last few minutes of Johnny Carson . . . or the Dave Letterman show. Where do you live?''

It was a short drive, and in just a few minutes, they were in the elevator. Peach ignored the blank expression on the doorman's face and was angry with herself for feeling clandestine. They probably thought she was a sex-starved widow with a young gigolo.

They entered Peach's penthouse, and Jason was suitably impressed. Sarah and Miles were still in the kitchen. Peach asked them to serve tea and cakes in the study. She then took Jason on a tour, and he was enthusiastic about everything. At last they settled on the down-filled couch in front of a giant television screen, and Sarah brought in a tray.

"Thank you, Sarah. You and Miles may retire now."

"What about the dishes, ma'am?"

"You can do them in the morning. By the way, Sarah, this is Jason Darrow, the star of *Sandman*."

Sarah's jaw dropped, her eyes bulged, and she lost her composure altogether. "Really, ma'am? Did you see the movie tonight?"

"Yes, and it's fantastic. Jason is going to be a big star."

"D'you think I might have an autographed picture? For my little niece, of course. She's only thirteen and loves American movies."

Jason stood up and kissed the flustered woman on her cheek. "Sarah, thank you. You're the very first person to ask. I'll always remember you. I'll drop it by tomorrow."

Sarah resumed her dignity and declared formally, "Thank you very much, sir. Goodnight."

Although the television was on, Jason and Peach paid little attention as they continued their conversation. He was stimulated and happy and eager to talk.

"Jason, you'd never seen yourself on the screen before, had you?" she asked.

"Never. Oh, I've seen myself on videotape in acting classes but never on the big screen."

"How come you didn't see the dailies while you were shooting?"

"Burt wouldn't let me. He and Don the director were afraid I might get self-conscious and change my performance, and they liked what I was doing. I sneaked into the editing room a couple of times and saw some stuff on the moviola, but the picture was so tiny I couldn't tell much about it."

"And how do you like yourself?"

He looked down at Peach's hand, which was resting on the couch beside him. He picked it up and looked at it, carefully examining her long slim fingers and polished nails. Then he turned her palm over and raised it to his lips and kissed it softly. Peach couldn't believe what was happening to her. A rush of warmth suffused her, and she tried to retain her composure and deny the desire she felt.

"You didn't answer my question, Jason."

He smiled impishly at her and said, "I know, but I want to tell the truth, and I don't want you to think I'm a conceited ass."

Gently he rubbed her hand across his cheek, and Peach found a longing welling up inside her that she thought had died with Drake. "You liked yourself on the screen, didn't you?" she persisted. She needed to keep the conversation going.

"What did you think of me?"

She smiled into the eyes that would melt the souls of millions of women. "I thought you were marvelous. I could see the movie over and over again and never be bored. I'll never forget this night. Someday I'll tell my grandchildren that Jason Darrow once held my hand and sat here beside me."

"And kissed you," he whispered.

He moved close to her, not releasing her hand as he put his arm across her shoulders. Her mind told her to resist, but the desire inside had taken control, and she responded. He kissed her eyes, her cheeks, and then softly, he pressed his mouth on hers. Although he was tender, his movements were purposeful. Peach realized that he intended to seduce her right there. Summoning all the power of her will, she pushed him away from her. "I can't, Jason."

He smiled. "You can if you want to. Do you?"

"Oh, God, yes . . . of course I want to."

"There's nothing stopping us. You're alone . . . and so am I. This is probably the most wonderful night of my whole life. It's a night I'll always remember . . . share it with me . . . be part of that memory."

He silenced her refusal with his lips again, and for the first time in her life, she felt the passion and the urgency of a young man's sexuality. She wanted him to go on, but still she resisted. "Jason, I've been a widow only two months."

"But how long has it been since you made love?" She felt the breath of his words in her ear as his hand softly stroked her breast.

"A long time . . . a very long time." She could not deny his or her own desire. The emotion he had aroused in her was overwhelming all her restraint. She wanted to hold him, to press her naked body against his, to open herself and gather him in.

Suddenly, he rose from the couch and stood at his full magnificent height. As tall as she was, he towered over her. He took her hands and pulled her to her feet and held her tightly against him. She could feel his hardness as he kissed her again and asked, "Are we going to your bed, or shall I have you right here on the rug?"

"The bed, by all means." She was not so mesmerized that she would risk her servants intruding. He lifted her off her feet, still holding her body against his. "Which way?"

As they entered the spacious bedroom, he closed the door behind them. "Lock it," she whispered. He insisted on removing her clothes himself, piece by piece, kissing and stroking her and admiring the smoothness of her skin and the beauty of her firm, full breasts. They made love three times before he fell at last into a deep slumber, and although she was exhausted from several orgasms, she was unable to go to sleep. Their lovemaking had stimulated rather than relaxed her, and she could not take her eyes off the incredible beauty of his face and body.

It was many hours before she was able to entertain the thought that she was perhaps old enough to be his mother.

_15_

Macbeth's Dagger

GRACE tried to keep her hands from shaking as Casey opened the envelope with the snapshots. It was not easy to feign casual interest. For the last two days, she had returned to the God who had forsaken her in the alley all those years before. She had prayed and begged Him to let her daughter's lover be some other Jerry Casey. She promised to forgive Him for abandoning her to those murderers and rapists, and she vowed she would tell Casey the truth and never lie again if only He would help her this one time.

"This is a good one, Mom. You can really see what he looks like. Isn't he sensational?" Casey asked as she held out the color print to her mother. Grace needed only one brief glance. She did not dare take the picture in her hand for fear of revealing her nervousness. Trying to control her voice, Grace responded with only a slight trace of acid, "You're right. He is . . . young . . . for his age."

Brusquely, she turned away and headed for the bedroom. "I really must go. I've stayed away from the shop too long. Everything will be in a mess if I don't get back." She left Casey, who was chagrined at her mother's lack of interest in the father of her grandchild.

Half an hour later she got into the car with Rudolfo and waved goodbye to her daughter, who stood on the lawn. As they drove away, she vowed never to pray again. There was no God.

She arrived at the salon amid a flurry of greetings and bitching. Everyone had a problem waiting for her return. The hours passed quickly, and at noon she found herself alone again with her agony. She opened the cabinet behind her desk and from the complete bar inside she poured herself a brandy. She had never been much of a drinker, but she needed something to lighten the heavy load that had settled on her mind. The heat of the first swallow seared her tongue and throat, but it felt warm and comforting. She rested her head on the high back of her chair and closed her eyes. It was good to get back to work, to put distance between herself and her troubles at home.

Suddenly, the door flew open, and Eve burst into the room, her face flushed with rage. "Jesus, Grace, that bitch at the desk has screwed up my book again. She scheduled two of my best customers at the same time, and Mrs. Bloomingdale just walked out in a huff!"

"Calm down, Eve. We'll work it out. I'll call her myself and apologize and tell her that the next visit is on the house."

Eve threw herself into a chair. She looked very unhappy. She noticed the drink in Grace's hand. "What're you drinking?"

"Brandy. Want some?"

"Hell, why not?"

Grace poured a drink for her then gestured toward the door. "Lock it so no one can walk in unannounced and catch us boozing."

Eve did as she was told, then returned to her chair and took a swallow of her drink. She made a face. "Whew, that's mean stuff for high noon. How come you're indulging at this hour? Something wrong with Casey?"

Grace reacted cautiously. "Why would you ask that? You saw her . . . she looks terrific."

There was a hint of exasperation in Eve's voice as she replied, "Grace, she told me she was pregnant and planning to get married."

Grace was caught off guard. It never occurred to her that anyone else knew. "Shit! Why would she tell you that?"

"Because she's happy and proud and very much in love."

"But she's not married."

"She's going to be as soon as the guy gets a divorce."

"Maybe, but remember we've only heard her side. He might be lying just to get her out of town."

"My, my, you are the cynical one."

"You know you can't trust a man when sex is involved."

"And when isn't it involved?"

"My dear young woman, you are the last person to defend men when you yourself won't allow one to touch you," Grace remarked nastily.

"Don't get personal, Grace. My sex life is not a point of discussion here, but as for that, how long has it been since you've been in the sack with a man?"

Grace was annoyed at the turn the conversation had taken. "I may not sleep with men, but at least I don't fuck women."

Eve slammed her glass down on the desk and stood up. "Goddamn it, Grace! It's none of your business who or what I sleep with." Her eyes filled with tears of anger, and Grace was ashamed. She got to her feet and hurried to stop Eve, who was fumbling with the lock at the door.

"Wait a minute . . . please. I'm sorry. Sit down now and finish your drink." She put her arm around Eve and guided her back to the chair and handed her a tissue. "Eve, your life is your own. If you prefer women, that's entirely your affair, and I appreciate the fact that you've been very discreet. It's funny how women accept the homosexuality of male hairdressers, but not female. I guess they're threatened, or something. Anyway, I understand your desire for secrecy, and I will never violate your trust. And I want to be your friend."

"I'm sorry I blew up like that, Grace. It's just been such a crummy day. This place falls apart when you're not here."

"Don't I know. But let's forget about that. I owe you an explanation. It's true, I don't sleep with men. Casey's father was the only man I ever . . . made love with. True, there was another man I wanted, but he was in love with someone else, and I loved him too much to tempt him to cheat on a wife who made him happy.''

"Drake Malone, right?''

"No comment.''

"Why nobody else?''

"When Casey was just a baby, I was gang-raped. I was beaten and used. They damn near killed me. I still have nightmares about it after all these years.''

"My God, Grace, how terrible!''

"I would never have survived the horror . . . and the disgust . . . and the shame of it if it hadn't been for my baby. While it was happening to me, I felt my spirit separate. It was almost as if my body had been so desecrated that my soul was trying to escape the filth that I had become.''

"Jesus, no wonder you're celibate. Did you ever, you know, try again?''

"Several times, but at the last minute, I'd pull away. I just couldn't go through with it. The last time I tried, the guy got so angry, he punched me and said I was a rotten cock-tease and that I'd be better off dead. I decided not to try again.''

"Don't you ever get horny?''

"Not often. I masturbate when I do.''

"But is that satisfying?''

"It has to be when you haven't got any alternative.''

"What about women?''

"Nope, sorry. That's not for me either.''

"Why are you so upset about Casey? Honestly.''

The cloud descended again. Grace took a long swallow of brandy and emptied the glass. "Because I think he's just an old fart who likes to take advantage of young women. Over the years, he's probably screwed everything in sight.''

"You're guessing, Grace. You don't know him. You wouldn't like anybody who threatened to carry off your precious daughter.''

"Not true. I want her to have a loving husband and a happy marriage, but this guy is old enough to be her father. By the time her kid is grown, he'll probably be dead.''

The last word seemed to hang in the air like Macbeth's

dagger, urging her to clutch it, promising a final solution. Grace lapsed into silent thoughtfulness. Eve watched her, waiting for her to continue the conversation, but she did not. Eve finished her brandy and stood up.

"Thanks for the drink. I'd better go. It's time to shampoo the toner out of Mrs. Stack's hair." She left, but Grace was not aware of her departure, so lost was she in thoughts of resolution and revenge.

"I'll kill him," she whispered to the empty room.

_16_

A Happily Married Woman

MAGGIE used the time-consuming drive to Long Beach to organize her thoughts and plan the next few hours. Could all this really be happening to her? It seemed only yesterday that she was a Brownie leader, and here she was being flown to New York on a private plane. She had been offered another job that would pay her in six figures. She pinched her arm and giggled. It hurt. She was awake!

She pulled the car into the driveway and rushed into the house. "Dee . . . Dee! Where are you?"

Dee hurried out of her office. "Right here. What's wrong?"

"Nothing! Everything's wonderful. I'm leaving for New York at six tonight."

Dee looked at her watch. "It's almost one now."

"I know. Find Kirk for me. Wherever he is, track him down as fast as you can."

Maggie hurried upstairs to her bedroom to decide what to pack. What was the weather like in New York now? She'd check the temperatures in the *Times*. She went into Dee's office. "Didn't you find him?"

"No luck. He called in the office half an hour ago and said he'd call again before five to get his messages. They had no idea where he was."

"Oh, no," Maggie wailed.

"You can't leave town without telling him, can you?"

Maggie saw disapproval in Dee's eyes, and it annoyed her. "Well, I certainly don't want to, but I may have no choice.

150

I'm not about to give up a job that's worth a hundred thousand dollars just to talk it over with my husband."

Dee gasped. "My goodness, again? In New York?"

"No, not in New York. I'll be back day after tomorrow. Check the weather there for me, then come into my bedroom and help me decide what to take."

At exactly five o'clock, Maggie picked up her tweed coat and overnight case and walked downstairs. Mrs. Cornwall's long silver Lincoln was parked in front of her house ready to take her to Burbank Airport, where the corporation's Lockheed Jetstar was waiting to fly her to New York. Maggie was nervous and upset. Kirk had never called the office. He still did not know she was leaving. She had written him a letter explaining the situation, but that was an unsatisfactory way for him to find out, and he would be hurt and upset. She briefly considered canceling out on Belinda, but she could not bring herself to do that. For twenty years, she had made accommodations for Kirk's career. Now he would have to find a place in his life for hers. She stopped in the office to say goodbye to Dee, who looked glum.

"Still no luck?"

"I've tried everywhere he could possibly be. I'm sorry," Dee apologized.

"It's nobody's fault. I'll call him from New York late tonight. I'll be at the Helmsley Palace at Fiftieth and Madison. When he calls, tell him there's a letter on his desk."

"Do you want me to wait till he gets home?"

"No, go home at your regular time."

"I hope he understands."

"He will, Dee. Don't worry. We've been married too long to let a little thing like this bother us."

At six-ten, the limousine drove into a private lot just a few yards from the sleek silver jet that would wing her across the continent. The driver carried her bag and escorted her to the stairway where two attractive young men in gray three-piece business suits waited to greet her.

"Good evening, Mrs. Hammond. I'm Tom Johnson, the pilot, and this is my copilot, Lars Stanton. All set?"

Maggie climbed up the stairs into the cabin where she was surprised to see four men in suits and ties sitting on two couches in the rear of the cabin. They were deeply involved in a conversation and barely acknowledged her arrival.

The copilot directed her to a chair up forward and told her to buckle up since they'd be taking off immediately. She did as she was told, the cabin door was closed by another young man in a gray suit, and the engines turned over. The young man leaned down, checked her belt, and introduced himself. "Hello, Mrs. Hammond. I'm Kevin, an employee of Cornwall's on my way to New York too. Can I get you something to drink during takeoff?" Maggie noticed that the other passengers had cocktails in their hands. "That would be nice. Do you have any wine?"

"There's a bottle of chilled Gewürztraminer. Will that be all right?"

"Lovely, Kevin. Tell me, who are those men?"

He answered as quietly as the noise of the engines would permit. "Middle-level company execs . . . nobody special." In moments, he returned with a cut-crystal hock wineglass on a small silver tray, a linen napkin, and a small glass bowl of mixed nuts. "There was a special dinner put on board for you. Mrs. Cornwall herself called Mr. Terrail at Ma Maison and had him send it over."

"Really?" Maggie was impressed with the royal treatment.

"Yes, but only for you. There are box lunches for the rest of us. She told me to see that you had a pleasant flight. Just let me know if you want anything."

The plane taxied to the runway and waited for clearance to take off. Maggie tasted the wine. It was exquisite, fruity and spicy. She looked around at the configuration of the cabin. She was sitting in one of four huge airline seats that faced each other with an aisle between. The couches on which the men were seated were aligned across from each other. The interior was done in blue, and the fabric on the upholstery was a dark, rich blue mohair. Bright chrome accented the color and gave a stunning effect.

The plane took off smoothly and began its steep ascent.

Kevin informed her of the altitude and explained that private jets were assigned to higher air lanes to avoid interfering with commercial flights. He realized that this was her first experience in a private plane.

"Kevin, did Mrs. Cornwall send some papers for me?" Maggie asked.

"Yes, I have the briefcase in the rear. Would you like to have it before dinner?"

"Yes, I'm not too hungry right now."

Seconds later, a rich leather attaché case was placed in her lap. She admired the quality. It must be a Mark Cross, she guessed. She set it on edge to open the shiny brass lock and was startled to see "M. Hammond" engraved on a small gold plate. She snapped it open and inside found a pale blue envelope addressed to her on top of a manila folder. She opened the envelope and withdrew the heavy monogrammed notepaper with its fine, firm, handwritten message:

My dear Mrs. Hammond,

I am delighted that you have decided to join me in this noble quest. It will be rewarding for us both, I am sure. Have Connor sign the papers where noted. As you will notice, the documents are personal. I am revoking certain trusts so that dear Bittsey will never inherit a cent of my estate. I have chosen to bypass Connor's generation entirely and set up trusts for the welfare of my grandchildren. Please read everything so that you will be conversant on the subject. Once the papers are signed, you can relax and enjoy yourself and get to know my son.

I understand the corporation's new jet is quite nice. I personally hate to fly.

I have arranged for you to have carte blanche at the hotel. Just sign your name, and I will pay for everything. I have complete faith in you not to take advantage.

If you have any questions, just pick up the telephone and call me. I look forward to a visit and personal report on your return.

> Cordially,
> Belinda Cornwall

Maggie quickly read through the papers, and then signaled that she was ready for dinner. Kevin served her a cold sorrel soup and poached salmon with cucumber and asparagus. He poured her a glass of Meursault. For dessert, there was a rich chocolate nut torte with coffee. Although she was offered a brandy, she refused. She had finally begun to relax and needed nothing more.

It was two in the morning, New York time, when the plane landed at La Guardia. There were two limousines waiting. One was for Maggie, the other for her fellow passengers to whom she had hardly spoken. Within thirty minutes she was in the lobby of the hotel, where she was whisked through registration and up to the twenty-fourth floor. The large room was done in pale green velvets. The lights of the city that never sleeps sparkled through the wide expanse of windows, and she looked down on St. Patrick's Cathedral and Saks.

As soon as the bellman left her, she picked up the phone to call home. It was after midnight there, but no one answered. After fifteen rings, she decided to unpack and get ready for bed. At four in the morning, New York time, she gave up trying to reach her husband, but anxiety prevented her from sleeping soundly.

The next morning she ordered breakfast sent in so that she would be available to receive calls. At nine, Connor Cornwall's secretary called to tell her that a car would pick her up at ten to bring her to the office.

She dialed home again, but still there was no answer. She was frantic with worry, thinking that Kirk might have been in an accident or had a heart attack. He might be lying somewhere needing her, and here she was gallivanting around New York playing big wheel. She awakened Dee who promised to find him and call her back.

Feeling a trifle better, she got dressed in her gray tweed suit with its matching silk blouse. She looked in the mirror to check her appearance. A petite woman with a well-proportioned figure, she had thick dark hair which showed only a few strands of gray. She looked like any well-cared-for matron in most respects, except for her eyes, which were large and dark and shone from her face like two smoky beacons. A high school teacher had once compared her to a Keane painting, and although she had felt embarrassed about it then, as she grew older she realized her eyes were an important asset, and she took pains to enhance them with subtle makeup.

She looked out the window and saw heavy cloud formations, but she realized she had nothing to worry about. She would be in buildings or limos all day. She supposed the very rich never had to wear rubber boots or raincoats.

At ten sharp, she entered the car for the ride through the traffic to the Cornwall Building in the financial district. Gripping her new briefcase, she experienced her first pang of concern for the little deceit she was about to practice. She must be alert and tell the truth as much as possible. Connor Cornwall must believe she was only a secretary. It would be a disaster if she was asked to type anything, but that was highly unlikely. Fortunately, Belinda had told him that she had just started to work for her, so her ignorance should not give her away.

She was ushered into his office immediately. Although it was spacious, it was simply furnished. There was none of the glitter and flash of California executive suites. This was old money, money that was taken for granted and did not need to be flaunted.

At her entrance, Connor Cornwall unfolded himself from a big, black leather chair. He was tall, an inch or two over six feet, slim and fine-boned, almost patrician, like his mother. His hair was light brown with some gray, and his skin had the pallor of a man who has sat behind a desk too long. His features were sharp, but he had the large dark eyes of his mother, and where hers were penetrating, his were soft and kind.

"Good morning, Miss Hammond. Did you have a good flight?"

Maggie returned his firm, dry, and bony handshake. "It was marvelous. I'm afraid even first class commercial will seem like steerage from now on."

"Good. Please sit down. Would you like some coffee?"

Maggie declined and opened her briefcase to retrieve the papers for him to sign. "Here are the documents. You can readily see where your signature is needed, and they should be notarized."

"No problem," he replied, buzzed for his secretary, and proceeded to sign the documents. There was a soft knock at the door, and an older woman dressed in dark, severely tailored clothing entered.

"Millie, take these down to Ethel and have her notarize them for me right away, please. As soon as they're ready, I'll be leaving for the day."

As the woman obediently withdrew, Maggie smiled. "You're very trusting," she said. "You didn't even read them."

"I didn't need to. I'm sure my mother inspected every comma and dotted every 'i.' She's compulsive about details, and I trust her completely. She's always looking out for my best interests. How do you like working for her?"

"I really don't know yet. Everything has been happening so fast since I took the job, I'm still a little disoriented. I can't believe that I'm actually in New York."

"We'll take care of that. Mother told me I was to devote the entire day to showing you around."

"I hope it's not an imposition."

"Not at all. I've been working far too much the last few weeks. I could use a little R and R myself."

"In that case, I accept your generous offer."

He leaned back in his chair and looked at her quizzically. Maggie felt uncomfortable. "I'm curious," he finally said, "why she was so insistent. I accused her of matchmaking, but she said you were a happily married woman. I gather she's told you that my wife and I are separated . . . and will probably be divorced before the year is out."

Maggie tried to divert his attention. "It's true, I am happily married . . . at least I was twenty-four hours ago. I couldn't reach my husband to tell him I was leaving."

"Mmm, too bad."

"I'm a little worried. There was no answer at home last

night. I did give my . . . uh . . . his secretary the message, but I never actually talked to him myself."

Connor looked at his watch. "It's almost seven-thirty on the coast. Here, sit in my chair and call. This is a WATS line." He got out of his chair for her. "I'll go see how the notary is doing. Take your time."

Maggie dialed her home number, and after eight rings, Kirk picked up the phone.

"Kirk, thank God, where have you been? I've been so worried."

"Where have *I* been? I've been at home where I belong. Where are you?"

"Didn't you get my note?"

There was a long pause. "Yes, I read your note."

"Kirk, why are you acting like this?"

"My wife flies off to New York without telling me, and she can't understand why I'm pissed off."

Maggie's fear had turned to fury. How dare he treat her like this! She restrained her temper. Long distance telephone calls were no way to communicate emotionally. "Kirk, I'm sorry if I hurt your feelings, and I don't want to discuss this on the phone, except to say that I'm relieved to hear your voice. I sat up all night trying to call you. Did you unplug the phone to punish me?" He did not answer. "Kirk, are you listening to me? How many times over the past twenty years has your office called to tell me you had flown off somewhere?"

"That was different."

"How? How was it different? Anyway, I'll be back tomorrow night. I have so much to tell you. Please, honey, don't fight me. I love you, and I need your understanding and support."

"What time will you arrive?"

"I'll call you tonight when I find out the schedule. The limousine will bring me to Long Beach, but if you feel like driving to Burbank, I'd love for you to see the plane. It's so beautiful."

"No, thanks. I've seen airplanes before. I'll meet you at home."

"Let's be friends. I'm doing a job just like you do, and I'm feeling so good about myself for the first time in years. Please don't spoil it for me."

"I'll see you tomorrow." There was a click on the line, and she knew he had hung up. She replaced the phone and saw that her h..nds were shaking. She felt awful. She took a handkerchief out of her purse and dabbed at the cold perspiration that had seeped through her makeup. "Stiffen up, old girl. Be a man. You're not a weepy housewife anymore. You're getting a pile of money for this job, so get on with it." She stood up and steadied herself, then walked to the door and opened it to signal that her telephone call was completed.

Within fifteen minutes, they were in the limousine and on their way to a destination Connor had not yet disclosed to her. "Is there anything in particular you'd like to see or do?" he asked.

"Not really. I was here once before when the children were young. We saw the Statue of Liberty, Rockefeller Center, you know, the usual tourist stuff."

"Thank God, we won't have to do that then. Would you like to see the original Cornwall's? Good, we'll do that first, and then we'll have lunch at Le Cirque after a quick drink and a look at Windows of the World. You don't have any problem with heights, I hope?"

"None at all . . . the higher the better."

"Terrific. Then, we'll stop at Bloomingdale's and Bergdorf's."

"That sounds like a busman's holiday for you."

"Not really. I enjoy sizing up the competition."

The day passed far too fast. While in the stores, Maggie tried to keep him in the furniture and accessory areas. She observed that he gravitated toward clean, simple lines and good design. At four in the afternoon, they were back in the car again.

Connor seemed to have an enormous amount of energy.

"Now, we have two hours until dinner. I have reservations at La Caravelle for the first sitting, then I've got two very hard-to-get tickets to Peter Shaffer's new play. After the theater, we'll stop in at Sardi's—"

"Oh, when do I take off my shoes and relax?" Maggie protested.

"Would you like for me to drop you off at your hotel now? You can rest for a while and change for dinner."

"That's an excellent idea."

"I'm worried that we haven't done enough. Is there anything, anything at all that you'd like to do?"

"I hope you won't think I'm being presumptuous, but I've never actually been inside anyone's home in Manhattan."

"That's too easy. I'll have the driver pick you up in an hour and bring you to my townhouse. It's a little bare now. Bittsey pretty well stripped the place when she left. We'll have a drink there and be on our way. All right?"

Maggie was elated. She was fairly certain that by the time she left New York, she'd have enough information to do the house for Belinda. Connor was such an easy person to know. His wife must be an idiot to walk away from him. He was warm and witty and sensitive, and Maggie had enjoyed every minute of her day with him. She was anxious to get back to her room and make notes before she forgot anything.

Late that night, as they rode back to her hotel, Maggie thanked him for his gracious and generous hospitality.

"Don't thank me, Maggie. I enjoyed it more than you did."

"Impossible. I can't remember when I've had so much fun." A pang of guilt struck her at the disloyalty of the words she had just uttered.

"Really?" He took her hand and held it, looking sad and wistful. "I wish my mother wasn't always right . . . just once I'd like for her to be wrong about something."

"And that is?"

"That you're a happily married woman."

Maggie didn't know what to say. She felt awkward. She

knew she must not take his compliment too seriously. She decided to play it very light, and she reached toward him and brushed his cheek with a kiss and pulled her hand away. "You say all the right things, Connor Cornwall, and I appreciate your gallantry."

The car stopped at her hotel, and Maggie got out immediately. Connor followed her. "Maggie, will I see you when I come to Los Angeles for the board meeting?"

She smiled and took his hand to shake it. He held it a beat longer than necessary. "I'm sure you will," she replied.

Once in her hotel room, she walked to the window to look out at the city below. She was amazed at her euphoria. She felt like a young girl with a crush. Connor was really quite special. No wonder Belinda wanted him back so badly.

It was almost two in the morning. She had to finish her notes and get to bed. She had learned a great deal, and she wanted all of her impressions to be recorded while they were fresh in her mind. She could wait to do it on the plane, but she was afraid she might forget something important.

It was three o'clock before she finally fell into a deep sleep. She had completely forgotten to call Kirk as she had promised.

_17_

That Extraordinary Burden

DEAR SHAN AND DAC,

How I miss you! The house is so lonely and quiet since you left for school. It's also a lot neater, but I'd welcome a few dirty sweat socks thrown around the place.

I enjoyed talking to you on the telephone last night, and I'm so pleased that you're beginning to enjoy college. Shan, don't worry so much. You've always been a good student, and you'll do fine. I know calculus is hard, but if you want to get into medical school, you'll just have to stick it out with those tough courses.

Now, I have something to tell you. I intended to do it when I called you last night, but I just didn't have the courage. I hope it will be easier to put down on paper.

Your father has moved out of the house. It seems that he has fallen in love with Ghilly Jordan . . . yes, the movie star. She's tired of living alone and being a sex goddess. She's convinced him that he is the one man in the world who could make her happy, and she's told him she's ready to settle down and have a home. Of course he believes her. What man could resist? He wants a divorce.

Please don't be too upset with him. I've gotten over the anger, at least most of it. When I first found out he was seeing her, I pretended I didn't know because I wanted everything to stay as it was. I was sure that he would eventually get tired of her . . . or vice versa . . . and would come back to me. I was wrong. How ya gonna keep 'em down on the farm, after they've seen Paree? Joke. Ha, ha.

These past two months have been hideous. Fear was my sole and constant companion. I took pills too, although I'm determined to stop taking Valium to get me through the long, lonely nights. The fear of losing your father has done strange things to me. Would you believe I haven't left the house in almost six weeks? Every day . . . well, almost every day, I get all dressed and ready to go out, but I can't bring myself to do it. I've even gotten into the car, but my heart beats so fast that I can't seem to catch my breath. It feels just like I'm having a heart attack.

I think I have agoraphobia. I've read about it in magazine articles. I'm sure it's just temporary. My difficulties with your father have made me afraid of everything, but I'm certain I'll be all right when I become accustomed to living alone.

Actually, your father's announcement that he was leaving came almost as a relief. For weeks now, I've been waiting for that other shoe to drop, and now that it has I have nothing more to fear. The worst has happened, and I'm still alive.

I don't want you to be hostile toward your father. Just because he no longer wants me does not mean that he doesn't love you. Please try to understand and give him your love. He needs it as much as I do.

I realize now that I cannot fit in with his new life-style, and I guess I don't want to. I fought the move from Long Beach, as you probably remember. I must have had some premonition of what was to come, but it was selfish of me. I was more interested in preserving my own happiness than doing what he wanted.

My only hope now is that this woman will do as much for him as he thinks she will. I hope she is prepared for that extraordinary burden. Or perhaps because of her beauty and fame, he will not expect as much from her as he did from me.

I don't blame your father. I really don't. If I had to choose between her and me, it would be no contest. She is the stuff of every man's fantasies.

Now don't worry about me. I have wonderful friends, and they watch out for me. Maggie Hammond calls all the time, and Peach Malone has visited me twice since she came back from Europe. I promised her that the next time she comes, I'll get into that Rolls with her and go shopping for something beautifully wicked and expensive . . . and charge it to your father.

My darling boys, accept the new arrangement as gracefully as you can, and remember, nothing is forever. We should all be thankful that we had as many years together as we did. Your father has assured me that there will be no problems with money.

Above all, don't worry! I'm going to be just fine. I'm sure that time will take care of my problems, and someday I will make a new life for myself. I expect you to help me keep all bitterness and recrimination out of my heart. You still have two parents who love you. That will never change.

I know the coming holidays will be trying for us all. Perhaps you can have Thanksgiving with me and Christmas with your father. If we're all generous with each other, we can work things out.

Please don't telephone me for a while. I know I'd break down and cry, and then we'd all be miserable. Give yourselves time to get used to everything, and then we'll talk.

All my love,
Mother

_18_

My Little Secret

PEACH sat across the room from the tall, rawboned man who had been a fixture in her family's life for ten years before Drake had become ill and housebound. Doug Dooley, ex-professional football player, Secret Service officer, and private investigator, had been her husband's and family's bodyguard. She had just finished telling him in detail the events in the Milan airport. "What do you think, Doug?"

Not given to many words, he just shook his head. "I don't know, Mrs. Malone. It's possible it was just a random attempt on a woman who obviously looked wealthy. On the other hand, it sure seems strange that the guy would shoot. I think we ought to take some precautions for a while anyway."

"Do you mind, Doug? I know you've got a successful agency to run."

"Mind? I'm happy to have you as one of my clients. I'll keep an eye on things around here. And I think it would be a good idea if one of my men drove for you all the time. Miles doesn't have any training in resistance or protection, and I have a staff of men who are very capable. You know all the businessmen at the top levels of big corporations try to protect themselves nowadays."

"I feel better already. But what about the children?"

"I'll take care of making some contacts where they are too. Just leave everything to me."

"I have a doctor's appointment this afternoon."

"I'll drive you there myself."

"But there may be times I'll want to go out with a friend . . . in his car."

"No problem. We'll just keep you under surveillance."

Peach sat in Jim Austin's office waiting for him to finish his telephone conversation. For the first time she was aware of how handsome he was. Heretofore, her entire relationship with him had been primarily as her husband's physician. Everett Allison, Drake's doctor and close friend, had died suddenly, and Jim had stepped in so competently and assuredly that she would forever be grateful to him. She was seeing him now not as the tender healer but a faulted human being. She needed to resolve her ambivalent feelings toward him if she was to continue as his patient.

Jim finished his conversation, perused her chart briefly, then asked, "Now, what's wrong? You had a complete checkup just before you left for Europe, and everything was normal except that little problem with the fibrocytic breast disease."

Peach was embarrassed, but she asked, "Well, I just wondered . . . am I too old to get pregnant?"

Jim could barely conceal his surprise. "Do you want to?"

"Oh, no! I want to be sure I don't."

Jim was incredibly curious to know who she was getting it on with. Good Lord, her husband had been dead for only a couple of months and she was already screwing around . . . or at least seriously thinking about it. "Peach, it's highly unlikely at your age, but not impossible. If I were you, I'd take some precautions."

"I see. Then, should I take the pill?"

"No. An increase in estrogen could exacerbate your breast problem. It would be better if you used a diaphragm . . . or let, uh, him use condoms."

Peach was not happy with the suggestion. "How much risk is there really?"

"Peach, there are more reasons than just your breasts. At your age, there's also an increased risk of heart attack. It would be like using dynamite to dig up an anthill. I'd rather you risked pregnancy."

"Isn't there something . . . easy?"

"There's the new sponge. It's not perfect, but your risk of conceiving is low anyway."

"You know, Drake and I never practiced any kind of birth control. He would have been happy if I'd had a child every year."

"Oh, well, then . . . abstain around the middle of your cycle. You're pretty safe."

Peach was relieved. She could not face up to introducing contraception into the spontaneous and marvelous lovemaking sessions with Jason. Their relationship was fragile, but she wanted it to continue, for a while anyway.

"How's Laura, Jim?"

"Fine. How are Anne and Steve?"

"Jim, I hear you've moved out of the house, and I'm worried about Laura."

Jim stood up and walked over to the window. After a long, thoughtful silence, he answered her. "I can't help Laura anymore. She won't leave the house. She takes too much Valium. She's lost interest in everything but her own misery. She has no desire to help herself."

"Jim, she needs you. She's given up because she feels that she's lost you. Can't you see that?"

"She has lost me . . . that's the problem. I can't live a lie. We're worlds apart now. She still wants to be a little housewife in Long Beach, and I'm pretty sure that this whole charade is meant to punish me for leaving her."

Peach was astounded at the anger and bitterness in his voice. "Jim, she's your wife . . . the mother of your children . . . how can you be so callous?"

"Laura is one of those weak people who uses her frailties to control those around them. She thinks that by making herself sick and weak, she'll make me feel guilty enough to come back. Our marriage is finished, and if you're her friend you'll try to convince her to accept it and make a new life without me."

Peach was furious at his insensitivity. She wanted to lash out at him, but she remained silent. In all fairness, she reminded herself of his quiet kindness during Drake's last ordeal, and she did not want to repay him with a lack of understanding for his viewpoint.

"Forgive me for prying into your life. It's just that I've been hearing all sorts of stories about you and Ghilly . . . and then I see Laura's distress . . ."

"I'm glad she's got good friends like you. She's going to need help."

"Don't you care about her at all?"

"Of course I care, even though it might not look that way." He sat down again before continuing. "Being a doctor, I know all too well the tenuous hold we have on life. Any moment something can go wrong with this marvelous and complex mechanism we call the human body and *pfft*, that's it, Charley . . . it's over and done . . . finished. That's all there is. I'm not immortal. Whatever I have left of my life I want to enjoy . . . to live it on my own terms . . . in my own way."

"Even if your way destroys what's left of someone's else life?"

"Peach, does anyone have the right to dictate to anyone else how they should live? Isn't that the really selfish position to take?"

Although she did not agree with him, she understood what he was saying. He was a man over forty and facing his own mortality. Who was she to condemn the direction he had chosen? "Jim, I think you're going to find that you've given up more than you're getting. Ghilly Jordan is beautiful and glamorous, but take my word for it, very temporary. Don't plan on her being around to comfort you in your old age. In fact, you'll be lucky if she's still around by Christmas."

"You've got her all wrong. She's a terrific lady."

It was time to leave. He had found his own truth. "Well, good luck, Jim. Thanks for your time."

"Peach, I'm happy to know that you've returned to a normal sex activity. I was afraid you'd have difficulty adjusting to life without Drake."

"I'm a little surprised myself. Perhaps those long years of Drake's illness made the separation easier. If he had died suddenly, the shock would have devastated me. He did everything for me, you know . . . including preparing me to be alone.''

''I take it you're not alone anymore. Who's the lucky man?''

Just because she had inquired into his personal life didn't make it mandatory that she reveal hers. She smirked as she replied, ''That's my little secret.''

She hurried home. Jason had promised to call from New York at four, and it was that now. *Sandman* was scheduled for a nationwide opening next week, and Jason was slated for the cover story of *Time* magazine, if nothing in world affairs happened to push him off. Everyone connected with the film was holding his breath in anticipation.

Sarah met her at the door with the news that she had just missed Mr. Darrow's call. Peach was crushed. ''Where is he? I'll call him back.''

''He said you couldn't reach him. He was on his way somewhere and said to tell you he was sorry he'd called too early.''

''Did he say anything else?''

''Yes, ma'am. He said to tell you that it was all set . . . those were his exact words.''

''Really? That's marvelous! That means *Sandman* will be *Time*'s cover story this week! Did he say when he'd call again?''

''No, but Mrs. Hammond called. She wants you to call her.''

Peach went into her study to call Maggie. ''Hi, this is Peach. Sarah said you called. What's it like working for Belinda?''

''I just hope I survive. She's one tough lady.''

''They call her the Iron Maiden, you know.''

''Peach, have you seen Laura? I've been so busy lately, I haven't had any time for her.''

Peach told her about her conversation with Jim regarding Laura. She was glad to share the load with someone else.

When she finished, Maggie let out a long sigh. "God, we've got to do something to get her out of that house."

"I think we need professional help."

"I agree. Do you know of a good psychiatrist or psychologist we could contact?" Maggie asked.

"Not really. Drake didn't believe in them, but I have a friend who knows everybody. Maybe we could find someone who would see Laura at her home."

"Let me know if there's anything I can do."

"You've got your hands full. Don't let Belinda scare you, but keep looking over your shoulder. How's your husband holding up?"

"Okay, I guess. We don't see each other too much. Oops, there's my other phone. I haven't talked to Belinda for two hours. She's probably wondering where I'm hiding."

"Go then. I'll keep you posted."

Peach dialed Arlene. She was delighted to have an excuse to talk to her. Maybe she could find out something about Burt's plans for Jason in the next few weeks.

Arlene answered the phone, but there was a palpable lack of warmth in her tone when Peach asked about Jason's schedule. The conversation was awkward, and Peach decided to discuss her reason for calling. She gave Arlene a quick sketch of Laura's troubles without revealing her name.

"Why don't you call Dr. Christine Sabatini?" Arlene replied. "She's a psychologist who has an excellent reputation. She specializes in women's problems, and I hear she gets good results quickly. Her office is in Santa Monica, but you'll have to look up the number yourself. I've never used her."

"Thanks, I'll call her right away."

There was a long silence, which was unusual in any conversation with Arlene. Never had Peach been treated so coldly by her. "Arlene, there's something wrong, isn't there?"

"Why do you ask?"

"You're . . . just not yourself. Have I done something to offend you?"

There was a pause, and then suddenly Arlene's voice, angry and hostile, blasted out of the telephone at her. "Jesus

Christ, Peach, what are you doing messing around with Jason Darrow?''

Peach was caught off guard by the directness and accusatory tone of the question. ''What do you mean?''

''You know damn well what I mean! Burt had one hell of a time keeping it out of Jody Jacobs's column. One of her sources saw the two of you nuzzling each other at Aux Delices in the valley. My God, he's half your age!''

Peach's hands were shaking, and she was numbed by the fury of Arlene's onslaught. ''Not really . . . he's almost thirty.''

''Do you want to ruin his career? He's not just any young stud, you know. He's going to be a big star. There will be millions of young girls all over the world fantasizing about him, but not if they find out he's screwing around with a woman your age.''

Peach was unprepared for the viciousness of the attack. ''Arlene, how . . . how can you talk to me like that? I thought you were my friend.''

''Somebody needs to talk to you. You're making an ass of yourself . . . and so soon after Drake's death too. How can you disgrace his memory like that?''

''I'm sorry you feel that way, Arlene. There's nothing I can say except I care very much about Jason, and I would never do anything to harm him or his career.''

''Then surely you must know that what I'm saying is true. He's on the threshold of stardom. Don't spoil it for him. Can you imagine what the *Enquirer* would do to you both if they found out? All the media would hop on that juicy little story, and Jason's remarkable performance would be buried in a pile of shit. Do you want to do that to him?''

''Are you thinking about Jason or the box office of *Sandman?*''

''Both, my dear, both. You know enough about this business to realize that without big box office there is no big career.''

''Arlene, I don't want to talk about this anymore.''

''I'm sorry if I've hurt you, Peach, but you'll be hurt

eventually anyway. Surely you know that even with all your money you can't hold a young man for long, especially Jason Darrow."

Peach hung up the telephone. She felt old and ugly and unclean. Her humiliation was so total that she fell on the bed and began to gasp for air. She knew she was hyperventilating, but she was unable to stop herself. Just before she fainted, she managed to scream one word that echoed through the house and was heard by Sarah and Miles. "Drake!"

Jim Austin was sitting beside her holding her wrist when Peach returned to consciousness. He smiled at her kindly and asked, "Feeling okay, now?"

She looked up into the concerned and kind face of her doctor, and the irony of it all swept over her. How fitting. Here was a man who like herself lusted for the body of a beautiful, young movie star. But Jim had a wife . . . and she was alone. There had to be a difference. She hadn't hurt anyone but herself . . . had she?

Arlene's stark, cruel words returned to sting her again, and she began to weep hysterically. She pressed her face into the pillow and sobbed great racking sobs that sent shock waves through her body. At first, Jim tried to hold her and comfort her, but when the hysteria grew more intense, he gave her an injection of Demerol. As the drug began to take effect, Peach's sobs became whimpers.

For the first time in her life, she had been exposed to harsh and unfair condemnation, and she was not prepared for it. Because she had been protected, first by her parents' love, and then by her husband's wealth and devotion, she had built no defenses. She was vulnerable, and she had been mortally wounded by Arlene's strident and cruel criticism.

Three hours later, she awakened from the drug-induced sleep to see Sarah sitting beside her watching over her anxiously. "What time is it, Sarah?"

"Almost eight. Do you feel better now?"

"Not really . . . but I'll be all right." Tears filled her eyes and rolled down her cheeks.

Sarah asked, "Shall I call Dr. Austin for you, ma'am? He said he'd stand by all night if you needed him." As she spoke, she tenderly wiped her employer's face with a cool, moist cloth.

Peach declined. "No, I don't need a doctor, Sarah. Just a little time."

"How about a cup of hot soup and some crackers? I'll have Miles come sit with you while I fix it."

"That's not necessary. I'll be okay. Take your time."

"Would you like for me to turn on the television for you?"

"Why not," Peach answered. Anything to turn her attention outward and away from the hemorrhaging in her soul.

Sarah opened the armoire and pulled out a shelf on which the set rested. She turned it on and placed the remote control on the bedside table. The evening news in full color filled the room, and Peach tried to concentrate on it. She welcomed anything that would blot out Arlene's vicious accusations, but she could not get them out of her mind. Although she wanted to reject everything that had been said to her, her conscience would not allow it. She had always known deep down that what she had done with Jason was wrong, but she had refused to acknowledge it because she enjoyed him so much, and he seemed to get equal pleasure from her. Nevertheless, she now knew that she had to terminate their relationship. She must forget him.

Suddenly she was startled to see the familiar face and form streak across the screen. Good God! It was a commercial for *Sandman*. At that instant, she knew how difficult it would be to put him out of her mind. For the rest of her life, she would see his beautiful face everywhere, in magazines, newspapers, television, and theaters. She could never erase him completely from her life.

The telephone rang, but she did not touch it. A few moments later, Sarah announced that Jason was calling from New York. There was only a moment's hesitation before Peach responded. "Tell him . . . I'm not here."

_19_

Imperfect Crimes

EVER since she had reached her decision, Grace had been at peace with herself. Now that she knew what she must do to straighten things out, the agonizing was over. She was in the planning stage, and she faced a challenge that was invigorating. It was only confusion and uncertainty that debilitated her. Even the choice she had made now seemed right and reasonable. Any guilt she might have had dissolved in the rationale that the world would be a better place without Jerry Casey.

He had inflicted the sin of incest on his own rejected child, reason enough for vengeance. Grace even found that hatred could be a fulfilling and satisfying emotion now that she had a plan for expiation. She was convinced of the righteousness of her course, as well as the need to remain undiscovered, for Casey must never see herself as the central character in a tragedy of such monumental proportions. Grace believed that Casey's sorrow in losing the man she loved would be minor in comparison to the humiliation of learning the truth.

Fortunately, time had erased all connections between herself and Jerry Casey, and she was thankful that she had never revealed his name to anyone, not even Drake Malone. Somewhere in her plans, she must be sure to provide protection for Casey. It would not do to commit the crime perfectly only to have suspicion fall on her daughter, who could be reasonably seen as having a clear motive.

Jerry's demise would solve the problem of the unborn child

too. Once the father was removed from the scene, the baby could be born and raised by his mother and doting grandmother. Of course there was always the risk of genetics. To her knowledge there were no serious diseases or abnormalities on her side of the family, and Jerry Casey was certainly a good physical specimen, but that was just a chance she would have to take. If there was something wrong with the child, well, she'd assume the burden of care.

Time was important now. Obviously he had not yet begun divorce proceedings or Casey would have heard from him. Grace strongly suspected he was just stringing her daughter along, but she couldn't be sure. The last thing she wanted was for him to show up in L.A. before she could set her plans in motion. It was important that his death take place before she had any known contact with him. She must try to act especially positive and supportive with Casey so that no trace of suspicion could fall on her. What a horrible thought! Nothing, even the situation as it now stood, could be half as bad as Casey's finding out that she had killed the man she loved so much. She had to be very careful.

Grace turned over in bed and looked at the clock. It was almost six-thirty. She had been awake for hours. In the last few days, she had learned that she could function effectively with little sleep. Now that she had committed herself to do what had to be done, she needed every waking moment to make her plans. She would commit the perfect crime, although she was not so naïve as to believe it had never been done before. The men who had almost killed her had never been brought to justice. It happened all the time. It was only the imperfect crimes one heard about. All she needed was intelligence, meticulous planning, and the will to do it. A little luck wouldn't hurt either.

She got out of bed and went into the shower. She did much of her creative thinking with the rush of hot water stimulating her senses. Perhaps it was a carry-over from the days after she was raped when frequent, scalding hot showers were the only means she had of cleansing her body of its misery. In the closed-in steamy compartment filled with a comforting cascade of water, she found the solace and relaxation that others more fortunate found in the arms of a loved one.

When she was dressed and ready to go to work, she carried a cup of hot Postum into Casey's room. Grace leaned over the bed and kissed her daughter on the forehead.

"Oh, hi, Mom. Are you leaving now?"

"I'm a little early, but you know what a hellhole that place is on Fridays. I want to go over the appointment book to make sure there are no goof-ups. Tonight is the big bash at the Century Plaza for the President, and everybody wants their hair and nails done."

"Can I help? I'll be glad to come in and answer phones or something. I'm getting stir crazy."

"I'll see. Have you made out a grocery list?"

"We don't need anything, and besides, I'm getting bored with all this nutrition stuff. Let's go out for a big spaghetti dinner."

"Sounds great. I'll talk to you later."

She left the house and got into the waiting car. No matter how erratic her schedule, Rudolfo always anticipated and was waiting, and she had long ago taken his presence for granted. Rudolfo had emigrated to the United States from El Salvador many years before, just after his wife and six children had perished in a fire. He had started work as a janitor in the shop, but he loved cars and spent most of his time washing and polishing hers. Soon he became her chauffeur, for Grace was ever fearful when traveling alone at night, and she found new freedom in having a driver. She had an apartment over the garage built for him so that he would always be available to her, and he took care of the garden, an all-year task in Southern California. He saw to it that she always had freshly cut flowers for the house.

Casey had grown to womanhood with both Rudolfo and Grace hovering over her, and because of the tragedies in their backgrounds, they were formidable guardians. Had Casey not been a willful child and fiercely independent, she would have been smothered by their concern for her welfare.

It was a busy day at the shop, and Grace had no time for anything but business until a call came in from Peach.

"Hi, Grace. How's everything? Are you enjoying playing mother to Casey again?"

"You know it! I just wish I could convince her to live here permanently."

"When's she going back?"

"I'm not sure. She's pregnant, and the guy's married. She's sure he's going to get a divorce, but you know how those things go."

"Are you awfully upset about it?"

"Not really. I'm so happy to have her home, nothing else seems very important. Whatever happens, I'll help her work it out."

"She's lucky to have you."

"I'm the lucky one. Now, what can I do for you, madam?"

"I've decided to fly up to the house in Napa for a few days and visit with Steve. I've been depressed the past few days, and he always makes me feel good about myself."

"Anything wrong?"

"Not really," Peach replied, but Grace detected the lie in her voice.

"I heard it rumored you had a new romantic interest, but I was sure it was just idle gossip."

"Grace, would you have time for dinner with me this evening?"

"Not tonight, Peach, I've already made plans. Suppose I come over to your place early in the morning for breakfast. I'll do your hair, and we can talk."

Grace dialed the airlines to find out the flight schedules to Chicago and Champaign, jotted them down, and tucked the paper into her wallet. She locked the door to her office so that she would not be disturbed and opened the safe. Although most of her clients had accounts or paid by check, she took in enough cash so that she could skim off some of each day's receipts, which she had been doing ever since the IRS audited her and accused her of doing it when she had not. She was so incensed at their unjustified accusation, she decided she might as well be guilty. She counted the money. Over seven thousand dollars. She had more than enough to pay cash for her plane ticket and expenses, and there would be no big telltale withdrawals from the bank.

There was a knock at the door. Quickly she put the money back into the safe and closed it. She opened the door for Eve. "What's going on in here?" Eve asked.

"I was just trying to adjust these control pantyhose. I didn't want anybody walking in on me with my pants down. God, they're cutting me in two."

"Why don't you take 'em off?"

"I may have to. So, what's up?"

"Nothing. Everything is moving along without a hitch, can you believe it?"

"Thank God for small favors. Say, would you like to join Casey and me for pasta at La Scala tonight?"

"Sure, what's the occasion?"

"Just an evening out for Casey."

When Eve was gone, Grace sat down at her desk once more to plan. Jerry's death had to be swift and certain and clean. She could not use a gun for the very reason that she was a skilled marksman and carried a small registered pistol in her handbag at all times. Years before, she had decided she would never be a victim again.

Jerry Casey was larger and stronger than she was, and Casey said he was in good shape. He must die in a way that would look accidental or natural. Her options were limited. She must think it through carefully and choose the method of execution wisely. The slightest mistake could destroy both her and her daughter.

_20_

One's Own Bed

MAGGIE settled in the limousine for the long ride from Burbank back home to Long Beach.

She was nervous and anxious to see Kirk. She was also feeling guilty about almost everything, particularly about enjoying herself in New York as much as she had. She looked at her watch. It was only three. With a little luck with traffic, she'd be home by four and could cook dinner for her husband. There was a telephone in the car. Why not? She'd call home and have Dee take some meat out of the freezer.

"Mrs. H.? Hi . . . where are you?"

Maggie lowered her voice so the driver couldn't hear. "Would you believe the Hollywood Freeway?"

"I hope you're in a car."

"It's the only way to go. What's new? Have you talked to Kirk today?"

"No, he was gone when I arrived, and he hasn't called in. Do you want me to try to reach him at his office?"

"No, I'll do it, but I'd appreciate it if you'd check the refrigerator and make sure there's stuff for salad and take a package of chicken breasts out of the freezer to thaw."

"Sure, anything else?"

"Put the telephone on the answering machine and drive down to the Swiss bakery in Seal Beach. Pick up a baguette of French bread and a white chocolate mousse cake."

"I'll have it all here before you get home."

Maggie rang Kirk's office and was relieved when his secretary put him on. "Hi, honey, I'm back in L.A. and on my way home."

"You must be in a limo, right?" His voice was friendly, and Maggie's spirits rose. "Yes, and this is so much fun. I'm going to have a phone put in my own car."

"How was the trip?"

"Very successful. I'll tell you all about it at dinner tonight. Let's eat at home." Maggie could hear him talking to someone else in his office, although she could not hear what he was saying.

He returned to their conversation. "Sorry, honey, but some men from Japan are in town, and I'm really busy. I have to take them out to dinner tonight. They're seriously interested in coventuring a shopping mall on that property in Valencia."

"Would you like to bring them to the house for cocktails first? I'd be happy to go with you if I could be of any help."

"Not necessary, but thanks anyway. The Japanese don't usually take their wives out socially, and you'd just be bored. I may be late, so don't wait up. These guys like to barhop after dinner."

Maggie was deflated. She had expected anything but business as usual. She had been worried that he'd be hurt and angry; she had hoped he would be glad to have her home. It had not occurred to her that he would be cheerfully indifferent.

When she walked in the door, Dee greeted her with the news that Belinda was on the telephone. "What timing," Maggie remarked ruefully as she dropped her suitcase and headed for her office.

"Hello, Mrs. Cornwall. I just this moment walked in the door."

"Did you have a successful trip?"

"I think so. I can understand your desire to bring Connor back home. He's a delightful man."

"I'll have the car pick you up at nine in the morning, and we'll drive out to Malibu to look at the house."

Maggie sensed that she would have to establish some boundaries or she would be a puppet on a string. "That's a little too early for me. I've been gone for a couple of days, and I'll need time with my secretary in the morning. Eleven would be better.''

"That's too late. It would be after noon by the time you stopped for me, and I'd planned to view the place with you, then talk about our plans over lunch back here at the house. Make it ten.''

"Fine, I'll see you tomorrow, then. And thank you for the arrangements you made. The trip was lovely.''

At ten that night, Maggie crawled into bed. She had tried to wait up for Kirk, but she couldn't keep her eyes open. She decided to get a few hours' sleep so that she'd be somewhat rested when he came home. As she snuggled down under her electric blanket, she mused over how nice and comforting it was to sleep in one's own bed. Yes, there really was no place like home. She fell asleep immediately.

Somewhere in the distance, she heard a bell ring, but her mind and body were heavy with sleep. The sound filtered through to her conscious again, and she forced her eyes open. Although the room was dark, she could see daylight seeping through the edges of the shutters. Suddenly alert, her adrenaline pumping, she sat upright and looked at the clock. It was nine! Dee must be at the front door . . . but where was Kirk?

His pillow and sheet were rumpled . . . he had been there. "Kirk!" she called, but there was no answer. She jumped out of the bed and hurried into the bathroom . . . he had been there too. She could see the tiny dusting of whiskers on the washbasin and his pajamas draped over the tub. She closed her eyes and inhaled the scent of his recent presence there. Perhaps he was in the kitchen having coffee. Without stopping for robe or slippers, she hurried down the stairs and into the kitchen, but there was no sign of his having been there.

The bell rang again, accompanied by several knocks on the door. Maggie opened it for Dee. Alarmed at her employer's dazed expression and dishabille, Dee asked, "Mrs. H., are you okay?"

"What time is it?"

"Nine, a few minutes after. I've been ringing the bell for a long time. I didn't want to use my key unless I was sure that no one was home."

"I overslept again, and I've got to rush." Maggie started upstairs and called back over her shoulder, "Get my husband on the phone. I've got to talk to him before I leave."

Maggie stepped out of her nightgown and got into the shower. The sharp sting of the heated drops of water failed to thaw the icy fear that penetrated her body and soul.

At ten sharp, she hesitated only briefly before entering the waiting limousine. "It wasn't your fault, Dee. Don't look so glum. When you do reach Kirk, tell him . . . I'll be home for dinner."

An hour later, Belinda was sitting beside her in the car. She was not wearing a wedding gown, but the wool suit she had on was white-trimmed in heavy satin braid, and the white silk blouse was ruffled and beaded with tiny seed pearls.

"Now, my dear, tell me all . . . every little detail about Connor. I want to see how much you learned about my son."

"It's hard to know just where to begin. He's so nice, in a very sensitive and gentle way. I was extremely happy when I found out that he's eclectic in his tastes . . . good design is more important to him than anything else, and that fits in perfectly with my philosophy of decorating."

Belinda nodded in agreement, and smiled as she said, "Go on, my dear. You can never bore me talking about Connor. It is obvious that you like him."

"I can't imagine anyone not liking him. He's such a gentle and considerate man."

"I hope you didn't get the idea that he is soft or a pushover. He can be very tough when necessary. He is my son, you know."

"Agreed. There is a great deal of quiet strength that one can sense in him, although there seems to be a lot of sadness in his eyes."

"Did he mention Bittsey to you?"

"Only in passing. I got the impression that he has closed the door on that part of his life."

"Really?" Belinda remarked, and turned her face to the

window. They drove in silence. Maggie too turned her eyes to the view as they sped across Sunset Boulevard toward the sea. In some ways, she likened this ride to the course her life had taken. Other forces were now in control, and she was being rushed along toward an unknown destiny.

The car turned north on Pacific Coast Highway, and the sun sparkled on the dark blue water. Maggie's spirits rose as the ocean came into view. "It's so beautiful," she murmured, and Belinda nodded her head in agreement.

"You know, Mrs. Cornwall, I was raised in Indiana, but as a little girl I always dreamed of living near the sea. There's something about that great, living, moving body of water that restored my soul."

"That's what Connor used to say . . . and please call me Belinda. All of my friends do."

The car finally arrived at the gateway to the Colony, the secluded community by the sea in Malibu where the privacy of the inhabitants was protected by guards and a gate. They were waved through, and the car drove slowly over the private roads and stopped at a large but unprepossessing house. It was built of plain, weathered wood, and the front yard was small, the landscaping sparse. Maggie was disappointed. How could she ever turn this barn into an irresistible invitation? The chauffeur opened the front door with a key, then he helped the women out of the car. Belinda stepped back and signaled Maggie to go ahead. "You first, my dear. I've already seen it."

Maggie stepped into the foyer, and her eyes widened in surprise and delight. The entire back wall was glass, two stories high, and there were the sea and the sand. It was glorious. To the left, on the beach, was a glittering swimming pool and patio completely surrounded by a glass windbreak.

Maggie looked down at grimy but beautiful floors and up above to the semicircular balcony which served all the upstairs rooms. A circular staircase led to the balcony. It was spectacular. Lost in the wonders of discovery, Maggie left Belinda to explore the house in detail. She was ecstatic.

There was a lot of work to do, but when she finished, this would be the most inviting house in the world.

When she returned to the living room, Belinda eyed her sharply, noting her rich dark hair with its few touches of gray and her large dark eyes ringed by thick eyelashes. Not a great beauty, certainly, Belinda observed, but a woman of taste and intelligence and charisma. "Do you like it?" Belinda smirked, inordinately pleased with herself.

Maggie laughed. "You know I like it. I love it! How much can I spend?"

"How much do you need?"

"I'm not sure. Why don't you let me make up some sketches and rough out a budget?"

"How long?"

"Two weeks."

"Ten days."

"Agreed." They looked at each other and smiled.

Late in the afternoon, Maggie called Dee from the limousine, which was taking her home. "Did you reach Kirk?" she asked.

"He came home about one o'clock. I helped him pack a suitcase. He said to tell you he would be in San Francisco tonight, and then he's going to Tokyo on Friday."

"Tokyo? For how long?"

"He didn't know. He said he'd call you late this evening, and if you wanted to go to Japan with him, he had made a reservation for you."

The coldness that had numbed her earlier returned. Japan! She had always wanted to go there to see that ancient and beautiful culture, and now Kirk was giving her the chance.

No, it was not a chance he was giving her, it was a choice he was forcing her to make.

__21__

Every Woman
in the World

DRAKE had once told her that the solution to one's problems could often be found in trying to solve someone else's. Peach decided to do something about Laura. She called Dr. Sabatini to discuss it, but she could not get through her secretary. She left her number and demanded that her call be returned as soon as possible. She looked at the time—almost noon. She'd give her until two-thirty.

Peach walked to the window to look out over the city. It was one of those rare cool days in Los Angeles when the air was clear, the sky was blue, and the view seemed to go on forever, but Peach couldn't shake the feeling of depression. Losing Jason had made her loss of Drake even more poignant. During her marriage, every low point in her life had been shared with Drake, and he had tried to carry most of life's burdens for her. Even when she miscarried their last child, Drake had managed to absorb her grief into his own. Now, here she was, longing for him to help her deal with the loss of her young lover.

God, she felt like such a fool! Arlene was right. She had behaved like a silly, love-starved woman. And worst of all, she felt guilty and disloyal for getting involved with another man in such a blatantly sexual way just a few short weeks after Drake's death. She couldn't continue seeing Jason without looking ridiculous. Their age difference was just too great. She would have to forget him.

The telephone rang and jarred her out of her brooding. It

must be Dr. Sabatini returning her call. She picked up the phone and said hello.

"Well . . . at last! I thought you were trying to avoid me." The sound of Jason's voice across the miles shook her. The moment was here, thrust upon her too suddenly. "Jason!" was all she could say.

"Ah, you recognize my voice . . . well, that's a start. I thought maybe you'd forgotten all about me."

"Where are you . . . calling from?" she stammered.

"Los Angeles," he replied, and her heart raced as she exclaimed, "No!"

"You're right. I'm still in New York, and they want me to stay for a couple more days. It seems everybody wants Sandman on their talk shows."

"I'm so happy the *Time* magazine story worked out."

"Yeah, really. I read the article, and it's unbelievable. It reads like a fan magazine."

"You sound like you're having a wonderful time."

"Not true . . . you're not here. Peach, I miss you."

She tried to keep her voice from quavering and her body from responding to him. "How . . . how are the interviews going? The TV spots looked wonderful."

"Boring, boring. Everybody asks the same questions over and over."

"When are you coming back to L.A.?"

"Wednesday. I'm taping the Carson show that afternoon. *Sandman* opens on Friday, but I also have to attend a benefit preview at the Museum of Science and Industry Thursday night. There'll be a dinner afterward at Jimmy's so get out your fanciest dress. It's black tie."

"I won't be in town, Jason. I'm flying up to Napa tomorrow to see my son." There was a long silence.

"Peach, something's wrong. You don't sound like yourself at all. Do you have to go to Napa right now?"

She decided not to play games. Honesty was always the best way. "Jason . . . I'm so sorry. I don't know how to say this . . . it's so difficult to find the right words . . ." To her dismay, she lost her composure and began to cry.

"Don't say it, Peach, please. Burt told me that Arlene had talked to you . . . just as he talked to me . . . but it's a lot of crap. What do they know about us . . . how we really feel about each other?" His voice was hard and angry.

"Oh, Jason, they're right, you know they are. You can't let the world know you're having an affair with an . . . old woman. It would ruin your career."

"You're not old! You're the loveliest, sexiest woman I've ever known. Besides, Burt doesn't own me. What I do on my own time is none of his business. I don't intend to sell my soul to be a movie star."

"Jason, I'll always remember the few hours we've had . . . but we have to face reality. I'm seventeen years older than you are." There, she had finally said it.

Jason's voice lost its hard edge and became persuasive. "Let's not make hasty decisions by long distance. When will you be coming back to L.A.?"

"I'm . . . not sure."

"Will you promise to tell Sarah to give me your telephone number up there?"

"Yes, if you want it."

"Then we'll drop this subject until the film opens and you've stopped bleeding from Arlene's knife wounds. What we have together is just too important to let someone else destroy. Are you listening to me?"

"Jason, no, please . . ."

"Now you promise you'll see me before you make any foolish decisions, or so help me God, I'll go on the Carson show and tell him everything . . . even your age."

Peach was aghast. "You wouldn't!"

"I would too. Johnny would love it." His voice was determined and threatening, and she believed he might do it.

"All right . . . I give up. Jason, you really are a handful."

"That's true, and if we keep on talking, pretty soon I'll be two hands full. How come just the sound of your voice makes me hard? I wish you were here to take me in hand."

"Jason, what am I going to do with you?" She laughed.

"Hmm, let's see . . . with three thousand miles between us, we can't very well let our fingers do the talking."

"Goodbye, Jason. Have a wonderful time in New York and at the premiere. I'll be thinking about you. You're going to be a big star. Every woman in the world will want you."

"But I don't want every woman in the world. I want you."

She hung up the telephone and walked to the mirror to look at herself. Her heart was pounding, and she felt shamefully sexy. She wiped away the smudges of mascara that her tears had made and looked deep into the reflection of her own eyes. "God, why do I now feel so deliriously happy?"

The telephone rang again. Was he calling back? A woman's voice greeted her. "Is this Mrs. Malone? I'm Dr. Sabatini. My secretary said it was urgent that I call you."

Peach had to come down from her high and attend to other things. "Thank you for calling. Yes, I have a very good friend in serious trouble, and I need your help."

Two hours later, Peach got into her car and directed the driver to Dr. Sabatini's office. She had given her a quick sketch of Laura's predicament, and Dr. Sabatini agreed to see her that afternoon since Peach was leaving town the next day. Peach had called Laura and told her she was coming but made no mention of bringing someone. Laura sounded happy and friendly, and she wondered if perhaps she was being hasty.

Christine Sabatini was ready when the car arrived for her. She was young, no more than thirty-eight, very tall and slim. Her skin was tanned, and her long brown hair was knotted at the nape of her neck. She moved with the grace of a dancer and had an air of serenity about her.

"Thank you for changing your schedule so that you could see Laura today," Peach said.

"No problem. I'm interested in phobics because they're mostly women, and my practice is geared toward them. I hope we can help Mrs. Austin before the phobia becomes too deep-seated. The longer they stay locked up in their homes, the more acute the symptoms become when they try to leave."

"Can this phobia be triggered by some emotional upheaval?" Peach asked.

"If the personality is susceptible, yes. Especially if she tends to be fearful in general. Has something happened to her recently?"

"Her husband left her for a beautiful young actress."

The psychologist nodded her head in understanding. "I see it all the time. You have no idea how devastating it is for most women . . . especially those who took pride in being good wives and mothers."

"Well, Laura was exactly that. She's a kind, sensitive person. I got to know her well when my husband was dying. She was so very thoughtful. Most of my friends stayed away. I suppose they thought I wanted to be let alone, but I really needed someone to talk to, and Laura was there. Her husband was my husband's physician, and in all fairness, I must say that he too was exceptionally considerate."

"I suspect she was married rather young."

"That's true. She worked and supported the family throughout Jim's medical school and training. They have two boys, twins, who left for college just this year."

"And now she's all alone."

They arrived at Laura's house and rang the doorbell twice before she answered. She was in a robe and slippers. Her face was pale, and she wore no makeup. Her hair was pulled back plainly in a rubber band.

"Peach, it's so good to see you," she said in greeting.

"Laura, I've been worried about you. This is Dr. Sabatini. She's been kind enough to come with me to see you."

Laura's expression reflected her alarm. "I don't need a doctor. I'm perfectly well."

"May we come in? It's been a long drive, and I would love to have a glass of water," Christine said, smiling and speaking in a soft, soothing voice.

Remembering her manners, Laura stepped back to allow the women to enter. "Of course, please come in, and I'll fix tea."

"That would be lovely," the psychologist replied as they walked inside. "My, what a beautiful home you have."

"Thank you. Peach, please show Dr. Sabatini into the living room, and I'll go put some water on to boil."

Peach was impressed with how skillfully Dr. Sabatini had guided them through an awkward moment. A few minutes later Laura returned with tea on a silver tray and a plate of homemade cookies. She had remembered the glass of water too. She served her guests gracefully, her fears submerged in domestic activity.

Dr. Sabatini began to question her about some of the antiques in the room, and the conversation drifted along comfortably. Peach wondered at the casualness of it all, but she was aware that Laura was gradually growing more at ease. There was a pause in the conversation, and after a brief hesitation, Laura asked a question. "Are you a psychiatrist, Dr. Sabatini?"

"No, I'm a clinical psychologist, and please call me Christine. I try to keep my relations with my clients on a first-name basis. Titles tend to put them in a subordinate role. In my profession, we try to help others to help themselves. We don't see ourselves as miracle workers."

"There's really nothing wrong with me. I'm fine, really I am."

"How long has it been since you've been out of the house?" Christine asked.

"Why, just yesterday . . . I went to the market."

Peach looked surprised. "Really? Oh, I'm so relieved. I've been worried about you thinking you had locked yourself up in here—"

"Where did you go?" Christine interrupted.

"Why . . . uh . . . just up to Ralph's on Ventura."

"Did you have any sensation of heart flutterings while you were out? Did the palms of your hand get damp and did you have difficulty breathing?"

Peach watched Laura closely. She was obviously uncomfortable with Christine's questions, although they had been asked in a kindly manner.

"No! I was fine," Laura protested defensively.

The psychologist looked at her and said, "Laura, let me help you . . . please."

Failing to maintain her composure, Laura burst into tears. Peach went to her and put her arms around the shaking shoulders of her friend and held her until the sobbing abated. "Laura," Peach said, "we're both alone now. We can help each other."

At last Laura regained her poise, but Peach stayed beside her. "Laura, come home with me for a few days. Then, if you're up to it, we'll fly to Napa together."

"I can't, Peach."

"Of course you can . . . if you'll just try."

"No, Mrs. Malone," Christine interjected, "she really can't now. But perhaps if we're lucky, she'll be able to do just that sometime soon." Laura looked surprised and interested as Christine continued. "You see, Laura, we're going to do it one small step at a time. It won't be easy, but your phobia is a relatively recent one. Let's get started right now. It will be much more difficult later."

"What do I do?"

"You can start by coming out on the porch now and waving goodbye to us as we leave. Then tomorrow, I'll be here at nine in the morning, and we'll take another small step. We'll have time to chat for a while. We'll set up a regular schedule for my visits until you're able to come to my office. All right?"

"All right," Laura agreed hesitantly.

When they left, Laura forced herself to step out onto the porch. As the car pulled away, Peach noticed that she turned quickly and hurried back inside.

"Christine, what do you really think?" Peach asked.

"Just what I told her. It will take some time. She's lost all of her self-respect and sense of worth. She's got to get some of it back before she'll be comfortable out in the world again."

"Losing a husband to another woman is almost as bad as becoming a widow," Peach commented.

"It's much worse. Her whole life was predicated on her husband and her relationship to him, but he stopped wanting her. A widow still has the benefit of knowing she was loved and not rejected."

"That's true. Drake's love was a constant in my life. It still is."

"Laura's existence revolved around her home and family. You can see that by the loving care she lavishes on the house. In spite of the fact that she herself looked untended, the place was immaculate. I would guess she has no servants."

"Right. She just could never find anyone who would do things as well as she wanted."

"And now, only the house needs her."

"Christine, I can't tell you how much I appreciate your help. Please have your office bill me."

"If I'm successful, she'll want to pay for everything herself."

Peach returned home with a sense of well-being. Drake was right as usual. Helping others was the best way to help yourself. Whatever happened with Jason, she promised herself she would not allow it to overwhelm her. She had learned an important lesson from Laura. Self-reliance and independence were not to be surrendered too easily. She would retain control of her emotional life, even if others had control of her fortune.

_22_

Someone to Hold Me in the Night

GRACE got into the car with only a brief nod to Rudolfo. She had taken Eve and Casey to La Scala the night before, and she had eaten too much pasta and drunk too much red wine. All night she had tossed and turned with visions of murder and violence tormenting her. Now, at a time when it was important for her to be alert and sensitive, she was tired and dragging.

"Grace, you look terrible," Peach greeted her.

"I had a little too much wine and pasta, too little sleep, I'm afraid."

"Oh, well, a hangover is rarely terminal. Come in and we'll have breakfast."

"Just coffee, please. I used up this month's quota of calories last night. Besides, I need to get your hair done in a hurry. I have to get to the shop."

As Grace started to work, Peach said, "Something's bothering you, Grace. It isn't just Casey's pregnancy. You're too realistic to let that shake you."

"Of course it's Casey's pregnancy. The son of a bitch that knocked her up hasn't called once. No matter what she says, I'm sure he doesn't intend to marry her."

"Has she considered an abortion?"

"She wants the baby. She loves the bastard and thinks he's going to divorce his wife for her."

"Maybe he will."

"He won't. He's made a career of fucking young girls."

Peach was surprised at the hatred in Grace's voice. "How do you know? Did Casey tell you that?"

Grace was on guard now after her outburst. It was imperative that she assure Peach that it was all surmise. "He's as old as I am. He's been married for a long time, and he's a college professor. I feel certain that Casey was not the first, and she won't be the last. He's probably taken up with some other young chick. No, I certainly don't want her to marry him, but then do kids ever do what their parents want them to do?"

"You'd rather she raised her child alone, like you did?" Peach queried and hit Grace's sensitive spot.

"She won't be alone like I was . . . she has me. God, I wish I knew what to do."

"Grace, you don't have to do anything. Casey is an adult. It's not really your problem. You can give her help and support, but you've got to stop playing God with her life."

Grace knew she had expressed herself too openly. She must erase the picture of hatred she had so vividly displayed. "You're probably right, Peach. I guess I'm just a meddlesome mother, and I have to back off. Thanks for the advice. I'm going to try to take it."

Peach was pleased with herself and accepted Grace's easy acquiescence as an indication that her advice had been right on target. Grace saw that Peach had taken her words at face value and was silently amused at how horrified her coddled and pampered friend would be if she knew she was in the presence of a potential murderer.

Peach related the story of Laura and the psychologist, and Grace commented, "Ghilly Jordan, by the way, is a regular client of Eve's."

"Does she ever mention Jim?"

"No, and that's strange. Ordinarily she gets her kicks out of telling the details of her sexual escapades, but she's been unusually quiet lately. Maybe she's really in love with him."

"I'd like to think so. If Laura's going to be torn apart, I guess it should at least be in a good cause. Personally, I think one day Jim Austin will wake up and realize what he's lost is a lot better than what he's got.''

"If he does, I hope Laura has the guts to turn him away."

"You don't think she should take him back?"

"Never. He'll just do it again, and she'll have to go through the whole thing twice. One day she'll take too many pills, and it'll be all over."

"Grace, you're a very cynical woman."

"Just realistic. Hairdressers see a lot of misery. Every day suffering women come into the shop for help, trying to hold onto their men and their security. They think they can hold their marriages together with a little bleach and a lot of makeup. We try to make them look and feel beautiful, which is usually an impossible job."

"God, that's depressing."

"Sorry. Now, have you considered letting me color those gray hairs . . . or do you like looking old?"

Peach laughed. "Yes, you miserable creature. As soon as I get back, I'll come into the shop for a complete renovation. Can you make me look twenty years younger?"

"For that you need a plastic surgeon. My skills are limited."

"Do you think I ought to?"

"I don't think so, but if you ever decide you do want a lift, by all means see a man named Pierre Senseney. I see a lot of reworked faces, and his are the best. He's the only man I'd let touch my face with a knife."

Grace was feeling better by the time she arrived at the shop with renewed determination to get the grisly job done. She checked over her appointment book, dealt with a few complaints, and at four o'clock announced that she was going home with a headache. Eve remarked that she had one too, and they promised each other that they'd refrain from drinking red wine in the future.

Instead of going home, she had Rudolfo take her to the shopping center in Century City, and she went into the hotel where she could find privacy in a telephone booth. Armed with a purse full of quarters, she called her older sister in Chicago.

"Blanche, it's Grace. How are you?"

"Fine, just fine. I got your check last week. Thanks, but you don't need to do that."

"When are you coming out for a visit?"

"You know I'm afraid of airplanes, Grace. Why don't you come visit me? You can see your daughter while you're here."

"Casey's back in California."

"I didn't know that."

"It happened suddenly. Listen, Blanche, I may have to go to Chicago on business, but I can't talk now. Will you call me tonight, collect, about ten your time?"

"Sure, why?"

"I need to take care of some things, but I don't want Casey or anyone else to know my business. I'd appreciate it if you'd call and invite me for a few days . . . okay?"

"All right. Ten o'clock . . . tonight . . . my time."

Now she would have an excuse to be away for a few days. The next thing was the clothing. She hurried back to the stores.

Everyone had gone when she returned to the shop to hide her purchases in the locked cabinets in her private office. She went through the hairpiece cabinet and took out a variety of wigs, hairpieces, and beards. So engrossed was she in trimming and shaping three of the wigs, she did not realize how late it was until the telephone rang. "Mom, are you coming home for dinner? It's all ready."

"Oh, God, it's almost seven-thirty . . . I'm on my way."

Stuffing everything away and locking it up, Grace hurried frantically. She had to be home when Blanche called in half an hour. She swept the hair off the floor and tossed it in the wastebasket. Flinging herself into the car, she exhorted Rudolfo to hurry home. "Casey says dinner is getting ruined. Move it."

Since he loved any excuse to drive fast, he maneuvered the car with skill and expertise. Within fifteen minutes, in spite of the still-congested traffic, they were home. Casey called to her mother as she walked into the house, "Mom, Aunt Blanche is on the phone."

Grace picked it up and said, "Blanche, how good to hear your voice. How are you?"

"Grace, Casey tells me she's pregnant."

Grace heard a noise on the line and realized Casey was still on the extension. "Still there, honey?"

"I was just telling Aunt Blanche—"

"I see, well, what's going on with you, Blanche?"

"I've been feelin' kinda blue lately, and I was hoping maybe you could see your way clear to coming for a visit."

"Is there anything wrong?" Grace asked.

"Nothing that a visit from you wouldn't fix."

"There's a hairdressers' convention in St. Louis next week. Maybe I could drop in there for a day or two so I can deduct the fare, then come up to see you. Okay?"

"Maybe I'll come too," Casey added.

"Are you sure it's okay to fly in your condition?" Blanche asked.

"No problem. I'd like to go down to the university for a day or two anyway."

"We'll discuss it later, Casey. Blanche, I'll call you tomorrow and let you know."

Grace was furious with herself for not realizing that Casey would want to get back there to see him. As they sat down to dinner, Grace broached the subject directly. "I don't understand your sudden need to fly back to see Blanche."

"Well, she is the only relative we have now."

"You saw her once, between planes, during the entire time you lived back there. The truth is you're only interested in seeing that asshole you're involved with." Grace abandoned the tactful approach in favor of a sledgehammer.

"Mother, mind your own business!"

"It is my business. You're the one who came home when you needed help. I just don't understand kids who want help from their parents, then get upset if they offer advice. You haven't heard from him, have you?" For a brief moment Grace felt a flash of hatred for this daughter who had brought so much misery into her life and who was now forcing her into actions which could destroy them both. Casey's face had become still and white, and she was staring into her plate, not moving.

Grace bored in with more accusations. "He hasn't called at all. He wanted you as far away as possible. He doesn't intend to divorce his wife, and you know it."

Casey got to her feet and walked away stiffly. Grace was further incensed by her refusal to fight back. "Casey, come back here. You can walk away from me, but you can't escape the truth."

There was no answer. Casey went silently into her room and lay down on the bed. She looked ill. Grace followed her, and her anger vanished in a wave of motherly concern. She sat down on the bed beside her. "Baby, are you all right?"

Casey answered with an outburst of tears. In mute and frustrating guilt, Grace held her daughter's cold hand until Casey started to talk through her sobs. "Mom, I love him so much. I don't want to face it, but I know you're right. He hasn't called me. I've got to go back and find out where I stand."

"Casey, there's still time for an abortion."

"I don't want an abortion, Mom. I intend to have this baby. Can't you understand that even if I can't have him, I still want his child? Someday he might change his mind and decide he wants us both, and we'll be here waiting for him."

"Oh, God, Casey, don't do that! Don't put your life on hold waiting and hoping for something that will probably never happen."

"Has it been so bad for you, Mom? You and I had a wonderful life together. You've been successful in a business that you love. We've had a happy home."

"There's a difference. You're closing the door on the possibility of ever loving someone else. I didn't do that. Through all those years, I had the hope that someday I'd find someone to share our life . . . someone to love me . . . someone to hold me in the night. It didn't happen, but it might have."

"I'll have hope too, Mom . . . and memories just like you had. We've both found security and love in Dad's memory."

Casey's words renewed Grace's will to do what had to be done. Jerry Casey had to die so that her daughter could begin again. As long as he was alive, he was a threat to them both.

"Maybe you should give him more time, baby. If you're prepared to wait a lifetime, certainly a few more months won't matter. He knows where you are. Call him on the telephone just to talk. Your sudden appearance may put too much pressure on him and make him feel trapped."

"I suppose you're right. I've got to have faith in him." She got up from the bed and headed for the dining room. "Come on, Mom, let's eat dinner. I'm starved."

Grace sat down at the table and looked at her food. She felt knots of tension in her stomach and envied the resiliency of the young. Casey had picked up her knife and fork and started to eat. Grace was sure that if she herself took a swallow of anything, she would most certainly throw up.

_23_

I Even Intend to
Mail It

DEAR PEACH,

Dr. Sabatini just left, and I had to sit down and share my happiness with you. For the first time in weeks, I feel good about myself. Well, maybe not really good, but not awful. I was able to admit aloud that Jim had left me, although I'd already written to the boys. I promised her I would reinforce my acceptance by writing to someone outside the family, and here it is. I even intend to mail it, which is something I don't often do.

I can't thank you enough for bringing her to me. She is an intelligent, warm, and understanding person. And so are you.

While she was here, we walked around the backyard. She's pleased with my progress, and I was actually able to walk down to the car to see her off. It wasn't easy, but I did it.

I'm going to wash and set my hair now. I took a good look at myself in the mirror and saw that I look like a witch. While it dries, I'm going to scrub the kitchen floor and bake some cookies for Dr. Sabatini's next visit.

Thank you again, dear friend. Have a wonderful visit with your son.

                                                            Love,
                                                                Laura

_24_

A Part-Time Wife

It was past eleven, and Kirk still hadn't called. All evening Maggie had been trying to lose herself in the blueprints and pictures of the house in Malibu, but she could not concentrate. When the telephone finally rang, she grabbed it, but it was not the voice of her husband but her daughter.

"Angie, it's so good to hear your voice . . . how are you?"

"Neglected, that's how. You haven't written me a letter in over a week. How come?"

"Hey, that's my line. You're the one who never writes."

"But I do call, don't I?"

"Yes, collect usually. How come this one is on your nickel?"

"Shit, I forgot."

"Watch your language. That kind of talk may be acceptable in the dorm, but it's still forbidden here."

"Honestly, Mom, you're so old-fashioned."

"Not as much as you might think. So, tell me, how's school?"

For over ten minutes, Maggie listened to Angie's tale of woe about dates and professors and exams, and then she, in turn, told her daughter about New York and Belinda Cornwall and the Malibu house.

"Mom, that's absolutely the greatest thing I've ever heard! Dad must be really proud of you."

"Well, I don't know about that. I think he's feeling

200

neglected. He's going to Japan and wants me to chuck the job and go along.''

''What a bummer.''

''Isn't it though?''

''What're you going to do?''

''I'm not quitting the job. Now that you're not here, I need to do something besides play bridge and golf.''

''Dad'll come around when he gets used to it, I'm sure. Mom, there's a group up here going to Heavenly Valley to ski over the holidays. Would you and Dad mind if I signed up to go along?''

''Do you have to know right away?''

''Yeah. We have to put a deposit on the condo soon or they won't hold it.''

''How much?''

''A hundred dollars. But I also need new ski equipment. Mine is so bad I might break a leg if I don't at least get new binders.''

''Well, let me ask your father . . .'' Maggie began and caught herself. Why did she have to ask Kirk for money or permission to buy something? She now had the power to buy things for herself. ''Okay, go ahead. I'll have Dee put some money in your account. How much will you need?''

Angie was astounded that her requests were being granted so easily. ''Great . . . should I check out prices and stuff and call you first?''

''Not necessary. I trust your good judgment. I'll put a thousand in your account, but be frugal with it.''

''Wow! Thanks. I'll go to the big ski sale in San Francisco next week. Maybe I can sell my old stuff there.''

''Good idea. It's been wonderful talking to you. Call me any time . . . collect.''

''Give Dad my love.''

At midnight the phone rang again, and she answered immediately with, ''Kirk?''

''How did you know it was me?''

''I've been waiting all evening for you to call. How's San Francisco?''

"Cold, and I've had way too much to drink. These Japanese sure like to party."

"How's everything going?"

"All right, I guess. I'll know more after I've talked to the people in Tokyo."

"Kirk, I want to go with you so badly . . . I really do, but I can't. Honey, I've got a job to do, and I want to do it. It's important to me."

"That job of yours has become more important than anything else."

"That's not true. I love you. It's not more important to me than you or Angie . . . but why do I have to make a choice? You never had to choose between me and your work."

"That was different. I was working for you. I had to support the family. You don't have to work."

Kirk's voice had grown cold and truculent. Maggie knew that reason would not budge him from a position he had assumed entirely from emotion. "Honey, it's late, and you're tired. I don't want to argue with you. Can't you come home for a day for two before you go to Japan?" she pleaded.

"No, I can't. You're too busy anyway. Have you got any more surprise trips to New York planned?"

"Of course not." Maggie was getting angry with him for being so childish. "That was a very special situation, and if you'd given me a chance to explain it, you'd understand. Do you realize we haven't talked to each other in days? Why are you acting like this?"

"Acting? I'm not the one who's acting. I'm doing what I always do. You're the one who's acting, pretending you're one of those rich people. You're not, you know. They're just using you, and when they're finished, they'll forget you ever existed."

"Of course they will! I know I'm not one of them. I just work for them. They're my employers, that's all. You're the one who's so blinded by jealousy that you can't see things straight."

"I'm not jealous! Why would I be jealous? I just don't want

my wife acting like a fool, chasing after a bunch of over-stuffed parasites.''

"Kirk, can't you get it into your head that I'm getting paid for what I do . . . just like you'll make money working with the Japanese.''

"And can't you get it through your head that we don't need the damn money? I make plenty for all of us. Have I ever failed to provide anything for you . . . or Angie?''

"No, you haven't. You've been a wonderful provider. I don't need the money. I need the work. I need to feel that I'm doing something useful.''

"Being my wife isn't enough anymore?''

"No, Kirk, it isn't.'' Maggie was exhausted. There was simply no way she could reconcile her views with his. "When are you leaving for Tokyo?''

"Day after tomorrow. If you change your mind, call me. I'm at the Stanford Court.''

"I won't change my mind. How long will you be gone?''

"It all depends. I'll let you know.''

The conversation was over, and Maggie's fury at his refusal to see her side gave way to a numb fear that chilled her. She began to shiver. She went to the large closet they shared and took Kirk's heavy bathrobe from the hook on the door. She put it on over her own thin peignoir and wrapped it tightly around her, then climbed into bed and turned on the electric blanket.

Throughout the long night, her mind searched for an answer to her dilemma. She drifted through the years of their marriage, reliving the good times and the bad. Sometime in the early hours of dawn, she made her decision. Twenty years was too big an investment to throw away. She had built her life around Kirk, and she needed him. She needed his love, his warmth, his protection. There was nothing in life that was worth the sacrifice of her marriage. Even if Kirk was being selfish and pigheaded, it was only because he loved her and felt threatened. She would call him in the morning and tell him, and feeling secure at last with her decision, she went to sleep.

Maggie awakened at eight o'clock. Her head hurt, and she felt smothered by the heavy robe and the heat of the blanket. She got out of bed and took a shower. Dee arrived just as she was sitting down to her toast and coffee.

"Dee, try to reach Kirk at the Stanford Court in San Francisco for me, will you? And, before I forget, deposit a thousand dollars from my account into Angie's."

"Is she overdrawn again?"

"No, it's just a little bonus from me for her being such a nice kid."

"Lucky kid, I'd say."

Ten minutes later, Dee signaled on the intercom that her call had gone through, and Maggie picked up the phone. "Kirk?"

"Yes, it's me."

"Darling, I just wanted to tell you that I've decided to give up the decorating business . . . if you really want me to."

"How come?" His voice was wary.

"I can't let you believe you're not important to me. You are. I love you, and I need you more than anything or anybody."

"Then you'll go to Japan with me? Great, I'll call my office . . ."

"No, wait, Kirk . . . I can't. I've agreed to do this job for Belinda. I've given my word. Just let me finish, and that will be it. I'll even give Dee her notice."

"You haven't made a decision, Maggie . . . you've just postponed it. Either you're getting out or you aren't. What's it going to be?"

"Please, Kirk . . . two months . . . is that too much to ask?"

"Maggie, you're kidding yourself. You're hoping I'll get used to it . . . that with time you can persuade me to accept your late hours and running around, but I won't. I hate it. The only place you've been a wife in the past couple of months is bed, when you aren't too tired. I don't want a part-time wife."

"I'm sorry, Kirk." The tears she had been unable to shed

during the night finally began to fall, and she had nothing more to say.

"Look," Kirk finally said, "let's not talk about this anymore on the telephone. I'll be home in a couple of weeks. We'll talk then." He was always touched by her tears, for she so rarely shed them. "Goodbye, honey," he said, but Maggie's sobs made her reply unintelligible.

_25_

A Woman's Touch

As THE helicopter carried her over the rolling green of the Napa Valley, Peach felt again the sense of renewal she had always found here, perhaps because her children loved it so much. Here they had found a freedom unknown to city children. Steve had always begged to stay longer when it was time to go home, and it was at his insistence that Drake had built a winery on the property so that the plump, juicy grapes they grew could be made into their own wine.

Drake, on the other hand, was restless when they were away from the city. He was only comfortable in the center of his active financial interests. Country life was a sometime thing for him, and he took no active interest in winemaking. Because it was a capital intensive business, it seemed that there was always more money going out than coming in, but he kept the place because his son loved it so much.

Peach had not visited in a long time. When Drake became too ill to travel, he turned over all the decisions regarding the property to his son. Steve assumed the responsibility eagerly, and college became a burden to him. He had his own vineyard and winery, and textbook oenology at the university seemed unexciting in comparison.

As she flew over her land, Peach saw her son running toward the helipad Drake had installed for his own use. Steve was waving his old cowboy hat in greeting. He had been wearing one sort of cowboy hat or another since he was three years old.

The helicopter touched down, and Peach jumped out into the arms of her younger child. As they hugged and kissed each other, she was aware of how much like his father he was physically.

"Mom, you look great!" he exclaimed.

"Oh, Steve . . . it's so hard to believe that you're a grown man . . . but you are. I still think I'm going to see a teenager with a sunburned nose who needs a haircut."

"Some things never change, Mom."

"I know. You still need a haircut." They both laughed.

As they walked arm in arm toward the imposing white farmhouse, Peach asked, "Have you moved into the house yet?"

"No, I'm still bunking in rooms at the winery where Raoul used to live. After all, the house is yours. We aired it out and dusted and stuff."

They walked up the steps and across the wide veranda where Drake used to entertain like a country gentleman. Inside the house, she took off her coat and sat down on the couch. On the coffee table was a silver wine cooler containing a bottle of white wine. Steve picked it up and pulled the cork. "Want to taste our new bottling of Chardonnay?"

"Is it good?"

"Taste it and tell me."

He poured a small amount into a balloon-shaped glass and watched eagerly as his mother swirled and sniffed expertly. "Hmm, wonderful nose," she murmured. Then she tasted it, rolling the bright, straw-colored liquid around in her mouth. "Oh, my goodness, this is wonderful. Big and buttery . . . it should age beautifully. I love it!" she exclaimed.

With a grin of pleasure on his face, he poured a glass for both of them and then slowly turned the bottle toward her so that she could read the label. She gasped. "Steve, I don't deserve such an honor."

"Yes, you do. You deserve at least that much. All the time we worked on this particular wine, I thought about you. It's a very limited bottling from that little vineyard on top of the hill. I decided to call it 'Peach's Tiara' because you like

Chardonnay so much. Now you have your own vineyard and its wine named after you. Those poor little vines up there really have to suffer to stay alive, and that's why the wine is so exceptional. It's the cream of our production.''

Flattered and touched, Peach raised her glass to drink a toast. "To Steve . . . who will make wine to remember." She took another taste. "Honey, is this really as good as I think it is, or am I being prejudiced by my name on the label?''

"Maybe, but Robert Lawrence Balzer was here for lunch last week with some of his students, and he said it was outstanding. He's going to include it in the Los Angeles *Times*' tasting next month, and he's also writing a column about it. He says it's an interesting story . . . boy winemaker produces sophisticated Chardonnay. How about that?''

"I'm so proud of you.''

"Mom, is there anything new . . . about the money?''

"No, only that Dom has agreed to give you six months more to try to make a profit.''

Steve exploded. "Six months? Six months is nothing when you're making wine . . . I need six years!''

Peach was upset at the anger and misery she saw. "I know, honey, but they're determined to sell the land. I think Dom was incensed about your spending so much money on that new crusher.''

"Do you know why I did that? Because I intend to make a sparkling wine next year . . . our first. The world's greatest champagne makers are coming here to California. Moët started with Domaine Chandon . . . Piper Heidsieck joined with Sonoma. They know that the future for champagne is here. We've got the land, the climate, and the technology. And France just can't make enough to supply the world. Everybody drinks champagne at some time in their lives . . . important times . . . times to remember. You love the stuff, don't you? Wouldn't you like to have a Malone champagne to celebrate the important moments in your life?''

"Steve, I think that's so exciting. Of course, I want you to do it, but I feel so helpless. Dom and Horace aren't interested in anything but a profit-and-loss statement. I think they've made up their minds to sell."

"I don't get it. Did they inherit Dad's money or did we? What goddamn right do they have to tell us how we should live? Or spend money that's ours? Dad promised me that this land would always be mine. Did he change his mind?"

Peach shook her head. "The trusts . . . he put everything in trusts . . . to avoid taxes, I guess."

"Exactly what do the trusts say? Did you bring them with you?"

"Why no, I don't have copies of them. I'm just going on what Horace told me." Inwardly she cringed as she realized how stupid she must look in her son's eyes. "But surely, Dom and Horace wouldn't lie to me. Drake trusted them completely."

Steve sat down beside her. "Mom, where money is concerned, nobody can be trusted. Let's get those trusts and see for ourselves what they say!"

"Steve, I feel like an ass. How could I be so gullible? Something's going on that's not quite right. I just know it. Dom's always had an abrasive personality, but he's become almost insufferable lately. I'll just bet there's something in those trusts that he doesn't want me to know about. Would you mind awfully if I cut short my stay and went back home tomorrow?"

"I think you ought to, Mom. And I hope you're right," Steve answered, and they fell into silence, finishing their wine before resuming their conversation.

Peach looked around her. The house was immaculately clean. There were fresh flowers from the garden in the cut-glass vases, and the napkins on the silver tray were her own beautiful Madeira embroidered ones. Obviously, there was a woman's touch here.

"Now, tell me, who is Penny, and why isn't she here with us?"

Steve sighed and walked over to the window. "She wanted me to prepare you. She refused to be here when I told you about us."

"Good heavens, does she have two heads?" Peach asked jokingly, and then her heart turned over. "My God, Steve . . . what's wrong with her?"

"No, she's only got one lovely and smart head, and well, there's nothing wrong with her, except maybe she's a little fat."

"Fat? Steve, what's the big joke? Come on, now, quit teasing. What is there about this Penny that I should know?" Peach demanded.

"Well . . . she's pregnant. Very pregnant. The baby's due in about two months."

"I assume it's yours. Are you married?" Peach began to feel apprehensive.

"No. I've been trying to get her to marry me for months, but she refused. She said we had to have your blessing or it would never work. She knows how close we are. She insisted that we wait until you came."

"I have a feeling there's more."

"Yeah. Well, you see, she's been married before. She has a twelve-year-old son from her first marriage."

"Twelve years old? Good Lord, Steve, how old is she?"

"Almost thirty."

Peach's suspicions and hostility were aroused. Her son wanted to marry a woman six years older than he was . . . a woman with one marriage behind her and obviously with designs on his money. Why else would she insist on Peach's approval? Suddenly, Peach felt ashamed for her thoughts. Did she really believe her son to be so unattractive that he could be loved only for his fortune? And as for the age difference, she was amused at herself. God, what was she thinking? The age difference between her and Jason was almost three times that of Steve and his Penny. Her reaction to the news mystified her son. Her frown suddenly turned to mirth, and she laughed. She set her glass down and stood up to hug him. "What's so funny?" he asked.

"Someday . . . not now . . . I'll tell you. Now, let's find Penny. I want to meet her. Let's go. I can't stay long, you know, and I have a grandson around here someplace. What's his name?''

"Dan, and you'll love him. His dad, by the way, died in an Air Force plane crash.''

They hurried through the rose garden to the winery and up the steps into the office. There sitting at the desk was a lovely young woman. Her long, dark, curly hair was tied in a ribbon, and her abdomen was so large she could barely get close enough to the desk to write. She had deep violet eyes and a sprinkling of freckles across her nose. She looked young and vulnerable. No wonder Steve was in love with her.

Peach approached her, and the young woman rose to her feet hesitantly. Without a word, Peach gathered her into her arms and hugged her. Penny began to cry. "Don't cry, my dear. I'm so happy for us all. Do you love my son?''

Her voice quavered, but she managed a soft and sniffly, "Yes, I do, Mrs. Malone.''

"I'm Peach, not Mrs. Malone, to you. And we'd better get this wedding accomplished as soon as possible. My goodness, child, you look like you could have this baby any day. What does the doctor say?''

"Six weeks, maybe more.''

Peach turned to her son. "Steve, why in the world did you wait so long to tell me?''

He shook his head in mock shame, but he was obviously overjoyed. "Just dumb, I guess. I didn't want to give you any more hassles than you already had, what with Dad being sick and then dying. I should have known everything would be okay with you.'' He opened the door and called out, "Dan! On the double.''

Within seconds, a lanky young boy with hair and eyes the color of his mother's raced in to join them. "Mom, meet Dan. Dan, this is my mother . . . and your new grandmother.''

Solemnly Peach extended her hand to shake his, and he took it. His fingers were rough and dry. "How do you do, Dan,'' she said looking him over. "I'd like you to call me Peach too, if that's all right. Do you think I might have a kiss?''

Dazzled by her beauty and graciousness, he quickly pressed his dry lips to her cheek. "That was lovely, Dan. Thank you. I suspect we're going to be good friends. Have you been to Disneyland yet?" He shook his head.

"No? How wonderful; then I hereby claim the privilege of showing it to you on your first visit with me in Los Angeles. Now, Steve, what about the wedding?"

"We've got the license, and Judge McIlheny said he'd come out and do it this evening, okay? I called John Parducci up in Mendocino and asked him and his wife to drive down to be witnesses. Is that all right?"

"How delightful. They've been friends since we first bought this land."

Later that evening when the ceremony and dinner were over and the guests had departed, Peach asked Steve to stay in the house for a private talk.

"Steve, I want you to move your family here into the house right away."

"I can't take your house. I know how much you've always loved it."

"It will be my wedding gift to you, and it will make me very happy if you'll accept it. I'll have that old schoolhouse Dad bought and put on top of the hill fixed up. You'll need a luxurious guesthouse to entertain wine people, and it will do nicely for me when I come to visit my grandchildren. In the meantime, have three good beds put in there for Sarah, Miles, and me, and make sure the heating and plumbing are installed properly."

"Mom, do you mind telling me why you acted so strange when I told you Penny's age?"

Peach could not as yet bring herself to tell the whole truth. "Well, a dear friend recently accused me of being an age-ist."

"I don't understand."

She laughed. "I didn't intend you to."

"Mom, Penny's a little nervous about that guy from Doug's office that's been prowling around here all the time. Is it really necessary?"

"Doug thinks so, but you know how paranoid he always was about protecting your father. I'm beginning to get tired of it myself. He insisted I be escorted all the way here . . . with an armed guard, no less. I had to wait an hour in the San Francisco airport while they checked out the helicopter."

"Has anything happened since you got home?"

"Absolutely nothing. Now, it's your wedding night, scoot. But don't do anything but kiss her, understand? We don't want that baby to be born before its time."

_26_

Not Alone

BELINDA proved all but impossible for Maggie to work for. She was besieged with telephone calls, criticism, and suggestions for changes. On more than one occasion, the two women lashed out at each other, although Belinda never allowed the dispute to get out of hand.

One night after two hellish weeks of unseasonable rain, Maggie was fighting her way home through the traffic on Pacific Coast Highway, which was jammed up because of a mudslide. She was cold and tired, her hair was damp and frizzed, and her boots were full of wet sand.

When she finally arrived home, she saw lights on in the house and figured that Dee had turned them on so that she wouldn't come home to a dark house. She was glad there would be no one to care for that night. She'd take a long hot bath and open a can of soup, and the rest of the evening could be spent on her paperwork.

Dragging her briefcase and bag of sample fabrics and tiles, she unlocked the door to the house. She smelled smoke, and it frightened her. Was the house on fire? Dropping everything, she looked around the kitchen, then raced through the hall into the family room. There was a fire in the fireplace. Good God, why would Dee . . . ? And then Kirk walked into the room carrying a drink and the newspaper.

"Kirk! You scared me," she exclaimed.

"That's a hell of a greeting. I thought you'd be glad to see me."

"I am, I am." She rushed across the room and threw her arms around him. Holding his glass and paper aloft for safekeeping, he received her embrace casually. "When did you get home?" she asked.

"This morning. I went directly to the office. Things were in a bitch of a mess there . . . that's why I didn't call right away. Thought I'd surprise you. I should have known you wouldn't be here. Where've you been? You look terrible."

"Malibu . . . and it's dreadful there. It rarely rains this early in winter. Everybody is scurrying around putting sand-bags in front of their houses."

"I hope old lady Cornwall doesn't expect you to do that too."

"No, of course not. But the damn roof is leaking and ruining all the new paint."

"Well, darling, welcome to the cold, cruel business world."

Maggie observed his aloofness as she released her hold on him, and he moved away to sit down by the fire. "Have you had dinner yet?" she asked.

"Not a thing since I got off the plane. I hope you've got something in the house for a change. I can't stand the thought of eating in another restaurant." He settled down to read the newspaper, as Maggie wondered what she could possibly fix. She'd had so little time while he was gone, and grocery shopping had a low priority. She went to the refrigerator. There wasn't much. "Kirk, how about a cheese omelet?"

"I've had a lot of eggs lately, but if you haven't got anything else, I guess that will have to do."

As she hurried up the stairs, Maggie called to him, "I'm going to take a quick shower and get out of these damp clothes. Then I'll fix us some dinner."

"Don't take too long. I'm starved."

She resented his attitude. After all, she was working too, probably harder than he was. This was not the time, however, to demand equal rights. She was glad to have him home.

Within an hour, clean, and dressed in a wool caftan, she carried a tray into the family room and set it on the large coffee table. "The fire is so lovely, I thought it would be fun to sit here on the floor and eat. I opened a bottle of Cabernet Sauvignon,'' she said as she poured the deep red wine into glistening glasses and served the omelets with sliced tomatoes and a loaf of crusty bread that Dee had baked.

Kirk's manner thawed from the combination of the fire and the wine and the food, but Maggie knew it was mostly because of the wifely attention he was getting. They talked about Japan, and he surprised her with a long strand of baroque pearls. Maggie was overwhelmed. "Kirk, they're beautiful . . . and huge. They must be at least nine millimeters.''

"Ten, actually,'' he said and smiled, and she could see that he was enormously pleased with himself as he tenderly placed them around her neck.

"Kirk, I missed you terribly. I put your old bathrobe on every night. It made me feel closer to you.''

She was in his arms, and he held her tightly. For the first time in weeks, he kissed her, beginning softly, then pressing her mouth open. Hungrily they explored each other's bodies with their hands and their mouths and within minutes, their desire became unbearable, and she opened her legs so that he could thrust his hardness inside her, bringing them both to a hasty but satisfying climax.

Lying together on the floor by the fire, Kirk continued to stroke her, running his fingers across her soft abdomen, along her thighs, and into the moistness of her vulva. They did not speak for a long time for they were savoring the closeness and the quietness of their reunion. When Kirk suggested they go up to bed, Maggie concurred. Once settled in bed with his arms around her, Maggie whispered, "I love you.'' Kirk repeated the words, and as they drifted toward sleep, he added, "You'll never regret it . . . I promise you.''

"What's that, honey?''

"Giving up your new career. I'm glad you finally came to your senses. And I'm really sorry I gave you such a bad time about the Cornwall job. I know you have to finish it, but as soon as it's out of the way, we'll take a vacation in Japan. Mr. Shibuyashi has invited us."

Maggie was too comfortable to feel any rancor or remorse. She had made her bed, and she would lie in it, but, thank God, not alone.

_27_

Marching Bands and Bugles

GRACE stood in the hallway looking at the face of the antique grandfather clock she had brought from her parents' home after they died. It was depressing, for it was ticking off the seconds of her life too fast. Unaware that her daughter was watching her from the doorway, she slowly ran her fingertips over the smooth wood frame around the clock face. Casey was alarmed by the ineffable melancholia she detected. "Mom, are you all right?"

Startled that she had been observed, Grace replied quickly, "Of course. I was just checking the time."

"Aren't you leaving awfully early? It's over two hours until your flight leaves."

"I have to stop at the shop and pick up a few things on the way."

"Are you sure you don't want me to go to the airport with you? I can cancel my doctor's appointment."

"Don't be silly. It's awkward waiting to see someone off. There's never anything to say. I'd much rather go alone."

"Mom, are you sure you're feeling all right?"

"Of course I'm all right."

"Well, you don't look all right. Why don't you call Aunt Blanche and tell her you can't make it? I have a strange feeling that you ought not to go."

Grace looked into her daughter's troubled eyes and was tempted to tell her the truth and halt this fool's charade she had made of their lives. Tell her, tell her, a small voice inside her screamed, but she could not say the words.

"Casey . . ." she began, and paused, "don't forget to pick up the turkey I ordered at Gelson's Market. I'll be home late on Wednesday evening. I'm sorry to put the whole burden of Thanksgiving dinner on you."

Casey realized that if there was something bothering her mother, she was not going to find out that day.

Grace continued, "I'm going to spend tonight and tomorrow night in Chicago, and I'll fly down to St. Louis on Sunday. It's only a three-day convention. For the life of me, I can't understand why they scheduled it during such a busy season."

Casey put her arms around her mother and hugged her. "Well, if I can't change your mind and get you to stay, I'd better let you go. I'm sure traffic will be bad, and Rudolfo doesn't need any more speeding tickets."

"That's for sure. I'd hate for him to have his license suspended. 'Bye now, sweetie. If you need anything, call Eve . . . or Peach." She left quickly.

"Eve, come into my office when you finish that comb-out," she said when she arrived at the salon, and hurried into her office. Once inside, she locked the door, then opened the cabinet where she had packed the clothes and hairpieces in a small, inexpensive suitcase. There was a knock at the door.

Eve entered, and Grace indicated that she should sit down. "Eve, you know I trust you, but I don't trust everyone who works here. Here's the key to my desk and file cabinet. If anything should happen to me, be sure that Casey gets the little brown leather box."

"Good grief, aren't you being a bit morbid? After all, you're just going to Chicago, not the moon."

"Nobody's going to live forever, not even me."

"Okay, okay. How come you decided all of a sudden to go to that convention? It's not even a big one, and I thought you hated those things?"

"I do, but it's a good way to visit my sister and let Uncle Sam pay for part of the trip."

* * *

Two hours later, the jumbo jet rolled down the runway for takeoff with Grace nervously settled in the front row of the first class section. Although she liked flying, this trip was different. She was embarking on an adventure so bizarre that she herself had trouble taking it seriously. Could she possibly do what she intended to do? Did everyone who ever plotted the death of another human being experience the sense of unreality and game-playing that she now felt?

She forced herself to concentrate on the plan and avoid thinking of the consequences of failure. It was like climbing a mountain . . . she didn't dare look down. She had no illusions about success either. If she failed, she would destroy her daughter and herself. If she succeeded, she would have another nightmare to add to her library of bad dreams.

The stewardess brought her a double martini on the rocks, and she sipped it slowly, gazing out over the clouds below. She wondered if she would be able to lure him into the trap . . . would he die quickly and easily?

She had briefly considered going to him and telling him the whole story, enlisting his cooperation and silence. But she decided against it. If he was as callous now as he had been in his youth, he was not the person to trust with her precious secret. He might even tell Casey. He might, in fact, enjoy telling her, knowing that the truth would get him off the hook permanently. If that happened, then the course she was now taking would be closed to her forever. He would live to mock her and his child.

Now, her only link to him was through her daughter. She did not think Casey would be suspicious about foul play. Casey's youth would find it easy to accept death by heart attack in a man so much older than she.

She reached into her purse and groped about until her fingers made contact with the lethal package. She held it momentarily, her fingers caressing it, reassuring herself that it was still there. If the rest of her scheme proceeded as easily as her purchase of the drug from her friendly neighborhood coke dealer, she had nothing to fear.

Rudolfo had passed the word that she would be in the shop

alone on Tuesday night with cash for a special buy. Finn, the old weasel who supplied coke to some of her customers, appeared at eight o'clock. Although she had, on occasion, referred people to him, she never bought the stuff herself. She'd tried it once and hated the feeling. She sent customers to Finn because he had a reputation for selling good cocaine, and he refused to sell anything to kids. Once he had sent word that he'd pay for the references, but she refused. If her wealthy, self-indulgent adult customers wanted to destroy their nasal membranes and brain cells, that was their business, but she had no intention of becoming part of it by making a profit.

Finn knocked at the back door, and she let him in. Although she was familiar with him and his activities, she didn't trust anybody in the drug business. Rudolfo was in the foyer waiting and listening for her call, and she had on a smock with large pockets. Her hand was inside her right pocket gripping her pistol throughout their meeting.

Finn was right out of a TV movie. He was small with a ferretlike face and eyes that moved constantly, always on the alert, always checking his surroundings. His dark beard, although closely shaved, cast a sinister shadow over his face. "Hi, Grace . . . watcha need?"

"Finn, I've got a customer who tells me that digitalis is great . . . better than coke . . . it gives a terrific rush. True?"

"Dunno . . . never heard . . . maybe . . . want some?"

"Yes. She'll pay very well. How much?"

"Letcha know tommorra . . . this time."

"Will you have it then?"

"Think so."

"I'll have cash."

"Credit's good."

"No, Finn. I pay cash for everything."

"Two then . . . easy."

"Two? Hundred? Thousand?"

What passed for a smile darted quickly across his face as if afraid to light on its poisonous countenance and be contaminated. "Hunder . . ."

"I want a stiff dose . . . and some reds, okay?"

" 'Kay." He turned and was out the door and gone béfore she could say another word.

The next night he appeared on schedule, handed her a small box and said only two words. "Jus' one."

With her left hand, she extracted a hundred-dollar bill from her pocket and handed it to him. "Thanks, Finn."

"Got some snow."

"No, thanks, but I'll send somebody who wants it to you. Are you still at Hollywood and . . . ?"

He interrupted her hastily, his eyes darting more rapidly. "No, too hot. Tell Rudy you wan' somthin'."

He left again so quickly that had she not had the package in her hand, she would have had difficulty believing the encounter had actually taken place.

Now on the plane, fingering it as she sipped her martini, she wondered at the strange memories that were stored away in her brain. She thought she had forgotten the morbid party game she had played over ten years ago in the house of Everett Allison. Each guest had been told to think up a novel way to commit the perfect murder. She remembered that Dr. Allison had proposed murder by excessive heart stimulation, which would probably be accepted without autopsy, especially if the victim had reached middle age. Funny she would remember that and also remember the drug he had named.

She had faith in Everett Allison ever since Drake Malone had called him in to care for her after the accident. If he said digitalis would work, she was certain it would.

Grace's arrival in Chicago was heralded by a terrible snowstorm. She had almost forgotten how wretched life could be in the Midwest in winter. The years of California sunshine had softened her marrow, and she was cold and miserable in the long, slow taxi ride through nearly stalled traffic to her sister's apartment. The reality of her mission had hit her the moment she set foot outside the air terminal into the freezing, blustering blizzard. It was merging her own special hell with one of nature's, and it left her nervous and shaking.

When she arrived at her sister's apartment, Blanche greeted her with the warmth and affection of one lone relative for another, and Grace responded in kind. The glow of the reunion sweetened the bitterness of the weather. "Grace, you look marvelous. Come in. Good heavens, you must be frozen."

Grace carried her suitcase into the apartment. She had left the one containing the wigs and clothes in a locker at the airport. "I am, Blanche. I'm not used to this miserable weather. How can you stand it?"

"Used to it, I guess. I'm sure I'd miss it if the sun shined all the time like it does in California. Take off your coat and sit down by the radiator over there. That's the warmest spot in the room."

Grace did as she was told and looked around at the neat clutter of Blanche's tiny one-bedroom apartment. Her poor sisters had never really had much of a life.

Blanche fixed two cups of hot tea and pulled another chair close to the radiator. Grace cupped her cold, trembling fingers around the steaming cup and drew warmth from it as she looked her sister over. Blanche looked damn good for her age. Her hair was still rich brown, although time had artfully frosted it with gray. Her face was lined softly, but her eyes were bright and dark behind the thick glasses she had always worn. Grace remembered Blanche quoting Dorothy Parker years ago—"Men seldom make passes at girls who wear glasses"—and she wondered how much influence that nasty little couplet had on Blanche's image of herself in that long-ago youth.

Later, when they had finished dinner and washed the dishes, they sat down again by the radiator to sip a glass of cream sherry. Blanche rolled her eyes in pleasure and smacked her lips. "Mmm, mmm, this is one of those little luxuries your check buys me, Grace. Every night, I have a small glass of this sherry after dinner."

Her pleasure made Grace feel ashamed. She had a wealth of material luxuries, yet she couldn't find a tenth of the joy in them that Blanche found in her glass of cheap wine. "Blanche,

I wish you'd reconsider and come live with Casey and me. We'd love to have you.''

"I know, but I just don't want to. I'm sorry, but that's it. All my life I've done things that maybe I didn't really want to do, but that's all over now. The day of Ellie's funeral, I decided that the rest of my life would be just for me."

"But, Blanche, I've got so much. Let me share it with you. I have a beautiful home, money, servants, sunshine. Just think, no more cold evenings by the radiator. We could travel . . ."

"No, sister dear, that's your life, not mine. My world is here. I've got a lot of friends, widows mostly. We play bridge together just about every afternoon. 'Course, we can't go out much in the evenings, too dangerous, but I have my little sherry and the TV."

"Blanche, how come neither of you ever married?"

For a long while there was no answer, and Grace wondered if she'd pried too much. Eventually Blanche said, "That's a question, all right. I'm not sure I have the answer to it. Oh, at first, I guess we both thought someday our Mr. Right would come along . . . but either he didn't exist or he couldn't find us. We just stopped thinking about it. We had each other. We always got along so well, not like most sisters. I can't remember ever fighting with Ellie. She was such a sweet, soft-spoken . . . lady. We had a happy life together."

"But didn't you ever think about . . . sex?"

Again Blanche was slow to answer. "Yes, I did, but look at the trouble sex got you into, little sister."

"Just because I made a mess of things didn't mean that you two should have forsaken it."

Grace was puzzled by Blanche's clipped reply and downcast eyes. "We didn't."

"I don't understand . . ."

Blanche raised her head and looked directly into Grace's eyes. "Ellie and I shared the same room, the same bed, for over thirty years. We loved and comforted each other. I knew her body as well as I know my own."

Grace was startled by the directness of her sister's admission.

She did not know what to say. "You surprise me . . . I never suspected . . ."

"Suspected what? That we loved each other? Ellie needed me all her life. She was shy and afraid. At first, I resented her constant dependence on me, and later, I realized I needed her as much as she needed me. We never considered ourselves . . . that way. I was never attracted to any other woman . . . and neither was she. What we did just seemed natural and loving, that's all."

"Her illness must have been very hard for you."

"It was, but life goes on. Everybody has to die sometime. I only wish she hadn't suffered so much." She stood up. "Well, better get to bed. It's ten o'clock, and they shut off the heat till six in the morning."

Later, as Grace settled herself under the electric blanket in the king-sized bed beside her sister, she thought how sad her parents would have been if they'd known the truth about their three daughters. She was glad she hadn't burdened them with her problems.

At six the next morning, Grace got up and found her sister already in the kitchen, sitting in front of the stove with the oven door open, reading the newspaper, and drinking coffee. "Come on over here. The heat will be coming on soon. Want some coffee?"

"Sure, black."

She huddled up against the oven door and shivered. "Blanche, I have to leave this morning."

"So soon?"

"I'd really appreciate it if you wouldn't tell anybody that I left here today."

"It's nobody's business what you do."

"Casey . . . especially Casey . . . or somebody from the shop might call. Tell them I'm . . . out. I'll call you tonight for messages . . . okay?"

At ten that morning, Grace kissed Blanche goodbye and got into a cab for the return ride to the airport. She had to be in St. Louis by noon Monday for the opening luncheon. That wasn't much time.

At the airport, she exchanged the suitcase she was carrying for the one in the locker. She took it into the nearest ladies' room, but it was too crowded. The next one was also full. She saw a door marked for employees only, and she decided to try that one. Providence was with her. Not only was the room vacant, but there was a small anteroom with a cot in it and a mirror.

She closed the door and unpacked quickly and changed into a man's suit. She washed the makeup off her face and donned the dark wig and heavy brows and mustache. Carefully, she unrolled a snap-brim man's Borsalino which she had found in a secondhand shop. There was a stain around the sweatband which served to make it look worn and natural. She pushed it down on the wig and adjusted it. Not too funny looking. She practiced taking it off, and the wig moved. She applied gum around the edges of the wig to fasten it securely.

When her appearance satisfied her, she packed everything she would need into a large blue nylon carry-on, put the clothes she had just taken off into the suitcase, which she then deposited in the locker beside her other one. That done, she practiced walking down the concourse, lengthening her stride and trying to move like a man.

She checked her watch. It was getting late. She would have to hurry to make the flight on Britt Airways to Champaign. Half an hour later, under a reservation she had made in the name of Malcolm Jensen, she boarded the jet for her destination. It was only a forty-five-minute flight, and she was soon on the ground in a city that at one desperate time in her life she had vowed never to see again. Who would have thought she would return to the scene of the crime to commit another one?

She got into a cab and directed the driver to a hotel near the campus. She checked in as Malcolm Jensen from Des Moines and paid for the room in advance, saying she would be leaving very early the next morning.

When she was alone in the room, she dialed Jerry Casey's telephone number for the second time in forty-eight hours. This time, however, she would manage to keep the quaver out of her voice. Casey picked up the telephone on the second ring.

"Professor Casey. Dr. Davis. I arrived just a little while ago. I'm in room 320 at the Sheraton." Grace spoke in her natural voice.

"Fine. I hope you had a good trip in spite of the weather. Would you like me to meet you there, or my wife and I would be happy to have you join us for dinner?"

"Thank you, but no. I'd prefer to have you come here, if you don't mind. I'm meeting another candidate for the board position in a little while. Would this evening about nine be all right?"

His voice revealed his disappointment. "Oh, I didn't realize when we talked the other day . . . well, uh, I assumed that I was the only one . . . from this campus, of course."

Grace's voice was sympathetic. "I'm so sorry if I misled you, Dr. Casey, but we have an awful lot of competition for these openings because they come up so rarely. The Masterson Foundation is heavily endowed, and not only are board positions prized for their prestige, they also provide certain fringe benefits . . . financially, you understand." Grace was glad she had listened when her daughter talked about her profession. The Masterson fellowships to graduate students in American literature were generous and in great demand.

"I see, well, I haven't mentioned it to anyone . . . as you stipulated," he replied.

"Good. Nine then. Room 320." She put down the receiver with a shaking hand. So far, so good. She unpacked and hung a lavender silk dress by Chloe in the bathroom. She took a brown sweater and necktie from the bag and a man's leather cap and earmuffs and stashed them in the cabinet under the sink. She undressed and took off the Borsalino and wig. "Goodbye, Malcolm Jensen," she whispered.

She took the package from the bag, and for an hour practiced inserting a hypodermic needle into the foam mattress on the bed. When she felt confident, she pressed the needle into her thigh several times to test her skill. She barely noticed the pain.

At seven, she showered and began her second transformation. Delicately, she applied a pair of lifts with spirit gum at her temples and pulled them until the folds around her eyes were taut enough to give them a slight upward tilt. She tied the attached threads together at the top of her head. She repeated the process with a second pair of lifts just behind her ears and pulled the jawline just enough to erase the telltale looseness that gave away her age. Satisfied that she looked younger, she then began the expert layering of makeup that would subtract more years. When she was finished, she covered her blond hair and the lifts with a curly brown wig, the color of her natural hair, and stepped back to observe the effect. Too bad no one would ever see the lovely young Dr. Davis except the doomed Dr. Casey. The skills she had learned working on movie sets had come in handy on more than one occasion.

She turned on the television set to hear the news, amused at her own coolness. She slipped on the sheer silk dress that showed her narrow waist and full breasts and then stepped into a pair of matching high-heeled sandals. She looked at her hands and regretted she'd had to pare her long fingernails.

Just before nine o'clock, she dissolved the contents of three red capsules in a little warm water and then filled the glass with ice cubes from the refrigerator under the sink. In another glass, she splashed a small amount of Scotch from a flask she'd brought and took a sip. She must be careful not to mix up the glasses.

At exactly nine o'clock, there was a knock at the door. She took a deep breath and opened it. She would not turn back now.

Jerry Casey looked startled. "Oh . . . I'm sorry, are you, uh, by any chance, Dr. Davis?"

Grace flashed him a welcome smile and replied, "Yes, I am. Please come in, Dr. Casey. Thank you for being so punctual." She threw herself so completely into the part that her anxieties began to fall away. This must be why they call revenge sweet, she thought.

"Well, I certainly didn't expect you to be so young, and

well, so beautiful,'' he remarked as he walked into the room
and removed his coat.

"Come now, Dr. Casey. I hope you're not one of those
chauvinists who think a woman must be unattractive to be
bright."

"No, on the contrary . . . I've often found that my bright-
est students were usually physically well endowed also."

"Please sit down. Would you join me in a drink? I always
carry a flask of good Scotch with me. Since you're my last
appointment, I think it would be nice to begin unwinding a
little."

Casey accepted the drink and sat down across from her at a
small table by the window. The conversation flowed smoothly
and easily, although Grace began to worry that he drank too
slowly. She finished off her drink and offered him more, but
he refused. "Thank you, no. I'm not much of a drinker,
really." It was not long before she realized that he was
coming on to her. People never change, she observed silently,
as she helped him turn the conversation to more intimate
topics.

"Would your wife accept your traveling frequently, Dr.
Casey? You know, our meetings are held in various parts of
the country. All expenses are paid, of course, but only for the
board members, not spouses."

"She'd probably be glad to have me out of the house. Are
you married, Dr. Davis?"

Grace smiled over her glass, her eyes meeting his, trying to
be as sexy as possible and feeling awkward. "No. I'm a
career woman, you see, and I like my freedom . . . to play
the field. There's so little time . . . and so many men."

He raised his glass and smiled wickedly. He knew an
invitation when he heard it. "Here's to freedom," he toasted.

"Bottoms up," she replied and laughed a deep, knowing,
seductive chuckle. The old fool thinks he's going to screw his
way into the appointment, Grace thought. He still believed
his cock could get him anything.

It wasn't long before he suggested they sit together on the
bed where they could be more comfortable. Grace was reluctant,

but having started the operation in motion, she could not very well back away. She prayed he would fall asleep before he got down to serious screwing.

As he put his arms around her, she tried to conjure up the feeling of ecstasy she had experienced the first time he'd touched her, but visions of her nightmare in the alley kept intruding. "Let's have another drink," she suggested, and emptied the flask into their glasses. She drank hers quickly, hoping the alcohol would alleviate some of the revulsion and fear that she felt. She tried to forget that the man touching her was her mortal enemy, but as his hand moved over the thin silk covering her nipples, she shivered, remembering the cold nights in the snow.

"You're cold," he whispered hoarsely. "Let me warm you up."

She tried to relax, to pretend she was enjoying it. Would that damn sedative never take hold? Had Finn sold her blanks?

He slid the zipper down in the back of her dress and unsnapped her brassiere. In seconds, her breasts were bare and his lips on them. Good God, could she go through with this charade?

"Come, let's get into bed . . . you'll be warm there."

"All right," she replied hoarsely. "I'll bolt the door."

They both undressed, he quickly, she slowly, and when she was nude, she got under the blanket, and he joined her. As he ran his fingers lightly over her abdomen, he asked, "What is that long scar across your stomach?" His fingertips traced the eight-inch ridge that ran from just under her left breast to her right hipbone. He deserved the truth, she decided. Maybe it would cool his ardor. "I was gang-raped when I was nineteen. That's just one of the scars they left me."

"Really?" he asked, his hands moving lower and more excitedly. "How many were there?"

"Hoodlums, you mean? Only five, but it seemed like a hundred."

"What was it like?" he asked, and she could hear his breath coming faster, and his fingers began to explore inside her body. The beast was getting turned on by her agony! Her hatred overcame her revulsion, and she allowed him to do as he wanted. It was fitting that his final conquest would be with the woman who would end his fucking forever.

When at last he mounted her and began his rhythmic movements in and out, she tried to concentrate on what she had to do. At long last, he came and quickly rolled off her onto the bed. Why had she ever thought he was a great lover?

"God, I feel dizzy," he said.

"Just close your eyes and rest," Grace replied, and through her teeth, "That was terrific. I'll wake you in a little while and maybe we can do it again."

When she was certain he was sound asleep, she got out of bed, picked up the glasses, and took them with her into the bathroom. She closed the door softly and removed the wig and lifts. Then she showered and bathed away all makeup and traces of her victim. When she was clean and dry, she put on the man's trousers again, the white shirt, and a brown tie and sweater. She covered her hair with a gray wig and applied a tapered beard and mustache. She filled in the creases around her eyes with gray shadow and daubed a bit more to hollow her cheeks. She pulled the brown leather cap and its earflaps over her head and donned a pair of rimless glasses. She then turned the reversible trench coat inside out so that the dark plaid was on the outside and unfolded a brown nylon totebag into which she stuffed all her belongings. She washed and dried the glasses, then, pulling on a pair of gloves, she thoroughly polished every spot in both the bedroom and bathroom where she might have left fingerprints.

When she was satisfied that the room was clean, she filled the syringe with digitalis. She turned on the light by the bed, but Jerry Casey was in a deep, drug-induced sleep. He had lost the game. But it didn't really matter. The prize was the same, win or lose. She had tried to make herself look as she did when she was young. She wondered if he had ever thought about her once in all those years, and she mocked her own sorry ego. Yes, she had wanted him to see her and remember. But he hadn't. And it was just as well. Nothing he could have said would have changed her plans.

She threw back the covers and found an artery close to the hairline at his neck and traced it gently with her fingertip into his hair where a tiny needlemark would not be seen even in an autopsy. With trembling hands, she inserted the needle and drew the plunger back slightly until a drop of blood rose in the syringe. Thank God, she'd hit it on the first try. Slowly she depressed the plunger until the syringe was emptied. She withdrew the needle and held a wad of toilet paper against the tiny wound until it sealed itself. Throughout the procedure, Jerry Casey did not stir. She hoped the digitalis would be as effective as the reds had been.

She threw the bits of paper into the toilet and flushed it, checked the room once more to be sure she'd forgotten nothing, and went to the door. Just before leaving, she looked once more at the sleeping figure of her nemesis.

"You bastard! You didn't think you had an enemy in the world."

She left the hotel unnoticed and walked to the bus station through the cold snowy night. There she took a cab to the train station where she boarded a Chicago-bound express. The trip was uneventful.

After two days of boredom, she headed back to Los Angeles. She was surprised at how normal she felt. Where were the marching bands and bugles heralding this important event in her life?

Weather and holiday traffic caused a delay in her flight, and she did not arrive home until late on Thanksgiving eve. Casey was waiting for her.

"Mom, I'm so glad you're home," she exclaimed as she rushed toward her and caught her in a bear hug.

"Whew, what a welcome. I've only been gone a few days."

"I have the most wonderful news! Jerry called me this evening. He's asked his wife for a divorce, and she's agreed. If everything works out right, we'll be married before the baby is born. Can you believe it?"

_28_

The Most Gorgeous Man

THE TURKEY, all twenty-two pounds of him, was stuffed and in the oven by nine in the morning. The pumpkin pies and jellied cranberry and port salad had been done the day before. She wanted everything to be ready so that she could enjoy this special day. Her boys were still asleep upstairs, and from the moment they arrived home late the night before, she had begun to feel human again.

Actually, the first encounter with her twin sons had not been as traumatic as she had feared it would be. There was a lot of hugging and kissing and reassuring. She tried not to be gratified at their anger with their father, but nevertheless, she was.

Dr. Sabatini had warned her they would forgive their father eventually, and she had encouraged Laura to help them to do so. She had been counseled it was in no one's best interest for her to punish Jim by trying to turn his sons against him, and indeed, her sense of worth and nobility increased with each word she spoke on her husband's behalf. It was, in fact, very satisfying to play the role of misunderstood yet very understanding wife, and her sons were terribly impressed with their mother's magnanimity and generosity. She wondered if her halo would glow in the dark.

Laura busied herself with setting the table, the job she always saved for last because she enjoyed it so much. She hummed as she polished the Baccarat goblets and admired the Buccellati sterling that Jim had insisted on buying when they

233

moved in. It had seemed so wasteful when she still had her mother's old silver, but he wanted everything to be the best that money could buy. She supposed Ghilly fell into that category too. Well, Ghilly might have her husband, but she'd never get her hands on anything else of hers.

"You sure sound happy, Mom," Dac said as he entered the dining room.

"I'm happy now because you're home. I missed you both so much. Want some breakfast?"

"Not yet. I'll wait for Shan to wake up. He's still zonked out. Mom, Shan and I talked last night before we went to sleep, and we've decided to spend Christmas with you, here at home. Dad really doesn't need us at all now . . . hey, don't interrupt, okay? We're not doing this to punish him or anything, understand. It's just that . . . well, you know . . . you're all alone, and he's not."

During the speech, which was an exceptionally long one for the usually taciturn Dac, Laura tried to keep eye contact with him but could not manage it. Her eyes filled, and she had trouble controlling her emotions. She did not want to ruin their beautiful day with tears, God knows she'd already shed an ocean of them, but she was touched.

"Come on now, Mom . . . please don't cry."

Laura dried her eyes as best she could, then she put her arms around her tall son and held him close to her. Feeling awkward and uneasy with such a close emotional display, Dac patted her on the back. "Okay, Mom, okay."

"Dac, thank you. I appreciate everything, and I want you to know I have not regretted a moment of my marriage. It was a happy one for years, and best of all, it gave me you and your brother."

"I'm glad you feel that way, Mom. Say, how about a little drive with me and Shan? Maybe you could do it with us. Want to try?"

"Let it be, Dac. I'll do it, but in my own time. Go wake up your brother. I want to get the kitchen cleaned up so I can get dressed early."

At two o'clock the doorbell rang, and Shan hurried to

answer it. The house was filled with the aroma of roast turkey and there was a crackling fire in the huge fireplace in the family room. The sun had remained hidden by a thick layer of clouds, and it was as close to a winter's day as one could find in Southern California.

Maggie and Kirk and their daughter Angie stood at the door with their arms laden with hospitality offerings. Laura and Dac joined Shan in greeting their guests, and everyone was happy and effusive and somewhat emotional. Kirk was seeing Laura for the first time since her break with Jim, and he felt a little uncomfortable and eager to keep the situation light and casual. He kissed her lightly and said, "Laura, you look more beautiful than ever. It's been much too long." Then Laura greeted Angie. "Angie, you're so grown up . . . how come my boys are still kids, and you've become a woman?"

"Come on, Mom, we're not still kids. Hi, Angie, c'mon into the kitchen. We're concocting something for us to drink," Shan announced.

"No, thanks, Shan. The last time I drank one of your specials, I threw up. I wouldn't mind a beer though," Angie replied.

"Hey, it's Thanksgiving, remember? You'll be having wine . . ." Laura said to the young people but was not heard. With Shan on one side of Angie and Dac on the other, the twins were too busy talking and leading their pretty former playmate away from the dreary adults.

Peach arrived as Kirk was opening the second bottle of champagne. Laura let her in and was again struck by the radiant beauty of her dear friend, a beauty that seemed more pronounced lately. "Peach, come in. I was afraid we'd all be smashed before you got here."

Peach was contrite. "I'm sorry I'm late. I was on the telephone with a close friend . . . and I . . . just couldn't seem to get away."

Laura was intrigued by Peach's unusual lack of composure. It was not like her to speak so breathlessly. Her eyes were sparkling, and her cheeks were flushed. Realizing that she was the target of all eyes and ears in the room, Peach attempted to direct the attention away from her own discomfiture as she walked toward Kirk with her hand outstretched. "At last, I'm finally getting to meet Maggie's other half. Kirk, how do you do? I'm so happy to meet you. Maggie has told me so many nice things about you."

Kirk was on his feet staring at her, dazzled by her beauty and warmth and the fact that she was one of the world's wealthiest women. Feeling like a schoolboy who has just been asked to dance by the prom queen, he was appalled at his own stumbling words. "Well, how do you do? You must be Peach Malone."

"Must I?" she teased. "Couldn't I be Bo Derek?"

Realizing he was being teased, Kirk tried to join her in banter. "Sure, but why would you want to? She's only a ten, and you're at least a fifteen."

Laughing, Peach turned to Maggie. "He's being so nice, and after the way I monopolized your time doing the penthouse. Aren't you proud of her, Kirk? Did you realize you were married to a genius? She is, you know."

Laura watched the exchange of pleasantries with the delight of a hostess who finds that her guests can carry on their own conversations without her orchestration. She smiled benignly at them as she passed the caviar mold and blinis and felt a surge of love for them, her dear friends.

It was especially nice to have Kirk here. When they used to play bridge in Long Beach, Kirk always insisted on being her partner, primarily to shield her from Jim's annoyance with her for not being as skilled as the rest of them. Although Kirk had as much desire to win as Jim did, he was sensitive to her feelings of inadequacy at the bridge table and on the tennis court. He gave her the confidence to play better, and consequently, their matches in both games were more even than when she played with her husband as partner.

Later, as they all sat down together at dinner, Laura herself offered the blessing. "Thank you, Lord, for my wonderful children and friends. Thank you for sending me a gift of love through these special people who helped to guide me through a long, dark tunnel into the light again. I promise to spend no more of my days feeling unloved and ungrateful for the blessings You have given me. This is a very special Thanksgiving.''

There was silence. Then Kirk picked up his wineglass to propose a toast. ''To Laura. . . . May the rest of your life be filled with more love and happiness than you've ever known.'' Everyone raised a glass, and the glow of their shared friendship seemed to light the room. If Jim could just be here now, Laura thought, he might realize what he is losing.

When dinner was over, and they were ensconced once more at the fireplace drinking coffee with brandy, Peach was restless in contrast to the others who were in a satiated, overstuffed trance. She kept looking at her watch and glancing over her shoulder toward the window. Laura finally asked, ''Peach, are you expecting Miles to pick you up?''

''Oh, no, I gave him and Sarah the day off.''

''Do you have a ride home? I'm sure that Shan and Dac would be happy to drive you when you're ready.''

Peach shook her head. ''Thanks, but that won't be necessary. Actually, I'm being picked up at seven.'' The atmosphere in the room crackled with curiosity.

''It's almost that now. Would you like for me to watch for the car while you go in the powder room to freshen up?'' Laura asked.

''Good idea. I must look a mess.''

''No way, Peach, no way,'' Kirk said from the depths of Jim's easy chair by the window. ''What kind of car should we watch for?''

''A red Porsche,'' she called as she hurried out of the room. Ten minutes later, the car stopped in front of the house. ''It's here, Peach,'' Kirk called.

Peach said her thank-yous and goodbyes quickly and rushed out of the house. Although it was dark outside, everyone in the room crowded to the front window. Straining their eyes to see who was helping her into the car, they were all frustrated until Angie's voice rang out. ''Oh, no! I'm gonna die!''

Impatiently, Maggie snapped at her daughter, ''Not so loud, the whole world will hear you. Who is it?''

"Sandman!"

The car drove away, and Peach's friends looked at each other in bewilderment. Kirk was the first to speak. "Who the hell is Sandman?"

Maggie laughed. "You've been out of touch. *Sandman* is the hottest movie in the country. They're standing in lines for blocks long to see it. And the star, Jason Darrow, is the new idol of teenagers all over the country."

Angie broke in. "Right. And he's positively the most gorgeous man I've ever seen. We went to see it the night it opened, and I stayed to watch it twice. I hid in the restroom so I wouldn't have to pay the second time."

"How old is this guy?" Kirk asked incredulously.

Shan answered, "Twenty-six or seven. For sure, no more than thirty."

"No kidding? What the hell is he doing with a woman Peach Malone's age?" The room was quiet as each of them pondered Kirk's question.

"She's a beautiful woman, Kirk," Maggie finally said. To which Angie replied, "Yeah, Mom, but she's old. She must be forty."

"But she's rich," Shan said.

Angie shook her head. "He doesn't need her money. He's a big star." She was perplexed and frowning, but the older women in the room did not find the revelation of Peach's new interest in life disturbing at all. On the contrary, both Maggie and Laura found it reasonable . . . and very reassuring.

_29_

Everybody Wants
to Be Somebody

PEACH hurried down the steps hoping to reach Jason's car before he could get out and be seen. Although it was dark, he was parked directly under the street lamp, and when he pulled his tall imposing frame out of the small car, she knew that anyone within a hundred yards would recognize him. He was big and handsome and had a star quality that surrounded him with an aura of excitement.

As he moved toward her, Peach shook her head slightly and hurried into the car. There had been three weeks and a tornado of emotions since they touched each other, and she wasn't sure what would happen when they did. She certainly did not want an audience, however, and she was aware that the eyes of curious friends were peeking through the shutters.

"Jason, get back in the car," she said urgently, and her eyes pleaded with him to comply. Reluctantly he did so, but when they were seated inside the car, separated by the gear shift, he put his long arm across her shoulders and pulled her close. For a long tremulous moment, he held her face close to his with his mouth barely brushing hers. "Peach," he whispered, and she could feel the warm moisture of his breath on her lips, "I've missed you."

Slowly he lowered his head toward hers until their lips touched, and desire ignited them both. After a long, deep kiss, he released her and started the car. As they pulled away from the curb, he whispered hoarsely, "Let's get out of here.

If this damn car wasn't so small, I'd have you right here in front of your friends.''

"Thank God it is, or I'd probably help you," she replied.

As he drove rapidly down through the winding road of Coldwater Canyon, Peach studied his profile and tried to understand the need she felt for this very young man. It was a desire unlike anything she had ever experienced with Drake, and she was mildly ashamed of it.

"It's been a long time, Peach. Why didn't you call me?"

"I knew you'd try to force me to go to that premiere with you, and I was afraid."

"Afraid? Of what? Me?"

"No, afraid of myself. I seem to have no will of my own when I'm near you."

"Terrific . . . let's keep it that way. . . . I love you, you know."

"Oh, Jason, how can you say that? I'm an old woman, and the world is full of beautiful young girls."

"True . . . but none as beautiful or desirable as you. I'm going to make love to you tonight until you beg for mercy. Then, I'll do it again."

Twenty minutes later, they entered the elevator at Peach's building, and Peach wondered if the naked lust she felt was visible to the doorman. As soon as the doors closed and the car began to move upward, Jason pulled her to him and kissed her until they reached her floor. The doors opened, and they hurried into her apartment. She had given Miles and Sarah the day off, but she called out anyway to be sure they were alone. There was no answer. Jason was busy undoing the buttons on her silk blouse, and within moments, he had her breasts exposed. She loved having his hands on her, and she urged him toward the bedroom.

"No, I want to do it right here on the floor . . . that's what I've been dreaming about these past weeks. I promised myself I'd take you as soon as we got inside the door. Right here!"

"It's too hard, Jason," she protested.

"I know . . . feel it." He took her hand and pressed it

against him, and she felt the imposing swelling at his groin. Quickly, as he pulled her clothes from her, she opened his shirt and belt buckle and then undid the zipper on his pants.

In moments, she was lying on the hardwood floor with his body pressed on top of hers. As he kissed her, he slid his erect and demanding penis inside, and they began to move together, slowly at first, and then urgently. Very soon, her body went taut in its orgasm and, feeling her climax shudder through his body, he too released in a spasm of desire and heat and sharing.

When it was over, he stayed inside her, kissing her eyelids, her cheeks, and her mouth. "Jason, that was wonderful," she whispered. "I don't ever want to let you go."

"Don't then. If we wait a little while, we can have an encore without my ever leaving your soft, warm pussy."

"No, we can't! Sarah and Miles could walk through that door any minute!"

"What do you think they'd say? A lovely evening, madam, would you care for tea?"

"Probably, but I don't want to find out."

Reluctantly, Jason stood up and pulled Peach to her feet. He ran his fingertips lightly over her body as she stooped to gather up her clothes. "Mmmm, that was a delicious appetizer. Now, let's have dinner!" With his long arms, he whirled her around and caught her behind the knees and lifted her. As he carried her toward the bedroom, she dropped her pantyhose and one shoe. "Jason, wait," she protested, "I dropped my shoe."

"Leave it for Sarah. Think what a thrill it'll give her." He laughed.

"I give up. Can we stop in the bar for a bottle of champagne?"

"With the main course?" He looked at her in mock disapproval. "No, we'll drink champagne with dessert."

At six o'clock the next morning, Peach came to full wakefulness. Although she had not fallen into a deep slumber, she had dozed on and off all night. She could hear Jason's deep breathing and knew he was in a sound sleep, but she was afraid to move for fear of disturbing him. His arm lay across her hip, and he was snuggled up to her back. Such a sleeping arrangement was foreign to her, for throughout her life with Drake, they had maintained separate bedrooms. Although he had insisted it was out of consideration for her desire to sleep later in the mornings, she had always known it was to accommodate his need to have the freedom to arise whenever he chose. Now, here she was cuddled up and comfortable with a young man just a few years older than her own son, and she was appalled at how very much she was enjoying it.

Someday she would have to get herself together and end this obsession with sex and Jason. She had been invaded by some nymphomaniacal spirit that was controlling her better judgment. She worried about their affair going public, for she knew she was risking her privacy every time she saw him. His face and form were being watched on the screen by millions of people everywhere, every day, and he was fast becoming an intimate part of millions of young women's fantasies. How could she have been so unfortunate in her choice of a lover?

Moving slowly so as not to disturb him, she disengaged herself and got out of bed. She tiptoed into the bathroom and closed the doors so that the sound of the flushing toilet would be muffled and she could turn on the light. As her hand hit the switch, she suddenly found herself revealed in the nude in the plethora of mirrors surrounding her. Curiously, she stepped closer, anxious to appraise the body Jason found so alluring. Perhaps the mirror could answer her questions. Mirror, mirror, on the wall . . .

She was tall and slim. Her breasts were not large, but they were round and full. Her rib cage was small, as was her waistline, and her hips were round. Broad where a broad should be broad. . . . Her body hair was scant and blond, and her pubic hair was not thick enough to hide the soft cleft in the mound of Venus. What were those white streaks? She looked down to examine them and found they were vestiges of dried semen. She smiled. It had been some night.

She turned to look at herself from the rear. Not bad. A little cellulite here and there, but not surprising since she had never been one to exercise much or pound herself into shape as most of her friends did. Why? Drake, of course. He was so much older than she was that he created a constant illusion of youth for her. Now that he was gone, would she grow old?

Enough of this narcissism. She had important things to think about. Jason could be nothing to her but a diversion. He could never be the center of her universe as Drake had been.

Since her return from Napa, she had been frustrated by her inability to reach either Horace or Dom. Both men had left town for the holiday week and would not return until Monday. Horace was in China, and Dom had gone hunting, damn them. And Horace's secretary had refused to knuckle under to Peach's demands for copies of the trusts. As she stepped into the shower, she reflected on the anxiety the delay caused her. The longer she waited, the more she dreaded the confrontation with the men in control of her life.

Half an hour later, she walked into the bedroom with a fluffy peach robe with a matching towel wrapped around her hair. Jason was awake and propped up on pillows watching the "Today" show.

"Hi, how long have you been up?"

"Not long. You slept well."

"Come back to bed," he demanded. Peach looked at him in amazement. "Really, Jason, not again."

"No, not again . . . at least not till after breakfast. I just want to hold your hand and watch Jane Pauley."

"Why Jane Pauley?"

"They're running the interview I taped with her last week, and I'm nervous. I need you to hold my hand while I watch me making an ass of myself."

"Jason, you never make an ass of yourself. All your appearances have been terrific."

"You're prejudiced."

"Well, that's true. Let's have some breakfast. Eggs okay?"

"Sarah and Miles back?"

"I'm sure they are."

Peach called in his order on the intercom as he watched in amusement. When she finished, she got into bed and tucked her body against his. "It must be great to be rich. It's like living in a fancy hotel all the time with room service," he commented.

Just before the interview was shown, Miles wheeled in a tray with everything Jason wanted and more. "Good morning, Miles. Just leave the cart there. We'll help ourselves. Are those fresh scones?"

"Yes, ma'am. Sarah got up early and baked them for Mr. Jason. She heard him say he liked them on the Merv Griffin show, and she wanted him to have some of hers."

As he withdrew, the two lovers exploded with laughter which they tried to muffle by putting their heads under the covers. "Do you think it was my pantyhose on the hall floor that gave you away?" Peach giggled.

"Probably. How many horny lovers have you got who screw you in the foyer?"

"Just one, and Sarah knows who it is. She's obviously a big fan of yours."

"And I'm a big fan of her cooking. Let's eat before Jane ruins my appetite."

Jason's interview was a good one. He had obviously charmed his interviewer, and she treated him with respect and warmth. When asked about his ambitions, he talked of the sea and his desire to own his own yacht. When asked about his love life, he replied, "No comment, except to say I have a wonderful relationship with a special woman who insists on remaining anonymous." Peach groaned. "Oh, God, Jason, how could you? Now everybody will be trying to find out who the mystery woman is! I can just see what those dreadful newspapers in the supermarket will do with that."

"I know," he said, and grinned smugly. Peach looked at him accusingly. "You did that on purpose. It wasn't a slip, was it?"

"Well, something's got to bring you out of hiding. We can't sneak around forever. I'm proud of our feelings for each other. You're the most beautiful woman I've ever met . . . of any age, except maybe Mother Teresa, of course, but you're a lot sexier than she is."

Peach scowled. "Terrific."

"Seriously . . . I want a career as an actor . . . not just as Sandman. I want to do demanding, exciting roles. I don't want to be just some teenybopper's wet dream. I'll always remember a line of Goethe's. He said, 'Everybody wants to be somebody; nobody wants to grow.' You see, being a star isn't enough for me. If I don't satisfy myself, what good is it if I satisfy the public . . . or the producers? And what good is any of it, if it takes you away from me?"

Peach loved the words he was saying, but they did not obliterate the specter of publicity. Drake had taught her to fear the press. Jason held her close to him. "Peach, don't worry so much. We'll work it out."

"Jason, you're young, and you'll be tired of me soon. You need someone who can give you a home and children. I can't do that."

"God, I hate to have people tell me what I want. I want you . . . now. Let's not try to plan our whole lives this very minute. We have no guarantee that we'll even be alive tomorrow. Isn't now all anybody ever really has?"

Peach tried to absorb his words and relax. Maybe he was right. Their feelings for each other might not last forever, but was that any reason to deny them altogether?

"Jason, I'll never marry you, you know."

"So, who asked you?"

"There's one thing I'd like to do, if you'll let me?"

"Depends. What is it?"

"I think I'd like to buy that boat you wanted."

"Whoa, don't play rich lady with me. That's not part of the deal. I want to fuck you, not your bank account."

"Jason!"

"Excuse the language. I just don't want you ever to get the idea that I have any interest whatsoever in your money."

"I know, but the boat will be mine. It would be a wonderful place for us to be alone together, and it will give you a chance to find out if reality is as good as your dreams."

"Okay, but it's your boat. You pick it out. You buy it."

"No! I don't know anything about them," she protested.

"Then you better damn well find out. It's a big investment, and you should know what you're buying."

"Aren't you going to give me any help at all?"

"Nope . . . can't anyway. Monday I'm leaving for another four weeks on tour in the States, then I'm off to Europe where the picture opens in January."

"Will you be here for Christmas?"

"Only for a couple of days."

"Good, then we'll celebrate here in my new home, and I'll invite a few of my friends."

Jason looked surprised. "Are you actually going to let me out of the closet?"

"They were all at Laura's yesterday anyway, so I'm sure they already know."

Jason pulled the towel off her hair and ran his fingers through it. Then he kissed her forehead, her nose, and her mouth. She could feel the hot wetness begin to burn between her thighs as his lips moved downward. His hand pulled at the knot holding her robe together, but it would not release. She inserted her own hand under his and undid the tie. He pulled the robe off her, and she could feel that he was aroused and ready. He pulled her close to him, and they lay side by side, her breasts touching his chest, the softness of her belly pressed against the hardness of his, with his erect penis between her thighs, and their legs intertwined.

"Jason, I can't believe this. I must be turning into a nymphomaniac. I want you constantly."

"I'll be your satyr. We'll fuck each other to death."

"I can't think of a better way to go."

He kissed her again, and slowly rolling over on his back, he lifted her on top of him. Her legs slid open, and she gasped as his penis penetrated her with a sensual thrust. Slowly they moved together, savoring the movement, neither partner anxious to reach a climax.

Suddenly, the telephone rang. Although it startled them,

Peach made no effort to answer. "Don't stop, Jason, Miles will get it," Peach whispered.

They continued, but within seconds the intercom buzzed twice, insistently. "It must be important," she said, and picked up the telephone. "I'm sorry to disturb you, ma'am, but Casey Gable is on the wire. She says it is an emergency."

"Thanks, Miles, I'll take it." She pressed the button and was immediately connected to the incoming call. She stayed on top of Jason, her body still merged with his. "Hello, Casey. Everything all right?"

"Peach, something awful's happened!"

"Casey, what is it?"

"I'm at Cedars Hospital with Mom. She tried to kill herself."

"Oh, my God. I'll be right there. Emergency room?"

"Yes, hurry, please. I'm so scared." She sounded terrified.

Peach slammed down the phone and rolled away from Jason. "Darling, I've got to go. A very dear friend of mine . . . and Drake's, just tried to kill herself. That was her daughter. She needs me."

"Who was it?"

"Grace Gable."

Peach called Miles on the intercom. "Miles, I need the car brought around right away. Grace is in the hospital."

Jason was on his feet and trying to gather his clothes together. "I'll go with you."

"No! Absolutely not! I don't want any media attention brought to the hospital. You're just too famous. God knows what's going on with Grace, but I'm certain it's nothing she'd want printed in the newspaper."

She saw the stricken look on his face, and she kissed him on the cheek. "Forgive me for being so abrupt. There's a long sad story involved here. I probably won't be back for some time."

Peach had almost finished dressing in a pair of wool pants, boots, and a sweater. She wrapped a silk scarf around her hair, and with her face clean and devoid of makeup, she looked young and beautiful. Jason sat down on the bed to watch her.

"You're lovely, Peach. Lovelier than any young girl I've ever known."

Peach paused briefly to look at him. He was so adorable sitting on the edge of the bed with no clothes on, his hair rumpled, and a fuzz of whiskers on his face. "Jason, I hate to leave you, but I've got to go."

"I know. Call me when you get a chance."

"I will. We've got unfinished business, haven't we?" Peach grabbed a suede jacket out of the closet, blew him a kiss, and was gone.

_30_

A Natural
Woman

MAGGIE slammed down the telephone and said to Dee, "Make sure that check comes back." Then she put her head down on the desk. She shouldn't lose her temper like that. She was tired and unstrung. Problems were piling on top of problems, and time was running out. Belinda pestered her constantly, and Kirk kept the pressure on too. She felt like shrieking at everyone.

Dee watched for a few minutes, feeling sympathetic and helpless. Finally, she decided she must intercede. "Mrs. H., mind if I make a suggestion?"

Her voice muffled, Maggie kept her head down as she answered, "Be my guest."

"Well, I was thinking maybe you should hire an assistant. Someone who could make that drive to Malibu for you occasionally, to be there for deliveries and check on the progress of the contractors. I'm worried about you. You look awful. Those circles under your eyes have gotten so dark, and you've been taking too much aspirin for those headaches. That stuff's not good for you."

Maggie lifted her head and looked at her secretary. Why hadn't she thought of that? Of course, she needed a helper. "Dee, that's a great idea. Why didn't I think of it?"

"Probably because most women think they're supposed to do everything themselves. We're just not programmed to delegate work to other people like men are."

"Dee, you surprise me. That's an acute observation."

"It's not original, I'm afraid. I read it in *Ms*. magazine."

"Well, here's to Gloria Steinem. Put an ad in the Long Beach *Press-Telegram* and the Los Angeles *Times*. Maybe the *Register* too. Let's hope there's a housewife out there yearning for a career in interior decoration. Be sure to stipulate that no professional experience or training is required . . . needs only good taste, ability to deal with people, and have a car. Okay?"

"What about pay?"

"Call several employment agencies. List the opening and ask them. Lower by about ten percent any figure they quote."

"I'll take care of it." Dee was pleased that her suggestion had been so well received.

Maggie smiled warmly at her. "Dee, I couldn't have made it this far without you, you know."

"Thanks, I really enjoy my work. I'm so glad that you got that job for Mrs. Malone and needed a secretary. I'm really looking forward to moving into a real office. That will be such fun."

Maggie felt a pang of conscience. She hadn't told Dee that she had promised Kirk she'd quit and go back to being a housewife and that soon she'd no longer need a secretary. She had convinced Kirk that it must be kept a secret or Dee might look for another job before the Cornwall contract was finished. It was a lie. She knew that Dee would never desert her if she was needed, but she could not bring herself to make the break final.

The telephone rang, and Dee announced that Mrs. Cornwall was on the line again. It was only ten in the morning, but this was already her third call. "Yes, Belinda?"

"I'm sorry to be such a pest, I really am, Maggie dear, but I just had to call you with some wonderful news." Her voice was sweet and tinkled like a bell, and Maggie knew she was about to be wheedled into something she didn't want to do. "Oh?" she murmured. Now what?

"Connor just called. He's decided to fly home for the holidays. He said he had no reason to stay in New York since the children were in California. They will both be here too. Isn't that just marvelous?''

"I'm very happy for you. How will that affect your plans for unveiling the house?''

"Well, that's what I wanted to discuss with you.''

Maggie had the feeling that her neck was about to be placed on the guillotine by Madame LaFarge herself. "Yes?''

"I was thinking how exciting it would be if I could take him to the house at Malibu right after dinner on Christmas afternoon. I could present it to him as my Christmas gift. We could have a beautiful tree decorated in the living room there . . . and lots of fresh poinsettias all around. It would be cozy and warm with a fire in the fireplace. We could watch the sunset together.''

"I can't do it, Belinda," Maggie said flatly. "It's impossible. I'm stretched to the limit as it is.''

"Nonsense. I'm sure you can work it out if you have to. Money is no object now. Spend what you have to spend, just do it.''

"Belinda, you can't buy time. The pressure on suppliers at this time of year is incredible. Everybody wants everything by Christmas.''

"Well, can't you get it almost finished? Can't you make it look warm and inviting even if absolutely everything isn't in place?''

Suddenly, Maggie realized she had an advantage in this new turn of events. Since Belinda was altering the terms of the contract, she could do the same. "Well, perhaps I could make it livable, provided, of course, that the deadline for total completion is removed altogether.''

Belinda had what she wanted. "Naturally, once he sees the house and likes it, you would then be working for him, and there would be no real rush. I do expect you to be there Christmas Day to greet us and explain any unfinished details to him.''

Maggie was indignant. "Christmas Day? Are you serious? I have a family too, and they're just as important to me as yours is to you.''

"Well, explain it to them. Business always comes first, and this is business. People who are really successful in life do not let holidays or anything else interfere. I'm paying you a great deal of money. A few hours on Christmas is not much to sacrifice."

"But, Belinda, you know exactly what the plans are. You can describe it as well as I can," Maggie said, trying to be more conciliatory.

"Connor thinks you are my secretary. He asks about you all the time. You made an indelible impression on your visit with him, and I think he will be utterly charmed to learn of your real part in this little exercise. I want him to love this house. Do you understand?"

"I'll see what I can work out. I'll call you tomorrow."

"Maggie, my dear, if this evolves the way I hope it will, I shall give you a bonus that will make Peach Malone look positively penurious."

The conversation was ended, but Maggie held the telephone for several moments in disbelief. She was stunned by the sudden insight that Belinda was using her to help lure Connor to California. No matter that she was happily married . . . well, not perfectly happy . . . but still very married. Belinda had implied that Connor was attracted to her, and she intended to exploit that interest for her own gain. Get Connor to California, no matter what lives, even his, are trampled to achieve that goal. Bittsey must have been quite a woman to have beaten Belinda on anything, especially when the prize was her beloved son.

Maggie tried to summon some indignation, but it eluded her. She was flattered that a man so attractive, intelligent, and sensitive found her interesting. She'd had only one man in her entire life, and she had been grateful for his love and caring. Now, here she was almost at middle age and still . . .

"Mrs. H, what happened? You look like you're in a state of shock. The old battle-ax didn't sack us, did she?"

Maggie snapped out of her trance, glad Dee couldn't read her mind. "No, not at all. As a matter of fact, we've got a reprieve . . . sort of."

Maggie gave Dee a quick rundown on the new turn of events and told her to get busy on the assistant, and then said, "Find Kirk for me. I have to tell him I'll be late for the dinner with the Driscolls tonight."

Maggie hurried into her room to dress. She had a million details to attend to, and the thought of being charming to Colonel Driscoll and his wife was almost more than she could stand. He had been an investor in a number of the limited partnerships Kirk had formed, and whenever he came to town, he expected to be entertained. He and his wife were a totally boring couple, and Maggie hated the way he referred to her as "the little woman." Kirk had wanted to invite them to the house for cocktails, but she refused. She had no time to get the house ready for any kind of entertaining. Now, since she'd have to go to Malibu and the Design Center, she'd really be pressed to meet them by six. Perhaps if she wore something that could be dressed up with a scarf, she could go directly there.

Dee announced that Kirk was on the line, and she picked up the telephone. "Kirk, honey, is everything still on for tonight?"

"You know it is. The Driscolls are expecting us to pick them up at the hotel at six. I've made reservations at the Ritz in Newport Beach."

"Kirk, please don't be angry, but I've got a problem. I don't see how I can make it back to Long Beach by five-thirty. Could you possibly change the reservations to a restaurant in L.A., then I could just meet you there?"

"Absolutely not. I've already told them where we're going, and it's too late to get reservations anywhere that's really good on a Friday night. Maggie, we've had this planned for a week! And besides, the Driscolls wouldn't understand having to change plans to accommodate your job. I haven't even told them about what you've been doing."

"Why not? I'm not working as a whore."

"Don't be crude. You know how conservative they are. If they knew you were working, he'd get suspicious about my financial stability. They simply would not understand, or accept, any wife working for . . ." he paused for sarcastic effect, " 'fulfillment.' In their world, a woman finds fulfillment in her husband."

Maggie's exasperation almost consumed her. Kirk never let up on her for a moment anymore. Everything they did together was like a battle in spite of all the negotiated settlements. All he wanted was total capitulation. "Kirk, just for once, help me. This will all be over in a few weeks."

"If you really cared about us and our marriage, you would have quit all this shit a long time ago."

"I thought we had an agreement."

"The agreement was your idea, not mine. My life has been one long marathon of unironed shirts and restaurant meals since you first got involved, and frankly, Maggie, I hate it. Don't expect me to be understanding all the time. Maybe some women can handle two jobs, but it's beyond you, face it."

Maggie couldn't fight anymore, and as usual she retreated. "Let's not get started with more insults, Kirk. It's very destructive to both of us. It may make you feel better, but it makes me feel very hostile. Can't you understand that?"

"Look, Maggie, are you going with me tonight, or do I tell the Driscolls that you're sick?"

"I'll be here at five-thirty, Kirk."

"Thanks. This is important to me. And dress up a little, will you? I'm tired of seeing you in pants, and Mrs. Driscoll thinks they're terrible."

"Don't worry. I've already laid out my organdy pinafore." In a feeble gesture of defiance, Maggie slammed down the telephone, fairly certain that Kirk had already hung up. She hated herself for being so spineless. Why couldn't she just tell him to go to hell? Because she knew that if she ever did, it would be all over. Throughout their married life, Kirk had been in control, and he was not about to give it up. She was married to a despot, albeit usually a benevolent one, but a despot just the same.

He had always been generous about the time she gave Angie, and he had been helpful and understanding when she was doing houses for him, but Angie was his child too and the houses were his ventures, not hers. She was sure he just didn't like her being independent of him. By striking out on her own, she had threatened him, and he was simply trying to protect his way of life. Natural instinct. Understanding his motivation didn't help much with her anger, however. She hated his lack of interest in her feelings, and she resented her mewling acquiescence. Were they destined to live out their lives as the conqueror and the vanquished?

After a quick check of the house and a brief argument with the tile-setter, Maggie headed for the Design Center to see a leather couch that had just arrived at Casa Bella from Italy. As soon as she saw its creamy butterscotch-colored leather and smooth linear modular forms, she made a snap decision to take it in spite of the ridiculously high price. She then hurried to Brunschwig & Fils to cancel the yardage she'd ordered for the couch she had planned to have custom-made. The fabric house was negative about her cancellation, but they became amenable when she offered to pay a hefty penalty. Had she really been dumb enough to believe that money couldn't buy time?

Late that afternoon, as she fought the freeway traffic home, she again returned to the long thoughts of the morning, but her spirits were higher. The house was coming along beautifully, and she was reluctant to leave it. When she was there, her personal troubles faded away. She wondered if it was like that for men. Did they find most of their satisfaction and happiness in their work? Or did most of them feel they were captives as she had been? She could never find any joy of accomplishment in cleaning toilets or vacuuming rugs. It was drudgery to be done again and again.

Years ago she had decided she was not a natural woman. Something was left out of her, some natural nesting instinct, and she had felt guilty about it all her married life. She had tried, but just keeping the house clean and tidy had always been an effort. When Angie was a baby, she had almost been done in by it all. The diapers and the crying never fit into the schedule for cooking, shopping, and cleaning. In her case it was true that woman's work was never done. She could never get it finished. She was constantly amazed by women who were able to sew their own clothes, wax their floors, and have a drink and a gourmet meal ready for their husbands. Even Laura made her ashamed of her inadequacies, but mostly she was ashamed because she hated it all, and that was very unnatural.

Decorating, on the other hand, made her feel good about herself. She loved it, even with all the anxieties and the frustrations. She was good at it, and now she would have to quit. She couldn't give up everything she had, her home, a successful and loving husband, for a job. The thought of Kirk leaving her was terrifying. The long nights, sleeping alone, dining alone . . . always alone . . . no, if she couldn't have both, she'd choose Kirk. No contest.

She arrived home shortly after five. Kirk's car was in the garage, and she hurried into the house. He greeted her at the door in his robe holding a glass of wine for her. "Good, you made it. Here, have a quick swallow of this and hurry upstairs and dress."

"The Friday night traffic was awful. I left Malibu at two-thirty." She gulped a mouthful of the wine. "Mm, good. What is it?"

"Some Alexander Valley Chardonnay. I picked up a case for you. We had it at Scandia, remember?"

"Lovely. I'll take the glass upstairs with me."

She showered and dressed in half an hour. She wore a low-cut chocolate brown French angora sweater with a beige silk skirt that she had splurged on right after she had started working for Peach. It was almost overpowering in its lushness and femininity. Even though she was rushing, she put on heavier eye makeup, and when she emerged, teetering on the extremely high-heeled brown suede sandals that Kirk called "screwin' shoes," she was gratified by her husband's quite obvious appreciation.

"You look terrific! When did you get that outfit?"

"I've had it for a long time," she lied, not about to ruin

256

his pleasure by pointing out that she had paid for it with her own money.

"Wear it more often, will you? Come on, let's hurry. Driscoll and his wife will be waiting."

It was an extremely successful evening for Kirk. Driscoll, a lecher behind his country gentleman manners, was extravagant in his appreciation of Kirk's "lovely little lady." For Maggie, the evening was eternal. The talk was boring. She tried to keep a vapid smile on her face and nod at appropriate times while her mind toyed with her own concerns, but Driscoll paid far too much attention to her, and it was impossible to concentrate. Although Kirk had warned her never to have more than one glass of wine because the colonel disapproved of women drinking, she ignored the dictum and allowed the waiter to keep her glass filled. Only alcohol would make her mellow enough to refrain from sarcastic rejoinders to the colonel's patronizing pronouncements. She wondered if other women found some men's attempts at flattery degrading. When Driscoll remarked on how well she filled out her furry little sweater, she resisted the urge to comment on how small the bulge under his fly was.

The dinner was good, and Maggie ate everything set before her. Consuming the wine and the food was her only salvation from boredom and irritation. She ordered an elaborate and filling pastry for dessert and almost choked on it when Driscoll commented that he liked his women to have a hearty appetite for food because that was always a good indication that they had a hearty appetite for other things too. Maggie looked at the thin, birdlike woman sitting across from her picking at her dinner with clawlike wrinkled fingers covered with huge diamond rings, and she wondered if the colonel had killed her appetite for everything, including food.

All the way home, after dropping the Driscolls at their hotel, Kirk was euphoric. Driscoll had indicated that he would be the linchpin in the new partnership he was forming. Maggie was miserable. She had eaten too much and drunk too much wine and coffee, and she'd have a bitch of a time getting to sleep.

When they got into the house, she wanted to take a warm bath to try to relax, but it was obvious that Kirk was exhilarated, and he would probably be as horny as hell. God, she was in no mood for sex. She was tired and angry with him, and it would be a cold and loveless coupling. She tried to quell the suspicion that she might want to punish him for ruining her day, destroying her evening, and making her unfit to work efficiently the next day. As she was stepping out of her skirt, Kirk grabbed her from behind and slipped his hand between her legs. "Come to bed . . . I want to see how big your appetite really is," he whispered in her ear, and his tongue flicked in, following his words. Maggie recoiled. "Don't! You know I don't like that."

Kirk was not to be deterred. He inserted his hand into the back of her pantyhose and down the cleavage of her buttocks. His penis was engorged and pressing between her legs. She tried to resist, but the more she struggled, the more he was stimulated. He snapped off her brassiere, lifted her in the air and kicked away the delicate silk skirt. "Stop it, Kirk! You'll ruin my dress."

"I'll buy you another one," he whispered, his right hand working inside her, his left arm around her waist holding her tightly to him. Gradually he managed to pull her pantyhose down around her ankles, and then he forced her to her knees with his body on top of hers. She tried to pull away, but he was big and strong and determined, and his grip was like a vise. She decided not to fight him. "Let's go to bed," she begged.

"No," he ordered, "I want to do it right here." Suddenly she realized that he intended to thrust himself into her anus. Like a battering ram, he tried to enter her, but she refused to let him. "Stop it, Kirk. You're hurting me!"

"Come on, don't be so tight-assed. Let go. Let's find out what it's like . . . maybe you'll enjoy it."

But Maggie would not give in. She pulled her muscles tighter and more taut, and the act itself became a contest of wills and bodies until Kirk became frustrated. Roughly he pulled her lower body up higher and quickly penetrated her vagina from the rear. She gasped in pain as he thrust himself deep inside her again and again, until at last he reached orgasm with a stroke so deep she felt it might penetrate her uterus. When he was finished, he stood up and pulled her to her feet. He turned her to face him to kiss her lightly, but she pushed him away.

"How could you do that to me?" she demanded angrily.

"What? What did I do?"

Maggie was appalled at the look of unabashed astonishment on his face. "You know what you did, goddamn it!"

"Come on, honey. Where's your spirit of adventure? Admit it . . . you enjoyed it too."

Maggie was too furious to say more. She walked away from him toward the bathroom to wash away as much of the struggle as she could when she heard him exclaim, "Oh, God, Maggie . . . I'm sorry. I didn't mean to do that . . ." The contrition in his voice was absolute and surprised her. She turned to see what had changed his demeanor so abruptly and saw that he was looking down at her legs and the floor. There was blood streaming from her rectum, and she had left a trail of spots on the rug. "Jesus, honey, I didn't mean to hurt you."

Without a word of reassurance or forgiveness, Maggie stepped into the shower and slammed the door behind her. She turned on the water full blast. Kirk hovered outside, worried and guilty. "Let me take you to the doctor, honey. Are you still bleeding?" Maggie refused to answer him. She had no intention of telling him that the blood was probably only from the small hemorrhoid she had developed when Angie was born. It troubled her very little and infrequently. Why should she alleviate his pain? Let the son of a bitch suffer.

_31_

Love and Support

DEAR SHAN AND DAC,

I can't tell you how much it meant to me to have you here for Thanksgiving. In spite of everything, I'll have to admit it was probably one of the happiest holidays of my life.

Happiness, like good health, is never appreciated until it's lost. Somewhere in the misery of the past few months, I learned to appreciate the good things I still have. Your dad may be lost to me, but I have you two, and I have wonderful friends.

Yesterday Kirk Hammond brought me a huge bouquet of roses in thanks for the holiday dinner. I couldn't believe he had taken the time to drive all the way up here to deliver them in person. He stayed for tea, and we had a wonderful chat about you and Angie and the marvelous times our families had together in Long Beach.

He told me he'd had lunch with Jim, and he was troubled by the realization that they had become strangers. It saddened me too, for he was a good friend to your father. Whatever Jim finds out there among the star-studded cast of thousands, I'm certain it will never replace what he has given up.

I talked to him on the telephone this morning. I must admit it upset me. I even had to call Dr. Sabatini. She assured me that my agitation was normal. I always feel better after I've talked to her.

The problem is that your father has taken a condominium at Aspen for the holidays. Apparently Ms. Jordan is an excellent skier, and he's anxious that you get to know her. He wants you both to go with them, and I do too.

As I've told you so many times, I don't want to deprive you of your father or his love. No matter what he does, he is your father, and he loves you very much. It would only add to the burden I already carry if I also had to bear the guilt of depriving my sons of a father.

Now, don't make a fuss. I know my decision is right, because I had a sign. Stop laughing. I really did. Right after I dried my tears and sat down to write this letter, Peach called. She asked me to spend Christmas Day with her. I said yes, and I'm determined to go. Maggie and Kirk will be there, and I suspect that young movie actor who plays Sandman will be there too. See, you don't have to worry. I'll probably be with far more exciting and illustrious people than you will.

I'm sure I can do it. Dr. Sabatini is too. (Yes, I called her again.) In fact, she is coming here next Monday, and we are going to the shopping center. Until then, I shall practice every day taking longer and longer walks in the neighborhood. My days of confinement will soon be over.

I love you both. As soon as I can, I promise to visit you at school.

All my love,
Mother

_32_

Private Agony

PEACH arrived at the emergency room at Cedars-Sinai Hospital and was almost knocked to her feet by Casey, who threw herself into her arms. "Casey, what happened? How is your mother?"

The young woman was weeping so hard she could hardly speak. Her hair was in disarray, and she was wearing a down parka over her pajamas. All she had on her feet was a pair of knitted socks. As gently as she could, Peach pulled her toward the leather couch and sat down with her. "Now stop this, Casey, and tell me what's going on."

Casey took a long shuddering breath and said, "I don't know. She's critical. It's . . . an overdose of sleeping pills."

Peach asked, "Can you tell me about it?"

Casey nodded and tried to explain. "She didn't get out of bed this morning. When I went in at seven, I knew something was wrong. She was anxious to get down to the shop today because she said everything was probably in a mess because she'd been away. Oh, God, she was so still and white. I was sure she was dead. I called the paramedics, and they got there right away."

"How do you know it was sleeping pills?"

"She left the empty bottle on the sink. God, why did she do it?"

"Are you sure it was suicide?"

Casey nodded her head. "She left me a note. It was lying on the pillow beside her head." She drew a rumpled and tearstained paper from her jacket pocket and handed it to Peach, who opened it and read it, her eyes filling with tears that made the words swim.

My darling Casey,

Don't try to understand what I've done. For some questions, there aren't any answers. My one regret is that I'm leaving you.

Since the day you were born, you have been my only reason for living. You brought light and happiness into a life filled with dread and despair.

Be happy and remember your mother with tenderness.

The letter said absolutely nothing. Typical of Grace, Peach thought, but why . . . and why now? "Honey, did anything happen yesterday . . . anything at all?"

"Yes, but it was wonderful news. Not the kind of thing that would drive her to . . . this. Just the opposite."

"What was that?"

"Jerry, the baby's father, called me. He was in the hospital. He'd had a mild heart attack. He said it wasn't serious at all, and he felt fine. He called me to tell me he loved me, and that when he thought he was dying, he realized how important I was to him and how much he wanted our baby. He told his wife everything, and she's agreed to a divorce."

Peach was mystified. "And what was your mother's reaction to the news? Was she happy?"

"Yes . . . God, I guess so. I was so caught up in my own ecstasy that I didn't really pay much attention. I probably just assumed she was happy because I was so delirious. The past few weeks have been perfectly miserable for me. I hadn't heard from him, and I had begun to think that what Mom said was true."

"What was that?"

"She was sure he was going to fade away from me and the baby."

They sat together in silence amid dozens of people who were also in some kind of distress. An hour later, a nurse approached Casey. "Miss Gable? May I have a word with you in here, please?" She indicated a small office behind a glass window. Both Peach and Casey felt a cold panic. "My mother . . . she's not . . . ?" The nurse took her arm and helped her to her feet. Peach stood up too, her knees shaking. Casey grasped Peach's arm and begged, "Don't leave me."

Inside the office, the nurse closed the door and asked them to sit down. "Dr. Austin is here now and asked me to have you wait in here for him. He's with your mother."

"Is . . . is she still alive?" Peach asked.

"Yes, but she's very ill. Would you like some coffee?"

Both women shook their heads. Swallowing anything would have been an impossibility for both of them. The nurse smiled and tried to be reassuring. "Don't worry now. She's getting the best care possible. If anyone can save her, our staff can, and Dr. Austin is highly regarded here. Now just try to relax and call me if you want anything."

The minutes passed like hours. Peach tried to fit the pieces of Grace's history together as well as she could remember them. It had been so many years since Drake had told her the tragic story that she was sure she had forgotten some important detail. She herself felt a sense of personal failure that her good friend had been in desperate trouble, and she had been totally unaware of it. If Drake had been alive, it would never have happened. Whatever demons had set upon Grace, she would have brought them to Drake, and he would have helped her to exorcise them. Why had Grace not taken her, Drake's wife, into her confidence?

The burden of guilt that each close member of a family feels when one of them attempts suicide fell especially heavily on Casey since there was no one else to share it. She alone felt responsible for what had happened, even though she had no understanding of it.

It was almost eleven when Jim Austin finally made an appearance. He looked tired, and there was no information to be gleaned from the impassivity of his face. "She's still alive, Casey, but I honestly don't know if that's good news."

"What do you mean?" Casey asked fearfully.

"She's gone into cardiac arrest twice. The team here is fantastic. They've resuscitated her, and she seems to have stabilized."

Peach interjected, "Why isn't that good?"

Jim kept his attention directed toward Casey. "We don't know if she's suffered any brain damage. She's still unconscious. Everything possible is being done. I've got the city's best neurologist with her now. We'll just have to wait and see."

"Can I see her?"

"Not yet, Casey. We've got her in intensive care. Peach, why don't you take Casey home and get some food in her? Remember, young lady, you have Grace's grandchild to think about."

"You can reach us at my place, Jim," Peach said.

Twenty minutes later they were at Peach's apartment, and Sarah was fixing lunch. Casey called the shop to tell Eve, and Peach retired to her bedroom to call Jason and explain to him that she could not see him until a resolution of some kind had been reached. When she hung up the phone, she reflected on how far away the night before seemed to be . . . a lifetime. Tragedy had a way of separating itself into a time frame all its own.

As the day waned and darkness closed in with its own special set of terrors, Jim called with some encouraging news. "Dr. Reinhardt did a scan and some other tests, and he's hopeful. She's still in a coma, but he's fairly sure that if she comes out of it, she'll probably be okay."

"Thank God," said Casey fervently.

"We're not out of the woods yet, Casey. Understand?"

"I understand, and thanks for everything, Jim. I'll be at home. You can reach me there."

"I think you ought to stay here," Peach protested.

"Thanks, but I've got to face that house now while there's still hope. Otherwise, I might not ever be able to set foot inside it again."

Peach felt a crushing sense of loneliness when Casey left. She decided to call Jason to see if he'd come over and spend the night. She let the telephone ring ten times before she gave up. It was almost seven-thirty. He'd probably gone out for dinner. Later, Sarah brought her a light snack on a tray, and she sat on her chaise longue watching television. Every fifteen minutes or so, she dialed his number again, but there was no answer. It was almost eleven when she gave up, thoroughly depressed. She tried to deny that she felt suspicious and jealous, but in honesty, she knew that was what she felt, and she hated herself for it. Her good friend lay near death, and she was absorbed in fear that her young lover was with another woman. Was she destined to be an old hag yearning for the arms of a young male?

She went to her vanity table and switched on the lights surrounding it. The magnifying mirror was merciless. She put both hands to her face and pulled the skin taut. A lift. Why not? She'd see that plastic surgeon just as soon as Grace's situation was resolved, and she'd whip her body into shape as other women did. If money and effort could make her young again, she was ready to expend both.

As she returned to the bedroom, the sound of Grace Gable's name coming from the TV newscaster caught her attention. Oh, no! The story of her attempted suicide was being reported. How vile that one woman's private agony could be so exploited. Grace was not a public figure. The only celebrity she had was the prominence of her customers, and it didn't seem fair. The telephone rang just as the newsman intoned, "Hospital authorities describe her condition as guarded." It was Casey calling.

"Peach, have you seen the eleven o'clock news?" she wailed.

"Yes, I just heard it on Channel Four."

"It was on Two also. How dare they do that? Who told them?"

"Now calm down, Casey. All the media have sources at the hospitals, particularly in the emergency room. It's a matter of public record anyway. Attempted suicides are always reported to the police. It's a violation of the law, you know."

"Jesus, what a mess. She'll hate it. She never told anybody anything."

"I know, honey, but she did it to herself."

"Peach, I'm feeling a lot of anger toward her. Isn't that awful?"

"It's perfectly natural, Casey. Listen, I want you to talk to someone soon. There's a wonderful psychologist—"

Casey interrupted her. "Forget it, Peach. Mom didn't believe in shrinks and neither do I."

"Don't be so definite. This might have never happened if your mother had consulted a professional about her problem. Whatever it was."

"Maybe. I think I'll call the hospital and find out if there's anything new."

Ten minutes later, Casey called Peach again. Her voice was excited and angry. "I just talked to Jim. God, Peach, I'm so happy and mad at the same time I could kill!"

"Why?"

"Mom opened her eyes at six-thirty . . . almost five hours ago, and nobody called me! She hasn't spoken yet, but the neurologist is optimistic."

Peach's mood lifted with joy and relief. "Thank God!"

"But do you realize, I could have been there if I'd known? Now she's asleep, and he said I shouldn't visit till morning."

"Wonderful. I'll meet you there . . . what time?"

"Eight, I guess."

"Fine, now you get some rest so you can get up in time to dress nicely. I want those people at the hospital to see what you really look like."

Casey laughed. "I didn't realize what I fright show I was till I came home and looked in the mirror."

As Peach began to get ready for bed, she looked at the telephone and was tempted to try Jason one more time, but she resisted. She must continue to let him be the aggressor. He was too young to be pursued. And she was too darned old to do the pursuing.

_33_

Are You with Me?

MAGGIE got up at six after a restless and almost sleepless night filled with anger and humiliation. She was still in an unforgiving mood. Kirk had ruined her day yesterday with his selfish demands, and then, when she had gone out of her way to help him, he rewarded her with brutish behavior. She moved quietly to avoid awakening him. She had a dim hope that she could get out of the house without facing him.

Quietly she gathered some clothes from the closet and sneaked out of the room. She'd used Angie's bathroom down the hall. Although she'd had a shower just a few hours before, she wanted to take another one. She was sore from the abuse he'd inflicted, and she needed the refreshment of a cascade of hot water. It would be a long day, and she was already tired.

After drying herself, she rummaged about in the drawer to find some of her daughter's cosmetics. There wasn't much. These young girls of today are so much smarter than we were, she mused. They let the world and their mirrors get used to their bare faces so that they had the freedom to face life without eyeliner or lipstick.

When she felt presentable, she tiptoed out of the bathroom and went to Dee's office to leave a note with instructions. Then she crept down the stairs, congratulating herself on having avoided Kirk when she detected the aroma of coffee in the air. Coffee? Who would be making coffee? Kirk didn't know how. He never did anything in the kitchen. Had Dee left the pot on all night? She'd better check it out.

When she arrived in the kitchen, she found Kirk standing at the sink slicing a banana into a bowl of granola. The table was set with grapefruit, toast, and coffee. He had even put some jam into a glass bowl. She couldn't remember this ever happening before. Even when Angie was born. Even when she came home from the hospital after her appendectomy.

He turned to face her. The uncombed hair and full night's growth of whiskers made him look humble, and the contrite expression on his face completed the picture. How dare he look so pathetic?

"I made breakfast for you," he mumbled as he turned back to finish the banana.

Maggie tried to conjure up the vision of hostility he had displayed the night before, but it eluded her. He was ashamed to a degree she had never thought possible, but then his behavior had been equally impossible.

"Thanks, but I'm in a hurry."

"You have to eat. You've been missing too many meals lately. You're getting too thin."

"You sound just like my mother," she said, and their eyes met tentatively.

"Good, that's what I was aiming for."

He poured the coffee, and they both sat down at the table. He offered her the front page of the *Times*, the section he always claimed first by divine right. Maggie shook her head. "No, I have to eat and run. The traffic will be bad, and I have to make up for the day I lost yesterday." She couldn't resist one small stab at his conscience.

She ate her grapefruit, half of her cereal, and took a sip of the strong, bitter coffee, then stood up to leave. "Thanks for the breakfast. I won't make it home until after the rush hour. If you want to wait, we can go down to the Marina for dinner." She smiled, continuing, "Unless you've gotten hooked on KP and want to try cooking it yourself."

"No way. It's not habit-forming."

"Thanks for the effort. I really appreciate it."

"Yeah," he sighed and raised his eyes to hers. He was not accustomed to humbling himself, and she could see it was a miserable experience for him. In other times, she would have taken pity, but not now. She was silent.

"Maggie, are you okay?" he asked, and then said, "I'm really sorry."

"I know you are." She paused. "So am I." She left the house immediately, relieved to escape the emotions roiling there.

She could not escape, however, for all during the long drive, her mind kept returning to her anger. Why would Kirk treat her like that? She had aborted her own plans in order to dress beautifully and be his doll wife. She had endured hours of death-defying boredom, and in return he had ravaged her. Never in her life had she experienced sex without consent until last night, and it wasn't sexy at all. She felt as if she had been brutalized by a hostile stranger, and in spite of his morning contrition, she knew that the anger was still in him. But why? She had agreed to give up a satisfying and lucrative career, an agreement she resented more each day. Now that she knew her capitulation had not pacified him, what was the point of it all? If he was going to continue to be nasty, why should she give up her work?

Well, damn it, she wouldn't do it. She'd tell him tonight. No, not yet. Better wait and see if she got any other good job offers and then deal with it. When push came to shove, she'd stop being a doormat and fight for what she wanted. After all, it was her life too. The time to test their marriage had finally come. She hoped it would pass, but when she thought about the man she'd seen the night before, she had doubts.

Once at the house, she was immediately plunged into a dispute between the landscaper and the carpet men, and the telephone was ringing. It was, of course, Belinda.

"Yes, Belinda, the color of the carpeting turned out fine. The shutters will be installed next week, right after they finish with the floors."

"Wonderful," her employer cooed. "I just knew you could do it."

"Belinda, I have a favor to ask, but say no if you don't want to. Do you think I could have that lovely desk you have in the anteroom off the library? I thought it would make the house very special and add a sentimental touch to put it in the alcove of Connor's bedroom."

"Maggie, my dear, that is an inspiration. I'm surprised I didn't think of it myself. Of course you may have it, and anything else you'd like. Why don't you come over today to look the place over. You may have anything I've got. After all, it will all be Connor's eventually anyway."

Bingo, Maggie said to herself. That's just what she'd had in mind. "Belinda, what a terrific idea. I'll be there just as soon as I can get away from here."

Maggie checked over the house. The bathrooms looked sensational. She had modernized them completely with sleek fixtures from Italy. The large tub in the master suite looked out through the huge window to the sea. She had planned to try it out by herself one evening at sunset, but she knew there'd never be time.

The telephone rang again, and it was Peach calling. "Peach, how nice to hear from you! Is everything okay?"

"I suppose. A very close friend tried to kill herself on Thanksgiving, but she failed, thank God."

"How terrible."

"Nobody knows why, and she's not the type for dramatic gestures. Anyway, I know you're busy. I called for two reasons. One business, the other pleasure. First, the business. Do you know anything about boats?"

"Not much, why?"

"Well, I don't know much about them either, so we'll have to learn together. I'm meeting with my financial advisers today, and if I can swing it, I'm going to buy myself a yacht. It will be very large, of course, and whether it's new or used, I will want you to decorate it for me . . . as beautifully and luxuriously as you did the penthouse. Are you interested?"

"Are you kidding? I'd love . . . absolutely love . . . to do that. But I've got to finish here before I can take anything else on."

"Of course. It may take weeks to find the right one, but I want you to help me make the final selection. We'll have fun doing it together. We may even have to fly to the East Coast or the Mediterranean or wherever. Are you with me?"

"You know I am."

"That's not all. As soon as you finish with Belinda, I want you to get started doing a little schoolhouse on our property in Napa. I'm giving my house to my son, and I want to refurbish the schoolhouse . . . it's a real one, by the way . . . into a guesthouse. Not a big job, but it needs your ingenuity to make it comfortable."

"Just as soon as this is over out here, I'll get started," Maggie replied eagerly.

"Now for the pleasure. I'd like for you and your family to join me for dinner here on Christmas Day. Can you come?"

"Drat," Maggie exclaimed, "I'd love to, and so would Kirk, but I've got to be here at sunset when Belinda shows the house to her son."

"On Christmas? Isn't she being a little selfish?" Peach asked.

"I tried to talk her out of it, but she's very determined."

"Well then, suppose we gather here at noon and plan to eat around two. You can leave whenever necessary, and the rest of us can sit by the fire and talk. Laura, by the way, says she intends to be here."

"That sounds perfect. Kirk and I will pick her up. I'm sure she'll feel more secure riding with us."

The conversation ended on a positive and happy note, and Maggie went back to work. It was not until she was in the car on her way to the Cornwall mansion that she realized she had just accepted another job. Her career was not to meet an untimely end, after all. And neither was her marriage, she hoped.

_34_

A Cave of
Her Own Fear

LAURA put down the Bullock's Christmas catalog in despair.
This would be the first Christmas in her whole life that she
would be completely alone. She wished she had kept in better
contact with her brother after her parents had died, but he was
a lot older than she was, and they'd never been close. A card
at Christmas was her only connection with him now.

She loved the holiday season. She put a lot of thought into
all the gifts she bought, because when she was a little girl,
her parents had never given her the things she'd asked for.
They gave her what they thought she should have. She'd never
forget the year she had pleaded for a puppy and got a new
snowsuit instead. She tried never to disappoint the twins, and
on many occasions, she'd had to defy Jim to give them what
they wanted.

This year they wanted new ski equipment and clothes, and
they had to choose that for themselves. Perhaps there was
some other gift she could buy to surprise them, but she'd
never find it in those sleek, brightly colored catalogs. She
needed to walk through the stores for inspiration. If only she
could leave the house.

Maybe she ought to try. What could happen? She'd get
dressed and get in the car and see just how far she could push
herself. The new mall was not too far away. Dr. Sabatini
planned to take her there next Monday, but she wanted to go
now, before all the merchandise was picked over. What could

she lose? If she did it, she'd be free. If she didn't, she'd be no worse off than she was now.

No, maybe she'd better not rush things. She sat down at the desk to write a letter to her sons, and when she was almost through, the telephone rang. It was Peach calling. "Peach, it's so nice to hear from you. Thank you for the beautiful plant, but you didn't need to do that."

"Yes, I did. It was a wonderful Thanksgiving. I'm sorry I had to rush off. Laura, do you think you could possibly manage to come to my house for dinner on Christmas?"

Laura took a deep breath and said, "I'll try, Peach. I really will. I can't bear the thought of being alone. The boys won't be here, you know."

"I know. I saw Jim at the hospital on Friday. He saved the life of Grace Gable, who is a very dear friend of mine. I'm hoping she'll be well enough by then to join us too."

"How come you're not going to Napa to be with Steve?"

"They'll see enough of me when my grandchild is born. Besides, they need some time alone together. Once a baby comes, things are never quite the same."

"How true. I'll never forget the sudden realization that suddenly there were two human beings that I was totally responsible for."

"Well, you got a big jolt having two all at once. How come you never had any more?"

"Jim, what else. He doesn't believe anybody should have more than two, and he said I blew it all on one pregnancy. Twins run in my family, not his."

The conversation went on for another ten minutes, and Laura was grateful for the warm and friendly exchange. She sat down and finished her letter, and her desire to go shopping returned stronger than ever. She had to buy presents now that she was going to Peach's.

Quickly she showered and dressed, although it took a while to put on her makeup. The weeks of being alone had left her uncertain about her appearance, and she wiped off the eyeliner twice before she felt it was straight enough. When she was ready, she checked her appearance. Not too bad, really.

She had lost ten pounds and looked slimmer and more shapely than she had for a long time.

She went downstairs to the hall closet and put on the buttery soft suede jacket Jim had picked out, and as she was putting it on, her gaze drifted up the stairs. She suddenly flashed back to that dreadful day when she had watched Jim and Ghilly. It was a ghost of a memory that would haunt her forever. She had tried to tell the psychologist about it but could not bring herself to put into words exactly what she had seen, although she remembered every vivid detail.

She must forget the past. Jim was dead to her now, and she must try to think of him that way. How she wished he really had died. How easy it would have been to be a widow. She could have held up her head to the world. Friends would have consoled her and sent flowers.

Dear Jesus, she was doing all the things she promised herself not to do. She must not let bitterness and hatred overwhelm her. She must stop cowering in the house like some frightened animal in a cage.

Quickly she picked up her keys and walked out to the garage. Her heart was beating faster. Her hands trembled so hard it took three tries before she could punch the correct six numbers and arm the security system. She must have the number changed from ten-sixteen-sixty . . . the date of her wedding anniversary.

She willed her shaking legs to get into the car, the Cadillac Seville she loved so much. Jim had wanted to buy her a Mercedes, but she had insisted on the Seville. All her life she'd considered the Cadillac to be the ultimate in transportation, and she had won out. Jim bought one for her but indulged himself in a Ferrari.

Once in the car with the door closed, she shut her eyes briefly and steeled herself. Before she could change her mind, she touched the control and opened the automatic garage door, and daylight filled the car. She inserted the key into the ignition, but the engine did not turn over. She ignored the relief she felt at the thought that perhaps the battery was dead and she couldn't go anywhere. She tried again, and the engine growled and began to hum. The palms of her hands were so wet they slipped on the steering wheel as she eased the car into reverse and backed out onto the driveway. Her heart beat faster, and she was afraid she would have a heart attack, but she forced herself to go on. If she was going to die, let it happen out here in the sunshine and not crouched in a cave of her own fear.

Cautiously, she drove on. It was Christmastime, and she would join the rest of the world in the shopping center.

She concentrated on her driving, and soon pulled into a parking space in the mall lot. Her heart was still pounding, but now it merely served to remind her that she was still alive. Perhaps she should go home now. She had already proved something, but a voice inside her urged her not to quit. Gathering her purse and keys, she pulled her weak and quivering body out of the car and tried to summon enough strength to go on. She put her hand on the roof of the car to steady herself, but she was faint. She rested her head on her arm and closed her eyes and remained that way until a hand touched her shoulder and someone said, "Are you all right, my dear?"

Laura looked up into the concerned expression on on elderly woman's face. "Yes, thank you, I'm all right . . . I think." She was embarrassed. The woman was at least seventy years old, her arms were full of packages, and she was worried about a stranger. "I've been ill, you see," she fumbled to explain, "and this is my first time out of the house."

"Wait a moment while I put these packages in my car here, and I'll walk you inside. Child, you're as pale as death. Are you sure it's all right for you to be out alone?" the woman said as she opened the trunk of the car parked next to Laura's and placed her packages inside. She closed it again and strode back to where Laura stood. "Come now. Take my arm. There's a lovely little coffee shop right inside. Let's go in there and have a cup of tea together, shall we?"

"I hate to impose," Laura apologized, "but I'm weaker than I thought. Just driving here has taken a lot out of me."

"I'd love to sit down and chat with someone. I'm tired too, but I wouldn't miss Christmas shopping for anything. I told my doctor that when I leave this life, I intend to go with my purse and charge card in my hand, and if it could be arranged, I'd like to be buried at Saks."

Laura was completely charmed by the spirit and good humor of the lovely stranger, and she allowed herself to be propelled into the mall coffee shop. Once inside, they both collapsed in a booth. The waitress took their order for two cups of tea, and Laura relaxed a bit. "My name is Laura Austin, and I'm so grateful for your friendly assist back there."

"How do you do? And I'm Cecily Baker, and I'm a stranger myself in this part of town. I live in Beverly Hills but I wanted to see the new mall. I do so hate moving my car about, and I'm getting too old to walk the distances between stores in my town."

"But you have such lovely shops there . . . Nieman's and the stores on Rodeo Drive."

The woman sniffed. "Rodeo Drive, that's for the Arabs and the Japanese and other tourists. We natives don't go there much. It's like Disneyland for the well-to-do."

Laura looked her good Samaritan over. She was dressed in an off-white Chanel suit. Her gray hair was fashioned in a tidy bun, she had a lustrous strand of pearls around her neck, and her aged fingers were adorned with several diamond rings.

Tea arrived and Laura learned that Cecily had four grown children, six grandchildren, and a great-grandchild on the way. She had been a widow for ten years. Laura tried to keep the conversation focused on Cecily as long as she could. "Tell me about yourself," Cecily finally asked. "You've let me do all the talking, and I am a terrible old windbag. Do you have a family?"

"Yes, twin sons, Shan and Dac. They're eighteen and away at school."

"And will they be home for Christmas?"

Laura hesitated before answering softly, "No . . . they're going skiing with their father."

Not wanting to pry, Cecily sensed her reluctance and did not ask her any personal questions. She waited for her to continue if she wished to do so. And in a few moments, Laura did. "You see, I'm in the midst of a divorce. Funny. I didn't really intend to tell you that. I've been sitting here planning to tell you that I was a widow, but I guess I just couldn't lie. You've been so kind to me, I wouldn't have felt right returning your sweetness with deceit. The truth is, he left me for another woman, and I'm so ashamed."

Cecily patted Laura's hand sympathetically. "That's nothing to be ashamed of, my dear . . . not at all." She paused a moment before going on. "Let me tell you a little story. My husband was a wonderful, kind, thoughtful man. I was sure that he was as devoted to me as I was to him until one day I got an anonymous telephone call informing me that he was having an affair with the nurse in his office. I didn't really believe it. I asked him about it, expecting a denial, of course, but he told me it was true. He said that he loved her and she was pregnant and pressing him to ask for a divorce. It was then that I knew I had fallen into a trap. It was she who had called me."

Laura was spellbound. This remarkably composed woman had endured the same disgrace and rejection. "What did you do?" she asked.

Tears were bright in the woman's eyes. "I gave him an ultimatum. Send the bitch away, or I would ruin him. Divorce was not so simple then as it is now. I told him that if he did not do as I said, I would take his children from him, and he would never see them again. I had all the weight of society, the law, and morality on my side. He capitulated, and we tried to resume our life together, but our relationship had been mortally wounded. I never shared the same bed again with him . . . or with any other man. I won, but it was a hollow victory. He died of heart failure ten years later."

"But you kept your marriage together, didn't you?"

"Yes, but sometimes it is better to just let go. If I could

have understood that then, I might have been able to go on and build myself a new life, perhaps even find a new love while I was still young. I didn't. I stubbornly clung to an old, worn-out one. It is not true that any marriage is better than no marriage at all. I've been much happier since Charles's death, and I've found peace and contentment living alone. You'll see. There's a lot to be said for independence."

Laura looked at her watch. It was getting late, and she did not want to stay out after dark. "Cecily, would you mind walking me back to my car? I'd better be on my way. This has been a big strain being out alone for the first time."

The two women, strangers until an hour before, walked arm in arm to Laura's car. The older woman felt Laura's arm tremble and asked, "Are you sure you'll be all right? I'd be happy to take you home."

"Thank you, but I'll be fine. I can't tell you how much I appreciate your kindness."

"It was my pleasure. Perhaps we'll meet again some time."

"I hope so. Goodbye, Cecily, and thank you for everything."

The drive back would be so much easier, Laura thought. She felt secure and comforted by her encounter with that extraordinary woman. She vowed that she really would try to make a new life for herself.

Cecily Baker got into her car after watching Laura drive away. Carefully she locked the doors and got herself organized for the drive home, but first, she closed her eyes and whispered a few words. "Forgive me, Charles. I hated to lie about you that way, but she needed help and encouragement so desperately . . . and you know what an awful busybody I am. I love you, my sweet, and I still miss you every minute of every day." She opened her moist eyes and drove slowly back to Beverly Hills.

_35_

How Much
Am I Worth?

PEACH got into the car after her usual morning visit to the hospital. "How's Miss Gable today?" the driver asked as they drove off.

"Not much change," she sighed. "Did you get in touch with Mr. Petrone and tell him I was on my way to see him?"

"Yes, ma'am. He said he was awfully busy after being away all week, but he hoped you'd be free to stay for lunch with him and Mr. Beller."

"Damn!" Peach exclaimed softly. She'd wanted to see him alone. Peach settled down in the back seat and tried to relax. She had been keyed up and nervous ever since returning from Napa and having to wait for her encounter with Dom. It was obvious that he and Horace considered themselves her guardians. She tried not to be angry with Drake for giving them so much control over her even though she had to admit it was probably her own fault.

From the moment she met Drake, she had allowed him to have complete control over her life. She rarely questioned his decisions, even in her own mind. If his ideas differed from hers, she usually felt it was she who was wrong.

Under such circumstances, Drake had probably assumed that she wanted him to make arrangements for her entire future, and now she found herself shackled. She did not want Horace and Dom to be her keepers. She was resentful of their patriarchal stance, particularly regarding the winery, and she was humiliated that she would have to beg for permission to spend money that belonged to her. She had intended to deal with the men one at a time, but good old Dom had out-maneuvered her by bringing in Horace to present a united front. She had made a tactical mistake, and as she got out of her car and entered the express elevator that would take her to the top of the skyscraper, she realized she should have made them come to her, as Drake always had. Oh, well, she was learning.

Dom's secretary escorted her into his office immediately, and he got out of his chair. They shook hands. Peach held herself aloof. No more kissing and effusive greetings. This was business.

"Would you like a drink while we're waiting for Horace?" he asked.

"No, thank you, and there's no need to wait for Horace to talk. Why did you tell me I couldn't buy a boat when we talked on the telephone this morning?"

"Because you can't afford it, Peach. It's that simple," he responded.

Peach felt as if someone had just stepped on her stomach. What did he mean? The word "afford" had simply dropped out of her lexicon the day she married Drake. Afford? They could always afford anything they wanted.

"I don't understand. Drake left me millions," she declared.

"In trust, yes, but those millions are not available to you to throw away frivolously."

"Frivolously . . . by whose definition? Yours, I presume?" she asked coldly.

Dom was not intimidated. Drake had been absolutely right in giving the power of the purse strings to him and to Horace. This woman and her son should not be allowed to squander the fortune their good friend had worked so diligently and cleverly to amass. "I'm sorry, Peach, you'll just have to trust me. Drake knew you had no knowledge of finance or economics, and that's why he set things up as he did. We have everything invested in good conservative investments that are aimed at growth and not high yield, and there is no reason whatsoever for us to invade those investments at this time. It would, in fact, be highly imprudent and costly to do so. I'm already having misgivings for allowing you to sway me regarding the winery. I know for a fact that Drake considered it a sentimental and unwise adventure.''

Peach was furious. ''Perhaps, but the fact is, he didn't sell, did he? He knew how important it was to Steve. Not everything can be measured in dollars and cents, Dom, and that's a direct quotation from my husband.'' The knot of anger tightened in her stomach as she continued. ''In all my years with Drake, I never, ever had to beg for anything. Not once did he ever refuse me, or our children, a single thing money could buy. Are you listening? Now, tell me why we're even contemplating selling away my son's life . . . and why I can't buy a damned boat?''

Dom was imperturbable. ''A yacht would be just another drain on your finances, just as the winery is. The initial cost would be only the tip of the iceberg. The expense of maintaining it, staffing it, and berthing would be enormous.'' His telephone rang, and he picked it up and in moments announced that Horace had arrived.

Peach's attorney entered, greeted her warmly, then sat down on the other side of the desk. She felt surrounded by hostile forces. These men were no longer her friends. They had become adversaries. Unless her husband in his final days had been outwitted by his own attorney, she was certain that he had never intended for his family to be controlled by outsiders.

''Horace, please explain to me how Dom has the authority to tell me how I can spend money that is mine?'' Peach decided on a frontal assault. She'd put them on the defensive for a change. She noticed a look of concern that bordered on the conspiratorial pass between the two men.

''Well, Peach''—Horace cleared his throat—''I'm sure Dom doesn't want to deny you anything within reason. He's just trying to protect you. Under the terms of the trust, that's what he's supposed to do.''

Peach was quiet for a moment, and then suddenly she

turned toward the banker and asked, "Dom, exactly how much am I worth?"

"You mean, how much the trust is worth. Well, that will take some time to assemble. The current values of the stocks at today's market, real estate appraisals and the like . . . it would all have to be calculated."

Peach was insistent. "How long will it take?"

Dom hedged, "A couple of days perhaps . . ."

She expressed surprise. "Really? In these days of computers one would think you could just press a few buttons and get a complete readout. Surely, you can give me a rough guess?"

"My dear, we have a whole network of banks and customers, and we administer a lot of trusts. Even a guess would take a bit of doing."

She got to her feet. "Good. Get somebody to work on it while we have lunch. Shall we eat? I'm famished." She headed toward the leaded glass door, and the two men followed her. They did not look comfortable. Dom called his secretary, who immediately entered. "Beatrice, tell Anton to serve lunch immediately. Also run a check on the Malone trusts and try to come up with an approximate value. Right away, please."

Peach was already in the richly appointed dining room. A highly polished mahogany table was flanked by eight magnificent Chippendale chairs. As soon as they were seated, a butler dressed in a morning coat served the first course, cream of watercress soup, and as she ate it, Peach took notice of the exquisite, embroidered linens, heavy silver flatware, and delicate porcelain. No expense had been spared in creating an atmosphere of wealth, privilege, and power.

As she sipped a Chassagne-Montrachet from a glass by St. Louis of France, she decided to continue her attack. "Horace, I want to transfer the ownership of the property in Napa to my son. It will be a wedding gift from me . . . and his father."

"Peach, you just don't seem to understand. The land and the winery are part of the trust, and in fact do not belong to you. You are simply a trustee."

Peach was learning. "How many trustees are there?"

Horace cleared his throat, a trifle nervously, and continued, "Well, the bank is one, and Dom represents the bank, and you . . . and me. By the way, I don't suppose you thought to have your new daughter-in-law sign a prenuptial agreement, did you?"

"No, and I'm sure it's not necessary anyway. She's a lovely young woman." Damn, she would not let herself be put on the defensive.

"Well, I'm sure she is, but there is a great deal of money in the estate, and you can never predict people's behavior where money is concerned," the attorney replied, a trifle sanctimoniously.

"I'm learning about that, Horace," Peach replied a trifle viciously, and then asked, "Why don't I have copies of the trusts?"

"I'm sure I must have left them with you," Horace answered defensively.

His answer surprised her, for she knew it was a deliberate lie. Horace was a meticulous person who never, ever neglected or overlooked details. That was the very reason he had been important to her husband, because Drake was a man who did not want to be distracted by the day-to-day minutiae.

"You're mistaken. Anyway, even if you did, I'd like another set, if you please. Send them to me this afternoon. I have some reading to do tonight. I think it's time I took my head out of the sand and started to learn about the real world, don't you?"

They finished their lunch uneasily discussing banal things like the weather, the new show at the Ahmanson, and the quality of food at the Regency Club. As coffee was served, Beatrice appeared with a sheaf of papers.

"Is that the information I asked for, Dom?" Peach inquired.

He nodded his head and briefly scanned the figures. After a few moments, he looked up and their eyes met.

"How much?" she demanded.

"Roughly, I'd say between eighty and ninety million, but that doesn't take into account any of the real estate holdings, which are extensive. You know how much Drake liked to buy land. There are oil wells too. I'd say roughly the entire estate is probably worth in excess of one hundred and fifty million.''

Peach raised her eyebrows. "Is that all? I thought there was more. I could swear that Drake told me we were worth more than two hundred. Have you been making some poor investments since his death?''

Her attitude startled both men. What kind of woman could accept the reality of that kind of wealth and be concerned because there wasn't more? Dom became extremely defensive. "Now see here, my dear woman, we have been extremely prudent and conservative in administering the trust. I personally have monitored it, and my time is valuable. Drake was a close friend of mine, and I will not be accused of malfeasance in handling his estate.''

Peach ignored his indignation. "Well, you're absolutely right about the boat, I must say. A woman whose only assets are less than two hundred million dollars had damn well better stay off the water and keep both her feet planted solidly on the ground.''

She stood up. "Horace, I want those trusts without fail . . . as soon as possible . . . today. Dom, please send me a detailed list of every asset in Drake's . . . my . . . estate. I also want a detailed account of every transaction that has been made by you or Horace in the past year, and I want that as soon as possible too.''

The two men had gotten to their feet. "Now see here, Peach, aren't you being a little dramatic? I'm sure if we sit down like old friends and not adversaries, we can straighten things out. Perhaps I was being a little conservative about the yacht. When the house is sold—'' Dom protested, but Peach cut him off.

"No, Dom, you did me a favor. Really, you did. It's time I stopped playing little girl lost and started taking charge of my life. Drake's gone now, and I don't intend to let him control me from the grave. Goodbye, gentlemen. Thanks for lunch.''

__36__

Let Her Be

IT HAD been three days since it was determined that Grace was experiencing a psychotic break, and her daughter was strung out and nervous from the uncertainty and the long hours of frustration at the hospital. Casey had been waiting a half-hour to talk with Dr. Winchester, and her head was throbbing. She had not felt well for two days, and she was concerned about a slight discharge of blood she had noticed that morning. She had called her gynecologist, but he was out of town for the week, and she detested the fat little man who was his associate. He was always making lewd comments, trying to be funny, when she was on the table with her feet in the stirrups.

Casey went to the vending machine and bought a can of orange soda, but its cloying sweetness made her nauseous. She needed her mother to help her through the weeks until Jerry could get there, but she was gone, hiding somewhere in the body of a woman who was a stranger to her.

Dr. Winchester arrived and introduced himself. "How is my mother?" Casey demanded.

"Well, Dr. Reinhardt and I have run some tests. We're fairly certain there is no physical damage to the brain. With your permission, we'd like to proceed with a complete psychiatric evaluation."

"Of course, do whatever has to be done. I want you to find out why she just lies there like a doll."

"Miss Gable, as I understand it, your mother never mentioned suicide and had manifested few outward signs of depression before she tried to kill herself. If that is true, I suspect she might have been facing some sort of crisis that she wanted kept secret and that she couldn't resolve. Now, having failed at suicide, she is experiencing a major depressive episode with some psychotic features. She's lost contact with the world that distressed her and has become mute. We'll have to keep her on the intravenous solution until she consents to eat and drink.''

"Well, if you're right, then if we find out whatever was bothering her and settle it, she might snap out of the state she's in. Correct?''

"Well, it's not as simple as all that, but it could happen.''

"Now all I have to do is find out . . . and I don't know where to begin,'' she lamented.

"Do the best you can. In the meantime, I've started her on an antidepressant drug, imipramine, and we may get results from that.''

When he had gone, Casey went to the restroom and was disturbed to see more of the brownish spots on her underpants. She decided to wait one more day before calling the doctor.

She went into her mother's room and found her propped up in the bed with her head turned to the window. She was passive and lifeless and so unlike the energetic mother she had known all her life. Was it possible that Grace had actually succeeded in killing herself, that this lifeless form no longer contained the vibrant spirit of her mother?

Casey stayed with her mother for two hours, brushing her hair, holding her hand, and talking to her. Grace failed to make any response.

When Casey left the hospital, she went directly home. She had been having a few abdominal cramps and decided she'd better spend the rest of the day lying down. That evening after dinner, she questioned Rudolfo about Grace's recent activities and contacts, but he offered no information at all. He was so totally unhelpful that she suspected he was suppressing something. "Hasn't anything happened lately that was different or strange? You're the one person who knows exactly where she goes and who she sees.'' Rudolfo remembered well the visits from Finn, but he felt it might cause Grace more trouble if anyone knew about them. He shook his head.

Casey got into bed and called Peach to tell her about Dr. Winchester and was surprised at her reaction. ''I think this is all really a little farfetched, don't you? It seems just too theatrical,'' was Peach's response.

''On the contrary, I think it's quite valid. She was running away from something, I just know it. Peach, you've known her longer than anyone. Surely there's something in her background that might give us a clue.''

''I'm awfully busy right now, Casey, and I'm afraid I just can't be much help to you.'' The conversation ended with Casey more suspicious than ever that her mother's friends were building a wall of silence around her. Her suspicions would have been doubly confirmed had she known how unsettling the call had been for Peach, who had been sworn to secrecy by Grace. If her friend wanted to take her secrets and lies to the grave, she would not betray her.

A call to Blanche in Chicago was equally unproductive, and Casey gave up for the evening. After a restless night, she arose early and called Jim. She was having more frequent cramping, and she was worried. She told him about Dr. Winchester's theory, and Jim agreed to look over Dr. Allison's old files to see if there was anything there that could shed light on the situation. He was concerned about her bleeding and cramping and told her to stay in bed.

Later in the morning the spotting stopped, and Casey decided to go to the shop and talk to Eve. When she arrived, she was greeted warmly, and everyone was eager to hear about Grace. Eve gave her a hug, and they retreated to the privacy of Grace's plush office.

''Eve, I can't thank you enough for taking charge like you have. The place is really humming.''

''Yeah, it's busy . . . too busy. The place is full of people who sense there's a juicy bit of scandal to sniff out.'' Her voice was bitter.

"Eve, I think you should be getting more money . . ."

"Don't worry about that, honey. When Grace gets back, I'll get even. How's she really doing?"

Casey filled her in on the doctor's theory and asked her help, but Eve shook her head. "There's nothing I can tell you. I just worked for her. She's been kind, generous, and forgiving. I never pried into her private life, and she stayed out of mine. Well, I've got to get back to work."

"Eve, please . . . don't shut the door on me. Help me find out what's wrong so we can bring her back."

"Maybe she doesn't want to come back," Eve replied.

"But I need her!" Casey said.

"Look, you're a big girl now. It's time you stood on your own two feet. Let her be. If she wants to come back, she will."

Casey sat in the office and felt cold and abandoned. There was a conspiracy of silence around her mother. All her life, Casey had been treated like a princess, and now she suspected it was all unreal. The life she was living seemed to have no relationship with her childhood. If she didn't know who her mother was, how could she be certain about herself?

_37_

You're a Fool

MAGGIE arrived at Belinda's, and they toured the house together picking out items of furniture and accessories to move to the beach house. When they were finished, Belinda invited Maggie to join her in the library for a glass of champagne.

"What a nice surprise. Are we toasting anything special?" Maggie asked as the butler left the room. Belinda raised her glass. "We are drinking a toast to me for having the good sense and intelligence and courage to hire an unknown decorator, who performs admirably and efficiently under stress and trying conditions." She smiled impishly.

Belinda was a master at backhanded compliments, Maggie thought. She was certainly not one for lavish praise.

"I'll drink to that . . . to you and Peach Malone for giving me the chance to show what I can do." Maggie couldn't resist bringing Peach's name in. In the past weeks, Belinda seemed to forget that Peach had actually been Maggie's discoverer and benefactor, preferring instead to see herself in that role.

"Belinda, I should tell you that this job has not been easy. My husband has been putting even more pressure on me than you have."

"I suspected all along that you were not getting a lot of encouragement at home," Belinda remarked.

"Mmmm, did it show? I thought I was concealing it rather well."

Belinda shook her head. "You misunderstand me. Your actions did not give you away. I just knew there would be trouble eventually. Men don't like their women to be wrapped up in anything that does not pertain to them, and I could see that this endeavor was consuming all your vitality. I hope that when it's over, you will go back to your first priority, your husband.''

"Oh, really?" Maggie retorted, annoyed with Belinda's smugness. "What would you have said if Kirk had ordered me to quit right in the middle of this job?"

Belinda bridled. "Well, fortunately he didn't."

"He didn't? How do you know that?"

"Because you're here, that's why."

Maggie turned to look out the window as she replied, "Well, you're wrong this time, Belinda. He did deliver such an ultimatum."

"You're a fool, Maggie Hammond. No job is worth risking a husband . . . even this one."

Maggie was discomfited. The words and tone of Belinda's voice contrasted sharply with the joviality that had prevailed just minutes before. "I still have my marriage, Belinda. And my career. I intend to find some way to reconcile them. I also have the right to spend my time pursuing those things that I find worthwhile and rewarding."

Belinda raised an eyebrow and observed her with sardonic amusement. "What planet are you living on, Maggie? Certainly not this one. Things just don't work that way. If our society were to allow women to be like men, everything would fall apart. Our entire social structure would collapse. Women were meant to be loved and cherished, and in turn, well, if we have to give up some things, it's a minor sacrifice. Don't think you can beat the system, my child. You may think you can win, but in the end, you'll lose everything. Sooner or later your husband will look elsewhere for the comfort you no longer provide him."

Maggie finished her champagne in silence and set the glass down. Her mood, which had been bright, had now gone dark and sour. She really detested this self-centered witch. "I hope you're wrong, Belinda. Shall we have lunch? I've got to get back to work."

Realizing she had gone too far, Belinda tried to appease

her. "I could be wrong, of course. After all, I've never met your husband. What do I know about your relationship with him? Come, I've had a special lunch prepared for us. I hope you can spare a few extra calories."

Over lunch they had an animated discussion about antiques and idealism in decorating, and Maggie set forth her views more passionately than usual.

"You amaze me, Maggie, you really do. You not only have the soul of an artist, but the naïve intolerance of one," Belinda commented.

"Intolerance?" Maggie felt insulted. "What do you mean?"

"You're approaching your work as an art, not as a business. I cannot believe you would actually refuse a commission because you didn't agree with the client's taste if you needed the money. Come back to me in five years when you have the overhead of an office to maintain as well as a payroll, and then you tell me how many jobs you turn down for artistic reasons. Unless, of course, your husband is still providing you with the security and freedom you have now."

In spite of herself, Maggie had to laugh. "Oh, Belinda, you do have a one-track mind. You never give up."

Before Maggie left, she called Dee for messages and learned that several women had responded to the advertisement, but only one was a possibility. Dee continued, "Your husband said to tell you he won't be home for dinner, and Mrs. Austin called while he was here, and he took the call."

"Is everything all right with her?" Maggie asked, and she was puzzled by the manner in which Dee said, "I guess you could say it was."

"What do you mean?" Maggie demanded.

"Well, Mr. H. told Mrs. Austin he'd be at her house tonight at seven for dinner."

"Don't worry about that, Dee. I'm delighted that Kirk is being kind enough to spend time with her. Really, it's okay." Maggie was glad he was being nice to Laura, and she was glad she wouldn't have to rush home through the heavy traffic for dinner.

At four-thirty, she left the Design Center and had a leisurely and filling tea at Trumps. As she drove along the freeway still busy with holiday shoppers, she felt a sense of tranquillity. The Malibu house would soon be finished, and if only Connor would choose to live there, she would have accomplished her mission.

By nine that evening, she had showered and donned her loveliest nightgown and peignoir. She poured herself a glass of wine and built a fire in the fireplace. She turned on the television to keep her company as she went over the invoices and ledger sheets Dee had meticulously prepared. She was pleased to learn from Dee's messages that she had interviewed a promising candidate for the job as her assistant. Perhaps if she organized her work in a more businesslike way, Kirk might agree to her continuing. After all, the money was outstanding, and they both loved to spend it. She promised herself she would be more warm and loving and convince him that working made her a happier, more complete person. She would make love to him tonight and let him know she cherished him and held no grudges.

Maggie did not see the eleven o'clock news or Johnny Carson. Curled up on the couch under the colorful old afghan her mother had crocheted, she went to sleep so soundly that she did not hear Kirk's arrival at two in the morning. Quietly, he turned off the TV and the lights and left her on the couch, sleeping alone.

_38_

To Old Friends

LAURA looked at the clock in the kitchen as she finished putting her breakfast dishes in the dishwasher. Although she lived alone in the house, she continued to observe the rituals of good housekeeping that kept everything in perfect order, even as she had tried to do during the first terrible weeks of her ordeal when she was trying to deal with Jim's infidelity by taking too many pills. When everything was tidy, she sat down at her desk to call Dr. Sabatini. "Good morning, Laura," Christine answered. "How are you today?"

"I have some exciting news for you. I went shopping yesterday. All by myself. I drove to the new mall and had tea with a lovely woman I met there, and then I drove myself home. Can you believe it?"

"Tell me about it," Christine responded.

When she had finished giving her the details, Laura announced triumphantly, "I'm going to do it again today, only this time I intend to actually do some shopping. Could you go with me?"

They agreed to meet in the tearoom at Bullock's at noon, and Laura went upstairs to bathe and dress. Carefully, she laid out the Anne Klein gray wool pants and cashmere sweater and tried to concentrate on what she was doing and not on the hours ahead. Although she'd had some success the day before, she knew that it probably wouldn't be much easier the second time. The only difference would be that now she knew she could do it.

When she was ready, she hurried down the stairs and into the garage. Moving as fast as she could, she tried to outrace the accelerated beating of her heart and the rapid intake of air into her lungs. Proceeding at a feverish pace, she focused her attention on the mechanics of departure, and she rushed ahead of the fears that threatened to block her path at every step.

Almost before the garage door opener had finished its leisurely lifting of the barricade between her and the outside world, she was in the car with the engine running. She fastened her seat belt, and put the Seville in reverse. She was on her way.

The drive was only a little less nerve-racking than it had been the day before, but this time, when she parked the car, she did not hesitate. She got out immediately and strode toward the stores, forcing her legs to move her forward, trying to turn the jelly in them to starch.

Although she walked from department to department and tried to lose her anxiety in the wonder of the beautiful merchandise, her palms remained icy wet and her heartbeat thundered in her chest. At eleven-fifteen, without having made a single purchase, nor even coming close, she decided she had to sit down. She would go to the tearoom early and secure a table before the crowds of Christmas shoppers filled the place.

Laura was seated at a table where she could see the entrance, and she sat down in relief. She closed her eyes and willed her heart to calm down, to stop frightening her and agitating her so. Suddenly, a hand was placed on her shoulder, and she heard Christine's voice say, "Are you okay, Laura?"

"Dr. Sabatini . . . you're early!"

The psychologist sat down and smiled warmly. "I began to worry about forcing you to stay in the store too long, but you did it. Really, you should be very pleased with yourself. I've never had a client exhibit more determination and self-control."

Laura preened at the compliment, and they ordered lunch. Christine reminded her that she was supposed to call her by her first name, and it was suggested that she seriously consider joining a weekly therapy group. Laura agreed to consider it.

As they were leaving, Laura said, "Thank you so much, Dr. . . . Chris. I can make it to the car by myself. I'm pretty much at ease now, although I'm tired. I feel like going home and taking a nap."

"Good idea. Your metabolism probably thinks you've been in the Boston marathon. Call me in the morning, and we'll talk about your next excursion."

When she got home and stretched out on the bed to rest, she found she could not relax. She was stimulated by her morning's adventure and wanted to tell someone about it. She called Peach, but she wasn't at home. Maggie wasn't at home, but Kirk was. "Hi, Laura . . . how are you getting along?"

"Wonderful, Kirk. I called Maggie to share a minor triumph with her."

"She's out as usual. Will I do?"

Laura ignored the rancor in his reference to his wife and plunged in with the details. It was a friendly conversation that flowed effortlessly between two people who had been friends for years and had respect and affection for each other.

"Laura, this calls for a celebration. Suppose I drive up there this evening and take you out to dinner. There's a great little restaurant on Ventura that's not far from your house."

"Oh, thanks, but two outings in one day might be a bit much. Why don't you bring Maggie up here to the house for dinner tonight? I'd love to have someone to cook for." She hesitated. "Or maybe that's too far a drive . . ."

"Laura, my dear lady, I would drive to Alaska for one of your home-cooked meals, but I'm afraid Maggie is too busy. Besides, I'm not even sure where she is or when she'll be home. Would it be all right if I came alone if I can't locate her? She never cooks anymore, and I'm wasting away to a mere shadow of my former self."

"Well, we can't let that happen. Is eight a good time? Traffic should have eased a bit by then."

"Eight, it is. Can I bring something . . . some wine maybe?"

"If you like."

"Good, I'll bring something special to celebrate."

Laura jumped out of bed and rushed downstairs to the freezer. She tried to remember what Kirk liked . . . lasagne, of course. She recalled how he was always needling Maggie because she couldn't make it like her Italian mother, and Laura, whose family was Scotch, cooked it to perfection.

She had ground beef in the freezer, but no ricotta or mozzarella cheese. She called the delicatessen that had a delivery service, but they had no ricotta. She'd just have to think of something else.

Nonsense. She was a free woman now, no longer a caged animal. She ran up the stairs, put on a velour warmup suit and tennis shoes, grabbed her purse and was out the door. It was a short drive to the supermarket, and she was back home with the cheese, fresh lettuce and tomatoes, and warm, crusty bread in less than half an hour. Her heart was racing, and her hands were shaking, but she had done it. This time had been the easiest of all. That was the secret . . . short fast outings. She was free!

By the time Kirk arrived, the aroma of baking lasagne mingled with the fragrance of freshly made carrot cake and the fire in the fireplace. Laura was dressed in a shimmering gold and white hostess skirt by Bill Blass with a gossamer gold silk tailored shirt, another of Jim's extravagant attempts to make her into a Hollywood wife. She had quickly shampooed her short hair and set it with hot rollers so that soft curls framed her carefully made up face. She looked happier and prettier than he had ever remembered seeing her.

"Kirk, it's so nice of you to come. Did you ever get in touch with Maggie?"

Kirk kissed her lightly on the cheek, and he noticed the scent of her perfume. "No, I tried everywhere," he lied, "but I'm sure she's happy and busy with her work and was probably delighted when she found out that I was being well taken care of. Mmm, you smell good."

"I know you, Kirk. You're talking perfume and smelling lasagne. My goodness, what a big bottle of champagne."

"It's a magnum. I bought it when I thought Maggie might be with us, but since we're alone, I suppose we'll just have to make the sacrifice, and drink it all by ourselves."

They went into the living room where the fire was going and where Laura had placed a terrine of her homemade liver pâté and crackers. Kirk popped the cork and filled the crystal glasses.

"Kirk, that's Dom Ruinart champagne . . . you shouldn't have spent so much money."

"Why not? I have a wealthy wife, and this is a very special occasion. Here's to one of the world's great ladies . . . and to her new life."

They clinked glasses as Laura responded glowingly, "And to old friends . . . the very best kind."

The evening passed leisurely. Kirk stuffed himself, and Laura enjoyed each bite he took even more than he did. As she sipped on the champagne, she watched him through the light of the candles, and her heart ached for the loss she felt. This was the way love and marriage was supposed to be, but she had lost it all.

Life was so unfair. All she had ever really wanted was to be a housewife and to have a happy, comfortable home and a loving husband. She was not like all those women who needed jobs and careers for fulfillment. She liked keeping house, but that wasn't a sentiment she ever expressed openly. Nowadays, people would think she was crazy if she admitted that cooking and cleaning made her happy.

When dinner was over, they carried their coffee and champagne glasses with them back to the living room where the fire had burned down to glowing embers, and there were no more logs in the basket. "Is there more wood outside?" Kirk asked.

"Yes, but it's way out in the back, and it's too dark and damp to go out there now. Besides, you might fall off the hillside." She giggled.

"No way, ma'am. We tough menfolk always bring in the firewood . . . got a flashlight?"

Laura laughed and brought a large, heavy flashlight to him.

"I've got lots of these . . . one in almost every room. You have no idea how scary it is alone in this big house at night."

Kirk was touched with sympathy for her. "You're very lonely, aren't you, Laura?"

They looked into each other's eyes, their souls touching in a brief moment of understanding. Laura looked down, embarrassed and naked in her vulnerability. "I'm learning to live with it, Kirk. I have no choice." Tears glistened in her eyes, and Kirk had an almost irresistible urge to take her in his arms and comfort her. Instead, he turned away. "Now point me in the direction of the woodpile, ma'am."

When the log basket was filled and the fire roaring again, they sat down on the floor near the hearth. "Laura, why don't you sell this big monster of a house and move back to Long Beach where your real friends are? I could find you a lovely and modern little condo on the water where you'd have a beautiful view and a lot of security."

"It's a perfectly sensible idea, but I haven't been acting very sensibly lately. This house, which I never liked and never wanted, became my refuge . . . as well as my prison. I'm not sure I'm ready to leave it yet. You see, it was here that I lost my life, and I sense that I have to stay here till I find it again."

"Laura, you don't expect Jim to come back to you here, do you?"

"It's quite possible," she replied, "that he'll get tired of the glitter and the tinsel, and you know, he loves this house."

Kirk set his glass down and picked up her hand and held it in both of his own. "Laura, look at me. I've got something to tell you. Maybe I shouldn't . . . but I can't stand to see you hurt anymore." There was a long silence, and he concentrated on her slim, white fingers in order to avoid her eyes as he spoke. "Jim's going to marry Ghilly Jordan."

The short gasp and slight tremble in her hands told him his arrow had hit its target, but he did not stop, for he knew that if she was ever to get on with her life, she would have to let go of her hope that Jim would someday come back to her. "I had lunch with him a week or so ago, and he told me. He says he's very happy."

Laura jerked her hand away from him. "Why are you telling me this . . . to make me miserable? Tonight was a celebration, and now you've spoiled it." She got up and began to gather the cups and glasses.

Kirk got to his feet, too, and took them out of her hands. "Laura, there's more. Look at me, don't turn away." He held her by the forearms and turned her toward him. Her face had gone white with anger, and she struggled to get away, but he would not release his hold.

"I don't want to hear anymore! Go home! Let me alone!" she exclaimed with hostility.

"Ghilly's pregnant," Kirk said, and her body and soul were impaled on his words. She could feel her life's blood seeping from the wound. She stopped struggling and wavered. Kirk quickly put his arms around her to support her. "Tell me . . . everything . . . please," she said weakly.

Gently he led her to the couch, and they sat down together. "Jim didn't want me to tell you just yet. He was afraid it would push you into a deeper depression if you knew. Your illness has weighed heavily on his conscience. He knows how much he's hurt you."

"But he did it anyway, didn't he," she said with bitterness.

"Yes, he did, but Laura, when a man reaches the age of forty, he comes to grips with his own mortality. He figures that he's got to grab for every single bit of what's left of his dreams, or there may not be enough time . . . and to hell with everybody."

"What about the people whose lives he ruins?" she asked.

"You've got to make your own life . . . find your own happiness. Don't expect someone to give it to you."

"When . . . are they getting . . . married?"

"As soon as the divorce is final. Ghilly is ecstatic about the baby, he says. *People* magazine is doing a spread on her when the announcement is made. They're looking at a house in Trousdale to buy. That's why he wanted to talk to me. He thought I might help him with the negotiations."

Laura's tears came as she began to mourn for her dead hopes. Kirk held her until she was exhausted and her eyes were red and swollen and her nose tightly clogged. Briefly, he left her to go into the kitchen and find Dr. Sabatini's number. Although it was almost midnight, she answered immediately.

"Dr. Sabatini, this is Kirk Hammond, a friend of Laura Austin's. She's just had some distressing news, and she's pretty hysterical. She needs your help.".

"Stay with her until I get there," she responded, and Kirk assured her that he would. Then he returned to Laura with a cool cloth to wipe her face. He was solicitous and tender, and she clung to him.

"I've called Dr. Sabatini, and she'll be here soon," he whispered reassuringly, but she did not seem to hear. "Don't leave me, Kirk. Please don't leave me alone," she begged.

"I'll stay as long as you need me," he replied.

_39_

For Any Reason

IT WAS two o'clock in the afternoon, and Peach was angry. Horace had not delivered the trusts to her the day before as she had told him to, and now he had not returned the call she had placed to him three hours ago. She had slept poorly, and she was anxious to find out exactly where she stood. Her telephone conversation with Anne the night before had reinforced her determination to wrest control of her business affairs and her money. Her daughter had been just as indignant as she was and had encouraged her to fight back.

She paced back and forth listening for the doorman's signal to her that there was a delivery. Finally, the telephone rang, and she snatched up the receiver. Could Horace have finally found time in his busy schedule to call her back? She must remember to take a good look at the balance sheets and find out just how much he was paying himself.

The voice she heard momentarily crowded finances out of her head. "Jason, where are you?" she gasped happily.

"In Miami, where else? Didn't you get a copy of my itinerary from the studio? I told Burt to have it sent."

"No, I didn't, but that's not surprising. I'm sure he thinks I might follow you around like a middle-aged groupie and spoil your sexy image."

"Hey, cut that out. I had a long talk with him. I told him he'd better make friends with you again, or I wouldn't do the sequel. I miss you."

"I miss you too, Jason. Sometimes I have this wild urge to charter a plane and fly to wherever you are."

"Why don't you?"

"You know why. We've got to live separate lives. There's no other way for us . . . in this life anyway."

"Peach, my love, my life is richer and fuller when you're with me."

"How's the tour?" Peach wanted to lighten the conversation.

"Dumb, boring. This movie star business is a bunch of dreck."

She tried to be reassuring. "The public relations bit will be all over soon, and you can go back to acting. I read in *Variety* that you'd been offered the lead in Alan Pakula's new film. True?"

"How would I know? That high-powered agent I signed with is so busy he never has time to call me. If it's true, he'd better not lose the deal for me by trying to get too much money."

"Don't be so cantankerous . . . or so eager. You're the hottest actor around now. I'm sure everybody wants you."

"Yeah, I guess so, but I'd like to work with Pakula. Maybe I ought to give that wretch of an agent another call."

"When does the *Sandman* sequel go into production?"

"Who knows? Burt hasn't even hired a writer to do the script yet. But what about you? Christmas at your house all set?"

"Definitely. I've been busy. Grace is not doing well. I stop to see her every day. By the way, I'm having some problems buying our boat." Peach proceeded to tell him the story of her discord with Horace and Dom, and Jason also encouraged her to fight back. After more than half an hour, the conversation came to a close. "I've gotta go, lovely lady. They're waiting in the limo downstairs to take me to another local talk show. Think about me sometimes, will you?"

"All the time, Jason. I promise." It was a very small lie. Peach walked to the window to look down at the city and think. For the first time since she became a widow, she felt that she had some direction in her life. She had two supportive and intelligent children who would stand with her in the battle. It was a myth that children who were indulged with material possessions became spoiled and greedy. Anne and Steve had grown up with all their values in the right order. They could have anything they wanted, but they had found happiness in working and creating. With Anne it was her art and her silver, and with Steve it was the wine he made from the grapes he grew.

It was Drake who had been their guide all along. He had never been too busy for them or their questions, and he had tried to impart to them all the knowledge of his own experience. He loved his children above all else.

Something had to be wrong. Never, never would Drake have given away control of his fortune. He trusted his son and daughter, for they were of his own blood. Maybe he hadn't been too sure of his wife's abilities, but he knew that his real wealth was to be found in his family and not in his millions of dollars.

Peach dialed Horace's number again. It was almost three, and her patience was coming to an end. Horace's secretary informed her that he was in conference and couldn't be disturbed and assured Peach that he had been given her message.

"Please interrupt him," Peach demanded. "It is important that I speak to him now, this minute!" Her voice was steely and terse. If this woman did not put him on the line immediately, she would storm his office in person.

"I'm sorry, Mrs. Malone. He left strict orders not to be—"

Exasperated, Peach exploded. "Don't give me any more of that nonsense. You put him on the telephone right now, or I'll get myself another lawyer!" Peach couldn't believe the voice she was hearing was her own. It sounded so deliciously forthright and commanding. She was even more gratified when she heard Horace's voice come on the line several seconds later. Whoever said honey was more effective than vinegar had lied.

"Peach, my dear, what's all this ruckus about? You've frightened the wits out of my secretary."

She tried to keep her voice at the level she found to be effective and forceful. "Horace, why in the hell haven't you sent those trusts over here as I asked you to yesterday?"

"Now calm yourself. I'll bring them over myself this evening. Perhaps we can have dinner together, and I'll explain everything—"

She cut him off, even angrier, and insulted by his patronizing manner. "I have another date this evening, Horace, and besides, I can read English . . . they are in English, aren't they? Send them over within the hour, or I'll come get them myself."

She slammed the phone onto its cradle and threw herself into a chair. There had to be something Horace did not want her to know. What a blithering idiot she had been not to insist on reading everything for herself long before now. She vowed it would never happen again. Never would she leave her affairs in the hands of others. Money and economics might not now be her area of expertise, but she could jolly well learn.

At five minutes to four she rang for Miles. "Miles, call for the car to pick me up in five minutes. I have a little errand to run."

She went into her dressing room and looked at herself in the mirror. She was dressed in aubergine wool slacks and a print silk blouse. Good enough for a confrontation, she decided. She ran a brush through her hair, put on some lipstick, and took a tailored gray jacket out of the closet. She looked into the reflection of her own eyes and hissed between clenched teeth, "Get 'em!" Then she strode out of her room toward the front door where Miles was waiting.

"Is everything all right, ma'am?"

"It will be, Miles. If we're not back in an hour, send the police to Mr. Beller's office. There might be violence."

Perplexed, Sarah opened the door, and Peach sailed out and into the open elevator. As she descended, she realized how much she was enjoying her own anger. For the first time in her life, she was allowing herself to experience full, unbridled, justified anger, and it was terrific. She was, in fact, looking forward to the confrontation. How dare that miserable man defy her? She exited the elevator in the lobby and hurried out to the car only to see Horace's car drive up. Hmmph. She was almost disappointed that she had won before the battle had properly begun.

"Horace, how come you came yourself? I thought you were in conference and too busy even to talk on the phone?"

"Peach, my dear, I got worried about you. You sounded overwrought. I came right away to make sure you were all right."

"I'm fine, Horace. And I'm not overwrought, as you put it. I'm just pissed off. Do you have those papers I asked for?"

"Calm down now. You look like you might have a stroke. Yes, I brought them. Now let's go back upstairs and not have a scene in front of the whole world." He took her arm to lead her back into the lobby, but she shrugged him off. "I don't believe you've been invited upstairs, Horace. Just give me the papers and go. I'll read them myself, and if I can't understand something, you can rest assured that I'll call you."

Silently, he handed her his leather briefcase. "Are all the trusts here?" she asked.

"Yes," he responded, his voice cold with fury, not trusting himself to say anything more.

"Good. Now just tell that secretary of yours to put my calls through immediately from now on. You may put the car away, thank you," she said to the driver.

Peach whirled around and walked back into the lobby. When she was upstairs again, she had some difficulty settling down to examine the trusts. She was exhilarated and triumphant. No wonder men were aggressive and forceful. It was fun, damn it.

Page by page, she read her way through the trusts, trying to make sense of the legalistic jargon, frequently exasperated at the verbiage that was designed to obfuscate rather than enlighten. She carried the papers to the dinner table with her as phrase by phrase she attempted to translate the documents into simple English. It was not until late that evening that she found what she was searching for, the key to her control, the lifeline that Drake had thrown to her. It was there, thank God, it was there!

She went to the telephone. She needed an impartial assessment to be sure she was right. She dialed Steve. He would probably be asleep, for he was an early riser, but this was his life too that she was trying to reclaim. The telephone rang several times, and then the drowsy voice of her beloved child answered. "Steve, darling, I'm so sorry to awaken you, but I need your help."

Instantly, he was alert. "Sure, Mom. What's up?"

"Now listen to this and tell me what you think it means." She read the paragraph to him. When she finished, he spoke without hesitation. "I think it means that as the surviving spouse you have the right to replace either or both of the other trustees at any time or for any reason, but read it again. It sounds too good to be true." Peach did so, and they both agreed that the trust gave the surviving spouse the power to do just that.

"Eureka! Steve, do you know what that means?"

"Sure I do. Dad never intended to have anybody in control except you, or in case of your death, Anne and me when we pass the age of thirty, right?"

"Right. Oh, God, you don't know how important it is to know that he trusted my judgment after all. He didn't think I was helpless and needed a pair of keepers."

"I feel exactly the same way. I've been having a lot of doubts. He'd always treated me with so much respect, not the way a lot of other fathers treat their kids. I couldn't believe he didn't mean it. What'll you do now? Get a new lawyer or a new banker?"

"Neither. I feel certain that Dom and Horace will toe the line now. They'd damn well better, or I'll fire them."

"Get 'em, tiger." Steve laughed.

"Good night, honey. Tell your lovely wife that I'm looking forward to that grandchild. How is she feeling?"

"Fat and clumsy. She's anxious to get it over with."

"I'll be there when you need me."

"Righto. I love you, Mom."

"I love you, too, Steve."

Peach went to bed that night, but it was difficult to go to sleep. She was stimulated and exultant, and for the first time in her life, she really felt like one of the world's richest women. Power, how sweet it was.

_40_

A Few Drops
of Blood

CASEY pushed Grace's wheelchair into the sunroom. Her mother had been taking the antidepressant drug for over a week now, and the improvement was noticeable. Although she did not speak, she was more responsive, and she would now allow herself to be fed. She would not yet, however, feed herself, and for that reason, Casey spent most of each day with her so that she could be sure she got enough nourishment to keep her off the intravenous solution.

The days stretched long in the hospital room. Casey talked to her mother a lot, hoping that somewhere in the abundance of her rambling reminiscences, she would touch a nerve that would release Grace from her prison of silence. She tried to be cheerful and encouraging at all times, but it was increasingly difficult and she was still bleeding slightly. Although the doctor had ordered her to bed for complete rest, Casey ignored his warning. She would not desert her mother now. She felt that she was the one who could be the most help in Grace's recovery.

It was almost time for lunch when Eve arrived, and Casey welcomed her enthusiastically. The monotony of her daily routine was depressing, and she was grateful for even the smallest diversion. "Eve, how great to see you," she said in greeting.

"Hi, how's the patient doing today?"

"Ask her yourself. I'm sure she hears you," Casey advised. Eve leaned down and kissed Grace's pale cheek. "Hi, boss, when're you going to get out of that chair and come back to work? We miss you."

Grace did not answer, but her eyes followed Eve closely, and she seemed to absorb every word that she said. Encouraged by Grace's attention, Eve continued to talk, relating all the gossip she knew, which was considerable, and giving a complete rundown on the activities at the shop, carefully deleting all the troublesome events. When she finally ran out of stories to tell, she turned to Casey and said softly, "You look godawful. Do you spend every waking minute here?"

Casey motioned her to step away so they could chat out of her mother's hearing. "I'm just tired, that's all. It's an ordeal spending every day here."

"Do you have to do that?"

"Well, she has to be fed. She won't eat unless someone puts a forkful into her mouth."

"Isn't that what the nurses are supposed to do?"

Casey shook her head. "She eats too slowly. And besides, I want to do it. It makes me feel useful. How's the shop, really?"

"It's that time of year, you know, and I'm starting to get the hang of running the place. Or maybe it's just that they're getting used to me as the manager. Anyway, the answer is fine . . . busy. Thanks for arranging for me to write checks on the account."

"I'd have had to fold the place if you hadn't been there to take over. Would you mind pushing her wheelchair back to her room? It's almost lunch, and I need to stop in the restroom here."

"Sure, say, are you all right?"

"I'll be okay. I've got a stomachache, that's all." She hurried away and started to run. She needed to get to a toilet quickly. Suddenly, she felt a gush of warmth between her thighs. She looked down at her brown wool slacks and saw a dark spot at her crotch that was spreading rapidly down her legs, and the pain in her abdomen became severe. The thought that she might be losing the baby flashed into her mind and panicked her.

She saw a nurse's aide and called out, "Hurry, help me . . . please. Get a doctor. . . . I'm bleeding!" She gasped, trying to keep her voice down so she wouldn't be overheard in the sunroom. The aide took her arm and led her into a room with a vacant bed and ordered Casey to lie down immediately while she summoned help.

Within minutes, a nurse and a resident physician were in the room, and Casey found herself being undressed. She was then rolled onto a gurney and rapidly wheeled into a cold, white-tiled room. Someone inserted a needle in her arm and hooked her up to an IV bottle. She was only vaguely aware of the activity because of the intense pain that ebbed and flowed throughout her body.

Her ordeal went on for more than an hour, but she was unaware of the passage of time until the last wrenching pain of expulsion, when she knew it was all over. She did not need to hear the words spoken to confirm her loss, and she tried to close them out as the young doctor leaned over her. "I'm so sorry, but we just couldn't stop it. I'm afraid you've miscarried. I'm going to give you something to relax you now. Can you give me the name of your doctor so we can call him?"

"Call Dr. Austin, please. Ask him to come as soon as he can," she whispered. Her tears lasted only a short time before the medication took effect, and she slipped into a hazy suspension of reality and then she was asleep.

Eve waited a long time for Casey to return, and when she finally went to the nurse's desk, she was told that Casey had become ill and was in surgery. Shocked, she hurried to the telephone to call Peach Malone. Someone close to the family should be there.

Five minutes after receiving the call, Peach was in her car on the way to the hospital. She arrived shortly after Dr. Austin. "Jim, thank God, you're here. Has Casey lost her baby?" Eve joined them, and the resident gave them the details of Casey's spontaneous abortion.

"Does Grace know about this?" Peach asked.

"I was with them both just before it happened. Casey left to

311

go to the restroom and never returned,'' Eve replied. ''There's no way she could know.''

''Thank heavens! Jim, don't you think we'd better call Grace's psychiatrist?'' Peach asked.

''Definitely. I'll call him right after I check on Casey. She apparently lost a lot of blood. If possible, I'd like to avoid transfusing her. She doesn't need the risk of hepatitis if we can avoid it. You two stay away from Grace until Dr. Winchester gets here. You both look pretty grim. Wait downstairs in the coffee shop for me.''

Meekly, the two women did as they were told. Over coffee, Eve said, ''I'm feeling a little guilty right now. Casey tried to talk to me about Grace to find out why she attempted suicide, and I turned her off. I told her to mind her own business and stay out of her mother's life.''

''Don't feel bad, Eve. I did the same thing. I know more about her past life than anyone, and I was afraid of betraying her secrets.''

''You know,'' Eve continued, ''Grace started acting weird right after Casey came home pregnant.''

''How so?'' Peach asked.

''She was out of things. She didn't have her mind on business, and you know that's really odd. She's always been like a tiger in that shop, watching everybody, keeping things on track. Then, there was that trip to the convention. Very strange.''

''She never went to conventions, did she?''

''Hell no. She hated them almost as much as she hated cold weather.''

''Very interesting.'' Peach thought a moment and then concluded, ''It's got to involve Casey. Unless there's something I don't know, her daughter is the only person she has any emotional involvement with whatsoever.''

''I agree.''

''I'm going to mention it to her psychiatrist. Do you mind if I tell him that you concur?''

''No, as long as I don't have to talk to him. I hate shrinks.''

Jim arrived and told them that they'd managed to stop Casey's hemorrhaging and that she was finally resting quietly.

"Any idea what caused the miscarriage?" Eve asked.

"No, but it's not an uncommon occurrence. She'd been spotting for several days, and she ignored orders to rest. The nurses told me she'd been here all day every day with her mother."

"She was probably torn between her mother's needs and the baby's . . . and the baby lost," Peach remarked.

"Jesus, I hope nobody ever lays that kind of guilt trip on Grace," Eve said.

"That would be awful . . . especially since she was so unhappy about Casey being pregnant in the first place," Peach added.

Later, Peach went upstairs for a visit. She found Grace sitting peacefully in a chair looking out the window. Peach sat down beside her, took her hand, and held it in both her own. "Hello, Grace . . . remember me . . . your old friend Peach? Of course you do. We go back so many years together. Please try to come back to us. We need you terribly," she urged softly.

The two friends sat in comfortable silence for a long while and Peach thought back to the days when she often sat quietly beside Hazel who lived without sight the last years of her life. As she always had, Hazel accepted the fate her God had decreed for her, and she was a loving grandmother to Anne and Steve, whose faces she never saw. It was in quiet moments that Peach remembered her, and she still missed her mother's love. Would it always be like this with Drake too? Would there be moments of poignant sorrow and regret that time would never completely heal?

When darkness fell, and the lights were turned on, Peach got up to leave. She gave Grace's hand a final squeeze and smiled into her eyes as she spoke. "Goodnight. I'll be back tomorrow. You know I'm never very far away." Then she kissed her on the cheek and left, feeling comforted and unusually tranquil. For the first time since Grace had tried to kill herself, Peach felt that she was going to be all right. She was a survivor, she assured herself. "And so am I," Peach whispered.

_41_

Nobody Wants to Eat Off the Floor

SHIVERING with the cold, Maggie awakened, but it was several moments before she realized where she was. The early morning light was filtering through the shutters, and the smoky smell of the now-dead fire filled her nostrils. Suddenly she realized that Kirk had never come home. Her nerves sprang to attention, and fear hit her like a tornado. She leaped off the couch in the family room, and clutching the afghan around her shoulders, she hurried up the stairs.

The bedroom was dark, but she saw the outline of his form under the blanket, and she could hear him breathing. Relieved, she slipped off her peignoir and dropped it on the floor with the afghan. She lifted the blanket on her side of the bed and inserted herself between the cool sheets, moving slowly so as not to disturb him. Although she did not touch him, she was warmed and comforted by his nearness.

Kirk awakened at seven, just as Maggie was beginning to drift back to sleep. He moved, and she was alert. "Honey, are you awake?" she asked.

"Yes, but I've got to get going. Stay in bed. I'll have breakfast out," he replied.

"Are you sure?" The bed felt warm and comfortable, but she too had places to go and things to do. "I'm getting up anyway, and we can have a few minutes over coffee together," she insisted.

"No, I haven't got time, but I think you ought to go see Laura today if you can."

"How come?"

He sat down on the bed beside her, and his voice was morose. "I did a dumb thing last night. Really shitty. I don't know what got into me."

Maggie was alarmed. Such admissions of human frailty did not come easily to him. What had he done that was so vile? Had he seduced the poor woman? She was appalled at the meanness of her thought, and she tried to smother it in concern. "Tell me. What happened?"

"Well, she cooked a terrific dinner, lasagne, and we drank a lot of wine . . . and she looked so lovely . . . and so damned vulnerable . . ."

"And?" The concern in Maggie's voice was clipped by suspicion.

"I told her the truth about Jim and Ghilly." Self-reproach and remorse dripped from his words, but Maggie was confused. "I don't understand."

"Well, of course you wouldn't. You're never around here long enough to talk to me. I had lunch with Jim last week. He wanted some advice about a house he's thinking of buying. He told me that he and Ghilly planned to get married as soon as his divorce is final."

"And you told her?"

"Yes," and his voice was a hoarse whisper. "I also told her that Ghilly was pregnant."

"Oh, my God, Kirk, how could you?"

Kirk had suddenly had enough of remorse, and his defenses bristled at her accusatory tone. "Damn it, it's all true. She has to face the fact that he's never, never, coming back to her. She's a beautiful, wonderful lady, and she deserves better than that bastard."

"Was she all right when you left her?"

"Not really. I called that psychologist who's been helping her, and she came over right away. She told me to go on home and promised to stay with her. So . . . I think you'd better check on her." He got up from the bed and went into the bathroom and closed the door.

All the warmth and love she'd felt for him ebbed away

with the morning light. Poor Laura. She was just beginning to pull herself out of a hole, and he had managed to shove her back in. She followed him into the bathroom where he was shaving and raised her voice to carry over the vibrating buzz of his electric razor. "Kirk, turn that damn thing off for a minute!" Her voice was curt and demanding, and he complied more in surprise than obedience.

"Why did you do it? What's happened to you lately? I can understand your lashing out at me, but why Laura?"

His eyes did not flinch from hers as he clicked the razor back on and went on shaving. "She'll get over it. We all have to face up to changes in our life-style. Some things are pretty hard to swallow, especially when the one you've loved betrays you."

"Are you insinuating that I've betrayed you?" she asked.

"Dee told me she was interviewing assistants for you. I thought we had an agreement that the Cornwall job would be your last."

He'd done it to her again. Just once in her life she'd like to be the aggressor throughout an argument, but it never worked out that way. No matter how belligerently she began, he always managed to put her on the defensive, but not this time.

"We're discussing Laura now. Let's finish that, and then I'll be happy to discuss anything you have time for. When were you appointed to be the bearer of bad tidings? What has she ever done that you'd want to punish her too?"

"You're crazy, Maggie. I wasn't punishing her. I like her a lot. In fact, I wish to hell you were more like her. Jim Austin is a damned fool for giving her up."

"What is this need you have to return kindness with cruelty? First it was me, and now Laura. What do I have to look forward to . . . wife beating?" She had hit the mark, and the pain on his face showed it. He put down his razor and walked back to the bed, where he sat down with his face in his hands. She felt no victory in his defeat.

"Maggie, what do you want from me? I'm sorry about the

other night. I really didn't intend to abuse you, and I didn't mean any harm to Laura either.''

Maggie decided it was time to discuss the important subject. "Kirk, let me continue working. I love it. I'm good at it, and I'm making excellent money. I have twenty or so good years left, and I need to spend them doing something that makes me happy.'' She sat down close beside him and continued. ''I'm going to hire an assistant and open a little office. I'll move Dee there, and then both of us can come home at night and leave everything else behind. We can make it work, if you'll just stop fighting me. There'll be lots of money, and we can enjoy spending it together.''

After a long pause, he shook his head and said, ''It won't be the same, Maggie. I'll try, but I won't promise anything. I've been a good husband. I've given you a beautiful home and filled it with expensive things. I've worked hard, and I don't like coming home to an empty house or a tired wife.''

She was determined to make him understand her viewpoint. ''Kirk, a good marriage is two people loving and caring for each other. It's compromising and sharing good times and bad times. Marriage is not homemade bread and a spotless kitchen. Nobody wants to eat off the floor.''

''I wish your mother was still alive . . . maybe she could talk some sense into you.''

''Kirk, for twenty years you've had this marriage your way. Let's try it my way for a while.''

He got up and went into the bathroom. She was sure she had made no inroads in his thinking, but she had one last parting shot left. ''By the way, I've got another job . . . two, in fact. Peach is buying a yacht, and she's asked me to do the interior as well as a guest house on their place in Napa.'' He made no comment as he snapped his razor on again.

Before going to Malibu, Maggie went to Sherman Oaks. Laura opened the door shortly after Maggie rang the bell. She was still in her robe, and her eyes were swollen, but she looked freshly showered and her hair was brushed and shining. Tragic, but lovely, Maggie observed.

"Laura, are you okay? Kirk told me . . ." Her voice trailed away as Laura shook her head.

"Don't say it, please, Maggie. I'm all right. Chris just left. She spent the night here. I cried and talked all night, and I'm exhausted."

"Didn't she give you something to relax you?"

"I don't take pills anymore. Come in. If I fall asleep, just cover me up and tiptoe out."

They went into the living room as Laura continued to talk. "Kirk called and said you'd be here sometime today. He was so relieved to find out I was all right, he insisted on driving up again this evening so that I could try going out to a restaurant for dinner."

"Do you think you can?"

"I hope so. I plan to spend the day, when I'm not sleeping that is, imagining myself at a lovely table eating while someone else cooks and serves me. It's what they call imagery. I hope it works. I think it helped me with the shopping excursion. Are you going to join us?"

Maggie was amazed at her control. Wherever had Laura found the lode of strength that had eluded her just a few weeks before?

"No, I'm afraid I can't, but I'm delighted you're going to try."

Laura sighed. "Well, I've done it three times alone. Going with Kirk should be easy."

"I'm so sorry about last night. It was very cruel—" she began, but Laura interrupted her.

"No! He did me a great kindness, really. I've been clinging to this barn of a house in the blind hope that Jim would come back. Now I know he never will."

Maggie was relieved by Laura's attitude and somewhat ashamed for the things she'd said to Kirk. "I'm so happy with the way you're taking all this."

"Thanks to Dr. Sabatini. She's helped me understand myself. You know, I've actually always hated this house. Why then would I lock myself up in it? To punish myself for being a naughty girl and losing my husband? Maybe. More likely, I just hoped he'd return.''

"But now you know that he won't?'' Maggie asked, and Laura nodded her head and replied, "Kirk gets the credit for that. You're lucky to have such a kind and sensitive husband. He's going to find a condo for me in Long Beach. If Jim wants this house, he can have it. It's brought me nothing but misery.''

As Maggie drove toward Malibu, she felt a singular loneliness and depression, but she didn't know why. Late in the afternoon after she had finished her errands, she got into the car to go home. But why? There was no one there. It was too late to call anyone to have dinner in town, and the evening stretched bleakly before her. She felt adrift, and for the first time, a pang of jealousy for her husband's preoccupation with another woman insinuated itself in her consciousness. This is nonsense, she scolded herself. If Kirk was going to get involved with anyone, it certainly wouldn't be with one of her good friends. He was being kind and helpful, that was all. Nevertheless, she decided it would be prudent to join them. It was foolish to be alone when the three of them could have a lovely evening together. She'd find a telephone and call Laura to find out what restaurant they were going to.

The traffic was sluggish. Christmas shoppers were out in full force, and the cars inched slowly along the clogged streets. She pulled into a gas station only to find that the telephone had been vandalized and would not work.

She got back into the car to head for Nieman-Marcus where she could leave it with the parking attendant and run into the store. Even on normal evenings, Wilshire Boulevard was a parking lot, but with the stores open later for holiday shopping, it was impossible. It was almost six o'clock when the store came into view, and at six-fifteen she was still waiting in a line of cars for the attendant. She was frustrated. Beverly Hills was a zoo, and she was an animal locked in a cage. She couldn't get out to make one damn phone call. What fools we are, she philosophized; we think a car gives us freedom to get about, but it becomes a jail when there's no place to park it.

At six-thirty, she finally dialed Laura's number, but there was no answer. She was too late. She walked idly through the store feeling isolated and lonely. She tried to concentrate on shopping for Christmas presents, but she couldn't focus her attention outside her own inner desolation.

For twenty years, her life had centered on Kirk and Angie. They were a family, dependent on one another, caring for each other, and as the wife and mother, she had always been at the center of their union. Now here she was, spun off into space alone, not by the force of fate, but by her own choice, and for the first time, she felt the cold consequence of that decision.

_42_

Don't Be Greedy

"SARAH, I hope you and Miles can handle all the preparations for Christmas," Peach said.

Sarah smiled. "Of course, ma'am. We'll take care of everything for you. We've ordered a tree from the nursery, and Mr. Jef himself is coming over to trim it on the eighteenth. I told him traditional. Will that be all right?"

"That will be fine. Put it near the window in the living room. Also call Laykin's and give them this list. I've written down all the items with the names of the recipients so they can put appropriate cards with each one."

Peach was in a hurry. She did not want to be late for her appointment at the doctor's office, and then she had to talk to Casey and visit Grace. She dressed quickly, and, at ten, she arrived at a professional building in Westwood.

Although Grace had recommended him, Peach had called several of the cognoscenti in town to be sure that Dr. Pierre Senseney really was a wizard in plastic surgery. She had made her appointment under the name of Lisa Brown. She wasn't at all sure she would go through with the procedure, but if she did, she intended to keep it a secret from everyone, including and especially Jason.

The waiting room was small and luxuriously appointed. There were no magazines or reading materials nor were there any patients waiting. Peach filled out the usual form and was immediately ushered into an examining room. A woman in a white uniform interviewed her. "Good morning, Mrs. Brown.

322

Dr. Senseney will be in to see you in just a moment. Could you tell me what kind of correction you are considering?'' she asked politely.

"A face lift, I guess. I don't think I need a tummy tuck yet," Peach replied lightly, somewhat embarrassed.

"I see. Then there will be no need to disrobe. Just sit on the edge of the table here. The doctor will be right in.'' She left and almost instantly the doctor entered. He was solidly built, of medium height, and he had a deep olive skin and black hair that was graying at the temples. His large brown eyes were somber and penetrating, and a slight smile passed across his mouth so rapidly that it was almost imaginary.

"How do you do, Mrs. . . . . Brown? I am Dr. Senseney.'' His voice was very deep and possessed a trace of a French accent. Very sexy, she observed, no wonder business was booming here. "Now, what can I do for you?'' he asked.

Peach hesitated. She was not comfortable with what she was doing. "I'd like to look . . . younger. I thought maybe a face lift would help.''

Without speaking, he moved a light over her head and turned it on. He took her face in both of his hands and moved it from side to side, stretching her skin up and down with his fingers. He scrutinized her briefly, and then abruptly let her go, snapped off the light, and turned to leave. "Come into my office, please. We'll talk there.''

Peach got down off the table and followed him, wondering to herself what incantations were read over these mortals that made them gods when they received their medical degrees. She resented it, but like most patients, she did as she was told.

Inside his office, which was small but opulent, he motioned her to a chair opposite the desk. When they were both seated, he leaned back in his chair and spoke. "Now, tell me why you want to look younger. You are a beautiful woman just as you are.''

Peach bridled at the intimacy of the question. "Well, I believe that's my business, isn't it?''

Again, the almost smile flashed across his countenance.

"Not really. It's mine too. Before I cut into your skin, I must know just what your expectations are. Perhaps they are of a degree that I cannot possibly fulfill, and my time would be wasted, and you would be disappointed, after having expended a lot of money and experienced much pain." Suddenly he leaned toward her, and his voice took on an impassioned tone. "This face lift you women treat so lightly is not a little tuck here, a little snip there . . . it is risky, serious, and painful. It is extremely delicate surgery. Now, tell me, why do you want it?"

Peach was thoroughly intimidated. She had never had a doctor speak to her so patronizingly before. Then she remembered that he did not know who she was. He wouldn't talk to her that way if he knew she was Peach Malone. Her hidden identity, however, would permit her to be honest.

"I have a young lover. I don't want the world to think he has . . ." She hesitated, the words were so difficult to find, but the doctor completed the sentence for her. "An old sweetheart, correct?"

Peach looked down at her hands. He was humiliating her with the truth. "Mrs. . . . Brown," his voice gentled, "go home, please. Forget the surgery. You are still beautiful. Your skin is still firm, much too firm to tamper with now. The only surgery that could help perhaps might be a blepharectomy, which is the removal of a little loose skin from the eyelids, but I don't advise it for you. It's painful, a little risky, and it will take three to four weeks for the swelling to subside. It just wouldn't be worth it for such a tiny improvement."

Peach was astounded. "Dr. Senseney, you'll never make money turning prospective patients away like this."

"Mrs. Brown, I don't consider surgery a business, in spite of what you might think. There are many people who lead happier lives with my help. I correct nature's mistakes and the fruits of man's follies, but I only take on those cases where the outcome is worth the risk. And contrary to what you and your friends think, a lift does not make everyone look younger . . . more rested, perhaps, unless, of course, there is a serious and premature deterioration of the skin tone. Then, I can help. But you, no. Nature has been very kind to you. Don't be greedy. Now, look up.''

Peach was bewildered by his final order, and he repeated it. ''Look up at the ceiling and tell me what you see.''

Peach looked up and found herself looking into a mirror that covered the ceiling of the office. ''What do I see? Why, just me . . . and you . . .''

''How do you look to yourself? Normal? The same as always?'' he probed.

''Why, I suppose so . . . yes.''

''Then, that is about all a face lift will do for you. When you looked up, the force of gravity pulled your skin back as far as it could go. If a surgeon took more, your face would be a mask devoid of expression, a death's head, taut and stretched and unattractive. You don't want that, do you?''

Peach stood up to leave. ''You've made your point, Dr. Senseney. Thank you, I won't take any more of your valuable time.''

He too arose, but his face was a thundercloud. ''Take my advice, Mrs. . . . Brown, there are surgeons who will do what you want for money, but believe me, the price can be more than you are prepared to pay. If you have a few moments, I'll show you some photographs that will convince you—''

Peach interrupted. ''That won't be necessary. I believe you. I won't shop around for a surgeon who will tell me what I want to hear.''

He smiled, and his face lighted with charm. ''Good. And don't be concerned about your young man. He has taste and discernment, and he is most fortunate. Goodbye. I hope we will meet again soon, socially, of course.'' My goodness, Peach thought, he is devastatingly sexy when he smiles.

Peach stopped at the desk on her way out, and the secretary asked, ''Shall I bill you or would you like to settle it now?''

''Now, please.'' Peach took a checkbook out of her purse and asked the charge.

''That will be two hundred and fifty for the consultation,

unless you're going to have surgery, and then it will just be included in the total."

"I'm not having surgery," she answered. She wrote the check, amused that her name and address would be revealed after all on the personalized check. So much for secrecy. She must remember to carry cash the next time she wanted to travel incognito.

Peach stopped in Grace's room at the hospital for a brief visit and then went upstairs to see Casey, who was still a patient. She found her weeping hysterically into her pillow. Peach rushed to her and put her arms around the sobbing young woman. "Casey, my dear, whatever is wrong?" She held her for several minutes. "There, there," she consoled her, "everything is going to be all right. You'll see."

"Oh, Peach," Casey moaned. "I've lost my baby, and it was all my own fault. I didn't do what I was told."

"Casey, you mustn't blame yourself. Some things were just not meant to be."

"But I was told to go to bed, and I didn't."

"Because you couldn't. Your mother needed you, and you did what you had to do," Peach insisted.

"I'm so afraid Mom will find out," Casey wailed. "She was so anxious to see her grandchild."

"Are you sure about that, honey?" Peach asked.

Casey wiped her eyes and blew her nose. "Why do you ask that, Peach? Did she say anything to you?"

"No, it was just a feeling. Eve thought so too." Peach handed Casey a washcloth. "Here, wipe your eyes with this. They're all red and swollen, and you don't want Grace to see you like that."

"You know, it hit me all of a sudden this morning. The baby's gone, and I'll have to tell Jerry. He'll never forgive me for killing his child." Her voice and manner were morose.

"Stop this nonsense right now!" Peach ordered. "You did not kill your child. Your body gave it up, for some reason we may never know, and this Jerry of yours will understand or he's not worth worrying about."

"I think I'm being punished, Peach."

"Good God, whatever for, child?"

"My pregnancy wasn't an accident. I planned it. I knew he'd never leave his wife just for me—"

Peach interrupted her. "Big deal, Casey. You're not the first woman in the history of the world to try to capture a man that way. It happens all the time. Besides, he was an eager accomplice. It wasn't an immaculate conception."

"Would it be awful if I didn't tell him about the baby until after his divorce?"

"Yes, it would be awful. You'd be piling one wrong on top of another. Casey, are you sure you want a marriage that's grounded in deceit? Do you really believe you could be happy with someone who has to be tricked into marrying you? Tell him the truth. Take the risk. You might win. But if you don't, it's better to lose now than later and leave a trail of broken lives behind you."

Peach paused and was sorry for lecturing her. She looked so childlike and woebegone. "Casey, when did Jim say you could go home?"

"Maybe tomorrow. My hemoglobin's still very low. He'd like to keep me here till the weekend."

"Then, I think you should stay. That house will be awfully lonesome."

"They might let Mom go home next Monday."

"That's a surprise."

"The psychiatrist said she might recover faster in familiar surroundings."

"Now that's something to be happy about. Give me a smile before I leave, all right?"

"All right. And I'll think about calling Jerry tonight to tell him."

"You don't want to live a lie, Casey."

"But I still don't want Mom to know, okay?"

"She's got to know sometime."

"Not now. When she's feeling better."

_43_

The Greatest Debt

Dear Kirk,

I can't believe it really happened. If I had to mark one day on the calendar of my life as important, it would probably be last night. After all these terrible housebound weeks of sorrow and fear and anger, I finally emerged and became a whole person again. Although I owe much to my friends and to Dr. Sabatini, it is to you to whom I owe the greatest debt.

Our dinner last night was . . . well, what words can I choose to best describe it . . . terrific? . . . sensational? . . . marvelous? . . . wonderful? Yes, all those and some that haven't even been invented yet. My heart didn't race with fear (not much, anyway). My palms stayed dry. I felt secure and comfortable and happy. Why? Because I was with you and because of you I have faced the truth and accepted it. I know that the happy years of my life with Jim are over, and I can now look forward to the future.

I intend to telephone Jim today and tell him I am ready to sit down with our attorney to make the final financial settlements. I am not at all upset or worried about it anymore.

I hate to keep imposing on your kindness, but I am eager to begin looking for that condominium you suggested. If you could pick out a couple for me to look at, I'll hire a car to bring me down to Long Beach to your office, and we can set out from there. I'm not quite ready for that long freeway drive alone yet. I hate to pressure you, but please hurry. I am extremely anxious to make the final break and get out of this house. I now feel like a prisoner waiting for parole.

It will be so wonderful to live near all my good friends again. Call me as soon as you can. You are a remarkable man, and I envy Maggie her good fortune in having you for a husband.

Love,
Laura

44

Delegate

CONVERSATION was awkward at breakfast the next morning. "How was your dinner last night with Laura?" Maggie asked.

Kirk did not lift his eyes from the newspaper as he answered, "Fine."

"Is she doing all right . . . really?"

"Uh huh."

"Where did you go?"

"Ma Maison."

"Really? Well, if I'd known the occasion was that special, I'd have joined you. Was the food good?"

"It always is."

"Kirk, we need to buy something for Angie for Christmas. It's just a few days away, and—"

He interrupted her. "I've already taken care of it."

"You have?" Maggie was surprised, for Kirk had always left all the shopping and wrapping to her. "What did you buy?"

"A new car. I ordered it last week."

"Well, you could have told me," she muttered.

"When would that be? You're never around here."

Oh, God, Maggie wailed inwardly, here it comes again. "Let's not get started with that, Kirk," she stated as she got up from the table and set her dishes on the sink, but Kirk had another salvo.

"You'd better quit leaving that garbage on the sink. I saw another roach there last night when I came in," he complained.

Maggie protested defensively, "But Imelda will be here to clean today. She'll wash the dishes."

"Yes, but she needs some supervision. She's been getting away with murder lately."

Maggie had enough. "Well, then why don't you do it? You're around here more than I am. If you don't like the way things are being run, be my guest, take over."

Without waiting for his retort, she rushed upstairs to dress. When she was ready to leave, she returned to the kitchen to apologize, but he was gone.

Dee arrived and reminded her that Elizabeth Haney would be coming at nine-thirty for an interview. Five minutes later the doorbell rang, and Dee ushered the woman into the living room where Maggie met her. "Good morning, I'm Maggie Hammond. You must be Elizabeth Haney. I didn't expect you to be so young."

"Oh? I'm almost thirty-five."

"Really? You don't look it. Are you married?"

The young woman shook her head. "Not anymore. We separated three weeks ago, and now I have to start supporting myself."

"I'm sorry. Do you have children?"

"No, I never would have left if we'd had kids. I'd have tried to work things out some way, no matter what. But since there were just the two of us, I left."

As she spoke, Maggie observed her. Her clothes were inexpensive but tasteful and well coordinated. She was thin and not very tall, and her red hair was curly in the current style. "Have you had any decorating experience at all?" Maggie asked.

"Not really. I took one of those courses at a department store a couple of years ago, and I enrolled in another one at City College last year, but I had to quit because Buck used the car at night a lot."

"Oh, you don't have a car?"

"Yes, I do. I let Buck keep all the furniture and stuff, and he gave me the car. It's only two years old, and it runs just fine."

Maggie was drawn to her. There was a desperation that she detected not far below the surface of the woman's smile and forthright responses. "Have you ever worked before? Outside the home, I mean."

"Not for a long time. I got married when I was eighteen. I was a waitress in a coffee shop, but Buck makes pretty good money at Douglas, and he wanted me to stay home and take care of the house. I sold Avon for a while and Tupperware, but I was never much good at selling. I like to do creative things. I got into painting plaster figurines, but the house filled up with that junk pretty fast. Then I knitted, and now I'm doing needlepoint. I just can't stand to be idle."

"Please forgive me for prying, but I'd like to know why you broke up your marriage after so many years. Is it perhaps just a trial separation?"

"No, I'll never go back. I can't." She looked down at her hands, and Maggie could see that the words were difficult to find. "You see, Mrs. Hammond, my husband didn't like . . . well, he's what you call . . . gay." Now that she'd finally said it, she relaxed and continued. "I didn't find out until just a year ago. I was pretty dumb, I guess. I just thought he was tired and working too hard. I probably would never have figured it out if he hadn't decided to tell me. He said he just couldn't keep up the pretense anymore. When his friend moved into the house, I left."

She said no more, but Maggie read in her face the rejection that she felt as well as a sense of personal failure. She would hire her. She needed the job to give her back some self-esteem, and Maggie intended to give her the opportunity.

"Well now, let me tell you about the job." Maggie gave her a quick history and description of what she was doing and what she needed from an assistant. When she was finished, she asked, "Now, that's all there is to it, Elizabeth. Are you interested?"

"Oh, yes! It sounds perfectly wonderful, and I'll work very hard. Hours don't mean anything to me. I haven't got anything else to do."

They discussed salary and expenses, and it was agreed that she would start that very day. Together they drove to Malibu, then on to Robertson Boulevard. Maggie found Elizabeth to be a quick and enthusiastic student. They were back in Long Beach at six-thirty, and Maggie gave her instructions to be at the beach house the next morning to accept delivery on the furniture.

Maggie entered the dark house. Dee had gone, and obviously Kirk had not returned home. She felt a measure of relief that she would have at least a little while alone. Tired as she was, she decided it would be politic for her to fix dinner and show Kirk that her career need not always interfere with their home life. She had just started when the telephone rang. It was Kirk. "Sorry, Maggie. I'm having dinner with some contractors. They're planning to bid on the mall, and I want to give them some information. I won't be late. They have a plane to catch."

She made no attempt to hide her disappointment knowing full well he would prefer her to be displeased.

"Darn it, Kirk. I've already got the chicken in the oven, and I put a bottle of wine in the fridge," she lied. "I was looking forward to having a quiet evening with you."

"Sorry. The guys are already here waiting for me. How about tomorrow, honey?"

Damn. Hoisted on her own petard. "Not tomorrow, I'm afraid. It's a big day for me. Everything's being delivered, and I can't be sure what time the last truck will get there."

The bitter edge of sarcasm returned to his voice. "Well then, check your calendar and make an appointment for me. If not this month, maybe next."

She was determined not to be goaded into replying in kind. "Please don't be angry, Kirk. I love you, and I need you. Our marriage is too important to both of us to let it degenerate into nastiness. I'll be waiting when you get home, okay?"

His voice softened only slightly. "See you later."

Maggie went into the kitchen and poured herself a glass of wine and then decided to call Angie. The sound of her only child's voice gave her a lift. "Hi, Mom, how's everything?"

"Fine. I just called to talk. Are you busy?"

"Not really. Finals started Monday, but all my papers are done, and I'm just reviewing notes. Did Dad tell you about the car?"

"That was a surprise. How did it come about?"

"Didn't he tell you about the transmission going out on the Ford?"

Maggie felt ashamed of herself for being so out of touch with her daughter's concerns. "No, I've been busy. We haven't had much time together lately."

"Yeah, I know. He's pretty upset, Mom. Maybe you ought to cool that working routine for a while."

"Not you too, Angie! I thought you were so big on women's liberation," Maggie teasingly protested.

"What's that got to do with it? Anyway, it's okay for other mothers, but I want mine in the kitchen doing her duty for Dad and country."

"What kind of car are you getting?"

"Would you believe one of those nifty new Mustang convertibles? God, he's the world's best father."

"When are you going skiing?" Maggie asked, but the real question was how come fathers always got the credit for giving.

"Christmas Day . . . late. I decided it would be nice for just the three of us to spend Christmas Eve together. Dad said we were going to Peach Malone's on Christmas, right? Any possibility Jason Darrow'll be there?"

"I think there's a good chance he will."

"Are you serious? I'd die to meet him! I'll bring my camera along. Nobody will believe it if I don't have proof."

The conversation lasted for another ten minutes, and Maggie enjoyed the closeness she had always felt with her only child. She vowed that she would call her at least twice a week.

She called Peach, and they talked briefly about Christmas, and Laura's unusually rapid progress. When the conversation ended, Maggie then dialed Laura. She felt guilty that she had been so busy that others, particularly Kirk, had managed to help her friend, but she had not had the time.

"Laura, I'm so pleased that things are going so well for you now. You had us all worried."

"God may have taken Jim's love from me, but he gave me good friends, Maggie, like you and your darling Kirk. If I live to be a hundred, I could never repay you all." Laura's words came out in a rush of gratitude. Maggie demurred, but Laura would not be denied. Words of praise for Kirk's deference and kindness poured from her lips in a flood that threatened to drown their friendship. The more laudatory Laura became, the more defensive were Maggie's reactions, until finally she became so irritated that she found it necessary to terminate the conversation.

"I really have to go, Laura. I'm so happy you're well again. We'll be picking you up on Christmas Day to go to Peach's."

"Christmas Day? Oh, I thought . . . well, Kirk invited me to join you two in Long Beach on Christmas Eve, but I had no idea you didn't know! I'm so sorry. Maybe we just ought to forget about it. . . ." Her voice trailed off in acute embarrassment.

Maggie felt guilty that she hadn't thought of it herself. Of course Laura couldn't be left alone on Christmas Eve. "I meant Christmas Eve, Laura. I just misspoke. Naturally we're planning to have you here. Angie will be home, and we'd like you to spend the night with us. I hope you don't mind sharing her room. It has twin beds. The guest room has been converted into an office for me, you know."

Maggie had recovered her equilibrium and was pleased at handling the difficult situation, but nevertheless annoyed with Kirk for being so fiendishly secretive about everything. He was certainly going to extreme lengths to demonstrate her lack of communication with him.

"Mind?" Laura responded. "It will be wonderful to see her again. Angie was always the little girl I never had. Now, what can I bring?"

"Not a thing. I've got everything planned," Maggie lied. There was no way housewifey Laura was going to preside over dinner here, she vowed. If she had to give up all sleep, she'd do it herself. When the conversation ended, however, she wondered at her own ridiculous pride. How in the hell was she going to do all the shopping, wrapping, cooking, and decorating . . . and still have time to finish the Cornwall project? Then, she remembered. She didn't have to do it all alone. She had Dee and Liz to help her. It was time she stopped thinking like a woman and began acting like a man. Delegate! She sat down to make a list. A gold monogrammed pen set for Kirk . . . a floppy Gucci leather tote for Angie . . . perfume for Laura . . . a *minaudière* for Peach, by Judith Lieber of course . . . a tank watch for Dee. Who else? Belinda . . . how could she forget her? She remembered an old etching of a bride and groom she had seen in an antique shop on Melrose. She'd have Liz pick it up and have it framed expensively.

She heard Kirk pulling into the garage. Pleased and happy with herself, she went to greet him. "I'm so glad you got home early," she said as she put her arms around him to hug him.

"Early? Are you kidding? It's almost midnight. What have you been doing?"

Maggie was astounded. The evening had flown by. "Midnight? Oh, my goodness, I've been gossiping on the telephone with Angie and Peach and Laura. Then I got involved making out my Christmas list."

"Finally? It's only a few days away." He returned her hug and kissed her lightly. "Hmm, you've been drinking wine, I see. Got some left?"

As they sat together on the family room couch, she began her campaign to convince Kirk she could do everything with a smile. "I'm so glad you thought to invite Laura for Christmas Eve."

"Sorry I forgot to mention it," he apologized, "but I knew you wouldn't mind."

Later, much later, after they had made love, and Kirk had gone to sleep, Maggie slipped out of bed and went downstairs.

Quietly, she squeezed the orange juice, set the table, and put the coffee and water in the coffeepot. She had to leave early the next morning, but she wanted to have breakfast with Kirk. She wanted him to feel cared for and comfortable when she told him about Elizabeth.

_45_

Lies and Deceit

THREE DAYS before Christmas, Rudolfo pulled the car into
the driveway with Grace and Casey in the back seat. Grace
looked at the house where she had lived for so many years,
and if she was happy to return, she showed no sign of it.
Casey got out first and turned to help her mother. "Come on,
Mom. We're home."

Grace took her daughter's hand and got out of the car. She
was very thin now, as was Casey, and their very slenderness
made them look even more like mother and daughter than
ever before. It was almost as if nature had stripped them
down to the bare essentials, and their basic likeness had
emerged.

"Are you glad to be here? Does it look the same?" Casey
asked, but Grace just smiled and nodded. There was no
spark, no hint that she was somewhere special.

The garden bloomed with seasonal flowers that Rudolfo
had planted, and when they went inside, there were vases of
lush red roses everywhere. The Christmas tree stood in the
living room emanating its fragrance of pine, and sparkles of
light from the sun came through the window and bounced off
the ornaments.

"Mom, Rudolfo did all the decorations himself. Aren't
they beautiful? Look, he put all the old ornaments on the tree,
even the ones Katie helped me paint when I was little."
Grace walked toward the tree and looked at it for a long time.
She reached toward a lower branch and touched a round

silver ball on which had been written "Casey–1963" in red glitter that was almost gone. She said one word, "Katie."

Casey moved close to her mother and put her arm around her and saw that there were tears in her eyes. "Katie," she repeated. Gently, Casey reminded her, "Katie's gone, Mom. She's been gone almost ten years now. She got sick and went home to Philadelphia, where she died. Remember how we cried, Mom?" Casey's eyes were brimming too as both women recalled the wonderfully warm Irishwoman who had tenderly cared for them.

Grace spoke again. "Drake's gone, too."

Casey agreed. "Yes, he is, but Peach is still here. Want me to call her and invite her over for a visit?"

Grace shook her head. "Not now. Where's Lily?"

"Lily? Who's Lily?"

Grace did not answer but walked to the couch where she sat down and wiped her eyes with a handkerchief. It was the most she had said in weeks. "Mom, did I ever meet Lily?" Casey persisted, hoping that perhaps it was a clue that would help solve the mystery of her mother's suicide attempt, but Grace just shook her head and said, "She's gone too."

Later that evening after Grace had gone to bed, Casey called Peach to ask her if she knew anything about Lily. Peach hesitated only briefly before replying, "I never met her, but she was a woman who befriended your mother years ago, before even Drake knew her. She was killed, murdered, I believe. She had a little boy that Grace tried very hard to adopt, but there was a silly prejudice then against single women adopting children." Quickly she realized her gaffe and amended it. "Grace was a widow then." One person's deceit makes liars of us all, she observed silently. Throughout the years, she had fervently encouraged Grace to tell her daughter the truth, and now here she was, lying to protect the lie.

"Was Mom upset about the murder?" Casey asked.

"Upset, yes, very, but that was years and years ago, my dear. I'm sure it had nothing to do with her recent problems.

Now, are you all set for Christmas dinner here? Is there any chance that your professor might join us?''

''How I wish he could, but I don't think so.''

''I assume that everything has worked out all right and that losing the baby didn't affect your plans,'' Peach said. There was a long silence, and an unthinkable possibility entered Peach's mind. ''You did tell him, didn't you?''

''I'll tell him when we're together. It won't make any difference. I know it won't,'' Casey answered defensively.

Like mother, like daughter, Peach moaned inwardly. They both complicated their lives so needlessly with lies and deceit. ''You don't believe that or you wouldn't be afraid to tell him, but then, it's really none of my business, is it? I'll see you at two on Christmas.'' Peach put down the receiver more abruptly than she intended, but her displeasure was obvious, and it rattled Casey, especially since she herself was nervous about Jerry's reaction to the sad news.

She just had to keep on thinking that things would work out when they were together again. Besides, once he saw what a beautiful life they had in California, he'd never want to return to the cold, dreary Midwest. The truth was, she didn't want to go back herself. She was a California girl, accustomed to a daily dose of sun. Besides, she could never get that far away from Grace again.

She must stop worrying and concentrate on her mother. Tomorrow they would take a little drive, stop at the shop for a visit, and then go to Scandia for lunch. If it all worked okay, they'd do it again the next day. Little by little, Casey intended to return Grace to the real world. Her only worry now was how the miscarriage would affect both Jerry and her mother. God, why did it have to happen? Life would have been perfect, if only she had not lost the baby.

_46_

I Can Make
Miracles

PEACH had not hurried to disclose to Dom and Horace the fact that she knew she was in control. She had deliberately not returned their telephone calls for several days. She wanted time to think, to determine just where she was going, and besides, she wanted them to worry for a while. But now, Christmas was almost upon them, and she did not want the confrontation hanging over her head during the holidays. It was time to put them out of their misery . . . or into it.

She dialed Horace's office, and his secretary told her he would be back shortly. Peach tried not to feel relieved. Maybe she really didn't have the fortitude for independence.

And why hadn't she heard from Jason? He'd said he'd be back for Christmas Eve, and that was tomorrow night. The telephone interrupted her worrying. "Mrs. Malone?" an unfamiliar deep masculine voice inquired.

"Yes, who is this?" she answered.

"Pierre Senseney. How are you?"

For a moment the name mystified her and then suddenly she connected it with the physician she had seen just a few days before. "Of course, Dr. Senseney. Why, I'm fine." Why would he be calling her?

"Please . . . call me Pierre. This is a social call."

"I see," she said, but she didn't see at all and waited for him to enlighten her.

"Please don't think me forward, Mrs. Malone, but I've been thinking about you constantly since your visit and I just had to find out if you would consider having dinner with me this evening . . . or any other evening?''

Peach was so startled that she was unable to respond immediately. ''Why . . . you surprise me. I don't quite know what to say.''

''Say yes. It's a simple and short word. Very easy to say, and it would make me very happy if you did, because I have never in my life asked a patient to go out with me.''

''Well, I guess technically I'm not a patient since you turned me away. But why me?'' Her meeting with him had been brief, and he had been blunt and impersonal.

''I don't know. After you left, the memory of your face and voice stayed with me. I can't really explain it except to say that I would like very much to know you better, and I would like you to know that I am not always the, how you say, abrupt doctor you met. Are you free for dinner this evening?''

His voice was compelling and his attraction to her extremely flattering. ''Yes, I am, but it must be an early dinner. I'm expecting an important call,'' Peach responded and was astonished at her acceptance. Why did she do it?

''Good! I'll pick you up at seven.''

The call was over, and Peach was left holding the telephone in amazement. Good grief, couldn't she have just said no? What would Jason think? Did it matter? Was he avoiding all contact with other women because he slept with her? Should she expect him to? The best way to keep from becoming a hovering, jealous woman was to have a social life of her own, right? Good. That was it. A reason to go.

The telephone rang again, and she hoped it was Jason responding to her thoughts, but it was Horace's secretary. As she waited for him to come on the line, she was irritated. She would tell him from now on she wanted him to call her directly. She detested the little power games men played on the telephone.

''Well, good morning, my dear. How are you? I've called you several times.'' His voice was friendly.

"Fine, Horace, but I'm busy. I need to talk with you. There are some things I want to discuss."

"Of course. Would you like to wait until after the holidays?"

"No, I want to do it today. Would three o'clock be all right?"

"Well, if you insist. I'll have to move a few appointments, but I'll be happy to do it. I'll expect you at three then."

"I'd prefer you to come here. And call Dom. I'd like him to come too."

With the rest of the day scheduled, Peach went to her closet to choose the clothes for the day's encounters. Mauve wool slacks and matching print suede overblouse would be perfect for conducting business, and a green sheer wool Oscar de la Renta that matched her emerald earrings and picked up deep green flecks in her eyes was perfect for dinner with Dr. Senseney. Her life, she reflected, was becoming more interesting every day.

Dom and Horace arrived at exactly three o'clock, and Peach was ready for them. They greeted each other with the usual warm and friendly enthusiasm, although Peach wondered how warm their manner would be when the session was over.

When the amenities were concluded and everyone had been served tea, Peach informed them that she had a limited amount of time and needed to get on with the business at hand.

Dom began, "Well, here are all the figures you asked for. As you can see, you're a very wealthy woman. The estate has slipped in value in the last year because of some extremely poor investments that Drake made in the months before he died. But as you can see, the trust is worth well over a hundred and fifty million. We've moved into more investments that have a lower yield but are considerably safer. The oil stocks are depressed now too, but believe me, they will bounce back strongly in the future."

"I'm really mystified about those poor investments you said Drake made," Peach said.

343

"Yes, so am I, but perhaps Horace can explain it. He was more involved in that area than I was."

"I feel very bad about all that," Horace said, "but I tried to dissuade him from speculating so heavily. You know how stubborn he could be though."

"Dom, what stocks are you talking about?" Peach asked. "Can you point them out to me on these printouts?"

Dom spread the papers out on the coffee table, and the three huddled over them. One by one, Dom pointed out a number of stocks. Peach tried to follow him, but he spoke rapidly. There was something wrong with all of this, but she couldn't put her finger on it until suddenly she realized something very important.

"Dom, are these dates of purchase right?"

The banker looked puzzled. "Well, sure they are. Why do you ask?"

"Because Drake was too ill at that time to make any decisions. There's no way he could have bought anything. He couldn't even speak then."

"It's quite possible that he made the decisions to buy into those companies long before he became too ill, and the buy orders just didn't take for a while," Horace explained.

"Seems damn strange. Who the hell was advising him on that stuff?" Dom demanded.

Horace shook his head. "I have no idea. He seemed to just pick them out of the blue."

"Well, it's possible the stroke could have had some effect, but his thinking was so clear in every other aspect, right up until the very end," Peach added.

"Horace," Dom said, "I'd like to take a look at all the backup on those investments. I don't have anything on them except the checks drawn to pay for them. Maybe there's some way to salvage something. At least we can have the Securities and Exchange Commission look into it to see if there's been fraud of any kind."

"Good idea," Peach remarked. "Now, Dom, I see that I hold major positions in several large corporations. Am I not entitled to sit on the boards of directors of those companies?"

"Well, not exactly, Peach. The trust holds the stock, not you personally."

"But I'm the trustee."

"Yes, my dear," Horace explained gently, "but you are only one of three. Dom and I are the others."

Peach's voice lost its docile tone. "I see. Then you two are holding those board positions, true?"

"Well, yes, but only because we are familiar with the business of those corporations, and we must act in your best interests," Dom declared.

"I'm sure you are, but I'm a big girl now, Dom, and I intend to run my own affairs. True, I've had little actual experience in your big world of finance, but I can learn. It's my fortune to use or lose as I see fit."

Horace responded. "That's not exactly true, my dear. Yes, you are the recipient of the benefits of Drake's estate, but he wanted to protect you and your family by placing everything in ironclad trusts that leave management in professional hands."

"Like yours?" Peach's voice went flat, and she allowed her anger to rise to the surface. They were deliberately trying to deceive her into thinking she was helpless.

"Exactly. Now Drake didn't want you to worry your pretty little head about anything," Horace cajoled her.

Peach stood up and rang for Miles. When he appeared, she asked him to serve cocktails. "Mr. Beller will have Scotch and soda, and Mr. Petrone will have it on the rocks with a twist." The two men tried to protest, but she waved them to silence. "Take the drinks. You'll both need something to hang onto."

When the beverages had been served, Peach raised her glass of champagne to them. "A toast, gentlemen, to the pretty little head you're both so worried about." She sipped the wine and then continued to stand, looking down at them. "Now, it's my turn. Dom, you know of course that I can replace you as trustee at any time and move all of my accounts and monies elsewhere. That would cause you and your bank a considerable loss, wouldn't it?"

Dom remained silent, but the muscles in his jaw rippled as

he clenched his teeth. Peach continued, "I can replace you too, Horace, and I probably should. You deliberately tried to mislead me, and if Drake is watching from somewhere out there, he is probably furious with you."

Peach looked at them both and laughed. "And all because of a damned boat! Thank God for that boat. If I buy it, I'm going to name it *Daylight* because it hauled me out of the darkness of my own ignorance. I'm a rich woman, and my wonderful husband taught me that if rich means anything, it means power. Both of you tried to usurp the power of my fortune. With good reason, I suppose. You thought all I needed to be happy was the trappings of wealth . . . cars, houses, servants, jewelry . . . but you were wrong. And you know, it's still stealing even if you only take something you thought I didn't want."

"Goddamn it, I resent the implication that we stole anything from you ever, Peach. Horace and I were doing exactly what Drake instructed us to do . . . watch over you and . . ." Dom exclaimed, but Peach interrupted him.

"I'm sorry. It was a poor choice of words, but hear me out. I think it's time you listened to what I want for a change."

Peach paused and realized she had begun to pace. Ideas were springing from her mind to her tongue before she could even digest them herself. She found herself eager to give voice to her plans for the future, and suddenly, it was all brilliantly clear. She sat down, and her voice softened.

"Drake loved the accumulation of money. It was his life until his children were born." She tried to find words to express what she felt. "But Drake is gone now. He couldn't take his money with him, and so it is no longer his. It is mine. All mine. Do you understand? None of it . . . not one cent of it belongs to either of you. And it is up to me to decide how to use it to make my life better and more meaningful."

Horace, clearing his throat again very nervously, asked, "What do you have in mind, Peach?"

"I'm going to do good!" She laughed triumphantly, and her words came out in a rush. "I'm going to start giving the damn stuff away. I'm going to be a fairy godmother. I'll wave my wand and make people's lives better."

The two men looked at each other with eyebrows raised at the insanity they perceived before them.

"Don't look at me like that, Dom. I'm not crazy. Ford did it. Rockefeller did it too. I'll call mine the Drake Malone Foundation, and I'll help young people, old people, and hungry people. I'll set up a staff to help me find them. What the devil good is money if you don't spend it?"

"Peach, I don't think you understand the gravity of what you're proposing to do. Our way of life is dependent on the preservation of holdings to maintain a sense of order in the economy," Dom began, but Peach snickered.

"Come on, Dom . . . as Drake would say, that sounds like something cranked out of the great American bullshine machine."

Horace interceded. "What will your children think of such a radical plan? After all, it's their inheritance you're planning to give away."

"I know that, and I intend to set up generous amounts aside for them. I intend to see that Steve gets all the money he needs to make the wine and champagne that is his dream. I intend to discuss everything with Anne and Steve, but I already know how they'll react. Great gobs of money, in and of itself, have never really impressed them all that much. Maybe because they've never been in need of it."

"When do you intend to begin?" Horace asked.

"In the new year, but I need your assurances that you will not try in any way to thwart my efforts. Don't worry, I'm not going to start tossing money out of windows, and I certainly don't intend to don sackcloth and ashes and live in poverty. I intend to do this efficiently and effectively. Are you with me, Dom?"

"I'll help in any way that I can. As a matter of fact, I advised Drake to set up a foundation years ago. It will be very helpful taxwise."

"What about you, Horace? Will you be as good a friend to me as you were to Drake?"

"I've always tried to act in your best interests, and I must say I resent the implied accusation. Of course, I'll do whatever you want."

"Look, I don't blame either of you. I've never really given you any reason to think I wanted more than I already had. I'm a little surprised with all this myself. When you walked in here today, the only goal I had in mind was asserting my prerogatives and wresting control." Her voice trailed off as her thoughts roamed. What did she really want? And as the answer came to her mind, it spilled from her lips. "Power," she said, "just like everybody else, that's what I really want. Drake got it by acquiring money. I'll get it by giving it away. You see, I'm not so different after all."

When they had gone, Peach sat in front of the window looking at the city below her as the amethyst of twilight faded into black, and she wondered at the direction her life was taking. Perhaps she had been less happy living in Drake's shadow than she realized. She was seeing a different self, a woman not content to live in seclusion behind the walls of affluence. Money would buy her more than physical comforts. It would buy her respect and influence. She would become a force to be reckoned with, a person with the power to make a difference in the world around her.

The days of being Drake's wife were over. It was time to develop her own identity. She wondered how many Kitty and Hazel O'Haras were out there struggling to stay alive and praying for a miracle.

"I can make miracles," she whispered.

_47_

Other Arrangements

MAGGIE arrived at Belinda's and found her out on the porch harassing the men from the delivery service as they attempted to load the precious cargo of antiques on the truck. "Thank goodness you're finally here to help me watch them. I'm so afraid something is going to get broken."

"Come inside, Belinda. It's a cold, damp morning, and you shouldn't be out here without a coat," she gently urged, but the older woman refused to budge.

"Look how they are carrying that cabinet . . . one slip, and the two-hundred-year-old piece will go smashing to the ground," she exclaimed.

"You must go inside and let them alone. They're professionals, I promise you." When she finally succeeded in getting her inside, she guided her toward the library. "Belinda, one thing I've learned is that you must have faith in the people you hire. Nagging usually has an effect just opposite to what you seek. You certainly don't want to make those men nervous . . . or hostile."

"Maggie, are you insinuating that I made you nervous or hostile?" Belinda asked belligerently.

Maggie laughed. "Not really, but you tried hard enough. Now get us some coffee while I take a quick check to make sure they picked up everything."

When Maggie returned, she found Belinda sitting in her wing chair weeping. "What's wrong?" Maggie asked. The old woman wiped her eyes with an exquisite lace handkerchief and answered tragically, "Oh, Maggie, I'm getting old, and I'm so afraid. I want my son with me these last few days of my life, and I just know he's going to refuse."

"Why do you say that? Have you talked to him?"

"No, I've been afraid to. He telephoned twice yesterday, but I wouldn't take his calls. Something just told me it was bad news."

Maggie felt sorry for her. "Don't worry, Belinda. I'm sure he'll stay. Tell him how much it means to you. He'll understand."

"No! I won't beg. If he wants to return to New York, I won't try to stop him. He has to live his own life, in his own way," she declared nobly.

"Belinda, if you won't tell him, I will."

The twinkle returned to Belinda's eyes. "Would you really do that for me?"

"I would . . . and I will."

"That's marvelous, Maggie." Belinda stood up, ready to go into battle again. "Now, get me a coat from the hall closet. I have to get back outside to make sure that desk doesn't get scratched."

When Maggie arrived at the house in Malibu, Elizabeth was directing the delivery service efficiently. When they had a chance to talk, Maggie told her she was pleased with her performance. "Oh, it's such fun, and the house is going to be terrific," her assistant replied.

"Let's hope the Cornwalls' enthusiasm is equal to yours. A recommendation from Belinda could mean a lot of jobs for us, Liz."

"How could anyone not love this place? It's like heaven."

"To you and me perhaps, but not necessarily to someone who can afford anything they want."

"It's hard to imagine. Sometimes I think that maybe having too much money wouldn't be all that great. There'd be nothing to wish for."

"Not true, Liz. Belinda wants her son, and she can't buy that."

"Isn't that what she's trying to do though . . . buy him with this house?"

"Yes, but the house won't do it. If he stays, it will be for love."

It was almost dark when the last delivery truck pulled away. The house looked magnificent with its new furnishings—warm, comfortable, and inviting. They could see the lights from the passing ships moving majestically across the horizon. Maggie walked through every room at least once, savoring the perfection of her efforts. She hated to leave.

Would she ever visit here socially, she wondered. Probably not. Unlike her relationship with Peach, she had never been anything to Belinda except an employee. Connor? No. She was a married woman, and custom did not allow friendships with the opposite sex. As difficult as things had been with Kirk, she still hoped to reconcile their differences. He was her husband.

She gave Liz the list of gifts to buy and have wrapped for her the next day, and together they closed up the house. Now it was time to get her own house in order. The florist would finish the rest here, and although she planned to check out everything on the morning of the twenty-fourth, there was not much more she could do.

She arrived home before eight-thirty to a cold and dark house. Although she had intended to tell Kirk about Liz that morning, he had hurried away, and she still faced the dreary prospect. Not tonight, however, and in fact, not for several nights. Angie would be home, and she wanted this Christmas to be a happy occasion.

She changed into a pair of jeans and a sweater and downed a quick sandwich and coffee. She had a lot of work to do. Sure enough, the bushy Douglas fir tree was in the side yard, just as she had ordered, and with great effort she managed to drag it into the house and set it up in front of the living room window. Sneezing from the dust, she climbed up into the crawl space under the roof where they stored the boxes of Christmas decorations and got them out.

After a long tussle with the tangle of wires and light sets

that stubbornly refused to light until every tiny bulb was jiggled, she began the tedium of decorating the tree, wondering where she had gone wrong. How come other families took joy in sharing the process of Christmas preparation and she had to do it all herself?

Kirk arrived home at ten-thirty to find her putting the last strands of tinsel on the tree. He looked around at the clutter of boxes. "God, what a mess," he remarked. A tiny voice of fatigue and irritation rose up from inside her, but she stifled it. There was no point in killing herself to make life serene, then stirring up a storm over unimportant remarks. "Yep, it sure is. I'm so glad you're here to help me clean it up. Doesn't the tree look gorgeous?"

"It does. You did a terrific job, as usual."

An hour later, the boxes were all stashed away, and Maggie was eager for a shower and bed, but Kirk wanted to begin celebrating. "Let's have a glass of wine and sit in front of the tree and talk," he suggested.

Maggie knew better than to refuse. "Sure. There's a bottle of champagne in the refrigerator. Why don't you open it while I take a quick shower and put on a robe? I feel awfully grimy."

"Okay, but is there anything to go with it? I didn't have much to eat, and I'm hungry." The urge to snap at him and tell him to feed himself almost surfaced. "I think we have a package of ripe brie in the cheesekeeper. I'll be down in ten minutes."

After the warm shower, the urge to sleep was almost irresistible, and she stretched out on the bed for just five minutes. She fell asleep immediately and did not awaken when, sometime later, Kirk covered her with the blanket and got in beside her.

"Do you want to go to the airport with me to meet Angie this afternoon?" A voice from above awakened her. She opened her eyes to see a naked Kirk standing over her with his shaving razor in his hand. Today? What was today? Oh, Lord . . . she'd left him alone with the wine and the Christmas tree!

"No, um, I think I'd better stay home and do the grocery shopping. I also have to wrap the packages," she replied, trying to get her adrenaline going. She pulled her body out of the bed and into a robe. "I'll have breakfast ready by the time you're dressed," she said. "Want some eggs?"

"Two. There wasn't anything to eat last night, and my stomach's gyrating."

"Poor child," she whispered, but too softly for him to hear.

When he had finally gone, she sprang into action. Imelda arrived at eight-thirty, but Dee did not show up until an hour later, and she looked sick.

"Is your face wearing that green for the holiday season or are you ill?" Maggie asked.

"Stomach flu. I was up all night," Dee replied.

"Why didn't you stay in bed, you ninny?"

"I just couldn't leave you in the lurch today, Mrs. H. I know how busy you are."

"Get out of here this minute! I can manage just fine. Go on now. I've got almost everything done," Maggie lied. "Take it easy. I'll see you the day after Christmas if you're feeling all right. I'll give you your Christmas bonus then."

When she was gone, Maggie's depression ballooned, but she didn't have time for self-pity. "I'll do what I can," she said, "and fuck everything else!"

Angie and Kirk did not arrive home until nearly seven because of the holiday traffic. Maggie was almost ready for them.

"Mom, it's so good to be home," Angie said as she rushed to hug her mother. "Dad said the tree was up. Let's go see it."

After dinner, Angie took off to visit friends, and Maggie did the dishes. She was about to start baking her pies for the next night's dinner when Kirk joined her in the kitchen. "Want to go to a movie?" he asked.

"Now? No way. I've got to bake the pumpkin pies and set the dining room table for tomorrow night's dinner."

"Can't you do that in the morning?"

She started to lie and then changed her mind. "I have to wrap the presents . . . and I also have to drive out to Malibu first thing to make sure the florist did everything right." Just as she was speaking, the telephone rang. It was Liz reporting on her shopping excursion. "Mission accomplished, Maggie."

"Terrific, Liz. I'll see you here at my house in the afternoon. I have to go to Malibu in the morning. Wait if I'm delayed. Dee's sick."

After she hung up, she realized that Kirk had been listening to her conversation. "Who's Liz?" he asked, and she knew that the moment had arrived, the crisis that always came too soon.

"My new assistant. She's working out fine."

"How long have you had her?" he asked.

"Just a couple of days," she replied. There was a nervous quiver in her voice, and her knees felt weak. Was it fear or exhaustion? "Kirk, can we talk about it? Without anger? Just like two adults who care about each other's feelings?"

"What's there to talk about? You've obviously made a decision without considering my—" he began, but she interrupted him.

"No! You've got it all wrong. You're the one who made the decision that I couldn't work without considering what I wanted. Can't you see it at all? Are you so blinded by your own self-interest that you won't see my side of it . . . even just a little bit?"

He raised his hands to signify capitulation. "Okay, okay, if that's the way you want it, I'll try for a while longer, but if it gets to be too much for me, we may have to make other arrangements."

Maggie's fear was turning to anger, and her voice mirrored her emotions. "Say it, Kirk! Don't pussyfoot around with innuendos and veiled threats. Say it, goddamn it, and get it out in the open . . . if you really mean it."

"Say what?"

Exasperated by his refusal to deal directly with the problem, Maggie decided to take the bull by the horns and throw it or be mortally gored. "Separation. Divorce. Isn't that what you're threatening me with? Only this time, I'm the one who's going to issue the ultimatum, not you. Yes, I'm going to continue with my work. I love it, and I can't let your childish peevishness deprive me of something so important. I love you too, and I want our marriage to go on, but not the way it's been for the past twenty years with my life devoted to the care and feeding of your ego. Can't we be partners . . . equally? Living and loving and caring for each other?''

When Maggie finished her tirade, it was several moments before he spoke, and his voice was tight but not angry. "No, thanks, Maggie. I don't need another partner. I need a wife, and if you don't want the job anymore, well, that's your privilege. Sorry. I thought our life together was more than just you feeding my ego. I guess I was wrong. As a matter of record, however, I've been a damned good husband. I've worked hard, and I've provided well for you and Angie.''

Maggie was stricken by his quiet, sorrowful manner and his words. "Oh, Kirk, I didn't mean you hadn't been a good husband. You have, and you've been a wonderful father.''

"I've been giving this just as much thought as you have, and I've come to a decision too. I want a wife waiting at home for me. I need comforting and warmth and love after I've spent the day beating my brains out to make a living. I can't cope with your career and mine too.''

A dull pain throbbed through her body. So this was it? The end of her marriage. Could she face life alone without him? She was sick with sorrow and fear. What in God's name had she done? Her throat was tightly closed, and she could not say another word. Kirk was the last to speak. "Maggie, let's keep this between us until after Christmas . . . all right? There's no reason to spoil the holidays for Angie. We'll tell her together when she gets back from her ski trip.'' Maggie nodded her head, and she heard him walk away.

Was this how marriages ended? A few words, ordinary everyday words put together in such a way to end a lifetime of love and sharing? A whimper . . . not a bang?

_48_

I Won't Need
You Anymore

LAURA dialed the number and prayed that a female voice would not answer, but it did, and although she was tempted to hang up, she held on. "Hello, this is Laura. Is Jim there?"

The sultry voice known to moviegoers the world over replied, "No, he isn't, Laura. This is Ghilly. Can I give him a message for you?"

Laura hesitated. She did not want to reveal her nervousness. She must be calm and composed, and she must not hate this woman. "Yes, if you wouldn't mind. Please ask him to call me at home when he gets a chance."

In a gush of friendliness toward the woman who had suffered so much because of her, Ghilly replied, "If it's important, I can have his service contact him for you."

"Yes, it's important, but not urgent. Just have him call me when he gets h—back. Thank you." She slammed down the receiver, thankful that the first ordeal was over. Christine had advised her not to direct her hatred toward Ghilly, but it was very hard to summon any charitable feelings for her. She looked at the clock . . . almost seven-thirty. Ghilly must be experiencing the doctor's wife's malaise of evening solitude.

Within ten minutes, the telephone rang, and Laura guessed that Ghilly had contacted Jim anyway. She snickered. Their curiosity must be whetted. She let it ring three times before she answered.

"Hello, Laura. Ghilly gave me your message." The sound of his voice plucked familiar chords of emotion.

"Yes, well, that was nice of her, but I told her there was no hurry. I just wanted to tell you that I'd like to talk to you sometime soon. I know you're leaving for Aspen, but when you get back, I think it would be a good idea for us to get things settled."

Jim sounded curious. "Well, fine, but maybe it would be better if we had our lawyers meet first."

"Really, Jim, do you want lawyers to decide what we're going to do with our lives? Can't we be two responsible adults and work things out for ourselves? It will be much easier than you think it will."

"Just what's on your mind, Laura?" He was wary, and she enjoyed it. She had a big surprise in store for him.

"Jim, we have two sons that we both love. No matter how much bitterness there is between us, Shan and Dac will always be there as a testimonial to the love we once shared. We can't wipe out what once was without destroying our children. We owe it to them to act decently to each other. I think we ought to meet and talk together. I'm not trying to trick you into anything." Her voice had become cool and serene as she talked, and she was enjoying the role she had chosen to play.

Puzzled and very curious, Jim could not resist the invitation. "Well, I'm at the UCLA Medical Center now. Would it be all right if I stopped in this evening?"

"Of course. Have you had dinner yet?"

"No, but that's not really necessary."

"I know, but it's really no problem at all. See you soon."

Her poise and composure vanished as she dashed into the kitchen to take a small fillet out of the freezer and thaw it in the microwave oven. She scrubbed two potatoes and put them in the oven with a bowl of frozen ratatouille she had made a few days before. She'd toss the salad and heat the rolls later.

She sprinted upstairs and changed into an outfit Jim had picked out and which Kirk had thought so beautiful when they had dinner together. She put her makeup on with a little heavier mascara than usual to make sure she didn't risk any tears, ran a brush through her hair, and dashed downstairs to set the dining room table. She opened a bottle of Bordeaux so it would have time to breathe, and she was lighting the fire in the living room fireplace when the doorbell rang. Life hadn't been dull lately.

As she walked slowly and calmly to open the door, she seemed to be viewing herself from afar. She was performing nobly in a part she had never expected to play. Tonight she would get back her husband's respect if nothing else, and she would forever lay to rest the cringing, self-pitying mouse of a woman she had been.

"Well, that was fast. You must be driving the Ferrari," she greeted him as he entered.

"No, actually it's in the shop again. Can you believe it?"

"That's too bad, but not surprising. Didn't I tell you not to buy a high-speed car in a fifty-five-mile-an-hour society?" Her voice was light and teasing.

"I know, I know. It's given me nothing but problems. I should have listened to you."

"Fast cars and fast women can get you into trouble," she smirked, but she smiled, and there was no acrimony in her tone. "Why don't you go into the bar and fix us a drink while I put the meat in the oven. Make yourself at . . . home."

"The usual?" he asked.

"No, just a little vodka on the rocks. There're too many calories in tonic."

"You don't look as if you need to watch calories anymore."

"But I like this new slim figure, and I intend to keep it."

When she finished in the kitchen, she joined him, and they sat down in front of the fire. She did not sit beside him on the couch, however, but sat in a chair facing him. She decided to be direct. "Jim, I know you're wondering what I'm up to. Well, I appreciate your coming here this evening. After the way I behaved the last few months, I'm surprised you still trust me," she began.

"Of course I trust you, Laura."

"How does it feel to be back in this house again? Do you still like it as much as you used to?"

"You know I've always loved this place. I was the one who insisted on buying it, remember?"

"Exactly. Well, I hate it. I always have, and I always will. I want you to have it with my blessing."

"Where are you going to live?"

"Kirk Hammond has offered to find a condominium for me in Long Beach . . . on the water. Now, here is my proposal. You buy the condo for me. We'll get an impartial appraisal on the house here and the furnishings, and we'll work out an equitable split of our holdings. I know there's not all that much. We were never good savers. Then, I'm going to ask you to give me an allowance that will support me comfortably for the next five years. I hope by then to be able to support myself. Perhaps I'll even marry again . . . I'd like to marry again. But . . . I don't intend to bleed you or be a burden to you forever."

Jim looked at her intently. "Laura, why are you doing this? What's your motive?"

"Motive? What a nasty thing to ask!"

"I'm sorry. I didn't mean it to sound that way. I'm just surprised, that's all. My attorney told me to dig in for a long battle."

"Yes, well, he won't make very much money if we don't fight, will he? I'll bet you called him before you came over here tonight, didn't you?" Her tone was accusing.

"Yes, I did."

"And he advised you not to come."

"Yes." He did not look at her.

"But you came anyway . . . why?"

"Because I still trust you more than anyone I've ever known. You're a kind, honest, caring woman, and I hate what I've done to you." His eyes were fixed on his drink, and as she watched him Laura felt her anger fading away. She longed to take him in her arms and comfort him, but she did not. Tenaciously, she held on to her composure.

"I did it to myself, Jim. I allowed myself to be a victim. I gloried in my martyrdom, but it was stupid. I have as much to be ashamed of as you do."

He looked up into her eyes. "I can't believe that I'm talking to the same woman I used to live with."

"You're not, thank God. I know myself so much better now. All my life, I was afraid. . . . I'm still afraid, but I'm learning how to deal with it."

"Are you able to leave the house at all?"

"Yes, but it's not easy. Every time I venture out the door, it's a real challenge. Do you know much about agoraphobia?" she asked.

"Not really."

"Most doctors don't. They call it 'housewife's disease,' because we're usually the ones who get it. They tend to diagnose it as nerves and prescribe Valium, which only makes it worse."

"You don't have much respect for the medical profession, do you?"

"I don't have much for you. Not anymore. But that's my problem, not yours. Just because I had a lot of naïve ideas about service to mankind and higher callings doesn't mean you're wrong. You're entitled to live your life any way you want. It doesn't matter that I think you sold out." She got to her feet. "Now, here's your very last chance for one of my delicious dinners. Will you pour the wine?" She hurried into the kitchen.

They ate dinner by candlelight, and she kept the conversation light, talking about the twins and old times. When dessert was over, the conversation was too. It was Laura who delivered the coup de grace to the evening.

"It's getting late, Jim, and Ghilly will think I've either seduced you or killed you. You should be getting home." Her voice was kind and tender.

He made no move but continued to drink his coffee. "I hate for the evening to end. It's been wonderful."

"I've enjoyed it too. I'm glad we can part friends. I want the boys to be comfortable with our divorce, and I hope they learn to like and accept Ghilly and the new baby."

"Kirk told you about that?"

"Yes, and I'm grateful to him. He's been a wonderful friend to me."

There was a prolonged silence as Jim seemed to be grappling with an unhappy problem.

"Jim, it's the house you hate to leave, not me. This is your home, and soon you can return to it permanently. Believe me, I'm anxious to move to my own place and start a new life. I won't stay here a day longer than I have to."

"There's no hurry. I'll talk to my attorney as soon as we get back from Aspen. You can be sure you'll have no problems with money . . . not while I'm alive and working. And as for the five years . . . well, I won't hold you to that. I'll always be there if you need me."

"I appreciate that, Jim, but I won't need you anymore."

They walked to the door together, and he turned to face her. "Goodbye, Laura," he said softly, and he reached down to kiss her, but she turned her head so that his lips brushed only her cheek.

"You're a great lady," he said wistfully.

"Goodnight, Jim . . . and good luck."

He walked out the door slowly, and she closed it and locked it behind him. As she walked past the mirror in the entry hall, she stopped to look at herself. "You did it, you phony! You did it!" she said to her image, and then she rushed upstairs to weep into her pillow.

_49_

The New Morality

ELATED by the triumph of her meeting with Horace and Dom, Peach got ready for dinner with Pierre Senseney. As she dressed, her mind buzzed with plans and ideas for the new course her life would now be taking. She'd tell Anne and Steve all about it when she called them on Christmas Eve.

When she was ready, she was pleased to see that she looked extraordinarily good. Why was the mirror always the first to reflect one's inner state of mind? She heard the telephone ring, and Miles called on the intercom to say that Jason was on the line. She picked it up immediately.

"Jason, where are you?"

"In Los Angeles, just as I told you I'd be. The limo is just now trying to get out of the traffic here at the airport. It's a zoo. I don't know how long it will take."

"It's so good to hear your voice. I've been worried. It's been days since you've called."

"We've been moving fast. They kept me so busy that I finally rebelled and made them schedule bathroom stops. They forget there are some things that can't be neglected. But I'll tell you all about it when I get there. If it's okay, I'll have the driver drop me at your place."

"Oh, Jason, I'm so sorry. I'm just on my way out for a dinner date. I wish I'd known when you were coming."

His voice reflected his disappointment. "I'm sorry too. I'd been looking forward to seeing you. I've missed you so much. Can't you get a headache or something and cancel out?"

"It's too late. He'll be here any minute . . . but if I'd known even a half-hour ago . . ."

"Well, that's the way it goes. When do I see you?"

She couldn't bring herself to invite him later in the evening. Somehow it was distasteful to have dinner with one man and spend the night making love to another one.

"Jason, dear, I've planned tomorrow, all day and all night just for us. Come here early in the morning for breakfast."

"Tomorrow? Well, if that's the way you want it." He sounded very disappointed.

"Jason, come tonight. I can't bear the thought of not seeing you until morning. I'll be home by midnight."

"Terrific! I'll be there at twelve, Cinderella. Don't turn into a pumpkin."

When she finished the conversation, Miles knocked at the door to tell her that Dr. Senseney was waiting in the library. She hurried in and offered him a drink, but he declined. "Thank you, but no. Our reservation is for seven-thirty, and they have promised me a view table."

Miles brought her sable coat, and they departed, making polite small talk until they were alone in his Mercedes sedan.

"Mrs. Malone, you are an incredibly beautiful woman. I have difficulty taking my eyes off you," he said as he put the car into gear and drove off.

"Is that a personal opinion or a professional one? And please call me Peach."

"Both . . . Peach. You have exquisite bone structure, glowing skin, and magnificent eyes, but I suppose you're accustomed to such extravagant compliments, are you not?"

"One never gets accustomed to them, do you think? Now tell me, how did you know who I really was? My name on the check?"

He laughed. "No, I knew who you were the moment you walked into my office. I was at the Silenzes' house the night *Sandman* was shown."

"I don't remember seeing you there."

"The handsome young star was monopolizing you. You had eyes for no one else."

"I didn't even know who he was until the movie started. Who were you with?"

"One of my patients, who shall be nameless for now. That evening was the debut of her face and abdomen, and she was so delighted that she insisted I accompany her and her husband and share her triumph. That week she got a very important part that everyone had said she was too old to play."

"Oh, of course that was . . ." but he shushed her with a finger to his lips.

"No names, please. My specialty promises confidentiality, even when the patient doesn't want it. Now, is Jason Darrow your young lover?"

"Well, now, since you're keeping names out of the conversation, so will I. Are you married?"

"I was. I am not now. I left France to come here to study plastic surgery. I fell in love with your country. My wife did not like New York, and she hated Los Angeles. She took my daughter when she returned to Paris. I had to make a choice."

"And you chose Los Angeles over your family? How terrible. Aren't you lonely without them?"

"I miss my daughter. She loved California as much as I did, and she intends to return to live with me next year. She was thirteen when my wife decided to leave, and although she begged me to let her stay, I could not bring myself to separate her from her mother. She visits me for a month each summer, and I go to Paris as often as I can. She considers herself an American, as I do."

At the restaurant, they were quickly escorted to a table at the back of the room by a window overlooking the lights of the city. Perched on the side of the hill, the restaurant had a commanding view to the south, and it was breathtaking.

"I'm so glad you suggested we come to this restaurant. I haven't been here in a long time."

They started the evening with a bottle of Taittinger champagne, and the conversation progressed effortlessly. They liked many of the same things, and they soon found that they knew many of the same people, and Peach found him to be a warm and easy companion. Only occasionally when she would look up to see his dark eyes staring intently at her face did she feel any discomfort, but she could not ignore the fact that he was powerfully charmed by her. It flattered her more than she wanted it to.

The evening passed quickly. The dinner had been superb and the service unhurried. They were extremely compatible about everything except the wine, and their lively discussion on the merits of French versus California wines stimulated them both.

"Pierre, you must be my guest in the Napa Valley someday. I'll take you to meet some of the finest winemakers in the world and prove to you that California is fast overtaking your châteaux in technology."

"Technology? But of course, winemaking is not technology . . . it is art!" They both laughed, and he continued, "And I accept your invitation . . . when can I come?"

"I shall be going up there very soon. My son's child is due shortly. Perhaps you can join us for a weekend when the guesthouse is ready?"

"Delightful. But when do I see you again here? Tomorrow? The next day? The day after that?"

She realized that she herself had made a commitment to the continuation of their friendship, and now she was uncertain what to do. "I'm sorry, Pierre. Tomorrow is Christmas Eve, and I'm pretty tied up for the rest of the year."

He reached across the table and took the champagne glass, which she had nervously begun to twirl by its stem, out of her hand and set it on the table. Then, holding her hand in his, he lifted it to his face and softly caressed his cheek with it. "That sounds so far away . . . the end of the year," he said softly. He looked up into her eyes as he kissed her fingertips, one at a time. "Spend the night with me," he murmured.

Peach was thankful Jason would be waiting for her to keep her from temptation. Pierre was a sexy and persuasive man, and she needed all the help she could get in resisting his efforts to manipulate her. "Please, Pierre, don't do that. Not now." She drew her hand away from him, and he did not persist.

. She decided to be honest. "I'm sorry, but I just can't cope with two relationships at the same time. I should not have accepted your invitation to dinner."

"Please," he protested, "I invited you only to dinner. The other . . . well, shall we call it an irresistible impulse?"

"The truth is . . . Jason arrived in Los Angeles today, and well . . . I'll be seeing him later this evening." Her voice trailed off in embarrassment.

He smiled at her discomfiture. "My dear, what an innocent you are. You women are just not prepared for true liberation. There is nothing wrong with dining with one person and sleeping with another. We men have been doing that for centuries."

"Well, I haven't, and I find it awkward even to talk about."

"Tell me, lovely one, is this Jason the only man you've slept with since your husband died?" She nodded her head. "And you were faithful throughout your marriage?" She nodded her head again. "You were also a virgin when you married, were you not?"

"I was, and I'm not ashamed of it," she replied defensively.

"Of course not, but you must not wrap yourself in it as if it were a badge of glory. Times change. You would not wear yesterday's fashions. Don't bind yourself in yesterday's moralities."

The conversation was beginning to annoy her. "This has been a lovely evening, Pierre, but I think it's time to go now. Would you ask for the check, please?"

Nothing more was said until he had finished paying and she rose to get out of her chair. He stayed her with a touch of his hand. "One more moment, please. I have more to say. I am infatuated with you, not only because of your physical beauty but because I find you charming and intelligent. My desire to possess your body is not, however, a barrier to our relationship. I will continue on any level you choose. Just do not exclude me from your life."

Without waiting for her response, he stood up, and they left the restaurant. When they arrived at her building and the doorman came to open the car door, Pierre snapped the central locking system so that he could not.

"I have one favor to ask of you . . . please," he began. "Ask your young man if he has been faithful to you. Will you do that for me?"

"Do you expect a report?" she snapped.

"No. I already know the answer. It is you who needs to know Goodnight. I shall telephone you soon."

She hurried up to her penthouse. It was almost midnight, and she wanted to change her clothes before Jason arrived, but it was too late. Miles informed her that he was out in the kitchen with Sarah. Suddenly, Peach found herself swept into strong arms and lifted off the floor. "Jason! Put me down," she gasped in surprise. Miles vanished so they would be alone.

"You're late, wench. . . . I've been here for ages." He set her down and turned her to face him. They kissed long and passionately. When at last they separated, she whispered into his chest, "Hold me tight. I missed you so much, and I've got so much to tell you."

"Let's take care of the important things first . . . we can talk later," he said, smiling mischievously.

"Good idea," she replied. "Come on, let's go into my bedroom."

He resisted. "Aw, can't we do it here on the entry floor?" he asked teasingly.

"We mustn't get into bad habits," she replied, pulling at his arm, "and besides, we're not alone tonight."

Behind the closed door of her room, they quickly began to undress each other. When she was naked, she began to take off her emerald earrings, but he stopped her. "No, leave them on. Jewelry looks sexier without clothes." Their love-making progressed rapidly and urgently. She was as eager to receive him as he was to enter, and it was not long before they both reached the pinnacle. When it was over, he pulled the blanket over them and cradled her in his arms.

"It's so good to have you with me again," she said. "How long can you stay?"

"I have to be in New York on the twenty-sixth. I've been offered the lead in the new Thompson play, and they're already in rehearsal. Jon Voight was going to star in it, but the film he's doing is way over schedule."

"Won't that interfere with your promotional tour in Europe?"

"My agent worked it out with Burt. If the play's a hit, I'll alternate weeks with Voight, and I can do one or two countries each week I'm not working. The film's already got so much press attention that it's not all that crucial whether I appear or not."

"You're going to be so busy we'll never see each other," she complained.

"Come on now, rich lady. You can fly to New York to be with me there. My play contract is only for twelve weeks."

"Jason, I can't do that," she said.

"Why not? New York is a wonderful, anonymous place. Nobody cares who anybody is there. We'll have all day every day together. You've already got an apartment there, haven't you?"

"Yes, but I've got things to do here now," she replied and told him about her meeting with Dom and Horace. He was impressed with her ideas and encouraging. They talked for a long time about the good she could do, and Peach found herself grateful that she now had some purpose in life. She certainly did not intend to be a camp follower.

After a while, Jason began to caress her sensually again, but the question Pierre had proposed was annoying her. She decided to ask it and get it out of her head once and for all. "Darling, will you tell me something? It's personal, and I don't want to offend you."

"You can ask me anything," he replied.

"Have you been faithful to me?" The moment the words left her lips she regretted them. She sounded stupid and Pollyannish.

There was a tiny pause, and she could feel him pull slightly away from her. "Have you?" he asked in response.

She was startled. "Me? Why, of course I have."

"What do you mean by faithful?" he asked, and she did not like the way his tone of voice had flattened. "Are you asking if I've screwed anybody else while I was out of town?"

Peach found herself pulling away from him too. "Well, yes, put crudely, I suppose that's exactly what I want to know."

"Do you want the truth? Or would a lie make you feel better?"

"You don't have to say anything else," she snapped.

"Now you're angry with me, aren't you? You should never ask a question unless you really want the answer. I thought we had an understanding. We'd love each other without strings or promises . . . no till death do us part. That was, I recall, your particular stipulation."

Pierre, you bastard, she thought, you knew this would happen. Now she'd have to find some way to salvage her pride.

"I'm sorry, Jason, but I had to know. You see, I've met someone. I had dinner with him tonight, and . . . well . . . I'm quite attracted to him, and I didn't want to . . . if . . . well you hadn't . . ." She fumbled for the words.

Jason pulled her close again, and his manner was once more gentle and tender. "And you didn't want to go to bed with him if I had saved myself for you, is that it?" He kissed her lightly, and she nodded her head. "You're an adult, Peach. Do whatever you want to do. You have as much freedom as I have."

There was little more conversation from then on. They made love again, but Peach could not reach another climax. Her mind had drifted away. She decided she just wasn't ready for the new morality.

50

Her Mother's Child

GRACE sat down behind her desk at the beauty salon as Casey had told her to. It felt strange to be here again. Eve had given her a stack of papers to look over, bank deposits, checks, invoices, but she couldn't concentrate long enough to make sense of them. Casey had told her she would have to come back to work soon, but everything was too confusing. Although she was quite aware that she was the proprietor of "Amazing Grace's," she could summon no interest in it.

Eve came in smiling as usual. Why was everyone always so damned cheerful when they talked to her? It didn't use to be like that. Everyone used to bitch at her all the time about something or other, and now everyone was continually smiling and mouthing treacly sweetness. It made her feel like an idiot.

"How ya doin', old girl? Making any sense out of that stuff I gave you?"

"Not really, Eve. I guess I'm just not ready for this yet."

"It's tough to get back into the swing of things. But we really need you here. The place doesn't run smoothly when you're not on top of things. Are you ready for Christmas?"

"Casey took me to Nieman's yesterday."

There was silence, and Eve was at a loss to continue. Grace was so passive and uncommunicative, Eve observed, she barely reacted to anything.

"Eve, how much longer before Casey will be finished?" She was tired and ready to go home.

"It won't be long. Benjie will have her hair done in ten minutes or so."

"My mind is like a sieve. I can't seem to hold onto anything for long. Now who is Benjie?"

"Benjie is the hairdresser you hired a month ago just before you went to Chicago." She sat down beside the desk. "Grace, don't get discouraged. You've been sick. Naturally it's going to take time to get back to normal. We almost lost you, you know "

"You know I feel like I'm looking through a camera, and everything's out of focus. I keep trying to turn the lens, but nothing ever gets sharp and clear."

"That's a good description. Have you told your doctor about it?"

"Eve, what happened to me? Do you know?"

"Have you asked Casey?"

"I'm afraid to." Her hands were clasped together so tightly that the whiteness of her knuckles threatened to burst through the skin. "Eve, I think I tried to kill myself. I did, didn't I?" She looked up into her friend's eyes.

Eve was afraid she was venturing into forbidden territory, but she obviously wanted the truth. "Don't you remember?"

"Yes, I think so . . . I was just hoping that maybe it was another nightmare."

"I won't lie to you, Grace. You took too many sleeping pills, but maybe . . . maybe you didn't intend to . . . maybe it was just a mistake."

Grace smiled, and Eve could see that she'd dropped the veil again. Her brief moment of insight had vanished. "Well, I'll go check on Casey and see if she's done." Eve hurried out of the office and back to where Casey was having her hair blown dry. "Benjie, shut that damn dryer off for a minute and leave us alone," she ordered. Muttering angrily that the hairstyle would be ruined, the young hairdresser stomped off.

Briefly, she gave Casey a rundown on her conversation with her mother. "You did well, Eve. That's the closest she's come to discussing it. She's making progress."

Later, as they drove home, Casey coaxed her mother into

talking again, but she was not responsive. Casey reminded her that it was Christmas Eve and they'd be celebrating alone at home and that they were going to Peach Malone's the next day.

"Who else will be there?" Grace asked.

"Maggie Hammond and her husband. She's the one who decorated Peach's new home. Laura Austin . . . you know her, she used to be a regular customer at the shop. Peach's new lover is expected . . ."

"What about Drake?"

"He's dead now. Peach is a widow. You remember, don't you?"

Grace shook her head as if to clear it. "My God, what am I saying? I know Drake is dead, maybe I just don't want him to be. Will anyone else be there?"

"No, I'm sorry to say. I had hoped that Jerry could be with us, but I guess that was just too much to ask for." It was the first time she had mentioned his name to her mother since Thanksgiving. Some inner voice had warned her not to.

"Jerry? Who's he?" Grace asked.

"Jerry Casey . . . you know."

The reaction to his name was instant and vehement. "Jerry Casey? What do you want him here for?" Grace's eyes blazed, and a flush appeared on her cheeks. She looked as if she might have a stroke, and her reaction frightened her daughter.

"Mom, don't get so excited. He's not coming," Casey said and was forced to acknowledge how powerful and negative her mother's feelings were toward him.

Grace was not appeased. "He can't come here! Never. I won't stand for it," she declared, and her voice regained the tone of authority that had lately been absent.

"Why not, Mom? Tell me," Casey pleaded, but it was too late. Grace's expression flattened out, and it was obvious she had withdrawn again, but Casey would not let go. "Answer me, Mom!"

Grace looked out the window, and her voice seemed to come from far away. "He doesn't want the baby."

Try as she would, Casey could not get her mother to say anything else. She just stared out the window with her lips pressed tightly together.

When they arrived home, Casey settled Grace in front of the television with Rudolfo to watch the news, and she telephoned Dr. Winchester. She was sure she had stumbled onto something important. Unfortunately, he was gone for the holidays, as was Jim Austin. She tried Peach too, but Sarah said she was out. Frustrated, she went into the kitchen to prepare dinner and ponder the problem. Was it possible that her illegitimate pregnancy had caused her mother so much pain that she'd try to kill herself?

At the dinner table, Casey tried to make the evening a warmly sentimental one. "I think it would be nice if each of us said what was in our hearts on this special evening. Rudolfo, since we don't go to church regularly and you do, would you mind saying a blessing?"

Bowing his head, he said in Spanish, "*Gracias a Dios para la vida de amiga mía.*" His eyes were brilliant with moisture of deeply felt emotion.

"Thank you, that was lovely. Mom, now it's your turn. Just say anything you feel."

Grace shook her head. "No, I don't know what to say."

"Say anything," Casey persisted.

"All right, I'll try. I'm happy to be at home with you both and not in that hospital where it was so cold. I'm happy that there's no snow. I hate the snow. . . ."

They waited, and when it was apparent that she was finished, Casey asked, "I didn't know how much you hated the snow, Mom. Is that why you moved to California?"

Grace nodded and said, "It causes so much trouble, and your feet get cold and wet if you don't wear galoshes."

"Tell me about the snow, Mom, I want to know more."

"I don't want to talk about it anymore. It makes me shiver. I don't know what made me think of it. Besides, it's your turn."

"Okay, here goes. My heart is full of love and gratitude for having my mother with me this Christmas. I can't mourn anymore for what I lost. I have to believe it was never meant to be. I'm so lucky to have been raised in a home filled with love, and I hope I can continue my life surrounded by the people I love.''

Although she hadn't intended to mention the loss of the baby, it was too important to ignore. She was concerned that she was not suffering the acute depression Dr. Austin had warned her about. She even found herself wondering if the baby had ever really existed at all, and her biggest fear was that Jerry would not want her without a child.

As they were eating dessert, Peach called. Casey went into the bedroom to talk. She gave her a quick rundown and described her mother's intensely negative reaction to Jerry's name and her odd reference to snow and galoshes. ''What do you make of all this, Peach?'' she asked.

''I don't know, but the time for lying is over. She's strong enough for the truth. Eve and I both feel that your pregnancy was not the blessed event you tried to make of it. Tell her.''

''I'm afraid to,'' Casey protested. ''Something awful might happen and ruin everybody's Christmas.''

Peach's exasperation caused her to make a serious slip. ''Casey, you're just like your mother. You both weave webs of lies around yourselves that complicate your lives and the lives of everyone around you.''

Casey was quick to pick up on Peach's thoughtless accusation. ''What do you mean? What lies has my mother told?''

''God, Casey, forget what I just said. It's out of the past . . . really . . . a long time ago.''

''The psychiatrist said everything about my mother was important. Are you hiding something that might help her? You know, if we don't find out what caused Mom's depression, she might try to kill herself again.''

There was a long silence. ''Some things are not mine to tell. Only Grace can tell you. Casey, please . . . don't make the same mistakes she has. Face the truth. Tell her there is no child now. Tell Jerry too. Maybe if you tell the truth, it will encourage her to do the same.''

When Casey returned, Grace and Rudolfo were clearing

the dishes. "I'll do that, Mom," she protested, but Grace refused to stop.

"I don't want to be an invalid. Maybe I'm a little confused and forgetful, but I can damn well do the dishes. Just make sure I put them in the dishwasher and not the oven or refrigerator, okay?"

Later in the evening, after they had listened to some children singing carols at the door and had settled down in front of the Christmas tree, Casey summoned the courage to begin. "Mom, I have something to tell you." Rudolfo got up to leave, but she stopped him. "Stay, Rudolfo, I need you here." Grace was troubled by the look of fear on her daughter's face. Was she ill?

"Ten days ago, I wouldn't have risked this, but I'm convinced you're well enough to handle it now. I hope to God, I'm right." She must say this quickly before her courage deserted her. "Mom, I had a miscarriage." It was short, blunt, to the point, and said.

Grace just looked blankly at her. "Mom, do you understand what I've just said? I was pregnant, remember? But something happened, and I'm not pregnant anymore. I hope you're not too upset, but I promise you, there'll be grandchildren someday."

"The baby's gone? Are you sure?" Grace finally responded, but there was no pain or consternation on her face, only curiosity.

"Absolutely sure. It happened in the hospital."

"Are you all right?"

"I'm fine. I didn't want to tell you, but Peach insisted . . ."

"You're not lying to me? You're not just telling me this to make me feel better, are you?" Grace had leaned toward her daughter and had taken hold of her arm. Her grip was tight and her voice tense.

"Relieve your mind? No! I wouldn't lie about something like that. One day when I was at the hospital visiting you, I had a terrible cramping sensation, and they put me on a table . . . and well, it was just all over. That's the truth."

Keeping her firm grip on Casey's arm, Grace turned to

Rudolfo. She needed affirmation. He would never deceive her. "Is she telling the truth? There is no child?"

Rudolfo nodded his head. *"Es verdad."*

Grace let go of Casey's arm and stood up. Her mind was flooded with so many images, she couldn't sort them all out. It was like a dam had burst, and she was being swamped in a flood of perceptions. She remembered Chicago, and Jerry Casey, and Finn, and Blanche . . . and the baby was gone! It was a miracle. She had done terrible things. She had lied. She had tried to commit murder. She had tried to kill herself and instead of being punished, she had been rewarded. Why? She had always known there was no order in the universe, but this occurrence demonstrated a perverseness that was totally incomprehensible. But, oh, God, how thankful she was for it!

"Mom, are you all right? I only told you because Peach said it was the best thing." Casey feared that the coldness with which she had received the news might only be the calm presaging the storm.

"I'm fine, honey. Really I am. I just need a little time to get used to all this. Peach was right. Thank you for telling me the truth. I know how unhappy you are about losing the baby, but it wasn't meant to be."

Grace gathered her daughter into her arms, and Casey knew that her mother was back at last. Perhaps someday when Grace was old and infirm, they might have to switch roles again, but that was a long time away. Thank God she could be her mother's child again. They both began to cry, and the past terrible weeks of misery were washed away with their tears.

Later that evening, when the fire had died down and the weeping had ended, Casey climbed in beside Grace in her mother's kingsized bed as she had done so many times when she was a little girl and afraid of the dark. Before she went to sleep, Grace made a silent promise to set things straight once and for all.

_51_

Time to Be Jolly

WHEN Kirk arrived to pick up Laura on Christmas Eve, she noticed the circles under his eyes. "Kirk, is something wrong?"

"Everything's wrong, but let's not talk about it now. It's Christmas and time to be jolly. Are you ready?"

"Yes, get that box in the kitchen. Even though Maggie told me not to, I made a coffee cake for breakfast tomorrow."

As Kirk steered the car onto the heavy traffic of the San Diego Freeway, he could sense Laura's tension. "Are you okay?"

"Not now, but I will be. Just give me a few minutes to do a few stress-reducing procedures that Christine taught me."

"It's really still hard for you, isn't it?" he asked.

"It may never be easy, I'm afraid, but I have to fight it, and I will. I know what my enemy is."

"Tell me about it."

"I'm really afraid of fear. My first full-blown attack happened on an airplane, although before that I'd had a lot of little ones that I didn't recognize "

"Like when?"

"Remember how I used to avoid driving the freeways?"

"Jim used to give you a hard time, I remember."

"And so did the twins. But I would have panic attacks just thinking about getting on the freeway, and I went out of my way for miles to stay on the surface streets. I knew my heart would start racing, my palms would get wet, and I'd get a helpless, weak feeling. Now, thanks to Christine, I know that the attack will come, but I also know I'll survive it. It won't kill me, so I must just go on and do what I have to do."

Angie greeted them when they arrived at the house. "Laura, you look terrific! I love your sweater," she said, fingering the bright red angora. "Will you give it to me when you're tired of it?"

"Why don't we share it? I'll keep it in the winter, and you can have it in the summer," she teased.

"Thanks a lot. Come on in. Mom's in the kitchen."

"Good. Maybe I can help her," Laura replied, and left Kirk to carry in her packages and overnight bag.

"Merry Christmas!" she greeted her hostess, and Maggie responded with a hug. "Maggie, what's wrong? You and Kirk both look tired."

Quickly, Maggie turned away to avoid her close scrutiny. "I'm all right, really. I've just been working too hard on the Cornwall house, that's all. Here, unmold this caviar thing for me."

Laura wrapped an apron around her skirt and set to work. In a short time, they had everything under control, and they joined Kirk and Angie in the family room for a drink before dinner. The conversation became less stilted as the liquor mellowed them, and everyone began to relax. During dinner, Laura told them about her meeting with Jim, and they praised her courage and poise. Kirk described a condo he had found for her, and they decided to look at it on the way to Peach's the next morning.

When dinner was over, they watched Mikhail Baryshnikov dance *The Nutcracker* on television. Later, Angie went to her room, and Kirk announced he was tired and was going to bed. Laura followed Maggie into the kitchen to help her with the dishes.

"It was a lovely Christmas Eve, Maggie. I can't thank you and Kirk enough for letting me be a part of your family tonight."

"Don't thank me. We loved having you. You made it possible, as a matter of fact, for us to have a decent evening together. I don't know how we would have managed without you."

"Maggie, what are you talking about?"

"I'm about to join you in the ranks of single women," she replied tersely, avoiding Laura's eyes.

"You can't be serious? I don't believe it."

"Believe it, all right. He gave me an ultimatum . . . either it's him or decorating," she replied bitterly.

"Surely you're not choosing decorating, for God's sake, over Kirk? Have you lost your mind?"

"The issue is control, not decorating. Does anybody, even a husband, have the right to impose his will on another, even if it's just his wife? Doesn't what I want to do count at all?" Maggie's voice betrayed a deeply felt anger.

"Surely you can work out some kind of compromise, can't you?"

"God knows I've tried. But I've committed an unpardonable sin . . . I've been too successful, and now I can't be content to play bridge and go to Cuisinart classes."

"You're making a big mistake, Maggie. Nothing, absolutely nothing in this world is more important than your husband. Believe me, I know."

"Okay, so you were the wonderful, devoted helpmate to Jim and look where it got you," Maggie said.

"That's not fair," Laura responded defensively. "Kirk and Jim are different men. You're luckier than I was."

"Look, even if I did give up my work, I have no guarantee that Kirk will stay around. He could follow Jim's example and trade me in for a younger model . . . or he could die. Either way I'd be left alone with nothing . . . like you are. You know if I quit now when my career is just getting started, I might never be able to get it going again. Remember old Will Shakespeare's line about the tide being taken at its flood?" Maggie slammed down a pan and continued, "Your whole way of life was destroyed because Jim wanted to screw some hot little bitch. Wouldn't you love to have a career right now to sustain you?"

"No, Maggie, I'm not like you. My career was in my home. I loved it, and I hope to God someday I'll be able to do it again. I just can't imagine trying to go out and apply for a job somewhere. The very thought of it scares me half to death."

They finished the dishes in silence until just before Maggie was about to turn off the lights, and Laura said in a doleful voice, "I just wish I had never introduced you to Peach Malone. I feel so guilty to think it was probably my fault." She was obviously very troubled. Maggie put her arm around her shoulder, and they walked upstairs together.

"Laura, stop trying to carry the burdens of the world on your shoulders. It wasn't your fault. Maybe neither of our marriages were as good as we thought they were. I hope I haven't spoiled your Christmas. I didn't mean to. I just needed a friend to talk to."

"Maybe he'll change his mind."

"I'm not counting on it, but it would be nice."

Angie was chattering on the telephone when she entered her room, and Laura was glad she would not have to talk to her. She was too depressed. She showered and got into bed before Angie was finished with her call. She closed her eyes and pretended to go to sleep, but she could not relax. She had barely come to terms with the dissolution of her own marriage, and now she was faced with a similar crisis her friends were creating. It frightened her. She needed Kirk and Maggie to help her through the next months.

Christmas morning was sunny and bright. As soon as Laura heard sounds in the kitchen, she got up and put on her robe. She brushed her hair and put on some lipstick and hurried to help Maggie. Instead, she found Kirk struggling with the coffeemaker. "Good morning, I thought it was Maggie in here," she said.

"She'll be out soon."

"Here, let me do that. Why don't you squeeze some orange juice and let me fix breakfast?"

"If you insist. By the way, Merry Christmas."

"And Merry Christmas to you too." She gave him a quick kiss on the cheek and went to work. In a short time, they had everything ready, and Laura made a suggestion. "Kirk, I've got a good idea. Why don't you get Maggie's wineglasses, and we'll have mimosas instead of just orange juice. There's a cold bottle of champagne in the refrigerator."

"Great idea. This will be a good day to spend in an alcoholic euphoria," he remarked, and she detected a slight bitterness in his attitude. Suddenly she noticed that Maggie was standing in the doorway, snd she felt awkward because she had no idea how long she'd been there watching them. "Well, Merry Christmas. I hope you don't mind my barging into your kitchen and helping Kirk fix breakfast?" she asked a trifle nervously.

"Why should I mind?" she answered with a notable lack of warmth.

"The omelets are ready," Kirk announced. "Is Angie out of bed yet?"

"She's in the bathroom. She'll be here in a few minutes," Maggie answered.

Kirk finished pouring the fresh orange juice and champagne into the glasses while Laura put the omelets onto a warmed platter with bacon and cut the coffee cake she had brought. Maggie made no attempt to join in the preparations. She poured herself a cup of black coffee as she dourly watched them bustle about in the kitchen.

Angie made her appearance, and put some Christmas music on the stereo. They all sat down to eat, and the adults seemed content to allow the youngster to dominate the conversation.

"I can hardly wait till it's time to go to Mrs. Malone's. Can you believe it? Jason Darrow? I've got two rolls of film, Dad. You've got to take lots of pictures of me with him. If we get a good one, I'm going to have it blown up to poster size," she burbled on.

"Angie, did you like the movie?"

"Are you kidding? I've seen it four times now."

"Is it really that good?" her father asked.

"Yeah, I guess so, but he's positively dreamy. He turns on the girls like you wouldn't believe."

"Well, I think we better go see it then, don't you think so, Maggie?" Laura asked.

"Oh, shit! This is awful," Angie exploded suddenly.

"Watch your language, young lady. What's so awful?" Kirk demanded.

"I'm probably the only one going today who's seen the movie. How embarrassing!" she wailed.

"I'm sure you'll be able to handle the conversation about Hollywood for all of us," Maggie commented dryly.

After breakfast they gathered around the tree to open their gifts. Maggie was surprised with Kirk's gift. It was a tiny lightbulb on a gold chain, and it was filled with small diamonds that sparkled as they tumbled loosely about. For the first time in many hours, she relaxed and smiled. "It's beautiful, Kirk. I've never seen anything like it. Thank you," she said, although she made no move to leave her chair to kiss him as Angie had done when she opened the package he had given her containing a gold key for her new car.

When the last gift had been opened, Maggie suggested they get ready to go, and Kirk volunteered to clean up the mess of torn wrappings. Laura noticed the diffident, almost formal manner which her hosts used in dealing with each other, and it depressed her. She vowed to try to talk some sense into Kirk. She'd had no luck with Maggie, but she'd become much closer to him lately, and she hoped she could influence him.

Angie was the first to get ready. Her long dark curly hair formed a thick halo around her head, and while her makeup was not obtrusive, even the little she used brought out the startling size of her large, dark eyes. She was dressed in a low-cut ruffled white cotton blouse and designer jeans so tight they might have come out of an aerosol spray can. Around her waist was a turquoise and silver Indian belt that emphasized her tiny waist, round hips, and ample breasts. The jeans were tucked into the handmade cowboy boots from Nieman-Marcus that she had wheedled out of her father for her birthday.

Laura was the next to emerge. She was dressed in a softly draped sheer lilac wool dress. Maggie appeared in a red silk pants outfit she had saved for the occasion. Laura noted with satisfaction that she was wearing Kirk's necklace.

Kirk protested that jeans were not appropriate attire, but both women defended Angie's clothes, and Kirk retreated muttering, "Well, do the pants have to be so tight? How are you going to sit down in them?"

Angie laughed. "I'll figure out something. C'mon, let's go."

Laura observed the affectionate display between father and daughter, and it worried her. Kirk adored his only child, and it was obvious from the overt and nubile sexuality of his daughter that she was a woman far more comfortable in the company of men than women. If Maggie let Kirk go, she might very well lose her daughter to him. It was a sad thought and was made even more so by the similarity that Laura had noticed. Angie, the darling little tomboy who had been the object of her sons' attentions for years, had grown into a woman much like Ghilly Jordan, a woman who wore her sexuality like a signboard that said to all men, "Look at me . . . I want it as much as you do." It might be false advertising but the lure of such women was irresistible.

Maggie's voice interrupted Laura's thoughts. "Kirk, I'm going to drive my own car, so if I'm delayed at the Cornwalls', you won't have to wait for me."

"Fine, I'll take Laura with me to the condo for a quick look. Do you want to go with us?"

"Please come, Maggie," Laura urged. "I need your expert advice. I can't pay the fees you're getting nowadays, but I hope you'll help me a little."

Maggie and Kirk avoided each other's eyes as she responded, "Of course I'll help you, and I'll be offended if you offer me any money."

After a short drive, they drove through the security gate into the seaside community where the red tile roofs and white walls against the azure sky gave it a true Mediterranean ambience.

"The one we're going to see is on the second floor, but it has a nice view." Once inside, Maggie couldn't help but contrast the smallness of the rooms and the quietness of the sea that was choked off by a breakwater, to the grandeur of the Cornwall house and the magnificence of the unrestrained tides of Malibu.

"Is this as large as they come?" Maggie asked.

"No," Kirk replied, "but it's the best value. There's a penthouse that's twice the size with a spectacular view from every room and has greenhouse windows, but it's three times the price."

"That's the one I want then," Laura declared. "Make an offer that will get it for me." All three Hammonds looked at her in amazement.

"Don't you want to see it first?" Kirk asked.

Laura shrugged her shoulders, but Maggie protested, "Well, I do even if you don't!"

"Good, I'll leave it up to you two to take care of it for me," Laura said, and laughed at the bewilderment on everyone's face. "Don't you understand? I'm trading it for that big house in Sherman Oaks. I might be soft, but I'm not a complete fool. Come on now, we don't want to be late."

On the way to Peach's, Laura rode with Maggie because Angie had wanted to drive her father's car. Although she was more nervous because Maggie's car was smaller and she drove faster than Kirk did, she decided to submerge her fears in Maggie's problem.

"Maggie, have you given any thought to Angie . . . you know, about your breakup with Kirk?"

"I should never have dumped my problems on you last night, Laura. Yes, I've given Angie a lot of thought."

"I guess you know she's partial to Kirk. You might lose her if she's forced to make a choice."

"She's a grown woman now. No one needs to have custody of her. There won't be any choices to make," Maggie protested but her voice lacked conviction.

Laura sighed. She could think of nothing more to say. Maggie was a stone wall. Maybe Kirk would be more responsive.

_52_

The Hearts
of Men

IT WAS Christmas morning, and Peach was lying beside her sleeping young lover having dark thoughts. She could not seem to erase from her mind the realization that he had been fucking other women. That word had never been part of her vocabulary before. Screw maybe, but she didn't use that either. Sex had always been an act she described as making love, but when she thought about him having his penis in another woman's vagina or mouth, it had become fucking, damn him.

What a sheltered life she'd had with Drake. He just hadn't prepared her for the real world. As tense and driving as he had been, he had always been tender and patient in his lovemaking. She couldn't remember a single time he had ever lost control of himself or initiated unusual sexual activity. He had put her on a pedestal in every way.

It was Jason who had introduced her to oral sex, bringing words like fellatio and cunnilingus off the written page into reality. Now that she knew how adventurous a man could be about sex, she wondered if Drake had found complete satisfaction in the pristine coupling that had characterized their marriage.

Had Drake had another woman . . . women? Grace? Was that the terrible secret that had driven her to suicide? Nonsense. If there had been someone else, it was no one she knew. Maybe that's who was after her . . . a woman wronged by

Drake . . . good grief, Drake was seventy-one, when he died. How dumb she was. Besides, nobody was after her.

Her eyes closed as she lay musing when she felt Jason's arm creep across her chest. She was still naked from their lovemaking the night before, and she was aroused when his hand gently closed around her breast and stayed there. "You're awake," she whispered.

Keeping his eyes closed, he replied, "No, I'm dreaming I'm in bed with the world's most beautiful woman, and I've got one of her breasts in my hand. Don't wake me up."

"Merry Christmas, Jason. Time to get up."

He wound his arms around her and held her close to him. "I'm already up. You know this will be our last time alone together for a while."

"You're not staying with me tonight?" she asked.

"I have to be in New York for rehearsal tomorrow morning. I'm taking the red-eye flight tonight."

"And leaving me all alone?"

"You can come along, you know."

She shook her head. "I can't. Steve's baby is due soon, and I've got to get busy on the plans for my foundation. It's important to me."

"More important than being with me?" he asked.

She pulled away and got out of bed as she retorted, "Is appearing in that play more important than staying here with me?"

He laughed. "Touché, naked lady. Your point. You will come to New York for at least one visit, won't you? Don't you want to see me tread the boards?"

Peach put on her robe and sat down beside him on the bed. "Jason, I have a question to ask you . . . and I'd like the truth . . . if you know it."

"I'm not going to like this, am I?"

"Where do I fit in your life?"

He slid down in the bed and lay on his back with his eyes fixed on the ceiling. "The truth, huh? Well, let's see. I like you. You're intelligent and interesting to talk to. You've got a funny sense of humor. You're beautiful and sexy . . . and incredibly innocent. I wish I was forty-five years old, because then I'd sweep you off your feet and marry you and we'd live happily ever after." He turned to look at her. "But I'm only twenty-eight, Peach. I've got too much to do. I've got places to go and people to meet. Can't I have all that and you too?"

She smiled and kissed him lightly. "That was the truth, Jason . . . and I thank you for it. I'll always be glad I knew you."

As she showered, she thought about her illusions. The one-man, one-woman arrangement sometimes was just not feasible. Would she have to dissolve her attachment to Jason before she could form one with another man? Pierre? Could she handle two romances at the same time? Would she find herself comparing one man's technique with another? Men enjoyed variety. Maybe she would too. Perhaps Pierre might like to join them for Christmas dinner. She'd call him as soon as she was dressed.

Peach and Jason were having breakfast when Miles entered the morning room and announced that Doug Dooley had arrived and needed to speak with her alone.

"Tell him to wait in the study. Jason, finish your coffee, this won't take long."

Doug was looking out the window when she arrived. "Good morning, Doug. And Merry Christmas. Miles said you wanted to talk to me."

"Yes, Mrs. Malone. It's important. I've uncovered a few things that you need to know. I had intended to wait until after Christmas, but I changed my mind."

"My goodness, you sound awfully serious."

"I found out that the attack on you in Milan was not a kidnap attempt. You were supposed to be killed."

"My God, are you sure?"

"When you're dealing with the underworld, you can't be sure of anything. I just know that the man who spoke to you in English has been identified. He's a hit man. He's not into ransoms."

Peach sat down on the couch. The idea that there was actually some person or persons who wanted her dead was frightening . . . no, more than frightening, terrifying. The kidnapping attempt had been easier to deal with, for it had a rationale, but why would anyone want her dead?

"Doug, I just can't believe it. Why in the world would anyone want me dead? For what reason?"

"I don't know. You've got to help me. Who stands to gain?"

"Nobody . . . nobody at all . . . except my children . . . and surely you don't suggest that!"

"Of course not, but there's got to be somebody else."

"Is the identity of the hit man the only reason you have to make such accusations?" She was beginning to feel hostile to him. He was disturbing her, and she wanted to reject his suspicions. How could she live with such a threat hanging over her every moment?

"Unfortunately, no. You probably haven't been aware of it, but I've doubled the watch on you for the past few days. During a routine inspection, we found that the brakes on the Rolls had been tampered with. Also, we've checked on the building's security guards, and we found one of them had forged identification papers. He disappeared right after we questioned him. We're sure he was a plant and that he was the one who messed with the car."

Peach looked down at her hands. They were shaking almost uncontrollably. "What do you want me to do, Doug? I'll do anything you tell me."

"First of all, I want you to stay here. We've got the place well secured, and we can check everyone coming and going."

"Good Lord, am I to become a prisoner in my own home?"

"Temporarily. Whoever it is won't wait too long. He seems a little eager. Are you sure there isn't someone you've crossed . . . someone you've become a threat to?"

Suddenly, she knew. "I just found out that my banker and my attorney were deliberately trying to mislead me about the terms of Drake's trust. I asserted myself . . . finally . . . and told them I was taking control of all my holdings . . . and that I intended to give it away . . . the money, I mean.''

Doug let out a low whistle. "Horace Beller and Dominic Petrone . . . those are the men we're talking about?"

"Yes, but I just can't believe that either one of them could mean me any physical harm."

Doug smiled bitterly. "Only the Shadow knows what evil lurks in the hearts of men. . . . Remember that old radio show? No, I guess you're too young. Anyway, those men would have the kind of bucks it would take for a hit . . . and your estate is worth a lot of money."

"Doug, they were close friends of my husband's. He trusted them completely, and you know what a good judge of character he was."

"It won't hurt to check them out. We don't have any other leads."

"I'm having friends here today for Christmas dinner. I can't change that now."

"Of course not. Go ahead and have a good holiday. I'll keep one of my men here in the penthouse, however, if you don't mind."

"I want him out of sight," Peach protested.

"Of course. And don't worry. If anything unusual happens, let me know right away, okay?"

"I will, Doug. And thanks for taking care of me. You're watching out for Anne and Steve too, aren't you?"

"Absolutely. I'll be going now. Merry Christmas."

"Thanks," she said wryly to his departing back. Surely he could protect her and her family, Peach tried to reassure herself. After all, he had once been entrusted with the life of the President of the United States.

Trying to get her mind off her jangled nerves, Peach went into the kitchen to go over the preparations for Christmas dinner with Sarah and Miles. "Miles, I'd like to serve some of Steve's Chardonnay with the turkey."

"I'm sorry, ma'am, but there wasn't any left when we moved the wine out of the cellar in the big house."

"You must be mistaken. You had a bottle iced for me on the bar the night I returned from Italy."

"Me, ma'am? I'm afraid not. I was too busy to get here at all that day. Perhaps Mrs. Hammond left it for you."

"No, it couldn't have been from Maggie. That was the limited bottling. We never put any of it on the market." Suddenly, the memory of Winnie drinking the spilled wine connected with the image of her tiny dead body . . . and Doug's warning. Good God, had her poor little dog drunk something meant for her?

Her knees shaking, Peach sat down again. "Are you all right, ma'am?" Sarah asked, concerned at the sudden stark paleness on Peach's face.

"Miles, quick, get Doug back here. Hurry. I have to talk to him right away."

The telephone rang. It was Dom calling. What did he want, she wondered, and although she was nervous about it, she took the call.

"Peach, I hate to disturb you on the holiday, but it's important that I see you for a few minutes."

"Can't it wait until tomorrow, Dom? I have guests coming in just a little while." She wanted to put him off. She hated the thought of facing him. Maybe he was the villain who had killed her little dog and was trying to kill her. He was the one, too, who'd cut off Maggie's money and was threatening her son's winery.

"No, it really can't, Peach. I'm sorry."

"Come on over, then."

She put down the telephone, and Miles signaled that Doug was on the other line. Relieved, she answered quickly. "Thank God Miles caught you, Doug. Where are you?"

"I'm still downstairs. What's up?"

"Dom Petrone is on his way here to see me . . . and I think maybe somebody tried to poison me."

"I'll be right there."

While she waited for him, Peach went into the bedroom to check on Jason. She found him lolling in the tub with the whirlpool and the stereo going full force. She decided not to disturb him. He was not destined to be one of the main characters in her life.

Doug arrived shortly, and he took up his position just outside the study, after carefully concealing a microphone on the desk so that he could monitor their conversation. Peach sat down and waited for Miles to usher Dom in. She felt like an actress in a bad play who didn't know her lines. She clenched her hands together tightly. Surely Dom would be suspicious if he noticed her trembling.

When Dom blustered in, it was obvious he was not searching for clues to her emotional state. He looked completely unhinged. She had never seen him look so rumpled and untogether.

"Peach, something awful's happened . . . and I feel totally responsible."

"What . . . what are you talking about, Dom?"

"I was at the bank all night. I haven't been home since yesterday."

"Christmas Eve?"

"Yeah, my wife's furious. Yesterday morning I got a call from a man named Saleem Talhami. He claimed he was the new owner of your house in Bel Air, and the security guards had refused to grant him access to the property. I called Horace right away, but his secretary said she hadn't heard from him since the day before yesterday. I called his home, but nobody was there either. I checked out the situation on the property and found out that the deed had been recorded the day before, and this guy was, in effect, the new owner of the house."

"I don't understand." Peach's fear had given way to curiosity and bewilderment.

"Yeah, neither did I. I went to see Talhami immediately, and I found out that he'd made a cash—cash, mind you—transaction with Horace personally . . . for eight million dollars! That house and grounds were worth at least twelve, maybe fourteen. Horace had an airtight power of attorney from you, and legally he had the right to sell it for any price he wanted to.''

"Do you think he stole the money?" She was aghast.

"That's just the tip of the iceberg, Peach. I've looked into some of those investments Drake made while he was ill. They were all dummy corporations. I think that Horace has been milking the estate ever since Drake got sick. God knows what we'll unearth when we really start digging.'' He put his face in his hands. He looked tired and much older.

Silently, Peach stood up and walked over to where the microphone was hidden. "Doug, please join us," she said quietly. She then walked over to Dom and put her arm around him. "Dom, I can't tell you how important it was for you to tell me this today. Now don't worry. It's only money.''

Doug entered the room, and Dom was surprised to see Drake's ex-bodyguard. Then Doug told him about the attempts on Peach's life that had been recently uncovered.

"It's my guess, Mr. Petrone, that it was Mr. Beller who was behind all this. When he realized it wasn't going to work, he made a quick cash sale and got out with as much as he could. Do you know exactly how long he's been gone?''

"No, I don't,'' Dom said wearily.

"This is all so hard to believe. Horace was Drake's closest confidant. He discussed everything with him. I can't tell you how many times Drake has told me how honest and bright he was.''

"When people die, people change, Mrs. Malone, especially when there's money involved,'' Doug remarked. "I'm going to get on this right away. I don't think you have anything to worry about now. That guy's probably too worried about saving his own neck to be thinking about wasting yours. We'll stay on the alert, however, until everything's settled.''

When he was gone, Dom and Peach talked for a long time. She tried to reassure him that she in no way held him responsible. He in turn vowed that he would not rest until Horace was behind bars.

"I'd really hate to see him get away with it," Peach said. "It's not just the money either. He betrayed all of us, especially Drake. But why did he try to kill me? It wasn't that I was asserting control . . . the first attempt was long before that."

"I'm sure it was the trust. He'd convinced Drake that if anything happened to you the kids shouldn't get the dough until they were thirty. With you gone, he'd have had complete control for several years."

"But he'd have had to deal with you still?"

"Listen, Peach, I'm not very proud of my part in this whole thing. The truth is, I just wasn't paying attention. I was letting him call all the shots."

"How much did he take?"

"God knows, millions, I guess. The estate was shrinking fast. That's why I was giving you and Steve a hard time. He was so much closer to it than I was. Jesus, I've got a whole banking operation to run."

"Drake trusted him completely."

"So did I," Dom replied.

When he left, Peach went to her room to begin dressing for the party, but her mind was awhirl with all the disquieting news. Soon, however, her depression turned to anger. Horace must not be allowed to get away! As her mind focused on him, she suddenly knew where he might be. Of course. Why hadn't she remembered sooner? She hurried into her study and closed the door. Quickly, she called Doug, who answered from his car telephone.

"Doug, I want you to check something out for me. There is a woman named Georgia Martin. She lives in San Diego, but she and Horace have been meeting for years at the Rosarita Beach Hotel in Baja. If it's not too late, you might still be able to find him with her."

"Great. I'll get on it immediately, Mrs. Malone. Don't worry, we'll get lots of cooperation from the police on this," Doug replied.

Peach put down the telephone, and congratulated herself

for remembering the sordid little story Drake had told her about Horace's mistress. Now that she thought about it, she wondered why the attorney had continued to keep her a secret after his wife's death. If he was still involved with her, maybe she had become his accomplice.

Well, whatever, Peach thought. She returned to her bedroom to get dressed. She vowed to put it all behind her and have a lovely Christmas. After all, she was still alive.

_53_

There Would
Be Other Christmases

EARLY Christmas morning, Grace awakened from a night of fitful sleep and painful memories that came to haunt. She had to bring some order to the chaos of her daughter's life, and she agonized over the words she would choose. Where to begin?

Casey awakened when her mother got out of bed. "Are you okay, Mom?"

"I'm fine, honey. Go back to sleep. It's early."

"No, I'm awake now. Let's have coffee."

Grace hesitated. Perhaps it would be better to tell Casey later and not spoil Christmas for her. No. She could not wait, or she would be tempted again to let it go. There would be other Christmases.

"Casey, I have something to say to you," she began, as she got back into bed. Courage, she told herself. Get this heavy burden off your back, but don't crush your child by dumping the load too fast.

"Casey, I have a story to tell you that I should have told a long time ago. One snowy night when I was just a girl, I met a handsome young man . . . it may sound like a fairy tale, but it isn't. He was smooth and crafty, and I was an eager little dunce all too willing to give up my virginity. I was a freshman in college, and although I would have willingly continued the affair, he lost interest. I chalked it up to experience. I was not in love with him . . . and then I found out I was pregnant. Even if abortion had been available to me, I would probably not have opted for that escape. The thought of killing a child in the womb is anathema to me now. Perhaps it would have been then too."

She paused and took a breath as Casey listened attentively. "Anyway, I forced him to give me two hundred dollars, but he made me sign a paper absolving him of all responsibility. I left Champaign. I couldn't tell my parents or ask them for help. It would have broken their hearts to find out what I'd done. I went to Chicago where my sisters gave me care and shelter until you were born. I was as proud of you then as I am now. As soon as I could, I took a bus to California where both of us could grow up in the sun."

Casey listened intently as the story of her life unfolded, and Grace spared her no details. Lily, Mrs. Goldhammer, and the night of the rape brought tears to them both, and Grace had to relive once more the night of horror. "Those scars on my body which I said were from an automobile accident were knife wounds. I should have died then, honey, but I had to keep on living for you." She went on to tell of the attempt at prostitution and the accident with Drake's car. "I was back in the hospital again, but nothing was ever the same. I had suddenly acquired a godfather to watch over me."

Casey listened intently, but at one point asked a question. "Was Paul Gable the guy who . . . fathered me?"

"I'm sorry, baby, there is no Paul Gable. My sister gave me the name Gable when I was pregnant. We pretended I had a husband in the Navy. Clark Gable was a big star then."

"But why . . . why did you tell me so many lies about him?"

"I could never deny you anything . . . even a father. You enjoyed the stories about him more than anything else. Pretty soon he became real to me too."

"I still don't understand why you tried to kill yourself."

"That's the hard part of the story, honey. You see, the father of your child was also the father of mine." There, it had been said . . . she could never take it back again. God help her.

Casey was confused momentarily, and then she made the

astounding connection. "Good God, no! Jerry Casey . . . my father. Where did you ever get such an idea?"

Grace was numb with pain and fear. This was a moment that might haunt her more than the nightmares of the past. This was the moment when she might lose her child forever. "It's true," she said, and reached out to touch her daughter's hand, but Casey pulled away.

"My God, why didn't you tell me?" Her voice was full of recrimination.

"Dear God, in all the world, how could I have known that you would meet him and fall in love with him? Is that a scenario that anyone could anticipate . . . or believe?"

"Are you sure it's him? You could be mistaken. You haven't seen him in almost thirty years!" Her daughter's voice was cold and hostile.

"Believe me . . . there is no mistake," Grace replied.

"Did you go back east to see him last month?" Casey demanded. Grace wanted to go on, to tell her the final truth about her attempt to murder him, but she could not. The words would not form on her tongue. If she told her daughter everything, she would also have to confess that she had seduced him . . . or been seduced. It was all too sordid. Casey did not need to know. What was one more lie on her soul?

"No . . . my trip back east was just . . . well . . . I needed to get away by myself to sort things out . . . to try to find an answer."

"You still haven't told me why you tried suicide."

"When I got home, you told me about his heart attack and his decision to divorce his wife. I just didn't know what to do. I thought I could take the whole mess to the grave with me . . . and you could live happily ever after." Her voice broke, and she began to cry.

Casey's anger and outrage evaporated in a wave of pity for her mother's suffering and attempt at self-sacrifice. Fearful that she might again break under stress, she put her arms around her and offered words of comfort. "Mom, I'm so sorry. It's okay now. I'm not pregnant, and I'm a grown-up woman . . . I hope. You don't have to shield me anymore."

After an hour of tears and consolation, Casey decided it was time to call a halt. "Mom, let's go have coffee. Please . . . we both have our lives ahead of us . . . let's leave the past where it belongs . . . in the past."

Later, after a light breakfast, Casey said, "I hope you don't mind if I ask a few more questions . . . but no tears . . . okay?"

"You're entitled," Grace said with a wan smile.

"Did you remember any of this while you were in the hospital?"

"Only in bits and pieces. I couldn't seem to get things in the proper sequence. Apparently, I was trying not to remember."

"But the news that I had lost the baby snapped you out of it . . . right?"

"I guess so. I think I would have told you about your father's identity if you hadn't been pregnant."

"I could have had an abortion," Casey remarked.

"That was no option, honey . . . I don't believe in abortion."

"I know it's hard for you to understand," Casey said gently, "but I believe a woman has a right to choose. I don't consider abortion in the first trimester to be . . . murder, as some people claim."

Grace covered her daughter's hand with her own, and said, "But I do. If abortions had been as easily available then as they are now, I might not have you."

"Oh, Mom, but look how you suffered for it. If it hadn't been for me, you wouldn't have been raped. You've lived a lonely life. I always wondered why you never had lovers."

"No, I never have, and I never will. But don't downplay my life . . . it's been wonderful. I've had the joy of being successful in business, which very few women experience. Life isn't a paperback romance, you know. It's a fiction foisted on gullible women that they cannot be happy alone."

"I read a survey that said the happiest people were single women and married men." Casey laughed, and then she asked, "Mom, are you up to going to Peach's today?"

"Are you?"

"I think we ought to get out of this house and start having a little fun."

"Good, then we'll go. But . . . she doesn't know about this Jerry Casey thing . . . let's keep it just between us, all right?"

"Mom, I love you." Casey put her arm around her mother's shoulder as they got up to clear away the dishes.

"Casey . . . doesn't the, uh, incest thing bother you at all?"

"I'm not devastated, if that's what you mean. After all, neither of us knew. Besides, as a student of serious literature, I know that it's happened in the best of families. In some cultures, it's condoned." She smiled ruefully. "I had a friend in undergraduate school who told me she'd been having intercourse with her father since she was ten years old."

"How awful," Grace gasped.

"She managed to survive it, but she hated him. One night she put a tape recorder under her bed, and she blackmailed him into letting her go away to school. She hated to go home for visits. She almost made me glad I didn't have a father to cope with."

"All men aren't like that, honey."

"I know, Mom. I enjoyed having Paul Gable as my father, and I'm glad you gave him to me . . . but I'm an adult now. Let's promise never to conceal problems from each other. Whatever happens, we'll face it together."

"What are you going to do about Jerry Casey?"

"I don't want to think about it now. I've got so much going on inside me right this minute. All kinds of things . . . happiness that I've got you back . . . misery about Jerry . . . I don't know whether to rejoice that my father is living or weep because he's no longer the man I love. I'm so confused . . . I just want to enjoy today, Christmas. I'll think about him tomorrow. Maybe I'll call him on the telephone and just say goodbye. . . . God knows. . . . I think that maybe I never want to see him again. Perhaps the best thing for us all would be just to close the door and start all over again. What do you think?"

"I think it's time I realized that you're a big girl now and capable of making your own decisions," Grace replied.

The years of pain and the burden of secrecy had been lifted, and as Grace dressed for the party, she looked forward to one of the happiest Christmases of her life. She put on her purple Halston wool dress that matched the diamond and amethyst pin Drake and Peach had given her for her fortieth birthday.

When they were both ready and met in the entry hall to leave, Casey looked her over. "Now you look like my mother again. Welcome back."

"It's good to be back. Merry Christmas, Casey."

_54_

The Advantages of Stardom

ON IMPULSE, Peach made one more telephone call before she started to dress. When she emerged from her room, Jason was inspecting the place cards, and he looked up and gave a long appreciative whistle. "You look sensational," he commented. "Are those things real?" He ran his finger lightly over her necklace of diamonds and rubies.

"They're paste, dear, just as they used to say in the movies."

"No, they're not. My God, I hope you don't wear them in public. They must be worth a fortune . . . or two or three."

"Don't worry, they're well insured, and they're not the most valuable pieces in my collection. Drake loved to buy jewelry for me. He once said I was his living Christmas tree, and it gave him great joy to hang ornaments on my branches. I think these are especially appropriate for the holidays, don't you?"

Jason looked her over admiringly. She was dressed in a white silk chiffon blouse with a long white wool Ungaro skirt, cinched at the waist with a cummerbund of bright red silk. The blouse was cut low in the neckline, and the necklace rested on her bare throat. He patted her on the behind gently as he said in mock tones, "But of course, every woman should wear her rubies on Christmas."

Peach approved of the casual elegance of Jason's dark tweed jacket by Giorgio Armani and the pale blue silk shirt he wore open at the neck. He was a beautiful animal, no doubt about it. She wondered wickedly if the new addition to her guest list might not ruffle his sophisticated sexual certitude.

"Who is Pierre?" Jason asked. "I don't remember your mentioning his name before. And how come he's sitting next to you?"

Peach was glad she'd had the bravado to call Pierre and invite him. She'd never played games like this with men before, but it was fun. "He's a physician I know," she replied. "He has no family here. His wife left him and went back to France. I thought it would be a nice gesture to include him. And I've put you in the host's chair at the opposite end of the table. You'll have a beautiful young woman on both sides of you."

The doorbell rang and Miles brought the arrivals into the library where Peach greeted them. "Casey! Grace! Merry Christmas!" The joy in her voice was tempered with caution. Was Grace as normal as she looked?

"Merry Christmas, Peach, you look fantastic," Grace responded, and Peach knew instantly that everything was as it should be. The two old friends threw their arms about each other in an outburst of emotion so intense that neither had words to express themselves.

Casey moved close to them and said softly, "You were absolutely right, Peach. I told her about losing the baby last night. It was something she needed to know, and everything's fine now."

Peach whispered, "Thank the Lord!"

As they separated, Grace added, "The Malone family came to my rescue again. I've been stupid, Peach. Someday when we're old and gray, I'll tell you how much." Both women dabbed carefully at their eyes with handkerchiefs to avoid smudging their mascara.

Through the entire scene, Jason had stood apart, but when it looked as if the drama had played out, he stepped toward Casey. "Hi, I'm Jason Darrow."

Smiling broadly, Casey extended her hand. "Of course you are. Hello, I'm Casey Gable, and this is my mother Grace."

Jason's eyes twinkled as he commented, "I have a good idea you're one of the beautiful young women Peach has placed next to me at dinner."

"I certainly hope so. If I ever go back to teaching school, knowing Sandman will give me a lot of status," she replied.

Soon the room was filled with the arrival of the Hammond family, Laura, and Pierre. The ebullient Angie zeroed in on Jason immediately, and everyone fell into a warm and spirited conversation that became even more lively as the Dom Perignon was consumed.

As hostess, Peach watched over the social intercourse with an alert eye to make sure that no one was left out. Grace and Pierre immediately got involved in what sounded very much like shop talk. Maggie and Casey discussed interior design, and Laura and Kirk were in a deep conversation about condominiums and financing. Angie had Jason all to herself on the couch by the window, and they talked about movies.

Peach was pleased at how easily Pierre had fitted into the group and was glad she'd invited him. He was so European. His manners were impeccable, and he was an attentive and interesting conversationalist. She looked at Jason and felt no twinge of jealousy. Angie was a sexy little doll, and if he was fascinated by her, so be it. She was not fool enough to put herself in competition with a child younger than her own daughter, and she was happy if he was enjoying himself. She was not worried that some woman would snag him . . . not in the near future anyway. He was a free and independent spirit and likely to remain that way. She was sure that she could resume her relationship with him any time she wanted.

Could it be possible that she was not too different from him, after all? Having spent her life under the control of one man, could she willingly surrender herself to the domination of another?

Dinner was announced, and she guided her guests to their chairs. At the table, Jason became the focus of attention as he regaled them with stories about the making of *Sandman*. He was a true actor in his love of attention, but he was witty and funny in a self-deprecating way, and everyone was enchanted with him.

After a while, Peach noted that Jason was addressing most of his remarks toward Casey rather than Angie. Casey was an attractive young woman, but in face and figure no match for Angie. She was exceptionally intelligent, however, and much closer in age to Jason.

When dinner ended, Maggie took Peach aside and told her she was leaving. She didn't want to make a big production out of her exit but would slip out while everyone gathered around the tree for brandy and the gift opening. Peach was aware that Kirk and Maggie had not spoken once to each other all afternoon. "Is everything all right?" Peach asked.

"I'll tell you about it later," Maggie replied. "Merry Christmas, and thank you for a wonderful party. It was a tremendous thrill for me to be a guest in this house."

"You did a magnificent job for me, Maggie. I shall always be grateful. This was my very first party here, you know."

"Are you still planning to buy the boat?"

"I don't think so. I've got other plans. I'll tell you all about them when we have time to talk. I want you to come up to Napa and get started on the schoolhouse as soon as possible."

"Another rush job?"

"I'm afraid so." They both laughed.

When Maggie had gone, Peach went back to her guests and observed Kirk Hammond more closely. He was a handsome man, the kind who improves with age. You could just never guess from outside appearances what went on between couples when the doors were closed, Peach mused.

As Peach walked toward the bar to get herself a brandy, she felt someone closing in. She turned and found herself face to face with Pierre. "Something's disturbed you. I can see it in your face," he said softly.

"You read faces very well, Dr. Senseney, but then that's part of the business, isn't it? You're right. Maggie just told me something was wrong, but she didn't explain."

"Christmas is not a happy time for everyone. And it is

quite obvious that our Mr. Hammond is interested in the other woman. Couldn't you tell?"

Peach was indignant at his implication. "You're quite mistaken. He's just being kind to her."

Pierre shrugged his shoulders in a manner typically Gallic and replied, "I bow to your greater wisdom. Now, why did you invite me here today? To compare me with your handsome young god?"

"I wouldn't do that. I wanted to see you again," she replied with a teasing smile, "but not alone . . . in the company of others . . . where it's safe."

"Do I frighten you?"

"A little, I suppose. You're so intense."

"You are afraid of the outcome," he said, and he stepped very close to her. "If we made love, you wouldn't be afraid of me anymore."

His voice was low, and although he did not actually touch her, he was so close that she could feel the heat of his body through the thin fabric of her clothes. She looked up and saw Jason across the room. If he should look at her now, could he see that another man had aroused her? She looked into the dark eyes Pierre had fastened on hers. "Come back after eleven tonight. I'll be alone then," she said. Quickly, she picked up her glass of brandy and brushed by him to join the group at the Christmas tree. Her cheeks were hot and flushed, as were unseen parts of her body.

A short time later, Pierre excused himself, explaining that he had to check on a patient whose face had been severely damaged in an automobile accident the day before. He graciously took leave of each person individually, and it was evident that the women were especially sorry to see him go.

Peach walked him to the door, and as they stood beside the bronze ballerina, Pierre lightly caressed the figure's round young breasts. It was a sensuous implication that did not go unnoticed by his hostess, who remarked, "You're a sexy man, Pierre." He took her hand and raised it to his lips, but instead of kissing the back of it, he turned her palm up and pressed his lips to it, lightly and gently flicking the tip of his tongue against her flesh.

"Peach, my dear, you have such poise . . . such composure. It would be so exciting to be the one to cause you to lose all control." Before she could comment, he turned and was gone. Peach smiled at his words and looked toward Jason. Sorry, Pierre, you won't be the first to do it, she reflected, somewhat amused.

She returned to her guests just as Miles summoned Grace to the telephone. No sooner had Grace picked it up than her face went ashen. My Lord, thought Peach, now what? Grace's hands trembled as she put down the telephone, and Casey hurried to her. "Mom, what's wrong?" she asked, putting an arm around Grace to support her.

"Jerry Casey . . . he's here!" Grace whispered.

"Who called?" Casey asked.

"Rudolfo . . . he's at the house. He . . . wanted to surprise you . . ."

Grace looked as pale as death, and Casey tried to reassure her. "Don't worry now. We can handle it. Don't be afraid."

Peach moved toward them, and although they had spoken so softly that she had not heard their conversation, she knew that Grace was extremely agitated. Casey looked up and said, "Peach, I'm sorry, but we've got to go. Would it be possible for Miles to take us home?"

"Is something wrong?" Peach asked.

"No . . . nothing. It's . . . well, we have unexpected guests at the house waiting."

"I see," Peach said, although she didn't, and she called Miles to get the car.

"Thank you so much, Peach. It was a lovely dinner. I'm so sorry to have to rush off. Please tell everyone goodbye for us."

Jason had walked up to them, and he joined in the conversation, addressing his remarks to Casey. "Going so soon? Don't forget now, I want you to come see the play. Is there any chance you could make it to New York?"

Casey shook her head. "I'm afraid not, although I'd love to. I have to get busy looking for a new job here."

"Tell you what," he persisted, "suppose I send you a copy of the script? Will you read it and give me a critique of the character I'm going to play?"

"Of course, Jason. I'd love to do that. I'm sorry, but we really have to dash. Merry Christmas. Thanks for everything, Peach." Quickly the two women left.

When they were gone, Jason and Peach looked at each other. "Don't toy with her, Jason. She's not for you," Peach warned.

"And how would you like it if I said that Frenchman wasn't for you?" he answered, but their conversation was interrupted by Laura and Kirk, who announced they were leaving too. Angie was still sitting on the sofa, making no move to join her father. "Angie," he called to her, "come on now. We've got to get going. The fog is rolling in."

"I'm not coming home tonight, Dad. Didn't Mom tell you? Sue Thomas has all my ski stuff at her house. We're leaving early in the morning from her house in Westwood. Jason's going to drop me off on his way to the airport," Angie declared, and the manner in which she made her declaration left no room for negotiation. It was an awkward moment for Kirk, since he had to concede or risk an embarrassing confrontation with his daughter, which he'd lose.

When Kirk and Laura had gone, Peach indicated that she wanted to talk to Jason alone. "Come into the library a minute, will you please? I'm sure Angie will excuse us?" He followed her, and when the door was closed behind them, she turned on him in fury. "How dare you humiliate me like that?"

"You mean Angie? I'm only giving her a ride."

"I know what kind of a ride it will be. Any idiot can see that she intends to fuck you!"

"You think so?" He grinned and asked, "Why would she want to do that?"

"So she can brag to all her little friends that she got it on with Sandman, that's why.'' Peach sat down on the couch and tried to control her temper.

"Do you think I don't know that by now? Damn it, Peach, she's nothing new to me. Everywhere I go, there are girls just like her . . . groupies . . . starfuckers . . . dying to get it from a celebrity. It's one of the advantages of stardom . . . you get more pussy than you can handle . . . or want.''

Peach put her face in her hands. She didn't want to hear anymore, but Jason continued. "Anyway, you don't have to worry about Angie. She doesn't interest me. Casey's more my type. She could seduce me with her brain.''

"And what about me, Jason? Did I seduce you? How?''

"The same way you're seducing Senseney . . . with that regal beauty that says come here go away all at the same time.'' His voice was tender and betrayed no hostility or bitterness. "You're going to bed with him, aren't you?'' he asked. Peach nodded her head. "When?'' he asked, and when she did not reply, he whispered, "Tonight.'' Peach could think of nothing to say, and there was a long silence. Finally, Jason sat down beside her and took her hand. She looked up at him, entreating him to tell her not to do it, but he said nothing, and she knew it was all over. They got to their feet, and he took her in his arms and kissed her tenderly, without passion. "Do what you have to do, my beautiful Peach. It won't make any difference in the way I feel about you. I'll still want you . . . any time.'' She pulled away and smiled enigmatically. She had no such reassurance for him.

When everyone had gone, and Sarah and Miles were finishing their clean-up, Peach sat down in front of the twinkling colored lights of the tree to await Pierre's return without enthusiasm. This, her first Christmas without Drake, had not been particularly happy. She'd be glad when it was over.

_55_

The Empty House

MAGGIE telephoned Belinda as soon as she arrived at the Malibu house. "I'm here now," she said.

"Well, I'm glad you finally made it," Belinda answered tartly. "We shall leave immediately."

Maggie turned on the heat and lit the fire in the fireplace. She switched on the Christmas tree lights and then went into the kitchen to make coffee. She remembered that Connor liked cognac with coffee after dinner, and the smell of fresh coffee brewing would add warmth to the house.

Room by room she toured the place, switching on lamps, and she was satisfied with all that she saw. It wasn't complete, but then no house is until it begins to take on the character of those who live there. It did look like Connor, however, if her memory of him had any validity.

As she stopped in the powder room to freshen her makeup, she heard the sound of a car door closing, and her heart raced. Why was she so bloody nervous? Within moments, the door chimes rang, and she forced herself to walk slowly to open it. There, resplendent in a white floor-length mink coat was Belinda, and behind her stood a startled Connor.

"Merry Christmas," Maggie greeted them.

"Well, this is a surprise," Connor said. "Mother told me we had to make a duty call on an old friend."

Looking like a feline gourmand who has just dined on chocolate mousse, Belinda swept inside triumphantly. "Come in, Connor. Don't just stand there letting the cold air in."

Bewildered, he followed her. Maggie extended her hand to shake his, and although he took it, he also leaned forward and kissed her lightly on the cheek. "God, you're a beautiful sight, Maggie. Merry Christmas."

Belinda was impatient to move on to her big moment. "Connor, come into the living room and look at this view. Tell me, what do you think of it?"

"Well, Mother, I'd say it was nothing short of magnificent." He turned to Maggie. "This is your home?"

Maggie shook her head but said nothing. This was Belinda's show.

"No, Connor, this is not Maggie's house, but you will see her in every room. She is not my secretary." She paused dramatically for effect. "She is my interior designer, and I commissioned her to do this house as a Christmas gift to you."

Connor said nothing, but a look of wry amusement slid across his face as he began to put things together.

"Well, don't you have anything to say?" his mother demanded.

"I didn't know you were finished with the presentation," he said slyly, and Maggie was amused and gratified at his perspicacity.

"Do you like it?" Belinda demanded.

"Does the presidency go with it?" he asked.

"You know it does."

"I haven't seen all of the house yet," he said, and both women could tell by the set of his jaw that he could not be pushed further. He was his mother's son, Maggie concluded.

"Maggie, show him around while I sit here by the fire and warm my poor, aching arthritis. This damp ocean air does fierce things to my tired bones. Do I smell coffee?" Belinda's voice had lost its imperious tone and had taken on a quavering quality. What an actress, Maggie thought. Some of the world's best performances are never seen on the stage or screen. A look of amused understanding passed between Maggie and Connor.

It took almost an hour to tour the house. Connor was

curious about every detail. Maggie saved the master bedroom and bath for the triumphant finale, and the effect was all she had hoped it would be.

"This is great! I can sit here in warm water up to my chin and look out to sea. That's undoubtedly the biggest tub in the world. Where did you find it?"

"This one was custom-made, but there are lots of them being used in California houses."

"Really? I'm sure there aren't many in New York. I take it that it's meant for two people, right?"

Maggie realized he was flirting with her, and she didn't know how to respond. "I guess so. I've never been in one of them myself, but I understand they're essential in bachelor pads."

"Oh? I suppose it's old hat to invite one up to see one's etchings. What does one say then? Come up for a . . . bath?"

"I wouldn't know. I haven't had any propositions in a long time."

Connor's bantering tone turned serious. "How's your husband, Maggie? I suppose he's not dead or anything, is he?"

"No, what a strange thing to ask."

Connor shook his head in disgust. "Oh, well, so much for voodoo. I guess I'll quit sticking pins in his doll."

Maggie laughed nervously. "You're teasing me."

Connor looked into her eyes and said, "Are you sure?"

Maggie's gaze fell. "Maybe that voodoo of yours worked better than you thought it would. We've been having a lot of problems lately."

"What kind of problems?"

"Kirk has given me an ultimatum . . . my work or my marriage."

"And . . . what did you choose?"

"Neither. I refused to let him back me into a corner."

"Good girl. Now what?"

"I really don't know." She walked to the window and looked out toward the sun, which was fast disappearing into the horizon.

"Maggie, don't be afraid," he said and put his arm around her. "I know just what you're going through, because I've already been there. I wanted my marriage to continue even though my wife was unhappy. I couldn't bear the thought of failing at something so important. I offered to do anything to keep us together, but Bittsey refused. She was much wiser than I . . . and much more courageous. She was right, and I no longer hate her for it."

Maggie relaxed. "I appreciate those words of comfort, Connor. I'm scared . . . I really am. Kirk and I had what I thought was the perfect marriage, but I guess I was wrong."

"No, you weren't. It probably was a good marriage, but one or both of you changed. Maybe you're no longer the woman he married."

"Do you like the house?" Maggie asked to change the subject. He did not answer immediately, but his arm remained draped across her shoulders as he gazed out across the ocean. Maggie guessed he was one of the quiet, self-contained individuals who could shut out the world when he wanted to.

"Was Mother a bitch to work for?" he asked finally.

"How did you know?"

"Why do you think I chose to live in New York?"

"Your mother blamed your wife for that."

The corner of his mouth twitched. "Poor Bittsey. I was too much of a coward to take the rap myself, but she thought it was amusing. She hated Mother and was glad to be away from her influence."

Maggie's expectations sagged. All her work would be for nothing. Connor wouldn't stay. "I see," she replied. "Then you're going back to New York?"

"Would it make any difference to you if I did?"

"Yes, it really would. It's important to me to have Belinda satisfied with my work, and I'm afraid she won't be very enthusiastic if the house fails to entice you."

His expression mocked her. "Is that all?"

Maggie shook her head. "No, but I'm so mixed up now that it's hard to separate my own concerns from my professional ones . . . honestly, that is, and I would never want to mislead you. Is that very presumptuous of me?"

"You could never be presumptuous, Maggie. Do you want to be my friend?"

Maggie looked down as she answered, "Yes. I've thought about you so much while I was doing this house that you've become like a part of me. I tried to visualize things as you would see them . . . to anticipate your likes and dislikes . . . to get inside your head and understand you."

"Maggie, that's the most seductive thing any woman has ever said to me. I probably couldn't be more turned on if you'd invited me to strip with you and get in the tub. Maybe your thought waves traveled all the way to New York and reached me, because you've been on my mind too."

"I'm flattered," she murmured, and she really was.

"Do you suppose it's infatuation . . . or just ESP?" he asked.

"We may never know," Maggie answered.

"Of course, we will. We'll have the rest of our lives to find out, although I'll probably be too busy to work on it much for a few weeks. This new job is going to be a pisser," he said.

"Then, you're staying?" Maggie could not believe what she thought she'd just heard.

"I fully intended to all along. I was acting the reluctant bride to extract a few concessions from the board, and dear old Mother did that for me. Now I'll have a stronger hand and better control. I intend to bring the company into the twenty-first century with up-to-date merchandising techniques."

"What about Belinda?"

"Remember what I said about people changing? Well, she hasn't, but I have. I can now see through the toughness and rigidity to the mother who loves me and who knows she is not going to live forever. I even regret the years I denied her my presence and my love because I was too selfish to stay here and fight it out with her."

"She'll be so happy, Connor."

"And you? Are you happy, Maggie?"

"I'm happy too."

"What about the tub? Care to make me an offer?" he asked teasingly.

"As a matter of fact, I intended to try that thing out before you came into town, but there was never enough time," Maggie answered, "and I'm afraid if I get in it now, I might drown. Give me a little time to find out if I can swim, okay?"

"How long?"

"A month . . . maybe less."

"One month from tonight, on January the twenty-fifth, I'll be up to my neck in hot water . . . waiting for you." He kissed her lightly on the forehead. "You're even lovelier than I remembered. Now, let's go tell Mother the news."

"She doesn't know?"

"I was going to hold out until next week, but now seems the appropriate time. Come on, enjoy it with me."

They hurried down the stairs and joined Belinda by the fire. "Well, you took long enough. Do you like it?"

Connor went to his mother and kissed her cheek. "It's the best gift I've ever received. I'll take it. Thank you."

Belinda smiled uncertainly. "Don't play games with me, Connor. Are you or are you not going to live here and resume your rightful position in the company?"

Maggie sat down to watch the drama unfold. Connor played his role to the hilt. One hand in his pocket, the other scratching his temple, he walked to the window to look out. Belinda's eyes snapped with anticipation as she watched his every move. "The truth is," he began, "this morning, I had about decided to go back to New York." Belinda's face recorded her anxiety, but she said nothing as he continued. "I thought, who needs it? It's a tough, demanding job, and I've never really hungered for power." He turned and smiled. "But then, you brought me here, and frankly, I can't resist. I knew I was home the moment I walked in."

Good God, Maggie thought, he is as much a manipulator as his mother, but in a much kinder way, and her heart rejoiced for the happiness she saw on the old dowager's face.

Belinda got shakily to her feet, and her eyes brimmed with tears. Dramatically, she opened her arms to her son, and Connor went to her. She held him and wept as she whispered, "Welcome home, son, welcome home."

The moment was charged with emotion, and Maggie found it difficult to keep her eyes dry, but since she felt she was intruding, she got up to leave. Belinda stopped her. "Maggie, my dear, can I ever thank you enough?"

"I'm as happy as you are, Belinda," she replied, but Connor interrupted her.

"You can thank her by getting on the telephone tomorrow to tell your friends that she's the best designer around. You might also add that she's going to be very busy heading up the new interior design department for Cornwall's in the near future, and they'll be lucky if she has time for them. Better call Paige Rense too at *Architectural Digest* . . . tell her she can photograph the house."

Maggie's expression went from joy to concern. "Wait a minute . . . I'm thinking about opening an office in Los Angeles, and it will take me some time to get settled in it. . . . I don't know about taking on . . ."

Belinda's expression changed as she realized the implications of Maggie's words. "Maggie, I hope you haven't made any rash decisions. Decorating is certainly never going to bring you the happiness and satisfaction that your marriage has," she stated.

"Mother, stay out of Maggie's affairs. It's none of your damn business," Connor warned her, and his voice was stern.

"Marriage is sacred," Belinda snapped, "and I don't think people should take separation and divorce so lightly."

"Oh, really?" Connor asked, amused. "I could swear that you weren't the least bit broken-hearted when Bittsey left me, were you? As I recall, you said something like 'good riddance' at the time . . . or was I just imagining that?"

The tone of his voice and his pointed words warned Belinda to back off, and she did. "Well, do what you wish, Maggie.

It's your life, and naturally, I will help in any way that I can. I'll see that your check is mailed to you this week."

"Thank you, Belinda. I must go now." Connor helped Maggie with her coat, and Belinda resumed her seat by the fire.

"I'll walk you to the door," Connor said. Fog was rolling in with nightfall. "That stuff is pretty thick. Are you sure you'll be all right driving alone?" he asked.

"I really don't need to see. My car knows the way, it's brought me here so many times."

"I hope it brings you back often. Will you have dinner with me tomorrow night? I've been anxious to try Spago's."

"I thought we had a date on the twenty-fifth?"

"Oh, that . . . that's for the tub. It can't hurt if we see each other occasionally before then . . . just to eat, you understand . . . and talk."

"Tomorrow night then, but let me meet you there. I'll be in Los Angeles all day tomorrow tying up loose ends."

"Fine . . . how about eight . . . at Spago's. . . . It's on Sunset, I believe."

"I'll call you if something happens, and I can't make it. Otherwise, I'll be there," she agreed, and got into her car. He closed the door and then tapped on the window for her to roll it down. When she did, he asked with a slight leer, "Do you believe in kissing on the first date?"

She laughed. He really was amusing. "I really don't know. Merry Christmas . . . and welcome to L.A."

She drove away, and her heart felt lighter than it had for a week. God knows, she'd have liked to preserve her marriage to Kirk, but life would go on. Maybe she had changed. She decided to have no bitterness for Kirk. After all, it was she who had moved away from the marriage, and she hoped that their relationship could be resolved peacefully for Angie's sake. If Kirk chose to do so, he might destroy her daughter's love for her, but she was certain he wouldn't. He loved Angie too much to deny her the love and affection of her mother.

Angie had not been an easy child to raise. Like Maggie's father, she was headstrong, temperamental, insensitive to those closest to her, but charming and affectionate. No, Kirk definitely would not want the sole parental responsibility for her.

She tried not to think of Connor. Whatever course she chose, she would let him have no influence on her. He was an intriguing man, not as handsome or dynamic as Kirk, but more sensitive and perhaps more intellectual. But he was not to be the big adventure in her life; that would be her work. She would not make the mistake of exchanging one master for another.

The fog was thick and murky, and it took her a long time to get home. As she walked through the empty house . . . empty of family . . . empty of love, she turned on the lights and thought that this was the way it would be from now on. There would be nobody to come home to.

"Dear God, I'm so afraid," she whispered into the stillness.

_56_

Our Night Together

WHEN Kirk and Laura got into the car to head for Sherman Oaks, their spirits were dampened by Angie's refusal to come with them. Both of them knew what Angie's motives were, and her father was furious. As he gripped the steering wheel of his car and peered through the windshield at the thickening fog, Laura saw the anger in the set of his jaw and the frown lines that were so deep between his eyes they seemed to have been chiseled there.

Now that she was away from the comfort and security of Peach's apartment, she was nervous again and anxious to get home. Fog was another hostile form her environment assumed, and it threatened her. She tried to relax with the procedures Christine had taught her, but she could not concentrate. In desperation, she reached out to Kirk for help.

"Kirk, I know you're upset, but please talk to me," she pleaded. Hearing the distress in her voice, he took his hand off the steering wheel and held her cold, trembling fingers in his.

"I'm sorry. I'm just mad at Angie. If Maggie had been there, she wouldn't have pulled that stunt with Peach's boyfriend."

"Are you sure? Maggie always contended that you were the only one she'd listen to."

"Really? I always thought it was the other way around." He turned to her and smiled. "But that's enough of that.

419

Let's talk about something else. Do you think Peach is more interested in Jason or that Frenchman?''

"It's quite obvious that they're both quite interested in her," Laura replied.

For the rest of the drive up fog-shrouded Coldwater Canyon, they rehashed the party, and although she relaxed slightly, she was nevertheless relieved when at last the car pulled into her driveway and stopped. Giggling and stumbling, they made their way up the steps to the doorway. When they finally got the front door open, Laura declared, "Good grief, I must remember to turn the porchlight on in the foggy weather. I couldn't see a thing." She turned to Kirk to say goodnight, but he was following her inside, and it was apparent he had no intention of leaving so soon.

"I could really use a cup of strong coffee, if it wouldn't be too much trouble. It's a long drive back in that crud, and I'm already half asleep from the wine and the food," he said.

"Come on in. Just make yourself comfortable in the living room, and I'll put a pot on right away."

When she returned twenty minutes later, she found him sound asleep on the couch. He had taken off his coat and tie and shoes and had turned on the gas logs. Trying to be as quiet as possible, she put the tray down and sat in the wing chair to wait for him to awaken. She too slipped off her shoes and curled up in the chair. She tried not to acknowledge the comfort she took in having him there, and she was in no hurry to awaken him. Relaxed and warmed, she too dozed off.

It was almost two in the morning when she awakened and saw that Kirk was still in a deep sleep. Her legs and back felt cramped. Stiffly, she got up and padded quietly upstairs. She washed the makeup off her face and brushed her teeth, and then she put on her nightgown and peignoir. Taking a blanket from the linen closet, she tiptoed back downstairs and covered Kirk with it. Just as she was about to straighten up and leave, his hand reached out and took hold of hers, startling her. "Kirk! I thought you were asleep," she gasped.

"I was until a moment ago," he answered softly. "You're in your nightgown."

"I was on my way to bed. You were sleeping so soundly, I didn't want to awaken you." She tried to pull away, but his hand tightened its grip. "Don't go away. You look beautiful in the gaslight. Sit down here beside me."

He moved over to make room for her, but she resisted. "Kirk, don't."

"Come on . . . you want to. You wouldn't be here undressed like that if you didn't."

"You're wrong! I just came down to cover you up. The fog is too thick for you to drive . . ." Her protests trailed off as he pulled her down to him.

"Don't talk. Just lie here beside me," he ordered, and she weakened and allowed him to press her body close to his until they lay stretched face to face on the narrow couch. With one arm under her head and the other across her hip, he cradled her comfortably. It had been so long since she had been held that she found herself incapable of resistance. Her mind and her conscience cried out to her to stop, but her body would not obey, and when his mouth found hers, she welcomed his kiss. Her long abstinence from bodily warmth and affection had produced a hunger that responded to each of his overtures with enthusiasm and abandon, and so eager were they both, that he was inside her quickly. The thrill of his body penetrating hers was enough to bring her to orgasm immediately with Kirk soon after.

When it was over, the reality of the act cast a shadow over them. "What have I done?" Laura whispered, too stricken with guilt to cry.

Kirk held her close to him, and his words were intended to reassure her. "It's not your fault. I'm the one who did it. You have nothing to feel guilty about." He pulled her chin up and looked into her eyes and said, "I'm not one bit sorry."

"How can you say that? Maggie has been a good friend to me and a loving and loyal wife to you," she protested.

In one abrupt movement, Kirk stood up and pulled her to her feet along with him. With his arm around her, he walked to the fireplace and turned off the gas, and then, pulling her along, he headed for the staircase.

"Where . . . where are you going?" she asked timorously.

"We're going to bed where sensible people our age should be. We're getting too old to make out in cars and on narrow couches. Come on. We'll do it again. It'll be better this time." His voice was teasing and persuasive, but she balked.

"No, we can't!" she said, but he continued to pull her along.

"Come on, Laura, neither of us lost our virginity tonight, and we haven't hurt anybody else either. As Chick Hearn would say, 'no harm, no foul.' "

"Kirk, you're awful. How can you tease at a time like this?" she exclaimed, but the cavalier approach he had adopted weakened the spell of guilt and horror, and her resistance faded. As they walked up the stairs, Kirk continued to persuade her. "Life's too short to take seriously, my love, and people make sex a lot more important that it should be. Take my marriage, for instance. It's over . . . finished. I've spent my last night under the same roof with Maggie."

"When did you decide that?" she asked.

"Ten minutes ago," he replied, and she was horrified.

"Dear God . . . Kirk, don't say that! I've already got more guilt than I can handle. Don't shovel any more on top of me."

They had reached her bedroom. Gently, Kirk pulled off her peignoir and gown and turned her nude body so she was looking at herself in the full-length mirrors. Standing behind her, he reached around and cupped his hands around her breasts. She could feel his erection beginning to press against her buttocks. "Laura, listen to me," he whispered softly in her ear, "there was nothing wrong with the sex in my marriage, but there was nothing right with anything else. Maggie needs her freedom, and I need someone who loves me and wants to be with me more than anything else. Do you understand?"

She tried not to listen. It was dangerous to let go. He might walk away from her just as Jim had and leave her in pieces Could she recover from another such cataclysm? "What want from me, Kirk?" she asked.

His arms released her, and she turned to face him. His strong, demanding features had suddenly crumpled, and his body sagged. He sat down on the bed and dropped his head into his hands. "Oh, God, Laura, help me!"

She could hear the throb of despair in his voice, and she saw that he was a man who needed to weep and couldn't. She sat down beside him and held him in her arms. "Kirk, have you told Maggie that you need her?"

He shook his head. "It wouldn't matter."

"Yes, it would. She loves you, you know that," she argued, hoping to comfort and encourage him.

"It could never be the same. There are too many things now that are more important to her than I am."

Laura could see that his anguish was real in spite of his self-centered point of view. She tried to reason with him. "Nothing ever stays the same, Kirk. I found that out. If you want to keep Maggie, you'll just have to make some accommodations, that's all. If your marriage is important, you'll try."

He lifted his head and looked at her. "I've already tried. The woman she's become infuriates me and makes me do and say cruel things. When we're apart, I promise myself I'll be understanding and kind, but when we're together, I act like a bastard and wind up hating myself again."

He took Laura's hand in his and examined it as he continued. "No, it's better for her and better for me to face up to it. It's all over. I want someone who'll be content just to be my wife . . . who'll take care of me and my home . . . who'll always be there when I need her. Someone like you."

She tried to deny the surge of elation she felt. "You're just lonely now and emotionally upset, but somewhere down the line, you'd regret such a hasty commitment, and I'd wind up being rejected again."

"I care about you, Laura, I always have. Besides you can't dismiss what we just did together. You liked it, didn't you?"

"I loved it, yes, for a lot of reasons. But not enough to build a dream on. As you just said, people make sex more important than it should be. Jim did too."

"Do you really think we can be lovers tonight and just friends tomorrow?" he asked.

"We can try. And no matter what happens, promise me that it will remain a secret. I don't want Maggie ever to know."

"If you continue to see her . . . to have her work on the condo . . . believe me, she'll know."

"Not if it never happens again. I didn't set out to deceive her. It was just one of those accidents of circumstance that happen sometimes."

"That's baloney, and you know it as well as I do. Tell me, Laura, why did you come downstairs in that sheer nightgown? You wanted it to happen as much as I did. I knew the moment Angie deserted us that this would be our night together . . . and so did you."

She wanted to deny it, but her own honesty made her realize that what he said might be true. "God, how could we do such a thing?" she exclaimed softly.

He took her in his arms and held her tightly. "Because we need each other more than Maggie ever needed anybody in her whole life."

He pressed her down onto the bed and pulled the blanket over them. As he kissed and caressed her body, she yielded to him, and it felt glorious. Oh, Maggie you idiot, she thought, how could you give him up so easily?

_57_

Silence and Ice

DURING the short ride home, Casey tried to reassure her frightened mother that the coming encounter would not be as bad as she feared it would. She did not know that Grace was primarily worried that Jerry Casey would recognize her as the woman who was with him in the hotel just before his heart attack. If he did, then Casey would know that she had not only attempted murder, but that she had lied to her . . . again.

"Look, Mom, all this happened between you and Jerry years ago. There's absolutely nothing to worry about. I'll do all the talking if you want me to."

"Are you going to tell him the truth . . . about everything?" Grace asked.

"What do you think?"

"I just don't know . . . maybe we shouldn't."

"I'll play it by ear, okay?"

When they arrived, Rudolfo told them that Dr. Casey was in the living room having a drink. As they entered, he got to his feet and moved toward them. He looked much older than either of them remembered him. He had lost a lot of weight, and his usual ruddy complexion was pale and lined.

"Surprise, darling!" He greeted Casey with open arms, but she ignored them and proceeded to introduce her mother.

"Jerry, I'd like you to meet my mother, Grace Gable."

Suavely, Jerry turned his attention to the older woman. "How do you do, Mrs. Gable? Well, it's easy to see where your daughter got her beauty. You look young enough to be her sister.''

Grace looked up into his eyes fearing the sign of recognition she might see flicker there. She met his gaze directly, but there was nothing there . . . no hint of remembrance and no sign of suspicion. She relaxed. She should have known. To him, women were all cunts . . . and didn't have faces.

"How do you do, Dr. Casey? Have we met somewhere before? You look familiar,'' she said, emboldened by the glint of amusement on her daughter's face.

"I'm sure we haven't. I most certainly would not forget a lady as lovely as yourself.''

"Come to think of it, perhaps you just remind me a bit of Paul Newman. He's a good friend of mine,'' Grace replied, enjoying the situation. She almost wished that she had not agreed to let Casey run the show. "Can I fix you another drink?''

"No, thanks. I shouldn't have had any at all. Doctor's orders, you know. And you're not the first person to say I reminded them of Paul Newman. It happens all the time.''

"Really? How flattering. Are you feeling all right now? Casey told me you had a heart attack.''

"I feel just fine. They're still not exactly sure it was an actual attack. Cardiac insufficiency, they called it. These medical men have a penchant for euphemisms. I just have to watch my diet and my weight and take the medication they gave me. It really took me by surprise. I felt so well when it happened.''

"Heart disease, I believe, is called the unseen killer, because it strikes without warning. Were you at home when it happened?'' She was curious to know, and only she understood the expression on his face as he answered, "No . . . I was attending a . . . meeting . . . at a hotel near the university. Fortunately, I realized something was happening to me . . . and I was able to call for help. The paramedics were there in less than two minutes, and I was rushed to the hospital.''

Grace went to the bar and poured herself a brandy, wondering when Casey would take the initiative and get things

FAME & FORTUNE

going, one way or the other. Her daughter had sat silently on the couch across from their visitor and had said nothing. The silence was awkward, and it was apparent that Jerry Casey was a little concerned with his welcome. He had expected to be greeted with warmth, love, enthusiasm, and gratitude, but instead, he had received silence and ice.

Grace sat down beside her daughter, and the three of them just looked at each other for a few moments, when Casey at last aroused herself and spoke. "Jerry, I have some very bad news. I just don't know how to tell you. I lost the baby."

It took a few moments for him to assimilate the announcement. "Oh, my God, when did it happen?"

"A couple of weeks ago. . . . I'm sorry I didn't tell you right away . . . but I had not idea that you would rush all the way out here to California to surprise me. I had intended to call you in the morning to tell you. I didn't want to spoil your Christmas."

Jerry took a deep breath and attempted to recover his poise. "Well, I see . . . that's . . . a big shock. How are you feeling?"

"I'm fine . . . now."

"Well, it's a setback, but we'll just go on, won't we? After all, there'll be more babies later . . . after we're married."

"No, I'm afraid not. I've given it a lot of thought, and I've decided that marriage is not in the cards for us, Jerry. It just wouldn't work."

The look on his face was uncomprehending. Grace saw it and wondered if Casey knew what she was doing to him.

"Darling, what do you mean? I've left my home, my wife . . ." he exclaimed, and his voice trailed away in confusion.

Casey said nothing more for a long, awkward moment. She just sat quietly staring at him. Finally, she spoke, and her words came out slowly, thoughtfully, and devastatingly. "I know, and I'm really sorry about that, but . . . I've decided that there's just too much difference in our ages." In spite of the sudden, stricken look on his face, she continued, "Jerry, you're old enough to be my father."

Good grief, Grace thought, doesn't Casey know that he'd

rather be accused of incest than be told he was too old for her?

Gathering together the shreds of his pride, he got to his feet. "Well, if that's the way you feel, then there's no reason for me to stay any longer."

"I really didn't mean to hurt you, honestly, I didn't."

"Hurt me? Don't worry about that. I was, after all, just trying to do my duty for the baby, you understand. I didn't want a child of mine to be born without a name."

Casey's lip curled slightly as she replied, "I appreciate that, Jerry."

Grace got up and went to get Rudolfo to drive him back to the airport. She was glad to get out of the room for a moment. When she returned, he was putting on his coat. "Goodbye, Dr. Casey. It was nice meeting you. Have a pleasant trip back. I'm sure you'll have no trouble getting a flight to Chicago."

Casey too was anxious to have him gone. "Goodbye, Jerry. It was nice knowing you. I hope your wife will understand and take you back."

When he was gone, Grace turned on her daughter and asked, "Did you know what you were doing to him?"

"Not at first. I felt sorry for him . . . he looked so much older. I was afraid if I dumped everything on him, he wouldn't be able to handle it."

"Well, don't worry about him anymore. He'll probably be screwing another young coed before the snow melts."

"Do you really think so?"

"Of course, I do," Grace said, "unless his heart trouble worries him too much." She tried not to laugh.

_58_

Two of Us

MILES came into the living room to check on Peach, who was slumped on the couch looking miserable. "Is there anything I can do, ma'am?" he asked, looking concerned.

"No, thank you. You and Sarah did a beautiful job today. The dinner was delicious, and the house looked lovely. I'm sorry you had to work so hard on Christmas."

"We didn't mind. We were happy to be with you, and Sarah loves to have someone appreciate her cooking like your guests did today," he assured her. "Shall I lock up now?"

"No." She hesitated. "A friend is returning later this evening. You and Sarah can go to bed now. I'll take care of things."

"Of course. Will Mr. Jason be staying for breakfast? Sarah will want to get up in time to bake fresh scones."

"No . . . no, he won't." Peach could not bring herself to let her servants know she would be entertaining another man in her bedroom. "He's leaving very early for New York."

When Miles left, Peach was angry with herself, not for lying to her servant, not even for caring what he thought, but angry that she had allowed herself to be so promiscuous. Why had she succumbed to the challenge? She did not want to make love to Pierre Senseney . . . not tonight, anyway. It was much too soon. She was still hurting from the separation with Jason. She wasn't ready to involve herself with anyone, particularly a man as singularly overpowering as Pierre. In her weakened and battle-scarred condition, he might well overwhelm her.

The telephone rang, and she rushed to answer it. Perhaps he was delayed at the hospital, and she would have a reprieve. It was not the doctor's voice but that of Doug Dooley.

"Good news, Mrs. Malone. You were right. Beller's at that hotel in Baja."

"Has he been arrested yet?"

"No, he doesn't know we're here. We've got to get cooperation from the Mexican government. Don't worry. He won't get away now."

"Doug, I can't thank you enough. I'm so sorry I've tied up your Christmas," Peach apologized.

"It was my pleasure. I'll keep you posted."

Peach went back to sit down and reflect thankfully on the close association she had shared with Drake in their marriage. Horace had probably assumed that she had never known about his clandestine romance, and he was safe with Drake dead.

The telephone rang again, but this time it was the voice of her beloved son, who said, "Hi, Mom."

"Steve! Merry Christmas. I tried to call hours ago, but no one answered."

"I'm calling from San Francisco. We flew Penny here this morning. Guess what?"

"She had her baby! Is she all right?"

"She's just fine. The baby was in a breech position, and they couldn't turn it, so they had to do a Caesarean. I didn't call you right away because I didn't want to worry you until we knew everything was going to be okay."

"Is the baby healthy?" Peach asked anxiously.

"Yes, thank God. It's a little girl, and she's beautiful. She weighs seven pounds, and is she noisy!"

His announcement had moved Peach to tears of bliss. "Honey, I can't wait to see her. Can I come right away?"

"We both want you here as soon as possible."

"I'll charter a plane and be there in the morning. Sarah and

Miles will be with me. Oh, my goodness, I'm so happy I can hardly stand it."

"Mom, we're going to name her Katherine . . and if it's all right with you, we'll call her Kitty."

Peach was dumbfounded. "I'm honored, Steve, but are you sure you want to do that? Kitty is an old-fashioned nickname."

There was no doubt in his voice. "We're sure. If it had been a boy, we'd have called him Drake."

When the conversation ended, Peach allowed herself a few moments of private, uncontrolled, and joyful hysteria. Then she called out the news to Sarah and Miles, who were as ecstatic as she was. Sarah hitched up her robe and set to work packing, while Miles got on the telephone to arrange hotel accommodations in San Francisco and a plane to get them there as soon as the weather permitted.

Peach went into the study to make two telephone calls. The first was to Pierre. By declaring it was an emergency, she persuaded his service to contact him at the hospital. When she explained to him why they could not rendezvous that night, he was extremely understanding.

"Congratulations. I know how important an event this is for you," he said, "as it would be for anyone."

"I'm sorry to call off our . . . engagement this evening, but I know you understand . . ."

"Let's not say we are calling it off . . . just a postponement," he insisted.

"As you wish. I think perhaps we ought to start all over, Pierre."

"The future is ours, and I am a patient man, Peach. You will call me when you return?"

Peach hesitated only briefly. "Yes . . . I will."

Before placing the call to Anne in Italy, she paused to think about all that had happened that day. It had certainly been filled with surprises and revelations. Horace had turned out to be a thief and worse, but she'd gotten even with him. And then, there was Jason. She had finally realized he was too young and too casual for any long-term relationship, but he had given her some pleasant memories.

Above everything else, however, there was Drake . . . still Drake. And he had turned out to be not perfect, after all. He had put his trust and his family in the hands of a crook and a charlatan. Why was she not disillusioned? Why did she still think of him with as much love and respect as she'd ever had? Maybe because it was comforting to know that even he could make big mistakes. Perhaps it had been more difficult living with a god than she had realized, and his fall from grace might give her more confidence in herself. After all, if he could make mistakes, it would be okay if she did too.

And now they had a grandchild. If only he could have lived to see her. "Drake, my love, she's part of you," Peach whispered, and she hoped he could hear her.

What a day! She called to Miles. "Miles, open another bottle of champagne . . . and bring three glasses. I want to propose a toast to the new Kitty Malone." Then, she added softly, "And now there are two of us, and we're both just beginning."

About the Author

KATE COSCARELLI, a native of St. Louis, Missouri, makes her home in Long Beach and Rancho Mirage, California. This is her first novel.